FORTY ACRES

A Thriller

Dwayne Alexander Smith

FABER & FABER

First published in the USA in 2014 by
Atria Books, a division of Simon & Schuster, Inc.
1230 Avenue of the Americas, New York, NY 10020

First published in the UK in 2014 by
Faber & Faber Limited
Bloomsbury House
74–77 Great Russell Street
London WC1B 3DA

This paperback edition published in 2014

Typeset by RefineCatch Limited, Bungay, Suffolk
Printed and bound by CPI Group (UK) Ltd, Croydon, CR0 4YY

The right of Dwayne Alexander Smith to be identified as author
of this work has been asserted in accordance with Section 77 of the
Copyright, Designs and Patents Act 1988

A CIP record for this book
is available from the British Library

ISBN 978-0-571-31670-0

FSC
www.fsc.org
MIX
Paper from
responsible sources
FSC® C101712

2 4 6 8 10 9 7 5 3

Forty Acres

Dwayne Alexander Smith is a screenwriter and author living in Los Angeles. *Forty Acres* is his first novel.

Follow him on Twitter @writtenbysmith
www.writtenbysmith.com

Praise for *Forty Acres*:

'Moving into more sophisticated territory *Forty Acres* . . . begins as a traditional legal thriller but opens out into something much bigger as a young New York attorney rises up through the black middle class to meet a supremely rich and powerful group who could buy up much of white America. But there is a price for entry into their ranks.'
Independent

'*Forty Acres* is an absolutely enthralling thriller, one that also has the capacity to challenge the readers' perceptions of right and wrong. With supreme confidence and a mastery of storytelling, the author asks hard questions, provides no easy answers . . . but delivers maximum suspense.

It's an unforgettable work by an amazing new voice. Easily my favorite of the year.' **John Ridley**, Academy Award-winning screenwriter of *12 Years a Slave*

'Wow! *Forty Acres* is a thriller in a class all by itself – brilliant and scary. The characters are masterfully well-drawn – Martin was so vulnerable and his confusion grew on me so that I ultimately cared and worried about him. I was on the edge of my seat!' **Terry McMillan**, author of *Waiting to Exhale*

'Bold . . . Entertaining . . . Intriguing.' *Publishers Weekly*

'I always enjoy books that challenge the complacency of any reader, and *Forty Acres* certainly achieves this. If, like me, you want a book that gets you talking, and results in differences of opinion, then this is certainly the book for you. I guarantee it will make you think, and stay in your head some time after you've read it. That's the sign of a good book.' Raven Crime Reads

'Up there with some of John Grisham's best work.' *Sport* (5 stars)

To the loving memory of my mother,
Barbara Ann Lewis

When I told her I wanted to make movies
she bought me a Super 8 camera.
When I told her I wanted to be a writer
she bought me a word processor.
When I told her I dropped out of college to chase a dream . . .
She yelled at me and told me to get a job.
Then she did everything she possibly could
to help me catch that dream.
Thanks, Mom.

PROLOGUE

Louis Ward walked across the Green Hill Mall parking lot in Southdale, Minnesota, reading the back cover of the *Seinfeld: The Complete Series* DVD box set that he had just purchased.

He did not notice the black van with dark tinted windows creeping up behind him.

Louis, who sported a T-shirt bearing the *Seinfeld* logo, was a huge fan of the show. So was his wife of nine years, Becky. Unfortunately, when the $250 box set was released seven years ago Louis was between jobs and they couldn't afford to splurge. They continued to watch the reruns on TV, of course, but what they really wanted were all those fun DVD extras. Today the Seinfeld box set was re-released, slimmer and less expensive, and Louis had promised Becky that he'd pick it up after work so they could watch it tonight. Both he and Becky were Irish Catholics. Neither one of them had ever been to New York City, so they had little in common with the characters in their favorite show, but that didn't matter. Louis and Becky both agreed that *Seinfeld* was the funniest show ever, period. Funnier than *Lucy* or *The Honeymooners* or any of those old black-and-white shows that people loved to bring up whenever Louis raved about *Seinfeld*. Those shows were great, sure, but *Seinfeld* was in a class by itself. Louis even credited *Seinfeld* with saving his marriage. When he and Becky went through that weird year of too little sex and too many fights, their shared love of *Seinfeld* kept them together when most couples would have just given up. For that reason alone, *Seinfeld* held a special place in Louis's heart.

Unfortunately for Louis, his *Seinfeld* obsession would be a contributing factor in the nightmarish turn that his life was about to take.

As Louis reached his beat-up old Honda Civic and fished for his keys, he noticed the black van easing to a stop in the lane. Despite the vehicle's opaque tinted windows, Louis paid no particular attention to the battered old vehicle. He just assumed it was some guy waiting to take his space. Sure, there were plenty of available spaces nearby, but some people were real particular about where they parked their car. Go figure.

Then Louis saw something crazy.

The side door of the van flew open and two men wearing ski masks rushed toward him. Louis only had time to think, *What the hell?* before the two men were on top of him. One of the men jabbed Louis in the chest with a stun gun. Louis shuddered as six million volts of electricity coursed through him. Another piercing jolt and suddenly the world spun and went dark.

The masked men tossed an unconscious Louis into

the back of their van, slammed the door shut, and sped away.

Two hours later a Green Hill Mall security guard would cruise by and notice a beat-up old Honda with its driver's side door hanging open. And even stranger, an unopened copy of *Seinfeld: The Complete Series* lying on the ground beside it.

1

Martin Grey stared out the backseat window at the crowd of reporters on the Foley Square Courthouse steps as the driver pulled the Lincoln Town Car to a stop. Martin watched as the first few newsmen noticed his arrival and bolted over, pursued by the rest. He watched as they swarmed around his car, tapping the windows, shouting questions, flashing their cameras. A pair of uniformed NYPD officers worked to hold back the mob, but they weren't doing a great job.

Martin couldn't believe it. The small civil rights lawsuit that he had begun working on two years ago had blown up into the biggest case of his career. And today was the finale. The closing arguments. Martin's last chance to sway the jury and win justice for his client—not to mention a hefty payday of $25 million.

"Want me to try around the back?" the driver asked.

Martin shook his head. "No. There'll just be twice as many back there. This is fine." Martin grabbed his briefcase and reached for the door.

"Good luck, brother," the driver said.

Martin couldn't help smiling when the driver called him "brother." Actually, they did look a little like genuine siblings. The driver appeared to be in his early thirties, like Martin. They were both average height with average builds. Even their neat, short-cropped hairstyles were similar. Martin noted that on the surface the only striking difference was that one gripped a steering wheel and the other a briefcase. Well, Martin was dressed a little sharper too.

Martin didn't see the driver's use of the label "brother" as a lack of respect, as some men in his position might. Martin took it instead as a sign of solidarity between two black men—something that Martin thought was sorely lacking in the African American community.

Martin slapped a ten-dollar tip into the driver's hand. "I work too damn hard to rely on luck," Martin said, "but today I'll take all the help I can get."

2

As Martin stepped out of the Town Car, the reporters closed in like vultures.

"Do you really think you have a chance against Damon Darrell?"

"Is it true Darrell offered you a last-minute deal?"

"Is Darrell the toughest attorney you've ever faced?"

There it was. The reason this case had skyrocketed into the media stratosphere. Damon Darrell, superstar attorney, jet-setter, and minor celebrity, was the opposing counsel. Every case that the flamboyant yet brilliant Darrell touched turned into a media circus. Especially a case like this.

Martin's client was suing his employer of twenty years, Autostone Industries, the largest manufacturer of automobile tires in the world, for blatant acts of racial discrimination. Several of these incidents had been caught by security cameras inside the main factory. One video clip actually leaked and went viral on YouTube. The evidence seemed insurmountable, but in a shrewd maneuver Autostone retained not just a brilliant attorney but a brilliant African American attorney to mount its defense.

The press ate it right up; the irony was just too delicious

to resist. And with Darrell fanning the flames with outrageous comments and courtroom antics, the crowd of reporters outside had exploded into a frenzied mob.

Martin knew that until he tossed the reporters a bone, they would make it difficult for him to pass. He paused and turned to face a cluster of lenses and microphones. "I'd prefer to reserve my comments for today's closing arguments. Thank you."

As Martin continued toward the entrance, a man shouted above the rest. "Better make your case out here, Grey, because inside you're going to get crushed."

Martin recognized that voice. He glanced back and spotted an impeccably dressed black man standing just outside the crush of reporters, flashing a familiar sly grin. The newsmen were so busy hounding Martin that they hadn't noticed Damon Darrell looming behind them.

Damon Darrell was about Martin's height and only eight years Martin's senior, but his patented supreme confidence made him seem taller and shrewd beyond his years.

Martin watched the reporters turn in unison to focus their electronics on the naturally telegenic Damon.

"Are you going to win, Mr. Darrell?"

"What's your confidence level, Mr. Darrell?"

Damon raised his hands to stifle the barrage of questions like a holy man beckoning his flock to order. "I only have one comment and that's for Mr. Grey."

Martin stood his ground as Darrell marched up the

steps, cutting through the mob of riveted reporters, and squared off with him.

"Be careful today," Damon warned. "I still have a few surprises for you."

"Of course you do," Martin answered. "Why would today's sideshow be different from any other day?"

As the reporters laughed, Martin noticed the devilish smile on Damon's face, the way Damon's eyes twinkled with the glee of a man who feeds on confrontation.

Damon stepped even closer to Martin and laid a fatherly hand on his shoulder. "Today I bring out my big guns. That's what's different, Mr. Grey." Then Damon continued up the marble steps and disappeared into the courthouse.

As the surrounding reporters clamored for a response, Martin could hear only Damon's warning echoing over and over in his head. Sure, Martin realized that Damon's posturing was just an act for the cameras, a shtick to nurture his legend, but there was still an intimidating air about the man. After all, behind all his shenanigans and theatrics, Damon Darrell was one of the best legal minds in the world.

3

Damon wasn't kidding about bringing out the big guns.

After Martin's concise twenty-five-minute summation, the entire courtroom sat enthralled as Damon Darrell delivered a closing that rivaled a one-man Broadway show. For ninety minutes he paced, pantomimed, and employed slick multimedia enhancements to underscore key moments.

Throughout the seven-day trial, instead of attempting to downplay the video evidence, Damon had embraced it. He argued that instead of filing a timely complaint, the plaintiff endured the abuse in view of the cameras with the intent of concocting a fat, juicy lawsuit. After summing this argument up in his closing, Damon drove home his case with a final statement designed to stick in the jury's mind. "Mr. Watson wasn't denied his civil rights," Damon said with a chuckle. "He's here trying to cash them in."

Laughter erupted, which the judge silenced with a sharp strike of his gavel.

Retaking his seat, Damon flashed Martin a smile that said, *Let's see you top that, kid.*

Martin knew Damon was right. How in the world

would he be able to follow such a phenomenal presentation? Martin could stick to the standard point-by-point rebuttal, as planned, but in the wake of Damon's fireworks he'd just bore the jury.

"Mr. Grey." The judge stared down from the bench. "It's eleven forty-five. Would you like to begin your rebuttal now or wait until after lunch?"

Even as the judge said it, Martin realized that this had to be another part of Damon's strategy. Eat up the clock so that Martin would have to wrestle with the lunch break. With only thirty minutes until noon Martin had two choices. He could deliver his rebuttal after the break when the jury, drowsy from full bellies, would be less attentive, or he could ask the judge to postpone lunch until he finished. Not a great choice either, because the jury would blame him for their sore butts and growling stomachs.

Martin's suspicion was confirmed when Damon suddenly stood up and addressed the bench. "Your Honor, if Mr. Grey would like to push back lunch so that he can deliver his closing, I'd be more than happy to comply—although my stomach might be less forgiving."

Laughter filled the courtroom and Martin could see that annoying smirk on Damon's face.

The judge turned to Martin. "Mr. Grey, how would you like to proceed?"

Martin was backed into a corner. The wrong decision now could do serious damage to his case. A case that, despite Damon's best efforts, Martin felt was leaning in his client's direction.

"Mr. Grey, I need a decision."

Martin had an idea. It was risky, but after weighing all the options he was pretty sure it was his best play. Only one thing made him hesitate. This was a high-profile trial. The world was watching. If his ploy didn't work, it could ruin his career.

"Mr. Grey!"

Martin stood up. "I'm ready to proceed now, Your Honor."

"Are you requesting a postponement of lunch?"

"No. That won't be necessary."

The judge looked surprised. So did Damon.

Glancing at the clock, the judge warned, "You now only have fifteen minutes. Are you sure, Mr. Grey?"

A troubled murmur rippled through the gallery. Mr. Watson could sense something was wrong and shot Martin an anxious look. Martin reassured him with a confident nod, then turned back to the judge. "Absolutely sure, Your Honor."

"Very well. Proceed."

Martin could feel every eye in the courtroom staring as he approached the jury box. The textbook would tell you to smile when you approach the jury. Look friendly. Martin did the exact opposite. He paused and looked each juror straight in the eye. Not in anger but in extreme seriousness. A stern look that said, *No more fun and games*. When Martin finally spoke, his voice was firm and authoritative. A voice that could not be denied.

"My colleague took an hour and a half to try to convince you of what he claims was in my client's mind. Something we can never know for sure. But what we do know for sure, what even Mr. Darrell agrees with, is that the video evidence clearly shows that my client, Mr. Watson, was a victim of repeated racial bias. I don't need an hour and a half because the truth is plain to see. You know what justice requires of you. Thank you."

As Martin strode back to his seat, he noticed that Damon's ever-present smirk had vanished, replaced by an expression he had never seen on his opponent's face before—uncertainty.

That was all the reassurance Martin needed.

4

The party filled the Jamaica, Queens, storefront law offices of Grey and Grossman. For nearly three years, Martin and his partner, Glen Grossman, had shared the cramped space with the two clerks they employed. With all the file cabinets and stacks of file boxes piled ceiling-high, there was never enough room, but on that glorious night, Martin's friends, family, and colleagues drank champagne and danced around the tiny space as if they were inside a ballroom.

Printed headlines from law blogs and news websites papered the peeling walls.

"Autostone Defeated in Key Race Discrimination Case."

"Autostone to Pay 25.5 Million for Civil Rights Violation."

"Storefront Attorney Slays Corporate Giant."

Martin, nursing a beer, stood back from the festivities in a fog of disbelief that had persisted since he watched the jury deliver the verdict. Martin had always believed he could win, but considering his legendary opponent, there had inevitably been a cloud of doubt. Still, Martin had pulled it out. He'd outfoxed the fox in front of the whole world and now nothing would be the same. His voicemail was already full with dozens of requests for television interviews. The publicity would attract bigger clients, not only for him but for Glen as well. Yes, sir, Martin thought, the clouds had cleared and now he could see forever. And forever looked pretty good.

"Why are you hiding in the corner?"

Martin turned and saw Glen Grossman approaching with his wife, Lisa, in tow. Both were holding drinks and were a little tipsy.

"This is all for you, amigo," Glen said. "You should be out there celebrating."

"I'm just taking it all in. You know, savoring the moment. Besides, this party isn't just for me." Martin wrapped an arm around Glen. "This is for us, partner. This is going to blow up Grey and Grossman, big-time. I hope you're ready."

Lisa chuckled. "Oh, he's ready all right. I just caught him at his computer searching for new office space on Craigslist."

Martin laughed. Yeah, that was Glen all right. Big dreams and an endless supply of energy to turn them into reality. Martin had met Glen while attending the NYU School of Law. Martin was an African American fresh out of Syracuse University. Glen was a New York Jew with an NYU undergraduate degree. They had differences too numerous to count, but one common thread shared by both their families was all that mattered.

14

In the sixties, Jewish lawyers played an invaluable role in the civil rights movement, and Glen's grandfather had been one of the most dedicated. On a few occasions he had even worked directly with Reverend King, a fact that Glen often found cause to mention.

Martin's grandfather owned a family bakery in Harlem but he had also been one of the movement's top leaders in the Northeast. When he wasn't pounding dough, he pounded the streets to organize marches and rallies. He was known not only for rallying protestors but for helping to feed them as well. It was at the famous '63 March on Washington that Martin's grandparents first met.

Trading stories about their ancestors' bit parts in history soon transformed roommates into great friends. After graduating, they clerked at the ACLU's New York office during the day and studied together for the bar exam at night. Just three years after they passed the bar, it was Glen's crazy idea for them to team up and hang their own shingle. Martin had concerns that they weren't ready, but Glen's answer to that was, "We'll get ready." How could Martin argue with that?

The first year and a half had been tough, but with hard work and lots of hustle, cases started coming in, and soon they were making a respectable living specializing in civil rights cases.

Then the Autostone case walked in off the street along with the great Damon Darrell and suddenly the world was at their door.

"Hey, what's Anna doing?" Lisa pointed across the room.

Martin turned and to his astonishment spotted his wife, Anna, climbing onto a desk, clutching a slip of paper.

"Stop the music," Anna shouted over the din. "I have something to read."

Martin watched, puzzled, as the radio died and everyone turned to face her. Even in the simplest of dresses Anna looked stunning. Every time Martin looked at her, he still couldn't believe that Anna was his wife.

Anna held up the slip of paper and addressed the crowd. "I just printed this from the home page of Law Watch. It's about Martin."

Everyone applauded. Law Watch was the number one legal website in the world. Anna flashed a smile across the room at Martin, then began to read.

> *Lawyers on both sides of the* Watson v. Auto-stone *race discrimination trial on Thursday delivered their closing arguments to eight jurors, capping two weeks of testimony in the highly publicized courtroom battle. Defending Autostone, the esteemed Damon Darrell was in his usual impeccable form. He delivered a ninety-minute point-by-point closing. But in a surprising turn the opposing attorney, Martin Grey, delivered his closing in less than two*

minutes: a daring appeal to the jury's common sense that brought down Darrell's case like a collapsing circus tent. Less than twenty minutes after the lunch recess, the jury returned a verdict in the prosecution's favor: $250,000 in compensatory and $25.5 million in punitive damages. The verdict is certain to be appealed but this David v. Goliath tale is already the break-room hot topic in every law firm in the land. With one keen swing of his slingshot, Martin Grey has thrust his tiny Queens firm of Grey and Grossman into the legal spotlight.

When Anna finished, her eyes were filled with tears and Martin was standing directly below her. The room erupted with applause. Martin eased Anna down from the table and into his arms.

"I'm so proud of you, baby," Anna whispered. Then Martin and Anna kissed as if they were the only two people in the room. A familiar voice suddenly boomed over the fading applause. "Martin, I had no idea your wife was so beautiful."

Everyone turned and stared at the sharply dressed man standing in the doorway holding two bottles of Dom Pérignon and wearing the biggest smile ever.

A puzzled Anna whispered to Martin, "Who invited him?"

5

Damon Darrell was the last person Martin expected to show up at the party, but of course, the man had a knack for doing the unexpected.

The crowd parted instinctively as Damon crossed the room to Martin. If Damon noticed the effect that his arrival had on those present, he never let it show. Damon handed Martin the two bottles of champagne, wearing a seemingly genuine smile. "I just wanted to stop by and convey my congratulations."

Martin did his best to conceal his surprise and thanked him for the gesture.

"Not at all," Damon said. "What happens during the trial is all business, right? Nothing personal. I'm here as a fellow attorney who admires your work. You're one hell of a trial lawyer."

"Thanks. You're not so bad yourself."

Damon laughed and Martin was relieved that he did. This was still Damon Darrell. Sure, Martin had just beaten him, but the list of important cases Damon had won was long and impressive. Hey, even Hank Aaron struck out sometimes.

Before Martin had a chance to do the honors, Damon

introduced himself to Anna. Damon didn't hide the fact that he was taken by Anna's beauty. He shook Anna's hand with a seducer's smile, then turned to Martin. "Mr. Grey, if I had known that you possessed the verbal skills to persuade a woman this beautiful to marry you, I never would have underestimated you."

Martin was surprised to see Anna blush at the remark. She was usually a tougher audience than that.

When Glen marched over, Martin grew a little tense. Throughout the trial Glen had made plenty of critical remarks about Damon. He respected Damon's skills as a litigator, but he couldn't get past the idea of the most powerful black attorney siding with the racists that ran Autostone. He was convinced Damon was only in it for the money.

Glen stuck out his hand. "I'm Martin's partner, Glen—"

Damon grabbed Glen's hand. "Glen Grossman. Of course. Nice to finally meet the other half of the dream team. You were on that class action against Texaco last year, weren't you?"

"Yeah, that was me," Glen said, surprised. Texaco had been the firm's biggest case before Autostone surfaced. They settled for five million and Glen was proud of every penny.

"You did a great job," Damon said. "Nice settlement. I doubt I could have done any better."

"Yeah, right." Glen chuckled. "I'm sure you would have squeezed twice that out of them."

Martin couldn't believe it. First Damon charmed Anna, and now Glen?

After Glen's introduction of Lisa and a few more minutes of conversation, Damon said he had to run off to some meeting, but there was one more reason he had crashed the party.

"My wife and I are hosting a little dinner party Friday night," he said to Martin. "And we would love for you and Anna to come. Fair warning, it's ridiculously formal, but the upside is my wife is an amazing hostess."

Surprised, Martin turned to Anna. He could see the excitement in her eyes as well. Darrell's great wealth and circle of celebrity friends were well documented in the tabloids. A chance to mingle in those circles, even for one night, sounded like great fun.

Damon said to Glen, "Really wish I could invite you and your lovely wife as well. Unfortunately, my wife plans these gatherings down to the smallest detail. I'm only able to squeeze them in because of a last-minute cancellation. Sorry."

"No, that's okay," Glen said, wrapping an arm around Lisa. They both hid their disappointment behind pleasant smiles. "Maybe next time."

Damon turned back to Martin. "So, shall I give my wife your RSVP?"

Anna glanced at Martin. She wasn't happy about it, but she understood what her husband had to do.

Martin frowned at Damon. "I really appreciate the invitation, but I think we'll wait for the next—"

"No, no, no," Glen said. "Don't be silly. You two go and have a great time. It's all right. Really."

"You guys have to go," Lisa added. "Then you can tell us all about it. Every detail."

"Good. Then it's settled," Damon said. He slapped Martin on the arm. "I'll have someone email you the information. See you Friday."

As Damon Darrell made a quick exit, Martin noticed the troubled look on Anna's face. "What's wrong?"

"He said the party was formal."

Martin rolled his eyes. "Let me guess. You have nothing to wear."

"Not just me," Anna said. "What about you? All you have are those old suits you wear every day."

"Have you two forgotten why we're celebrating?" Glen said as he grabbed a bottle of champagne from Martin. "The law firm of Grey and Grossman is about to receive a big, fat contingency check. I'm sure you two can afford to do a little shopping."

They all laughed as, *pop!* Glen freed the cork and let the champagne flow.

6

Behind the wheel of his Jeep Grand Cherokee, Glen double-checked his rearview mirror, then turned to Lisa. His voice was urgent. "This is going to sound nuts but I think we're being followed."

"What?"

"That van behind us. I think he's following us."

Lisa turned in her seat and peered out the back window. She spotted the battered black van in the lane behind them. The van was two car lengths back, which seemed about right for the speed they were traveling, and nothing seemed menacing about the way it was being driven. Lisa turned back to Glen. "What makes you think it's following us?"

"It's been right behind us ever since we left the party."

Glen and Lisa had slipped out early because Lisa had a flight to catch the next morning. Lisa ran a small decorating business and was headed to Vegas to attend a big home show. From the moment they drove off, Glen had noticed that black van trailing them. At first he didn't pay much attention to it. Just another pair of headlights in the dark streets of New York City. But after traveling fifteen minutes on the Long Island Expressway, crossing the

Midtown Tunnel, and heading downtown on Second Avenue, the same route he took home every night, that black van was still behind them.

Lisa sighed. "Are you sure it's even the same van?"

Glen glanced in the rearview mirror. The van's front bumper had an Obama sticker on it. He'd noticed the sticker the first time he spotted the van. "Yeah, it's definitely the same van."

"Glen, I'm sure it's just a coincidence."

"For a few blocks maybe, but every single turn for the last fifteen minutes? Doesn't that seem odd to you?"

"Okay, it's a *weird* coincidence. But it's still just a coincidence."

Glen shot his wife a look. He knew he had a tendency to see a conspiracy in every shadow—his nightly weed smoking didn't exactly help his paranoid tendencies either—but this was different. This was real.

"I'm telling you," Glen said. "That guy is following us."

"Glen, why would anyone be following us?"

"I don't know. Maybe to carjack us."

"For this old piece of junk? Be for real."

Then it struck Glen. It was so obvious that he was surprised he hadn't realized it before. "Of course."

Lisa could see the fear building in Glen's eyes. "What? What's wrong?"

"My law firm just beat one of the biggest corporations in the country out of $26 million. Maybe they want revenge. Huge companies like Autostone kill people all the time. They have hit men on the payroll to take care of anyone who gets in their way. Eliminate the competition. How do you think they get so big in the first place?"

Lisa rolled her eyes. "Do you even hear yourself?"

"Yes. And it makes perfect sense. Martin is probably being followed too. Shit! I better warn him."

Glen reached for the cell phone on the dash, but Lisa grabbed it first. "That's it, stop the car."

"What?"

"There's only one way to settle this craziness," Lisa said. "Pull over and see what happens."

"Are you serious? What if I'm right?"

"Glen, if you don't stop this car right now, I'm going to scream. I swear."

Glen frowned, then swung the Grand Cherokee over to the curb and pulled to a stop. They watched in silence as the black van sped by, continued down the dark street, and disappeared around the corner.

Glen looked almost disappointed to see the van drive off without incident.

"You see?" Lisa couldn't help rubbing it in a bit. "No corporate boogeymen. Can we go home now?"

Glen frowned as he shifted the SUV into drive and pulled away from the curb. "I still think they were following us."

"I know. That's the sad part. I keep telling you to cut back on that stuff."

If Glen had been watching the road instead of glaring at his wife, he might have spotted the black van parked just around the nearest corner. Idling in the shadows. Headlights off. Its occupants watching as the Grand Cherokee zoomed by.

7

As Martin wheeled his Volvo into his leaf-strewn drive-way, he saw with new eyes the handsome two-story brick house that he and Anna called home. Two years ago, when they had closed on the Forest Hills property, they were thrilled as could be. For both, it was their first experience purchasing a property. The price matched their budget, the square footage exceeded their expectations, and although the neighborhood was predominantly Caucasian, there were enough nonwhite households in the area to make Anna and Martin feel comfortable. Most of all, though, the little brick house symbolized that Martin's career was finally taking off and held the promise that someday soon they'd be able to start a family. But now, with Martin looking at undreamed-of success, he realized that in a few months he'd be able to afford three or four houses just like it and could live in almost any neighborhood he wanted.

*

Martin headed straight for the kitchen and started rum-maging through the refrigerator. Anna frowned. "Why didn't you eat something at the party?"

"I did," Martin said. "I'm still hungry."

Anna shook her head as Martin pulled the makings for a sandwich out of the fridge.

"I can't wait to see what's on the menu at Damon's house," Martin said as he put the finishing touches on his sandwich.

Anna frowned again. "I feel kinda guilty about Glen and Lisa. Don't you?"

Martin tugged Anna into his arms. "Damon's party is nothing," Martin assured her. "Lots of exciting things are going to happen for us now. For Glen and Lisa too. Trust me."

Anna purred, "Would one of those exciting things need to be potty-trained?"

Martin smiled. "Besides being beautiful and smart, are you a mind reader too?"

"Absolutely. You didn't know?"

"Okay, tell me what I'm thinking." Then Martin kissed her. Long and deep. "Well?"

Anna wore a wicked smile as she pressed her body closer to his. "I don't need psychic powers to tell what you're thinking. I can feel it."

Martin grabbed Anna by the hand and pulled her up the stairs toward the bedroom.

8

"Whoa! Check that out!" Martin pointed to a sleek black helicopter perched on a stretch of rolling lawn as he drove through the gates of Damon Darrell's Bedford, New York, estate. Other residents of the affluent hamlet, like Donald Trump and Ralph Lauren, might not be impressed by such a sight, but Martin gaped like a kid at the Macy's parade.

After passing the aircraft, Martin wheeled his Volvo around a broad circular driveway lined with luxury automobiles.

"That one cost almost as much as the helicopter," Martin said, pointing to a midnight-blue Bugatti Veyron.

"That's wonderful," Anna murmured without looking up from her dress. She was way too nervous to give a damn about rich boys' toys. She and Martin had decided to crack the piggybank and splurge on new outfits for the dinner party. Martin bought himself an Armani tuxedo, which he looked fantastic in, and Anna found the perfect Chanel evening gown. The simple black dress was the most expensive piece of clothing that Anna had ever owned. But now, as they wound closer and closer to Darrell's magnificent home, Anna had the sinking feeling that her little Chanel just wasn't enough.

Martin noticed Anna's anxious expression. "Don't worry, baby. You look fantastic."

"You're my husband, you're supposed to say that."

"You're right. Actually, you look terrible."

"Not funny."

Martin chuckled as he pulled to a stop in front of the sprawling Georgian gray-stone mansion. The ivy-laced columns that lined the facade were so tall that they seemed to hold up the night sky.

Two uniformed valets assisted the couple out of their car. As Martin and Anna approached the elegant wrought-iron front door, Martin whispered to Anna, "You really do look beautiful."

"Thanks." Anna took her husband's hand and held her breath. "Here we go."

A smiling servant opened the door before they could ring the bell and beckoned them inside with a sweep of his hand. Martin and Anna stepped through the door.

9

They were all black. That's the first thing Martin noticed when he and Anna entered the parlor where the other guests were chatting while enjoying wine and hors d'oeuvres.

The house was even more beautiful inside than Martin had imagined. He didn't know the first thing about interior design, antiques, or paintings, but he was certain that everything inside the Darrell home was the best. But as fantastic as the mansion was, nothing impressed Martin more than the roomful of guests.

There were four other couples besides Martin and Anna in attendance. The men wore perfectly tailored tuxedos. The women were all draped in designer gowns and adorned with glittering jewelry.

And they're all black, Martin kept mentally repeating to himself. He just wasn't expecting that. Of course, with Damon Darrell hosting, he knew that at least a few of the couples would be of African descent. But all of them? The idea had just never entered his mind.

The queer smile he got from Anna told Martin that she too was surprised by the complexion of the guest list.

"There they are," Damon bellowed as he strode across the room with a beautiful woman by his side. Damon thanked them both for coming, then introduced his wife, Juanita.

Martin had seen photographs of Juanita Darrell in magazines, but nothing had prepared him for just how stunning she looked in person. *Statuesque* is the word that popped into his mind. Like a fashion model in one of those two-inch-thick women's magazines that Anna always thumbed through but never seemed to read.

Juanita welcomed them with a smile worthy of a queen and complimented Anna on her gown. Anna countered by praising Juanita's beautiful home, and their hostess seemed genuinely flattered by the comments.

"I apologize for rushing off," Juanita said, more to Anna than to Martin, "but there are still a few fires to put out. We'll chat later." Then she was gone.

Damon took Anna's arm. "Come on, let me introduce you two to everyone." He ushered them to where the rest of the guests were gathered. "Attention, please," Damon proclaimed in a booming, formal tone that made Martin smile. "May I present Martin Grey and his beautiful wife, Anna."

Martin and Anna were greeted with smiles and warm hellos. The oldest couple in the group was the first to step forward. They were probably in their sixties but wore their age well. The distinguished-looking man shook Martin's hand firmly.

"A pleasure to meet you. I'm Solomon Aarons and this is Betty, my wife."

Martin paused, surprised. Did he hear right? "Did you say Solomon Aarons? CEO of AFG?"

Solomon smiled kindly. There was a calmness about the man, as if he owned the world and it wasn't a big deal. "That's what it says on my office door."

Martin couldn't help appearing a little stunned. The financial world wasn't something that he kept track of, but even he knew that American Financial Group was a big deal. After the recent economic meltdown, it was maybe one of the biggest brokerage firms on Wall Street, and Solomon Aarons, its savior CEO, was known as a financial genius.

"Everything okay?" Solomon asked.

"Sorry," Martin said, "it's—well—"

"Say it," Damon prodded Martin with devilish grin. "You didn't know that the CEO of AFG was black."

Martin smiled sheepishly to Solomon. "He's right. I mean I've heard of you, but wow, I had no idea."

Solomon laughed along with other guests. "No need to apologize, young man. Believe me, I'm quite used to it."

Martin noticed Anna smiling at him along with the others. "Did you know Solomon Aarons was a black man?"

Anna nodded. "Of course I did. He was profiled in *Time* and *Fortune* last year, baby."

Betty Aarons chuckled at Martin's touch of embarrassment, then bowed her head to Anna. "Good for you, young lady. Looks like us girls take the early lead tonight."

A man sporting a mane of shoulder-length dreadlocks, wire-rim glasses, and an African beaded necklace over his tux stepped forward and laid a sympathetic hand on Martin's shoulder. "Don't sweat it, my brother. The sad truth is 57 percent of black males over the age of thirty would not be able to name the CEO of any corporation."

"Black CEO, white CEO, doesn't matter," the attractive woman at his side added.

"Is that a fact?" Martin said, intrigued. "I must admit I've never heard that statistic before. I wonder if the numbers would be different for whites."

"Ah, now there's an interesting question," the man said with a smile. He stuck out his hand. "Kwame Jones. And this"—he gestured to the woman beside him—"is my queen, Olaide."

Olaide's gown was a unique mix of a haute couture cocktail dress and African tribal ceremonial dress. Anna gushed over the outfit, and Olaide confided that it had been made for her by an up-and-coming designer who only worked with 100 percent natural fabrics and dyes.

Martin noticed that unlike the other guests, who were all sipping wine, Kwame and Olaide were drinking sparkling water.

"Kwame and Olaide are co-owners of one of the biggest advertising firms in the country," Damon said. "They specialize in the African American market. You want to sell something to black people, you have to go through them."

"Got it," Martin said. "That explains the statistics."

"Statistics, demographics." Olaide shrugged. "Same difference."

"True, true," Kwame said. "And to answer your question, the white male in the exact same economic subset is far more likely to be familiar with—"

"Kwame, for Christ's sake," a tall bear of a man interrupted. "Give the man a chance to anesthetize himself with a few drinks before you pummel him with one of your social science lectures."

Kwame laughed along with the others. "Fine, fine. Just trying to elevate the conversation a little."

Damon introduced the big man as Tobias Stewart, founder and owner of Tobias Media. Martin didn't know much about the company except that they owned and operated an insane number of cable networks, radio stations, and newspapers in every corner of the United States and Europe.

The media giant was something of a giant in the flesh as well, but despite his three-hundred-plus pounds, Martin thought that Tobias appeared quite dignified in what could only be a custom-made tux. The svelte beauty dangling from Tobias's arm, his wife, Margaret, helped a great deal to tame the burly man's appearance.

Tobias gave Martin a slap on the arm. "I'm ten grand richer because of you."

34

"Glad I could help. But I have absolutely no idea what you're talking about."

"I placed a little bet on the trial," Tobias explained. "I knew Damon couldn't win 'em all."

"You bet on the trial? I didn't even know that was possible."

"You gotta get out of the courtroom more often, counselor. People will bet on anything. You just gotta know who's taking the action."

"Let me guess," Martin said. "I was a thousand-to-one shot and you dropped ten bucks on me."

Tobias's thunderous laughter was as jolly as he looked. "No. It wasn't that lopsided, but close. Hey, tell you what, next time you got a sure winner, you give me a call. I'll cut you a percentage."

Martin wasn't quite sure if Tobias was joking or not, but he decided to give him the benefit of the doubt and just laugh it off. "Thanks but no thanks. Disbarment's not exactly good for business."

Everybody laughed, Tobias louder than all the rest combined. The big man swatted Martin on the arm again. "You're all right for a lawyer."

Martin winced and resisted the urge to rub his arm. "Ah, thanks."

Finally Damon introduced the last couple, Carver Lewis and his wife, Starsha. They were the youngest couple at the party. If Martin had had to guess, he would have said that they were both in their late twenties.

Various tattoos peeked from beneath Starsha's clingy gown as if they were anxious to come out and join the party.

For Martin, Carver Lewis needed no introduction. Whenever Martin burned the midnight oil to prepare for a case, he liked to leave the muted television on for company—something other than a legal document or law book to glance at once in a while. Often when Martin would look up, he'd see Carver Lewis on an infomercial hawking his get-rich-quick real estate books and DVDs.

Carver was a high-profile real estate speculator who had found a lucrative niche by specializing in what some of his competitors called insanely risky deals. Then Carver got really clever. Instead of selling properties, Carver began to peddle his reputation as a real estate guru. Martin remembered reading somewhere that Carver Lewis had made ten times the money from his late-night infomercials than he ever had with his broker's license.

"I recognize you from TV," Martin said as he shook Carver's hand. "You're very convincing."

Carver replied wearing a strained smile. "Thanks . . . I think. I'm not sure 'convincing' is a compliment."

"I just mean that you're a good salesman," Martin said.

"The only thing I'm selling is a way for ordinary people to dramatically improve their quality of life," Carver said. "It's a legitimate business like anything else. I've made a lot of people rich. No 'convincing' needed."

"I'm happy for you," Martin said, with only a twinge of sarcasm. It was obvious that the young entrepreneur felt a need to prove something to his older and more accomplished friends, but Martin was not about to let the insecure punk walk all over him. Martin reached into his jacket and pulled out his wallet. "In fact, you totally sold me. Do you take Amex or MasterCard?"

While the other guests laughed, Carver's eyes drilled into Martin. "Funny. That's real damn funny."

"Carver!" Solomon barked at the younger man. "Enough."

Carver deflated, his deep respect for Solomon apparent.

Damon broke the tension by wrapping an arm around Carver. Then Damon winked at Martin. "Don't mind Carver here. He works too hard. I keep telling him, 'Relax. Take it easy.'"

"What do you mean?" Carver said with a smirk. "Easy's my middle name."

They all laughed, including Martin and Anna.

Juanita glided into the parlor. "So, is everybody nice and hungry?"

10

Two years before, for their third anniversary, Martin had decided to splurge and take Anna out to a five-star restaurant. At the time, the firm was three years old and past all the growing pains that come with starting a new business, and Martin's bank account was beginning to reflect the fact.

Martin picked an elegant restaurant near Central Park called San Domenico that people raved about. He and Anna were not disappointed. The atmosphere, the food, and the service were all perfect.

Martin remembered that magical evening at San Domenico as the best dining experience of his entire life. Until that dinner party at Damon Darrell's house.

He experienced a seven-course gourmet tour de force, served by a crack team of uniformed waiters. The menu favored fresh, local ingredients. Several of the dishes were delicious modern interpretations of Southern classics, as though an elderly aunt's cookbook had been translated by a five-star French chef. It was intoxicating, and Martin found himself anticipating each course, waiting to be surprised by whatever came out of the kitchen.

The conversation at the table was light and pleasant

for the most part. Much of it focused on Martin and Damon's courtroom skirmish. Surprisingly, despite their all being guests in Damon's home, no one seemed hesitant to voice delight at Autostone's defeat. Tobias went so far as to exclaim, "Those rednecks got what they deserved. Amen." Damon, meanwhile, did not appear to be in the least offended by these comments. The seasoned attorney just kept smiling and stayed true to his role as the gracious host.

As the dinner went on, it struck Martin that several of his fellow guests almost seemed to be studying him. Whenever he looked up from his plate, he would notice one or more of the men watching him. Not in a glancing way, but in a more intent, inquisitive way. There was even an awkward moment when a passing glance at Carver turned into a brief staring contest. Flooded with self-consciousness, Martin finally looked away. What the hell was going on? Had he said something wrong?

Anna, seated opposite Martin, shot a look across the table that asked, *Are you okay?*

Martin pivoted his face side to side to show both cheeks and gestured to the front of his tux, hoping his wife might spot a crumb or stain that would explain the odd attention.

Anna shook her head, then silently mouthed the words, "*Relax. You're fine.*"

Anna's reassurance had the effect of a soothing neck rub. She was right, of course. In such distinguished company, who wouldn't feel a little paranoid? *Chill out, Mr. Grey,* a little voice in his head said.

Martin winked at Anna, then picked up his wineglass and took a long, relaxing sip.

11

After dinner the husbands and wives split into two separate groups. The wives retired to the living room for after-dinner cocktails, while the men followed Damon down a long hallway to what he called his game room.

It was a rich man's playpen. Plush leather furniture, vintage pinball machines, a high-tech home theater setup, a beautiful hand-carved billiards table, and the centerpiece of it all, a fully stocked bar that would rival the city's finest watering holes.

Damon proceeded to play bartender, a role he appeared to enjoy very much. He prepared each of his guest's favorite drinks without asking them. For Solomon, Damon cracked open a bottle of thirty-year-old single-malt scotch. For Tobias, he poured a tall foaming glass of imported beer. For Carver, a straight double shot of Stoli. And lastly, for Kwame, a tall glass of tomato juice with a sprig of parsley and a fresh carrot stick.

After receiving their drinks, each man helped himself to a fat Cuban from the antique humidor at the end of the bar, then flopped down onto the plush leather furniture and kicked his feet up.

Martin noticed that this entire evening seemed quite

routine to the other men—the conversation before and after dinner, the way the men automatically separated from the women after the meal, and having Damon mix their drinks with barely a word spoken. Martin had assumed that the dinner was a special event, but this was clearly a gathering that occurred quite regularly.

"And what will you have?" Damon asked Martin, the only guest still standing at the bar.

"Vodka tonic."

"Stoli, Belvedere, Grey Goose? You name it, I got it."

"Stoli sounds good."

Damon mixed Martin's drink and garnished it with a perfectly cut double helix of lemon and lime peels. For himself Damon poured another glass of scotch. Then Damon pulled open his humidor with a flourish.

"Help yourself. Cubans. Best in the world."

Martin waved them off. "No thanks. I don't smoke."

Someone snorted. Martin looked over and saw that it was Carver. The young millionaire shook his head in dismay, as if Martin had just turned down a million dollars. "A good cigar isn't smoking; it's more like living."

The other men nodded in agreement as they blew smoke at ceiling.

"The kid's right," Damon said to Martin as he unbanded and snipped the ends. "Nothing like a good cigar." Damon held out the ready-to-be-lit Cuban. "Are you sure?"

Martin was tempted to give in just for the sake of

fitting in, but the risk of choking on the smoke and looking like a total pussy was too high. "No. Maybe another time."

"Suit yourself." Damon shrugged, then he flicked flame from a gold lighter and puffed the cigar to life.

Martin noticed framed photographs hanging on the wall behind the bar. Shots of Damon, Solomon, Tobias, and Kwame on various white-water rafting trips. The changing waistlines and hairstyles visible in the different photographs told Martin that these images were taken over a span of at least a decade. Carver appeared in several of these vacation shots as well, but only the more recent ones. Martin guessed that the oldest photograph that included Carver was only about three years old.

Damon noticed Martin looking at the photos. "You ever been white-water rafting?"

Martin laughed at the very thought. He was a city boy, born and bred. The closest he ever came to white-water rafting was a thrill ride at Great Adventure amusement park called Roaring Rapids. And he'd hated that. "Nope," Martin said. "Not much white water in New York."

"We sneak away a few times a year," Damon said. "Nice change of pace, you know?"

"Looks fun."

"Oh, it's fun all right." Damon smiled at the other men. "I can honestly say it has changed my life."

Wearing grins, the men all nodded in agreement.

Martin found their enthusiasm a bit odd; none of these

guys, with the exception of Tobias, looked like the rugged outdoor type. More than likely, Martin thought, these trips were just an excuse to get away from their wives. They probably spent more time drinking and gambling than taming the rapids.

Instead of crossing the room to sit with the others, Damon insisted on giving Martin a tour of his game room. Damon showed off his billiards table, which he said had been custom built for James Brown and acquired when the deceased Godfather of Soul's estate was auctioned off. Next Damon showed Martin his collection of vintage pinball machines dating back to the fifties, all fully restored and in perfect operating order.

"And over here are my most *significant* possessions," Damon said, leading Martin to a large glass display cabinet. It took up an entire wall and looked like the sort of thing that you would find in a museum. And, indeed, the strange array of items inside that cabinet would have been right at home in a museum.

Heavy iron restraints, rusted and corroded with age. Chains, leg irons, wrist shackles, steel collars, wooden neck and wrist stocks. Crude, medieval hardware all used for one purpose.

Martin knew what the items were before Damon spoke.

"All of these objects were used to capture and imprison African slaves," Damon told him with heavy eyes. "These very devices may have been used on my ancestors. Or yours."

Staring at the items, Martin couldn't help wondering what it would feel like to be burdened with one of those inhuman devices. To be collared like a wild animal. The mere thought sickened him. "Why do you collect these things?"

"A reminder. A motivator. Black men have an anger in them. Many are consumed by that anger and it ruins them. It's undeniable. Just watch the nightly news or visit a prison. All my life I've used that anger to drive me."

At the center of the display a framed antique document glowed in the beam of a warm spotlight. The paper was tinged and cracked with age. The old-style cursive writing was faded and difficult to read. Damon gazed at the document with a gleam of pride. "Do you know what that is?"

Martin could only make out a few words and numbers and a signature, but even for a document so old, the format was unmistakable. "It looks like some sort of contract."

Damon smiled. "That's right. It's the contract used to purchase my great-great-grandfather when he was first brought over here on a slave ship." Damon pointed to one name among a column of blurred names. "It's hard to make out, but that's him right there."

Martin's eyes widened. "How in the world did you find this?"

"It wasn't as hard as you'd think. They documented everything back then. Of course, it was pure luck that the document was still around."

Martin stared at the antique contract with new eyes. He knew intellectually that the slave trade had been a thriving and very lucrative industry, but to stand before a legal record of such cruelty was, for a lawyer, a vivid reminder of how integrated African bondage had been with everyday American life for centuries.

"Inspiring, isn't it?" Damon said. "Our ancestors were dragged here in chains. Now look at us." He gestured toward the other guests lounging in his high-tech playpen.

When Martin turned, he noticed that the other men were all watching him. Fixed on him.

"Every last man in this room," Damon went on, "could buy the bastards who enslaved our forefathers a thousand times over."

"I'll drink to that shit," Carver said, raising his glass. Damon and Martin walked over to join in on the toast as crystal clinked.

Martin had to admit to himself that he had been more than a little intimidated when he first walked in the door and found himself in the company of some of the most powerful men in the country. Who was he really? A storefront lawyer with some recent success but nothing compared to these titans. But at that moment, in the presence of a ghost that haunted all their pasts, he was beginning to feel like he belonged.

Martin stared back at the cabinet of slavery artifacts. "It is inspiring. Especially now that we have a black president."

This comment did not get the reaction Martin expected. To Martin's surprise, a couple of the men snorted. Others rolled their eyes. They were reacting as if he had just said he'd voted for McCain or Romney.

"I say something wrong?"

"Not wrong," Kwame said. "Just ignorant. And I mean that in the truest sense of the word, brother. Not an insult."

The others nodded in agreement.

"You're saying nobody here voted for Obama?"

"Of course we did," Tobias bellowed at Martin. "You're missing the point."

"Okay, what is the point?"

Damon wrapped an arm around Martin's shoulder. "Look, we all support brother Barack, but there's a bigger picture. And in that bigger picture his presidency does more harm than good."

"I can't wait to hear what you mean by that."

Solomon gestured to an empty chair. "Have a seat, Martin, and allow us to enlighten you."

12

"Your Martin seems like a wonderful man," Juanita said through a perfect smile as she sat down beside Anna on the sofa. "You're very lucky." The women were all gathered in a cozy sitting room decorated with Darrell family photos. Juanita and Damon had two boys, both from Damon's first marriage. Both were in college studying pre-law to follow in their dad's formidable footsteps. As they sipped wine and martinis, the wives traded stories on two topics: their children and their latest shopping adventures. Anna politely engaged in some of this idle chitchat, but her thoughts were nagged by how provincial it all seemed. A hundred years ago, maybe even fifty, having the men and women split into two camps after dinner might have been acceptable, but in the twenty-first century it just seemed a little backward. After making the rounds and spending time with the other women, Juanita had finally made it over to Anna.

All the women seemed to agree that Martin was handsome and smart and that Anna was very lucky to have him. Anna did not disagree, of course. Martin was terrific, and hearing a roomful of beautiful women gush over him only served to remind her just how fortunate she was.

Their praise also reminded Anna to keep her man happy—or else some young thang or an unhappy wife would be more than eager to snap him up.

One of the wives turned to Juanita and asked, "So, what do you think? Will they ask him? Martin seems to fit right in."

Juanita shrugged. "It's hard to tell, but Martin does seem like the perfect candidate."

"Perfect candidate for what?" Anna asked.

The wives all exchanged an uncertain look.

"What? What is it?"

Juanita leaned closer to her. "You see, Damon and the fellas have this little club. Every three months or so they go on these so-called male bonding trips to prove how macho they are."

The wives shook their heads. Anna could see that this was not their favorite topic. "Where do they go on these trips?"

"Would you believe," Juanita said, "white-water rafting?"

Anna's brow furrowed. "Wait . . . you mean like in those flimsy little rubber boats?"

"That's right," Juanita said. "And no river guide or survival expert along with them either. Just a group of black desk jockeys splashing around on some violent river in the middle of nowhere. You ever heard of anything so crazy?"

Anna had expected to hear camping or fishing or, at the very worst, hunting, but nothing as arduous as white-water rafting. Juanita was right. Their husbands weren't athletes, they were businessmen. "That does sound pretty dangerous," Anna said.

Juanita snorted. "Yeah, well, you just try telling them that. Sure, they swear it's safe, but you know men—always pushing to prove their manliness."

"She's right," Olaide Jones said. "And that especially applies to the ones who just push paper all day. I've seen actual studies."

Tobias's wife, Margaret, shook her head. "Men are so damn dense."

From their faces, Anna could tell that these wives had been down this road a million times.

Juanita made an almost imperceptible signal with her hand, and a server began to refill their wineglasses. "We can't stop them," Juanita said to Anna, "so instead we've found a distraction."

"And what's that?"

"When they go on one of their little jaunts, we take a trip of our own. A shopping trip. Paris. Rome. Milan."

Anna stifled a gasp. "Halfway around the world just to shop?"

"Oh, we get in a few sights and museums between boutiques. But shopping is key. You wouldn't believe how it calms the nerves. Right, ladies?"

The wives laughed and clinked their glasses.

"So, what do you think about Dubai?" Juanita asked Anna. "That's where we were thinking about going next."

"You really think they'll ask Martin to join?"

"Are you kidding?" Juanita said. "Damon will ask him for sure. If only to have Martin around so that he can get some revenge. My Damon is not a good loser."

13

Damon refreshed everyone's drink, then rejoined the other men in the sitting area. A haze of tobacco smoke lingered over the group like a brewing storm.

Martin was the only one seated with his back to a wall. So, despite the fact that the sofa and chairs were arranged in a cozy, informal circle, Martin could not shake the irrational notion that all the men were facing him. He almost felt as if he were on trial.

"Look at it this way," Solomon said to Martin. "Now that Barack's in office, a lot of white people are thinking, *Now we're even. Now we can forget slavery and racism is finished. Our hands are finally clean.*" Solomon slapped his hands together as if brushing away filth. "Of course, everyone in this room knows that that's far from the truth. Not even close."

"The Zimmerman case is a perfect example," Tobias said.

"Exactly," Kwame said. "Or how the Supreme Court recently gutted the Voting Rights Act of 1965. Some protestors gave their life to get that bill passed."

"Look," Martin said, "I agree with everything said. But you guys can't deny that electing a black president is a huge step forward."

The men all shook their heads. Wrong.

"Think about it, brother," Kwame said, leaning forward. "The accumulated wealth and power of the Caucasian race is so vast that it would take centuries for us to even get close. When you put it all into perspective, Barack's election is just a drop in the bucket of history. A significant drop, no doubt, but still just a drop."

"Damn straight," Carver said. "It's going to take a hell of a lot more than sticking a black man in a White House to even up the score."

"I'm not sure I see things quite that way," Martin said.

"Really?" Carver smiled condescendingly at the new guy. "And what *way* would that be exactly?"

"You know. That attitude that white people owe us something. Our energies are better focused on the here and now, on improving things for this generation and the next, not on trying to be compensated for an injustice committed centuries ago."

"Brother, you're either living in a dream, or you're a goddamned—"

Solomon stifled Carver with a pointed stare, then turned to Martin. "Let me ask you a hypothetical question. Let's say you owned a truck and a crook stole it. If that crook is caught years later, would you feel that he owed you anything?"

"Sure," Martin said. "He'd owe me a truck."

"Now," Solomon went on, "what if you couldn't afford another truck? What if the loss of that truck resulted in you and your family living in poverty, while, at the same time, that crook used that stolen truck to make his family wealthy? When this crook is caught, does he still owe you just a truck?"

Martin gave it a moment's thought. "I see where you're going with this, but I think your analogy is too simple for something as vast and complex as slavery in America."

"Are you sure about that, Martin?" Solomon said. "Let me frame it in real terms. In 1889, twenty years after slavery was abolished, the United States government opened up the Oklahoma Territory to any American citizen who wanted to go west and tame the land. Imagine that. Free land. Now, do you think that our ancestors were allowed to participate in that bonanza? Of course not. Do white families, to this very day, profit from that land rush?"

"You better fucking believe it," Carver said.

The other men murmured in agreement.

"And that's just one example," Solomon continued. "American history is littered with events in which our ancestors were robbed of opportunities that white people profited from." Solomon leaned forward and squeezed Martin's arm. "Now, I'm not sitting here asking you to change the way you think or what you believe in. I'm just asking you to consider what I'm saying and decide if there's any truth in it."

Martin couldn't deny that Solomon's argument stirred something inside him. An uneasiness that felt almost like fear. As if he was being forced to confront some terrible suppressed memory that he'd kept walled off for his entire life.

"Will you?" Solomon asked. "Will you think about it?"

"Of course," Martin said. "You have an interesting way of looking at things. Very persuasive."

"Oh, please," Tobias said. "Old Solomon here is just a lightweight. You should hear Dr. Kasim lay down the science. That man will make your ears tingle."

Martin noticed that the instant Tobias mentioned Dr. Kasim, the other men shot him a scolding look, like a group of monks who had just heard the Lord's name spoken in vain. Tobias shrugged off their stares and reclined in his seat.

"Who's Dr. Kasim?" Martin had to ask.

A moment of hesitance among the men was ended by Damon. "Dr. Kasim's hard to describe. I guess you could call him an . . . underground philosopher."

Martin couldn't help smiling. "Underground philosopher? Has he written anything I might have heard of?"

The men flashed amused smiles at the question.

"Dr. Kasim has written many books, brother," Kwame said. "But you're not going to find 'em in your local bookstore."

"Okay." Martin was becoming more and more intrigued. "Does he have a website? YouTube videos? A Facebook page? What?"

The men shook their heads, as if mentioning Dr. Kasim

in the same breath with the Internet was the craziest thing they had ever heard.

"Actually, Martin, I'm a little surprised that you've never heard of Dr. Kasim," Damon said. "I mean, considering your activism in college."

The comment gave Martin pause. In the handful of times that the two men had spoken, during and since the trial, he was certain that he had never told Damon anything about his past.

"Don't look so surprised." Damon smiled. "You think I became the best lawyer in the universe by sitting on my ass? Preparation is everything. I probably know more about you than your own mother. Let's see . . . you attended Syracuse on a full academic scholarship. Majored in black studies. Your junior year, your roommate was harassed, humiliated, and arrested for nothing more than *shopping while black* at an upscale department store. While helping your friend win a settlement against the store, you also founded the Black Board, a small but aggressive group that took on the businesses around campus that had discriminatory policies against the black students. Despite being arrested four times for various marches, you were still successful in getting most of those businesses to change their practices." Damon winked at Martin. "Pretty good, huh?"

"Perfect," Martin said, impressed. In legal circles Damon Darrell's case preparation was legendary, but Martin had no idea that Damon's research extended to the opposing counsel's life history. "And you're right." Martin chuckled. "If my mother had known half the crap that I was up to on campus, she would've had a total breakdown."

The men laughed.

"The point I'm trying to make," Damon said, "is that it seems as though someone as involved as yourself would have at least heard of Dr. Kasim."

"So this Dr. Kasim is an activist as well, then?"

"Activist, motivator, educator," Solomon said. "All of those things and more."

"The brother is a straight-up genius," Kwame said. "His ideas nurture the black soul."

"I'll tell you one thing," Damon said to Martin, his voice earnest. "No one on this planet has inspired me more. No one."

As Martin listened, a troubling question formed in his mind. His first notion was to let it pass, but his desire to know the answer burned as hot as the sincerity in Damon's eyes. "Don't take this the wrong way," Martin said to Damon, "but what do you think Dr. Kasim would say about your law practice?"

Damon beamed at Martin, like he had anticipated this question all along. "I assume you mean because I frequently defend corporate conglomerates against racial discrimination suits. Am I right?"

"Yes," Martin said. "Especially, it seems, in cases where the plaintiffs are African American. You know as well as I do that some of these companies blatantly take advantage of minorities, and yet you allow them to use you to put up a good front. From what I've heard tonight, that seems to go against everything you believe in. So why do you do it?"

"That is an excellent question," Damon said. He reclined in his chair and took a few easy puffs on his cigar before continuing. "Please excuse me for answering your question with a question. What do you think would happen if I turned down those cases? Even better, what if every conscientious black attorney refused to defend any corporation accused of racial discrimination?"

"Those corporations would lose more often," Martin said. "I know that much."

The men all laughed, Damon right along with them.

"True, true," Damon said, "but what I'm getting at is this: those corporations would just turn around and hire a white firm."

"So let them. At least they're not putting up a false front of diversity to confuse the jury."

Solomon shook his head. "No, no, no. You're not seeing the big picture, son."

"You gotta look deeper, brother," Kwame said. "It's not as simple as black and white."

"Not much ever is," Martin replied.

"Think about it like this," Damon said. "My firm employs over two dozen lawyers. Every last one of them is black—and a millionaire. In a slow year our billing easily exceeds one hundred million. Every year I donate twenty-five percent of my firm's profits to numerous black charities. College funds, food programs, recreation centers, housing initiatives, even campaign contributions to black politicians."

Martin's eyebrows rose. "That's very impressive. I had no idea."

"I don't do it for publicity, Martin, I do it to reach back and help my people. But here's the thing. If those corporations pay their multimillion-dollar legal fees to a white firm instead of me, none of that amazing stuff happens. What the corporations siphon away from our people with their discriminatory practices, I take back tenfold when they get my invoice. What would Dr. Kasim say about my practice? I'll tell you what he told me personally. 'Keep up the positive work, brother.'"

While the other men nodded in agreement, Damon sank back into his chair and took a long satisfying puff of his cigar.

Martin took this in in silence. Then something chilling occurred to him. Something that made his gut tighten. "Are you saying that you lost to me on purpose?"

"Did it seem like I was taking a dive?" Damon said.

"No, but—"

"Think about it. It doesn't matter if I win or lose, my bill's the same. Why would I risk ruining everything I've built? Hurt the people I want to help? Trust me, Martin, when I step into a courtroom, I fight with every ounce of my ability to win for my client, but I will tell you this."

Damon leaned closer, wearing a conspiratorial smile. "In my heart, I'm always pulling for the little guy. I was rooting for you the whole time, Martin, and you did not disappoint. Now those racist bastards have to pay twice."

Martin tried to smile in agreement, but he still had an uncomfortable feeling in the pit of his stomach.

Seeing the look on his face, Damon said, "Relax. Sympathizing with your opponent isn't unethical."

"And besides," Carver added, "we have one unbreakable rule. Anything said between us, stays between us."

The men nodded.

Carver studied Martin through the smoke curling from the fiery tip of his cigar. "Is that cool with you?"

Damon, Solomon, Tobias, Kwame, and Carver all watched Martin, waiting for his answer. Martin understood why. These were important men. These were titans of industry. African American role models. Men under constant scrutiny by the media and the government. They had reputations to protect and images to uphold. Martin did not feel that anything they discussed was hateful or malicious, but he could see how, outside that smoke-filled room, the complexion of their words and ideas could be misinterpreted in ways that could harm them all. "Agreed," Martin said with a nod.

The titans of industry smiled and puffed their cigars and drained their glasses . . . and Martin couldn't help feeling that he had just passed some sort of test.

14

By two a.m. Martin and Anna were speeding home along Interstate 684. There were few cars out, so Martin pushed his Volvo a little harder than usual. Martin wasn't a speed freak, not even close, but sometimes he did enjoy the rush of acceleration and the roar of the engine. What real man didn't enjoy burning a little rubber?

That was part of it too, Martin realized. That hour spent in Damon's game room, in the company of giants like Solomon and Tobias, had put him in a manly mood, as if some of their power had rubbed off on him. And perhaps it had. Friends like that not only could open a lot of doors, they could move mountains. As Martin pushed his Volvo even faster down the dark highway, he had a heady feeling.

"Why are you driving like a crazy man?" Anna said.

"Feels incredible, doesn't it?"

"Would you slow down, please?"

Anna's tone took Martin off guard. He slowed to the speed limit. "Are you okay?"

"It's nothing. I'm just tired."

Martin didn't pretend to understand Anna's myriad moods, three times more than the average woman by his estimate, but he did know when she was itching to talk about something. "I thought you said you had a good time."

"I did," Anna said. "I had a great time."

"Then what's wrong?"

Anna hesitated, then said, "What about your civil rights work?"

"What do you mean?"

Anna sighed. "You know I always support you, right? Your work, I mean."

"Of course," Martin replied. Back when the firm wasn't earning a penny, it was Anna's nursing job that paid the bills. Once, when things really looked bleak, Martin and Glen were tempted to close shop and take secure positions at an established firm, but Anna wouldn't have it. She convinced both Martin and Glen to keep going. Anna had never doubted him or his dream for a second. "You know you're my rock, baby," Martin said. "Just tell me what's wrong."

"It's just . . ." Anna frowned. "You're so excited about working with these men you've met tonight, and a part of me is really happy for you . . . but another part of me is worried that they're going to take you away from your real work. Do you know what I mean?"

Martin reached over and took Anna's hand. There was a time when Martin scoffed at the term *soul mate*. But that had all changed when he met Anna.

"Listen," Martin said. "Tobias and Solomon mentioned

that they had a couple cases that they could steer my way. Nothing major, I promise. Besides"—Martin chuckled—"it's not like the firm is overbooked."

"Not now you aren't. But rich men have rich friends, and their rich friends have rich friends, and once they see how good you are, you won't have time for anything else."

Martin smiled. He hadn't extrapolated the benefits of the night's events to that extent, but Anna did have a point. It could happen. If he and Glen played their cards right, in a few years, they could have a five-star client list. "I hope you're right," Martin said.

"What?"

"Baby, if the firm becomes that big, imagine all the pro bono work that I could do. I could devote an entire floor to nothing but civil rights cases."

"Floor?"

"Have you seen Damon Darrell's offices?"

"Martin, I do not want you to turn into Damon Darrell."

"Never," Martin said. "And no matter how big the firm gets, civil rights cases will always be a priority."

"You promise?"

"Cross my heart and hope to—"

Anna grabbed his hand. "Stop. You know I hate that. Just promise me. That's all."

"I promise, I promise, I promise. How's that?"

Anna smiled and gave Martin a big kiss on the cheek.

"Hey, hey, I'm driving here."

"And I promise," Anna said, "not to turn into a mannequin with a credit card."

"Huh?"

"Juanita's really nice, but those other women . . . they're kinda scary. Seriously."

Martin laughed.

"Oh, and one more thing," Anna said. "I beg you, no crazy rafting trips."

Martin gave her a puzzled glance. "How do you know about that?"

"Juanita told me all about it. Do you know how worried I would be? I wouldn't sleep a wink the whole time you were gone."

"Well, relax, they didn't invite me. Even if they did, you know I wouldn't be interested. You know that's not me."

"Not normally," Anna sighed. "I just have this feeling that after tonight . . . everything will be different." Then Anna sank back into her seat and stared out at the dark highway.

15

Damon Darrell sat in his wood-paneled study at a cluttered desk typing an email. According to the decorator, the desk was hand carved, extremely rare, and a perfect complement to the room's imported wood paneling. It was Juanita who had selected the desk, of course. Damon didn't care about any of that. He was too busy to care. As far as Damon was concerned, any desk that had space for his seventeen-inch Sony VAIO notebook, a telephone, and a sizable mug of coffee was good enough for him.

As Damon paused to take a sip from his steaming cup, he was surprised to hear a voice behind him. A playful whisper, "Knock, knock."

Damon turned and nearly dropped his coffee. Juanita stood framed in the doorway, naked. Juanita was almost forty, but thanks to a personal trainer and a private chef, she had the body of a twentysomething bikini model. Slender legs. Luscious hips. Perfect pert breasts. Cocoa skin so evenly toned that she seemed airbrushed. Nine years of marriage, and Damon was still floored by his wife's beauty. He beamed as he drank her in. "Guess I don't have to ask if all the help has left."

Juanita shook her head with a naughty smile. "There's

only one thing dirty in this house, and you're looking at it." Then Juanita licked her pouty lips.

Damon responded with a lustful moan. Before he had married Juanita, and even after, Damon had his choice of beautiful women. When you're rich, famous, and influential, top-shelf pussy isn't something you look for—it finds you. But with only a handful of exceptions, Damon had steered clear. What set Juanita apart from all the other pretty faces was her unmatched sexual appetite. The woman loved to fuck. Even better, she loved to be fucked good and hard by Damon. Damon knew countless miserable husbands whose sex lives had fallen into a rut or vanished altogether. He didn't have that problem because making love to Juanita never got old. Unfortunately, tonight Juanita's timing couldn't have been worse. Damon had an important phone call to make, one that required complete secrecy. The call was scheduled for two a.m. and it was already two ten. Damon knew that the man waiting for the call would not be happy.

Juanita deflated when she saw a frown appear on Damon's face. She knew her husband's *I'm too busy* look all too well. "But it's two in the morning." She pouted. "Can't it wait until tomorrow?"

"Unfortunately, it can't. I'm sorry, baby. I'll make it up to you. Promise."

Where some women might feel rejected and react with resentment, Juanita just smiled and said, "Well, try not to work too hard. Good night." Then she blew Damon a kiss and closed the door behind her. That was one of the things Damon loved most about Juanita. She wasn't one of those idle women who constantly competed with their husband's career for attention.

As it happened, the late-night conference that Damon was about to have had nothing to do with his career or a business deal, but Juanita didn't need to know that.

Damon cocked his ear toward the door and listened carefully. When he heard Juanita padding up the winding staircase toward their bedroom, he crossed the study and locked the door. The only reason he'd left the door unlocked in the first place was that he knew Juanita would peek in to say good night before going to bed. He had no idea that she would be in such a playful mood, especially after hosting a dinner party. While Damon was waiting for Juanita to pop in, he had replied to a few unimportant emails and checked the overseas stock quotes. Now that Juanita was headed off to bed and there was no chance of being interrupted, Damon could finally make the scheduled call.

Damon glanced at the clock. Two fifteen a.m. He just hoped it wasn't too late.

Damon hurried back to his computer and clicked on an icon labeled WhispeX. WhispeX was a teleconferencing program with one feature that set it apart from the rest. WhispeX employed an encryption algorithm that, the designer claimed, even the CIA couldn't crack.

A large video window bloomed onto the screen. With

no active connection, the screen remained dark. In the lower left corner of the window, another box, a quarter the size of the main window, displayed live video of Damon's face. The existing light was adequate but Damon had to center his image by adjusting the tiny webcam perched on his monitor.

Damon slipped on a microphone headset, then slid the cursor to a sidebar that featured a contact list of ten buttons. Nine of these buttons were labeled with a contact's name. Solomon, Kwame, Tobias, and Carver were among the names listed. One button was different from the rest. The very first button at the top of the list was labeled not with a name, just a number and a letter: 40A. Damon clicked the first button.

Connecting flashed in the main video window and the computer speakers issued a series of low electronic tones. The beeping ceased and the stern face of a black man filled the main window. Oscar Lennox's shaved head and meticulously groomed goatee gave him a striking look, but it was Oscar's eyes that wielded the fire. Two piercing gray orbs that seemed to see all and rarely blinked. Even through the monitor, Damon thought that Oscar's stare was more than a bit unnerving.

"You're late, brother," Oscar said, in a deep, calm voice.

"Juanita's party ran a bit later than expected," Damon explained. "I apologize."

Oscar nodded. "Understandable. Now what about the prospect?"

"He did well. Better than expected, in my opinion." Damon wasn't surprised that Oscar had jumped right to the chase. Oscar wasn't one for small talk. He was never rude, but he wasn't what you would call amiable either. He was all business all the time and never missed a trick — which made him perfect for the position that he held.

"And the others," Oscar asked. "Are you all in agreement?"

"Yes," Damon said.

Oscar raised an eyebrow. "Mr. Lewis as well?"

Damon frowned. "Carver doesn't like anyone but Carver. You know that. But yes, he did agree to proceed to the next step."

Oscar's eyes narrowed with interest. "Really. Tell me Mr. Lewis's thoughts — exactly."

"For what reason? I just told you, Carver agreed with the rest of us to move forward."

Oscar did not respond. He just stared at Damon from the video screen.

"Sorry," Damon said with a frown. He regretted that he had even asked the question in the first place. Oscar Lennox was Dr. Kasim's personal assistant and, more importantly, the doctor's spokesman in the outside world. Oscar was to be trusted, no questions asked. "I meant no disrespect," Damon tried to explain. "I just don't want to lose a solid prospect because of one irrational kid."

Oscar frowned, ever so slightly. "You might not think much of the young man's opinion, brother," he said, "but the doctor views Mr. Lewis's suspicious nature as an asset to our security. Now, do you have Mr. Lewis's card?"

Damon nodded and removed four business cards from the center desk drawer. Kwame, Tobias, Carver, and Solomon had each jotted down their individual impressions of the prospect on the back of their business cards, then surreptitiously slipped the cards to Damon before calling it a night. This was the secret voting method they always used. A little awkward, but simple and immediate.

Carver's card, with its full-color glossy finish, was the flashiest of the four. Damon flipped the card over and read aloud what Carver had written. "White partner could be trouble. Watch him carefully." Damon then held the card up in front of the webcam to allow Oscar to read it himself. "That's it. That's all Carver wrote."

Oscar frowned and thought a moment. Finally he looked back at Damon. "Dr. Kasim also has concerns about Mr. Grey's partner, as you know. But you don't?"

"Means nothing," Damon said. "I have a few white attorneys on staff as well. It's good for business and keeps up appearances."

"It's their friendship that mostly concerns the doctor."

"Of course. To be thorough I had Mr. Grossman surveilled for the last few days, physically and digitally. No red flags. Beyond their business relationship there's no substantial ties between the two. At least nothing compared to what we offer."

Oscar nodded. "That's good."

"He's young, smart, conscious, and his future, financially speaking, is limitless. Martin Grey is the strongest prospect that we've seen in a while. He's exactly the kind of man we need to keep what we have alive."

Oscar's video visage just watched Damon a moment, as if he were able to peer into Damon's soul from two thousand miles away. "Dr. Kasim trusts your instincts," Oscar finally said. "Feel free to move forward."

"Thank you."

"But I caution you, brother. Dr. Kasim does not want any mistakes. Not like the last prospect."

Damon nodded. "I understand."

"Use the best people. Double-check everything, then check a third time."

"I will. I promise."

"Dr. Kasim looks forward to meeting your Mr. Grey," Oscar said without even a hint of emotion. Then the encrypted teleconferencing connection winked out.

16

"Okay, how was it?" Glen asked, breezing into Martin's office and plopping down in a chair. "I want to hear everything that happened."

Martin set aside the trial transcript that he was reviewing. "It was fun. A lot of fun."

Glen frowned. "Come on, you can do better than that. I've been waiting all morning to hear this."

After Damon's party Friday night the rest of Martin's weekend was uneventful. When he returned to the office Monday morning, there was a significant uptick in new consultation requests, a direct result of the firm's recent victory.

Their two paralegals, Akiko and Meg, fielded the extra calls with ease, allowing Martin and Glen to get back to business as usual. They rarely took lunch breaks, but around noon there was usually a lull. That was when Glen found the opportunity to grill Martin about the party.

Martin threw up his hands. "What do you want me to tell you? Damon's house was amazing. The food was unbelievable."

"No, no, no. Who was there? Any possible future clients with bottomless pockets?"

Martin ran down the list of guests. With each name Glen's eyes grew wider and wider. "Solomon Aarons too? What was he like?"

"Brilliant," Martin replied. "You can sense it. Like an old wise man."

Glen nodded, then, struck with a thought, he said, with a huge grin, "Ooh, now I get it."

"Get what?"

"All the guests at Damon's party were African American. Come on, you had to notice that."

"I did. So?"

"So, don't you get it? That's probably the real reason Damon didn't invite me. Lisa and I would've been the only white couple there."

Martin was about to deny it, but he couldn't. Up until that moment Martin hadn't made the connection between the power chat in Damon's game room and Glen's exclusion from the party—not explicitly, but now, hearing it aloud, Martin saw it clearly.

Glen shrugged it off. "Hey, I don't think Damon did it maliciously or anything. He probably just didn't want us to feel awkward. Know what I mean?"

Martin felt a twinge of guilt as he nodded in agreement. "Sure. I guess that's possible."

"So what did all you big shots talk about?" Glen asked.

Martin tensed. It wasn't that he feared that anything discussed would upset Glen—in fact Martin was pretty sure that Glen would agree with most of what was said. What kept Martin silent was his promise. He gave his word to a roomful of very powerful men to keep their discussion private, and he wasn't about to break it. That and the fact that Glen was terrible at keeping his mouth shut.

Martin said, "We just discussed the case mostly."

Glen looked doubtful. "Come on. All those power brokers under one roof. They had to talk about more than just your case. Give it up, partner."

One of the attributes that made Glen a great lawyer was his tenacity. Once Glen latched onto something, he shook and shook until he ripped it apart. Martin realized that if he didn't distract his partner with something juicy, Glen would be drilling him for details about the party for weeks. "Actually," Martin said, "Tobias Stewart and Kwame Jones expressed interest in steering some business our way."

Glen's eyes lit up like a tot's on Christmas morning. "Bingo! Now that's what I wanted to hear."

Martin laughed.

"Martin, do you know what this means?"

"Slow down," Martin cautioned. "Nothing's certain yet. Could just be party talk."

"Either way, we have to be prepared, right? I mean, if those heavy hitters see this dump, they could get second thoughts. Martin, come on, it's time."

Glen had been pushing for a new office for over a year,

but Martin insisted on waiting until the firm's finances were more certain. With the fat contingency check on the way and the very real potential of landing two huge clients, it appeared that the time had finally arrived. "I think you're right." Martin nodded. "We'll start looking for a place tomorrow."

"*Yes!*" Glen slapped Martin high five. "Damon Darrell is all right with me. I mean, he had to realize that this could happen if he invited you into his circle. We're talking primo contacts here."

Martin shrugged. "Damon's plate is full, I'm sure."

Glen snorted. "Yeah, more like a huge serving platter."

Akiko's voice blared from the phone on Martin's desk. "You have Damon Darrell on line two."

Martin and Glen exchanged a look. Glen gestured to the phone with a little flourish. "Speak of the devil and he comes calling."

Martin stared at the flashing line two button, reluctant to take the call with his partner listening in. If Damon brought up anything discussed in the game room, things could get awkward.

"Come on," Glen said. "Don't keep our benefactor waiting."

Martin picked up the phone. "Hey. Damon. What's up?"

"Martin, how are you? Hope you and your wife had a nice weekend." Martin could hear the chatter and clatter of a restaurant in the background.

"I did," Martin replied. "And thanks again for Friday night. Anna and I had a great time."

"Listen," Damon said, his voice changing. "I have a very strange question to ask you."

Martin paused. What the hell did he mean, "strange question"? Their relationship was too fresh for any strange questions. "Okay," Martin said hesitantly.

"Are you and Anna, by any chance, Stevie Wonder fans?"

17

The following evening the Handyman sat in the front seat of a van parked across the street from Martin Grey's house, watching. The Handyman wore a blue workman's uniform with a photo name tag that identified him as Curtis Goins. The company patch on the sleeve of the Handyman's uniform read Cable Com in sleek lettering. The same logo adorned the outside of the work van along with the cheesy slogan "We bring smiles into your life." The entire facade was designed to render the Handyman invisible to the casual observer, as familiar as the corner streetlight or a mailbox. But if some henpecked husband dragging out the trash or some fat housewife out for a power walk did happen to take notice, all they would see was a cable guy goofing off. Those soft and clueless suburbanites would have no idea that they were in fact observing a man of rare talents, a true criminal artist.

The Handyman checked his watch: 6:33 p.m. The limousine was late. True, it was only three minutes, but for the task at hand every single minute was crucial.

The client had assured the Handyman that Martin and his wife would be out of their home for a minimum of three hours. For your typical garden-variety burglar three hours would be more than fine, but the Handyman was nothing like a typical burglar. In fact, the Handyman resented that vulgar term. He didn't consider himself a burglar at all. Burglars smash doors and break windows, whereas he had mastered the delicate skills to pick any lock and disable all security systems. Burglars ransack homes. The Handyman meticulously searched every inch of the property and took the utmost care to leave no trace of the intrusion. Burglars haul away valuables like jewelry and electronics. The Handyman had no interest in that junk. What the Handyman was after was far more precious. Financial records, medical records, bills, receipts, credit cards, family photos, keys, even hair follicles and nail clippings to extract DNA. With an array of high-tech gadgetry the Handyman would scan, copy, download, or photograph every shred of personal information that he could find—and he made it his business to find it all. To work his magic usually took about two hours, but if something went wrong, like a hard drive crashing while being cloned, three hours could be cutting it close.

Finally the limousine glided to a stop in front of the Greys' house. The Handyman checked his watch again: 6:35. Five precious minutes wasted.

The Handyman watched as the uniformed chauffeur hurried up the walk to the front door and rang the bell. A moment later Martin Grey and his wife, Anna, emerged. Martin was dressed in a suit and an open-neck shirt and Anna wore a clingy black dress. The Handyman recognized the couple from the photos emailed to him from the client. They looked like nice, honest people, and for all he knew they probably were. The Handyman had no idea why the client had targeted the Greys and he didn't care to know. He was hired to do a job and that was all that was important. He just wanted them to hurry up and leave so that he could get started already.

As the Handyman watched the Greys make their way to the limousine, something unexpected happened. Martin glanced across the street and stared directly at the Handyman. The Handyman just smiled and nodded. Martin simply returned the friendly gesture, then climbed into the limousine with his wife.

The Handyman frowned at his watch: 6:37. Usually he'd wait until the occupants were gone for a full fifteen minutes before entering a home. That way if they forgot something, like their tickets or wallet, there wouldn't be any surprise encounters. But the Handyman couldn't wait that long. Too much time had been lost already. The Handyman applied pressure to a precise point on the driver's side door panel, and a small hidden compartment sprang open.

If the Greys did return early, he would make every attempt to conceal himself. He was under strict orders not to harm them. But if by some unfortunate chance his presence was discovered, he would have to take matters into his own hands.

From the hidden compartment the Handyman removed

a nine-millimeter handgun and a silencer. The steely aroma of gun oil stung his nostrils as he twisted the silencer into place.

Throughout his eleven-year criminal career, the Handyman had never even come close to getting caught. He attributed this amazing streak to one rule that he lived by: no one could ever know what the Handyman looked like. Not the clients who hired him through phone calls and email and certainly not the victims. No one.

The Handyman placed the silenced handgun in his toolbox, slapped on his Cable Com cap, then jumped out of the van and strolled across the street toward Martin Grey's house.

18

"I hate to tell you this," Martin said to Glen over his cell phone, "but you're too late. We're already on our way to the concert."

"Shit. I was hoping to catch you guys before you left. I gotta be in court at eight a.m. tomorrow. What am I going to do?"

Martin and Anna were in the rear of the speeding limousine, riding in plush leather style. When Damon had extended an invitation to the Stevie Wonder concert, which included after-show drinks with the legend himself, Martin could not refuse. Damon even insisted on sending a limo, and in true Damon Darrell fashion, he spared no expense. The marble wet bar was fully stocked with only the best liquor and several bottles of chilled Cristal champagne. A silver platter of jumbo shrimp cocktail and another with a crystal dish of caviar were laid out for their noshing pleasure. A plasma-screen TV played Stevie Wonder music videos in crisp high-definition. Before Glen's call had interrupted them, Martin and Anna were sipping Cristal and singing "My Cherie Amour" with their mouths full. Anna tried to get Martin to ignore the call, but when Martin saw Glen's name on the caller ID, he felt a distinct pang of guilt. Here he was cruising around in a stretch limo while Glen was stuck back at the office preparing for a trial. Glen didn't seem to care that, once again, Damon had excluded him. The promised opportunities to come from Martin's association with Damon were enough to squelch any feelings of envy.

Martin had assured Anna that he would get off the phone quickly, but when Martin heard the urgency in Glen's voice, he feared that he had spoken too soon. Glen had a mini crisis on his hands.

Two weeks ago, after doing some preliminary research, their paralegal Akiko had handed Glen a typed list of dockets that he should review to prepare for the trial. Glen stuck that list into a case folder but never had time to get to it again—until twenty minutes ago when he noticed that the list was missing. It didn't take Glen long to figure out what had happened. He and Martin routinely exchanged duplicates of their case folders so that in case of an emergency each would be up to speed on the other's work. But instead of giving Martin the duplicate folder, Glen had mistakenly given his partner the original— along with the only list of docket numbers. Not a major problem if the folder was inside Martin's office, but it wasn't. Two nights ago Martin had taken the folder home to go over at his leisure.

"The folder's right in my study," Martin said. "If you had called just ten minutes earlier, I could have read you the numbers over the phone."

Glen groaned. "I don't believe this."

"Did you call Akiko? Maybe she made another copy."

"I tried. Believe me. For some reason she's not answering her phone."

"Did you look for the file on her computer?"

"Come on. You know I can't find shit on her computer. I can't even find shit on my own computer."

"Look, don't panic. As soon as I get back home, I'll just call you with the numbers."

"And that'll be when? Midnight? One? Great! I'll be up all night reading. I'll be a zombie in court tomorrow."

"I'm sorry. I just don't know what else I can do."

"Couldn't you just turn back real quick?"

Martin groaned. "Glen, there has to be another solution. We're already halfway there. We'll be late if we turn back now."

The instant Anna heard the words "turn back," her shoulders sagged.

"I'm sorry, man," Glen said. "I screwed up and I feel bad about it, I do—but Martin, you know how important this case is to the firm. Besides, what concert ever started on time? How late would you really be? I need you, partner. Please."

As irritated as Martin was, he also knew that Glen was right. The case was important. All their cases were important. Anna would just have to understand.

But before Martin could tell Glen that he would turn the limousine around, he remembered something. Two years ago, while Martin and Anna spent a week in Charlotte with Anna's mother, Glen did them a favor and checked in on the house a few times. Removed circulars from the doorstep, that sort of thing. "Wait a minute, don't you still have the set of keys I gave you?" Martin said.

There was a pause on the phone as Glen searched his memory. "Yeah! Yeah I do. But man, that was years ago. Do those keys still work?"

"The front lock I know we changed, but I'm pretty sure the back door is the same."

"That's great. What's the alarm code?"

"Two two three four."

"Two two three four. Got it. The file's in your study, you said?"

"Yeah. Should be right on my desk. Don't forget to reset the alarm when you leave. Same code."

"Really sorry I bugged you. You and Anna have a good time."

The instant Martin snapped his phone shut, Anna grabbed it, shut it off, and jammed it into her handbag. "No more calls."

"Hold it. What if Glen has trouble getting into the house?"

Anna rolled her eyes. "Please. How hard could it be to open a door?" Anna grabbed a bottle of Cristal and re-filled Martin's flute. Tiny bubbles swirled in the golden liquid. "Now quit worrying," Anna said, sliding closer to Martin. "Your partner will be just fine."

19

The Handyman sat at Martin Grey's desk waiting patiently as his Micron 1-terrabyte solid-state drive cloned the entire contents of a Dell XPS desktop at the amazing speed of one gigabyte per second. The SSD's pulsating work light and the shimmer from the computer monitor painted the walls of the dark study with a ghostly glow. A progress bar on the monitor indicated that 64 percent of Martin's computer had already been copied. In just ten more minutes, the Handyman estimated, his night's work would be complete.

Stealing the Greys' information was turning out to be one of the easiest jobs that the Handyman had ever had. Their home security system was one of those popular brands that advertised on television incessantly. The consumer-grade alarm circuitry was so easy to disable that it was almost laughable. Defeating the front door locks was just as simple. All it took was the insertion of a specially cut bump key, a few taps with the handle of a screwdriver, and the tumblers clicked open with ease. While lock-picking tools left microscopic scratches on the keyhole, when executed correctly the use of a bump key was undetectable. The Handyman had used bump keys for years, but when the surprisingly simple technique popped up all over the Internet, he was certain that home owners everywhere would scramble to have their flawed locks replaced. But to the Handyman's utter surprise, the scare never happened. Despite nightly news reports and magazine articles, the bump key secret had been widely ignored. It was rare when the Handyman encountered a door lock that he could not bump open in under ten seconds flat.

Once he'd gained entrance, the search of the Grey residence also presented very little challenge for the Handyman. When it came to record keeping, the Handyman put his victims into three distinct categories: organized, disorganized, and paranoid. The disorganized victims, the biggest group by far, presented the most trouble for the Handyman because they tended to keep their records wherever they set them down last. Sometimes the Handyman would have to search a home for hours to find and duplicate all the documents he needed. The paranoids, because they squirreled their valuables in some secret location or secured them inside a home safe, always presented a significant challenge, but only at first. Once the Handyman found their loose floorboard or cracked their wall safe, all their documents were right there for the easy picking. The organized victims were the easiest by far. They kept their records in filing cabinets or in boxes, neatly labeled. Sometimes even in alphabetical order.

Martin and his wife definitely fell into the organized

category. It did not take the Handyman long to discover that a walk-in closet inside Martin's study served as a kind of in-home records room. Stacks of cardboard boxes filled the rear of the four-by-four space. The boxes were each labeled with a year, the oldest being 1989, and every single one was jam-packed with old bills, bank statements, and receipts. Just inside the door of the closet stood two tall metal filing cabinets. These cabinets were of much more interest to the Handyman because they contained the Greys' most recent documents. Martin's filing system was excellent, making the Handyman's job simplicity itself. In under an hour the entire contents of both filing cabinets were digitally duplicated and stored on a tiny flash drive in the Handyman's hip pocket.

Cloning the computers found in his victim's homes was usually the most unpredictable and time-consuming part of the Handyman's work. Besides the desktops and laptops that were used by the victims every day, many homes contained several older computers as well. These were obsolete machines stubbornly hoarded because the owners refused to discard an item that cost them a small fortune just a few years ago. To do a thorough job, the Handyman liked to clone every computer in a victim's house. Older computers were usually slower or had faulty hard drives that required the installation of special software to coax their data free. Sometimes these computers also had passwords that had to be cracked, requiring even more precious time.

The Handyman encountered none of these technolog-ical obstacles inside Martin Grey's home. The Handyman found only three computers—a Dell desktop located in Martin's study and two MacBook Pro notebooks in their bedroom. The MacBook decorated with an Apple rain-bow sticker belonged to Anna, and the other belonged to Martin. Neither machine was password protected and they each took mere minutes to clone. Martin's desktop was a different story. The Dell XPS did require a password to gain access, but with the use of a sniffer program that the Handyman wrote himself, he was able to decrypt Martin's code in no time: LAWMAN. The Handyman almost laughed when Martin's password flashed on the screen. His victims' lack of imagination never ceased to amuse him.

What brought the Handyman the most relief about the evening's work was that neither Martin nor his wife had returned to the house—leaving him to complete his work in peace. Only twice had the Handyman been forced to kill his victims in order to make a clean escape. He didn't like killing, but like everything else that he set his mind to, he was good at it. No, the Handyman liked it best when he was able to complete his work quickly and quietly, then vanish into the night as if he had never been there at all.

The Handyman checked the hard drive's progression bar again: 85 percent complete. Only five more minutes to go. Maybe he'd get back to his hotel room in time to catch his favorite television program, *Crime 360*. It was one of what seemed like a million cable shows that focused on police forensic techniques. What made *Crime 360* stand out was its amazing level of detail. The very latest methods in crime scene analysis were exposed for the viewing public's entertainment every Saturday night at nine p.m. The Handyman often wondered if the producers of these shows ever worried that they were teaching crooks and murderers how to evade detection and prosecution. The Handyman, of course, was already well familiar with most of the techniques demonstrated on the show, but occasionally he did pick up a trick or two. Like the episode about—

What sounded like a vehicle pulling into the driveway seized the Handyman's attention. He grabbed his silenced handgun from the toolbox. The study was situated in the rear of the house with no view of the driveway, so he bolted into the living room and stalked to the nearest window.

The Handyman inched back the curtain and peeked out.

A blue Grand Cherokee crept to a stop in the driveway. The Handyman recognized the car. It belonged to Martin's partner, Glen Grossman. The Handyman had already done a level-one investigation on Grossman for the same client. Level one was just a basic background check with one day of surveillance. The Handyman's investigation of Martin began as a level one as well, until the client opted to upgrade the probe to the Handyman's most invasive tier of service, level three.

As the Handyman watched Grossman climb out of the SUV his mind raced. What the hell was Grossman doing here? Didn't Grossman know that Martin wasn't home? Then the Handyman saw something that answered his question. As the lawyer started across the lawn, he pocketed his car keys and pulled out another set of keys. Keys to Martin's house. What else could they be? No, this wasn't a casual visit where Grossman would be turned away by an unanswered doorbell. For whatever reason, Glen Grossman was about to let himself into Martin Grey's house.

20

The key ring that Martin had given Glen two years earlier held just three keys. The first two keys Glen tried on the rear door of Martin's house did not turn the lock. The last key did the trick. Glen pulled open the door and stepped into Martin and Anna's spacious kitchen. Soft moonlight through curtained windows glistened off chrome, marble, and tiles. Glen locked the door behind him, then reached for the security keypad to punch in the code—and froze. What Glen saw made no sense. The small LED screen on the keypad read Disarmed. Martin and Anna must have forgotten to set the alarm before they left. But that wasn't like Martin. Not even close. Glen's partner was a cross-all-his-Ts kinda guy. Glen couldn't imagine Martin forgetting something as important as securing his home. The excitement of the concert must have really gotten to him.

Glen headed into the living room. Just enough light bled through the windows for Glen to find his way around the furniture. Even in the dark, the place looked great, Glen thought. He remembered when Anna and Martin had first moved in. Martin got a great deal because the house needed a lot of work. And boy, did it ever. It took them a while, but Martin and Anna had done a fantastic job of transforming a neglected house into a beautiful home.

Glen moved past the stairs and headed down the short hall that led to Martin's study. The door was closed. Glen hoped it wasn't locked. He had no reason to believe it would be, but since he had no idea where to find the key, he couldn't help the worry. He had to get those docket numbers.

Glen smiled when the doorknob to the study turned with ease. But when Glen pushed open the door and switched on the light, he saw something that made his heart stop.

21

Hidden inside Martin's walk-in closet, the Handyman watched through the cracked-open door as Grossman entered the study and switched on the light. Even before Grossman entered the study, the Handyman had surmised that there could be only one logical reason for the lawyer's unexpected visit. Grossman was there to pick up something. Something important related to their work that could not wait. Of course, suspecting this as he did, the last place the Handyman wanted to be was inside Martin's home office, Grossman's likeliest destination, but he had no choice. By the time the Handyman had returned the desktop computer to normal and cleared Martin's desk, he could already hear Grossman moving through the house. The only place that the Handyman could readily conceal himself was Martin's records room. He just hoped, for Grossman's sake, that the lawyer would find whatever the hell he came for and leave promptly. Unfortunately, the shocked look on Grossman's face was not a good sign. Why was Grossman staring at Martin's desk like that?

The Handyman watched puzzled as Grossman rushed over to the desk and searched it frantically. He rifled every drawer, not once but twice. Grossman even looked under the desk.

What the hell was he looking for?

Grossman gaped at Martin's desk as if something had vanished right before his eyes. It was at that moment that the Handyman realized his mistake. *I took too many*, he thought.

To simplify the scanning of Martin's personal documents, the Handyman had removed any pertinent file folders from the closet and used Martin's desk as a work space. After he was done, instead of immediately returning the folders to the closet, he left them stacked on the desk with the intention to refile them after he completed cloning Martin's computer. Then Grossman showed up.

When the Handyman rushed to hide in the closet, he grabbed the stack of folders, but he took too many. When he had first entered the study, besides the computer and telephone, there was a lone folder on Martin's desk. Now it was gone. The Handyman glanced down at the stack of file folders that he still gripped tightly. There was no time to refile them without making a racket.

In the confined gloom he could just make out that all of the folders were light in color—except one. The folder at the very bottom of the stack was darker and thicker than the others. How could he be so stupid? There was no doubt that this dark folder was what Grossman searched so desperately for.

The Handyman's eyes glazed over with cool resolve as

he watched Grossman dial his cell phone. He heard Grossman leave an urgent voicemail message for Martin to return his call, then saw him slap his phone shut in frustration.

Then, just as the Handyman expected, Grossman turned and stared in the direction of the closet. The Handyman could see the unfortunate realization take shape in Grossman's head. What better place to search for a file than inside a closet filled with files?

As the Handyman watched Glen step toward the closet, he cocked his handgun.

22

Glen paused outside the closet door. He didn't like the idea of rummaging through Martin's personal stuff and he was pretty sure that Martin and Anna wouldn't like it. But wasn't this situation Martin's fault? Martin assured him that the file was on his desk, when it clearly wasn't. To make matters worse, Martin's phone was off or had no service, so there was no way to contact him. Glen glanced at his watch. It was already after nine. If he was going to get his minimum requirement of four hours' sleep, he had to be in bed by two. Reading time was burning up fast. He had no choice. Glen twisted the doorknob.

Brinnnng! Before Glen pulled the door open, his cell phone chimed. Glen grabbed it fast, expecting to hear Martin's voice, but it was his assistant, Akiko.

"Sorry," she said in her perpetually chipper voice, "I just got your message."

"Where were you?"

"It's Thursday. Hello? Yoga. You know I turn off my phone during class."

Glen did recall something about Akiko teaching a yoga class. The trouble was Akiko was involved with all sorts of new age nonsense. Everything from astrology to zombie parties. "I was looking for the docket numbers you looked up," he said.

"I know. You ready to write them down?"

Glen grabbed a pen and paper from Martin's desk and jotted down the six docket numbers. He promised to take his assistant out to lunch and then ended the call with a phrase that, at that moment, held more significance than he would ever know. "Akiko," Glen said, "you're a lifesaver." Then Glen flicked off the lights and exited Martin's study.

*

The Handyman watched from the living room window as Grossman climbed into his SUV and sped away.

It upset the Handyman that he would have to remain inside Martin Grey's house longer than expected to complete his work. But sparing the lawyer, that pleased him. It made the Handyman feel like a God.

23

The limousine ride was fun. The concert was amazing. Having drinks with Stevie after the concert was incredible. But making love to his beautiful wife inside a hot, steamy shower at two o'clock in the morning? Priceless.

Martin nestled Anna from behind as his soapy hands glided over her curves. The press of her pert bottom against his hardness was almost too much to bear. The heat from the rising steam combined with his coursing lust made his head swim. Unable to stand it any longer, Martin bent Anna forward beneath the hot spray and entered her from behind. Anna gasped and clawed the slick tiles as Martin pumped and pumped. *Smack!* He slapped Anna's ass cheek and Anna issued a little whimper that he liked very much. *Smack! Smack! Smack!*

"Yes," Anna moaned as water dribbled from her mouth and she pushed back with her hips. "Yesssss!" Anna's entire body shuddered as she climaxed, causing Martin to cry out and explode as well.

*

Martin and Anna cuddled beneath the sheets on their

king-sized bed, both bleary with sweet exhaustion. Anna's head nestled on Martin's chest. "So this is what happens when you hobnob with power? You beat your wife?"

"Guess I got a little carried away."

Anna moaned at the memory. "It was nice." Anna pecked a surprised Martin on the cheek, then she shut her eyes and drifted off to sleep.

24

"What about his African ancestry?" Oscar asked via the WhispeX teleconferencing window on Damon's computer monitor.

"Give me a second." Damon slid his cursor to another window on his screen that had a PDF document simply titled "M.GREY." This 103-page dossier contained an exhaustive examination of Martin Grey's background. The report had a polished academic look with a table of contents, twenty-three numbered chapters, photographs, charts, a few maps, and even footnotes. The research spanned four generations before Martin's birth right up until the present day. Of course, with a price tag of $30,000 cash and a waiting period of thirty days, Damon expected nothing less.

While Damon waited for Martin's background report to arrive by encrypted email, he had continued to nurture their budding friendship. Since the night of the concert they had gone out to lunch twice, and each time they split the bill. Damon always offered to pay, but Martin wouldn't have it. Damon genuinely liked Martin Grey. He liked Martin's smarts and drive and skills in the court-room. He reminded Damon of his younger self, before he met Dr. Kasim. A young black man filled with extraordinary potential and untapped power, but stymied by an invisible disease that afflicts all black men. The sickness. Damon was confident that Dr. Kasim would see in Martin Grey what he did and welcome Martin into the cure.

Damon continued to scroll through the report until he reached chapter eleven, which was titled "DNA Analysis." Along with a breakdown of the racial makeup of Martin's DNA, there was a tribal map of the African continent. Each color-coded territory was labeled with the name of its native tribe and a percentage number. These numbers represented the likelihood that the subject's ancestors descended from that particular region. One tribe scored strikingly higher than the others. Damon stared in surprise when he saw which tribe it was.

Even over the webcam Oscar could read Damon's reaction. "Well?" Oscar's cool voice blared from the computer. "Which tribe is it?"

"The Zantu," Damon replied, and he saw that Oscar's interest was piqued. Just as he knew it would be.

"Zantu? Are you certain? By what percentage?"

"Ninety-three percent." For a moment, Oscar's image on the computer screen just stared in astonishment. Damon had never seen this level of emotion from Dr. Kasim's assistant. And Damon knew exactly why. Many tribes were ravaged by the African slave trade, but to Dr. Kasim, a tiny, forgotten Ivory Coast tribe called the Zantu held special meaning. Damon couldn't help gloating a little. "I knew it. I knew Martin would make an excellent prospect."

Oscar nodded. "Indeed. I still have to discuss the details of your report with the doctor, but I think it's safe to say that Dr. Kasim will be very anxious to finally meet a member of his ancestral tribe."

25

The poker game in Damon's game room had been going for hours and Martin wasn't doing so well. Martin had started the game with $200 in chips, then watched helplessly as his stack dwindled down to a little over twenty bucks.

They were several rounds in by now and the competitive tension in the room loomed as thick as the lingering cigar smoke. Tobias was doing best, but Martin chalked that up to the big man's sheer recklessness and crazy luck. Damon, who had the second biggest stack, seemed to play with the most skill and focus. Kwame and Solomon shared a very relaxed style of play and both still possessed a decent number of poker chips. Carver, who barely had more chips than Martin, seemed to grow more and more ornery with each hand. When Martin lost yet another hand to Tobias, Carver shook his head in disgust. "Man, your game is weak. Save yourself some time and just give Tobias all your chips."

"Shit," Martin drawled casually, "I thought that's what I *was* doing."

All the men cracked up. Except Carver.

Damon passed the cards to Carver to shuffle. "It's his first time playing with us. Give the man a break."

"Yeah, Carver," Tobias said. "If I remember correctly, the first time you played with us you weren't exactly Phil Ivey."

"And he's still not," Kwame said, pointing to Carver's feeble chip stack. "Your ammo's looking a little weak there, my brother."

Solomon shook his head at the pitiful pile of chips. "Weak, nothing. He's on life support."

When the men finished laughing, Carver turned to look at Martin. "I just hope he paddles better than he plays cards. That's all I'm saying."

"Paddles?" Martin said. "What does that mean?"

"Oh, Damon didn't tell you? My bad."

Martin turned to Damon. "What's going on?"

Damon relit his cigar. "We're planning another trip and we want you to come along."

"Another trip? You mean rafting?"

"White water. Yes. We always have a great time. Trust me, Martin, you'll love it."

Martin shook his head. "I don't think so. I told you I'm a city boy. I'd be a complete klutz in the woods . . . not to mention on a raft."

"Don't worry about that. We'll help you pick out the gear, give you some instructional books to read. We'll teach you everything you need to know. That's part of the experience, learning from your fellow men, trusting them, and eventually becoming a teacher yourself."

"Yeah," Tobias said, wrapping a friendly arm around

Martin. "We'll turn you into a real outdoorsman in no time."

"I don't know, guys. It's just not who I am."

"I hear you, brother," Kwame said. "I really do. Before I went the first time, I felt exactly the same way. I didn't want to be anywhere that didn't have a toilet and cable TV. But let me show you something." Kwame got up, grabbed a photo from the wall, and handed it to Martin. The photo showed Kwame and the others, dressed in hiking gear, standing at the base of a towering waterfall. They were all smiling, but the expression on Kwame's face was nothing short of elation, like he had just had some sort of religious experience. "That was taken after my first trip. Look at my face. That's the look of a changed man."

Solomon took the photo from Martin and smiled. "What you see in this photograph is much more than a rafting trip. It's a reaffirmation of our manhood. It's reconnecting to our roots. It's spiritual bonding. But most of all, Martin, it's freedom. Freedom like you've never felt freedom before. This is our thing. Something that we do only for us. And we are inviting you to join us. To be a part of our thing. And, son, believe me when I say it, we do not extend that invitation to everyone."

Solomon's speech was a little sentimental, but Martin could tell that the old man meant every word. They weren't just inviting Martin on a rafting trip. They were extending their hands and inviting him into the fold.

Opening a door that did not open very often, and would not stay open for very long. Martin realized that if he refused their invitation, he might still get invited to a poker game or dinner party once in a while, but he would never truly be a part of that exclusive inner circle.

Solomon laid a supportive hand on Martin's arm. "We won't badger you, son. Just let us know if you're coming or not by the end of the week."

26

The following afternoon Martin stepped off an elevator on the forty-fourth floor of 1114 Avenue of the Americas in midtown Manhattan. Martin's heels clicked as he moved down a short marble hall and pushed through a set of hissing glass doors. He entered a chic waiting area with an angular slab of glass and black marble that served as the reception desk. Over the desk, a backlit brushed-steel sign declared "Darrell and Associates."

Two young receptionists, one male, the other female, both African American, tag teamed the nonstop phones. The girl, while chirping into her headset, flashed Martin a welcoming smile and raised a *just a second* finger.

Martin was there to meet Damon for lunch.

The receptionist returned her attention to Martin. "Please have a seat, Mr. Grey. Mr. Darrell's assistant will be with you in a moment."

Martin's brow wrinkled. "Thanks, but how did you know who I am?"

She smiled. "You're kind of famous around here."

*

The receptionist's statement was confirmed moments later when Irene, Damon's executive assistant, escorted Martin through the firm's sprawling halls. Curious faces popped up from cubicles and peeked from office doorways. Martin noticed a definite drop in the clatter of office work as he passed. He also noticed something else. Although he did spot a few white, Asian, and Latino faces, by far the majority of Damon's employees were black.

Irene, a Halle Berry look-alike in a slim business suit, gave him a teasing look. "So, how does it feel to be in enemy territory?"

It felt awkward, Martin thought. A few weeks ago most of these suits were probably working overtime to help their boss best him in court. Now here he was strolling through their ranks like a conquering general.

"I'll look out for flying paper clips," Martin said, to a chuckle from Irene.

They approached a wooden door flanked by two busy secretaries. Both women paused to greet Martin with a smile, then got back to work. Irene opened the heavy door and waved Martin forward. "Mr. Darrell's right inside."

As Martin expected, Damon's office was huge. Glass walls offered a dizzying view of the Empire State Building and downtown Manhattan. A legal library took up one corner, and in the other a spacious lounge area was anchored by a fully stocked bar. Damon, dressed sharp as always, rounded a desk cluttered with case folders, his hand out. "There he is. Pretty nice, huh?"

"It's like I've entered executive heaven."

Damon laughed and led Martin into the lounge. Martin noticed the large pizza box, plates, and utensils waiting on the coffee table.

"Hope you don't mind if we eat here," Damon said. "Something came up. I only have about twenty minutes and I didn't want to cancel."

Martin assured him that he didn't mind at all.

Damon opened the pizza box and groaned when he saw that the pie was uncut. He returned to his desk, grabbed a letter opener, and used it to cut two slices. He handed one to Martin, then raised his own to make a toast. "To Autostone Industries."

Martin blinked. "Why Autostone?"

"If not for them," Damon said, "you and I never would have met."

They bumped slices and ate. The pizza was as good as everything else Damon had presented to Martin so far.

"One day," Damon said, between bites, "you'll have an office like this. Even bigger. I'm serious. You'll see. Remember this moment."

Martin set down his pizza. "Why are you doing this?"

"What am I doing?"

"This. Hanging out with me. Introducing me to your friends. You setting me up for some sort of revenge?"

Damon chuckled. "Nope. It's much cornier than that."

Martin waited as Damon took another bite. Finally Damon said, "You remind me of me."

Martin made a face.

"I warned you it was corny. But it's true. Before all this, I was like you. Talent, smarts, and more passion than most, but stuck."

"I wouldn't say that I was stuck."

Damon smiled. "I know. But point is, someone showed me, and I want to show you. It's that simple. You okay with that?"

Martin gazed out the windows at the rushing city below. *Does this really happen?* Was this how you went from an average career and an average life to—what? Is this how you reached the top of the world?

Martin nodded. "I'm fine with it," he said.

"Good. Have you thought about the trip?"

"Of course."

Damon stopped eating to give Martin his full attention. "Look, this is more than just a white-water rafting trip. You know that. These men, they don't extend this sort of invitation lightly. This is an opportunity. A beginning. And I'll be right there for you." Damon patted his arm. "Kind of like your big brother."

Martin watched as his host finished his slice, then used the letter opener to cut another. A few weeks ago Damon Darrell was just a name in the newspapers, just a mouth barking into banks of TV microphones, a figure larger than life. But now, somehow, this man was his friend and, odd as it seemed, his mentor.

"Pizza's getting cold," Damon said. "You all right?"

Martin nodded. "I am. It's just—I don't know what to say."

"That's easy," Damon said. "Say you'll come on the trip."

27

"You're going *where*?"

As Martin recoiled, it occurred to him that maybe it would have been better to wait until their dinner with Glen and Lisa had concluded before breaking the news to Anna. Martin had assumed that Anna wouldn't make too big a fuss in front of their guests at the dining table. But judging by the ice in Anna's eyes and the way she clenched her steak knife, Martin had assumed wrong.

Glen was surprised by Martin's news as well, but his reaction was the opposite. "Holy shit." Glen looked up from the steak he was cutting. "That's big. When were you going to tell me?"

"They just asked me at the poker game the other night."

"So, give me some details. Where? When?"

"In two weeks. We leave Thursday the twenty-fourth. Return the following Monday. The Wenatchee River. It's in Washington State, somewhere outside of Seattle. That's where they always go. And get this—we're taking Solomon's corporate jet."

"Nice. Now that's the way to travel."

"Yeah, it should be fun."

Anna, having heard enough, slapped down her fork and knife and glared at Martin. "I don't believe this. Don't you remember our talk in the car? No crazy rafting trips. You promised me."

Martin shook his head. "No, I think my exact words were 'I'm not interested in going.' Can you actually tell me when I used the word *promise*?"

Anna bristled. "Don't do that. You know I hate it when you do that."

Nothing drove Anna crazier than having Martin shift into lawyer mode during one of their spats.

"Look, Anna, I'm sorry. I truly am. I knew you wouldn't be happy about the trip, but this is more complicated than it looks. When they invited me, I had to accept. I had no choice."

"What do you mean, you had no choice? You just say, 'Sorry. No thank you. I'd prefer not to risk my life playing macho man in the woods. Next subject.'"

Lisa nodded in agreement. "Sounds easy enough to me."

Glen shook his head. "No. It doesn't work like that. Not with these men. When power brokers invite you on a golfing getaway or to go fishing or partake in any activity that takes up a great deal of their very precious time—that's when they're ready to talk some real business."

"Exactly," Martin said to Anna. "Just try to think of this as a business trip."

"A golfing getaway I don't have a problem with. But this rafting business . . . I don't know. Martin, it's too risky."

"Come on, Solomon is nearly seventy and Tobias is like three hundred pounds. How risky can it really be?"

"I'm not married to them. I'm married to you. And you have to grow old with me. That's your duty."

Martin reached across the table and squeezed Anna's hand. "It's just four days. I'll get a little wet, and be back before you know it."

"Just promise me that you won't get yourself killed."

Martin raised his right hand. "I promise not to get myself killed. And you got Glen and Lisa as witnesses, so the promise is legally binding. I can't break it."

What Anna said next sounded playful, but her eyes were earnest. "You better not." Then Anna rose from her seat and, with Lisa's help, she cleared the plates and went into the kitchen to get dessert.

Martin turned to Glen. "Hope you won't have a problem holding down the fort for a few days. When I get back you can take a few days off."

"Partner, I have an even better idea. Why don't you ask Damon if I can go too? I'm sure there's enough room in the woods for one more."

Martin's stomach suddenly felt like a hollow pit. This was the question he feared Glen would ask. Glen loved anything that had to do with the great outdoors: camping, fishing, horseback riding, even sport shooting. Back in

NYU, Glen had almost convinced Martin to join a rock-climbing club until Martin realized that instead of a rock wall in some gym, Glen meant real rocks. Big rocks. Martin knew that the instant his partner learned about the rafting trip, Glen would once again hear the call of the wild. Martin thought about lying. He could tell Glen that the raft only held six men or that, because of all the gear, Solomon's jet had already reached its weight capacity. But Martin didn't feel comfortable deceiving his partner.

"I've been itching for something exactly like this," Glen said as he drained the last remaining drop from his wineglass. "And it's the perfect way for them to get to know me better. What do you think?"

"Honestly, I don't think it's a good idea."

"Why not?"

Martin frowned. "Come on, Glen. Do you really need me to spell it out? You wouldn't fit in."

"I wouldn't fit in? What the hell does that mean?"

"It means what you think it means. If we're going to do business with these men, everybody has to know exactly where they stand. I'm sorry, man."

A kaleidoscope of emotions played on Glen's face, but before either man could say another word, Anna and Lisa returned from the kitchen with coffee and dessert.

Glen threw up his hand to get their attention. "Both of you need to hear this. Martin has just told me that I am not welcome on his rafting trip because I'm white."

Anna and Lisa turned to Martin. "Is that true?" Anna said.

Martin rolled his eyes. "Oh, come on. Don't everybody act so shocked. These are hugely successful black businessmen. The key word being *black*. That's what makes them unique. That's the special bond they share." Martin turned to Glen. "It's not that they dislike you or anything. It's just that this group is special. It's a black thing."

Glen laughed. "A black thing? Are you serious?"

"Yes. A *black* thing. I don't know what else to call it."

"What would you call it if a bunch of my friends didn't want you around because you're black?"

"That's completely different."

"Oh, really? How?"

"It's different because of history. There's no shortage of rice-whitepeople clubs, believe me. Come on, Glen, you can probably explain why it's different better than I can. You're just offended because it means you can't go for a ride in Solomon's jet."

Glen sat silently a moment. Then he nodded. "Martin, you're right. It is different. I can't argue with you there." He got to his feet and turned to Lisa. "We should go."

"Would you stop being so dramatic?" Martin said. "Try to remember why I'm doing this. For us. For the firm. You really think I want to go on a stupid rafting trip?"

"It's cool, Martin. Everything is copa. I'm just not in

the mood to sit here and eat cake with you. And listen, don't worry about the firm. While you're off bonding with your brothers in the woods, I'll keep things running. No worries, partner."

The instant Anna shut the door behind Glen and Lisa, she turned to her husband, shaking her head. "He's not just your business partner, Martin. He's your best friend."

"Glen will be fine," Martin said, slicing himself a piece of cake. "He understands. You heard him."

"*I* heard him loud and clear. And if you think he's fine with this, then you didn't hear him at all."

28

Between making her morning rounds and passing out meds, Anna decided to sit down for a few moments at the nurses' station. Maxine, the unit secretary, was away from her desk, leaving her computer terminal unattended.

Anna stared at the monitor. At the bobbing Elmhurst Hospital Center logo screen saver.

What are you waiting for? Anna thought. *That's why you waited for Maxine to leave, isn't it?*

Anna didn't want to do it; in fact she was kind of proud of the fact that she had resisted for two weeks. But today was different. Today was the day before Martin's rafting trip and she was finding it impossible to resist any longer.

"Screw it."

Anna jumped into Maxine's chair and hit F9 on the keyboard, bypassing the patient database. Next she clicked the Google icon and waited for the search page to load.

After Martin dropped the bomb about the trip, he had showed Anna some YouTube videos of rafting trips on class III rivers just like the river that Martin and his "gang" would be riding. When Anna imagined river rafting, the first image that always popped into her mind was the opening sequence from the Saturday morning television show *Land of the Lost*. The one where Rick, Will, and Holly, on a routine expedition, go plunging over a waterfall. The other images that popped into her mind weren't much tamer. Little yellow rafts jammed with helmeted paddlers swept helplessly by raging water, flung against jutting rocks, and overturned by surging waves. But the clips that Martin showed Anna of hooting and hollering tourists bobbing along on calm rivers were nothing like that.

There were dozens of these clips on YouTube and they went a long way to soothe Anna's fears. But not far enough. Because there was one thing that Martin did not show Anna. The accidents. Every clip was sunshine and good times, but what about the accidents? Anna wasn't unreasonable. She knew that everything involved risk. Hell, people died in their own bathtubs every day. But some activities were riskier than others, and she wanted to know how risky this one was. River rafting on a class III river looked like a damn good time on YouTube— but every year, how often does that good time end in death?

The Google search window waited for Anna's query. Anna typed "class III river rafting accidents," then clicked on a few of the results. Story after story of accidents on class III rivers. What Anna found surprising was that only one story involved a death and that was five years ago. The vast majority of the accidents involved capsized rafts and weren't very serious. Anna could feel some of her tension dissipating, like the loosening of a noose. Maybe she was overreacting, letting the memory of a cheesy kids' show cause her to behave irrationally. Just to be certain, Anna decided to modify her search. Just ask the question directly and get it over with.

Anna typed "river rafting death statistics." Anna decided to leave out class III this go-round because she wanted to get more hits and assumed that statistics would automatically separate the incidents by river types.

Anna took a deep breath and clicked on the search. Dozens more links appeared. Most were articles about how safe river rafting was. Anna scanned a few of the articles and discovered to her relief that most of the deaths that occurred in the sport involved class V rivers and above, or some other outside factor like a heart condition.

A smile creased Anna's lips. But as she reached to close the browser, she spotted something on the monitor that made her pause. A link to another story about a rafting accident. But this link was different from the others. This link contained a name that she recognized.

Anna clicked on the link and a new page loaded. A three-year-old article from the *New York Times*. Anna began to read and was immediately stunned. "I—I don't believe it." With each shocking sentence she felt panic welling up inside her—and something else. Her breakfast.

Seized by a wave of nausea, Anna clamped her hand over her mouth.

"Anna, are you okay?" It was Maxine, returning to the station.

Anna shoved past her coworker and fled down the corridor toward the bathroom, clutching her mouth and stomach.

29

Martin peeked out the living room window and frowned at the empty driveway. He didn't really expect to see Damon out there, since Damon was due at 8:00 a.m. and it was only 7:47, but Martin was anxious and just wanted to get this party started already.

Working extra hours at the firm to get ahead of his legal work helped the two weeks leading up to the trip fly by. During that period, because of Damon's schedule, Martin and Damon met just once more for lunch. Martin tried to milk Damon for details about their upcoming adventure, but oddly, Damon showed little interest in discussing the topic. Instead Damon did what he loved to do, tell war stories. He entertained Martin with firsthand accounts of his legendary courtroom conquests. Martin remembered the headlines, of course, and found every word fascinating, but he would have preferred to discuss the trip. Even Martin's request for a list of needed rafting wear was blown off by Damon.

"Everything you need will be provided," Damon said, then he catapulted onto something else.

Despite Damon's assurances, Martin spent a Saturday afternoon shopping for items he thought he might need.

He purchased a pair of hiking boots, some new jeans, a waterproof jacket, and a backpack. He considered charging the items to the firm as a business expense, but Martin wasn't sure if Glen would agree. Considering the chilly mood in the office lately, Martin decided to just eat it.

Before turning in last night, Martin, prickly with anticipation, packed for the trip. Now, like him, his new backpack waited near the front door, ready to go.

Martin checked his watch, 7:54, and frowned out at the empty curb again. Then a thought occurred to him. *Where's Anna? Doesn't she know it's almost time?*

Martin knew that Anna wasn't thrilled about the trip but there was no way that she would let him leave without kissing him good-bye. *Would she?* At first the YouTube rafting videos that Martin showed Anna really seemed to do the trick. For the last two weeks Anna seemed fine. Her fears had been calmed. But last night something had changed. While Martin packed his gear, Anna was quiet and sullen. Martin knew that Anna had left the hospital early because she wasn't feeling well, but he had the distinct feeling that her bout with what appeared to be a mild stomach flu was not the source of her sour mood. He asked her repeatedly if she was okay, he even asked if it was the trip that was bugging her, but each time Anna just smiled and said that she was fine. Martin didn't believe her but there was no point in pushing. Martin wouldn't exactly describe his wife as a delicate flower. If something was bugging Anna, she was going to let him know sooner or later.

Three sudden blasts of a car horn threatened to wake the entire neighborhood. Martin looked out and saw Damon's shiny black Range Rover creeping to a stop in the driveway. Damon, dressed in a windbreaker, waved from the driver's seat. Martin waved back, signaling that he'd be right out. *But where is Anna?* When Martin turned from the window to call his wife, he found Anna standing directly behind him. The look on Anna's face was a troubling mix of reluctance and guilt.

"What's wrong?" Martin asked.

Anna sighed. "I wasn't sure what to do. I lay awake half the night thinking about it."

"Thinking about what?"

"I know how much this trip means to you, I really do. So I didn't want to say anything, but if I don't and something happens—"

"Anna, what are you talking about?"

Anna held up a piece of paper. A printout of a newspaper article. "I found this on the Internet yesterday. You should read it."

Damon's horn beckoned Martin outside.

"Listen, couldn't I read it when I get back?"

Anna shook her head. "No, you need to read it now. Before you leave. Please."

Martin frowned and took the printout. There was a

photo of a bespectacled middle-aged black man beneath the headline "Writer Dies in Tragic Accident."

Martin sighed and tried to hand the printout back. "Anna, come on, I really thought we were past this."

Anna crossed her arms. "Just read it, Martin."

Martin sighed, knowing there was no way in hell that Anna was going to let him leave until he read that article. End of story.

The article was about a novelist named Donald Jackson, the man in the photo, who went on a river-rafting vacation in Wenatchee, Washington, with some friends and drowned when their raft capsized. Now Martin could see what was so troubling to Anna. Martin had to admit that the coincidence was a bit disturbing. How many black men go on river-rafting trips to Wenatchee? But that's all it was: a coincidence. Martin tried to explain that to his wife, but she wouldn't have it. What Anna said next blindsided him.

"It's them, Martin. Damon and his friends took that man on one of their crazy trips and he got killed."

"You can't really believe that."

"Five friends. Doesn't it sound like them?"

"This says that it was a class VI river."

"Maybe they were lost. Maybe they're lying to you. Who knows?"

Martin shook his head. "Anna. Just because this guy is black—"

"This guy? You mean to tell me that you never heard of Donald Jackson before?"

The name did sound familiar but Martin couldn't place it. He shook his head.

"Donald Jackson wrote a huge best seller about four years ago. It was a big deal because it was his first book. They were going to make a movie and everything."

"Okay, that sounds a little familiar. So what?"

"Doesn't Donald Jackson sound like someone that Damon and his rich friends would want to rub shoulders with? Young, black, up-and-coming. Sound familiar?"

Beep, beep, beep! Damon's horn was losing its patience.

"Anna, think about what you're saying. Damon, Solomon, Tobias—these men are famous. Captains of industry. If just one of them was involved in this accident, it would be national news. Hell, it would be international news." Martin held up the article. "Do you see them mentioned anywhere in this article?"

Anna shook her head. "No. In fact, none of Donald Jackson's 'friends' are mentioned by name. Don't you find that a little odd?"

Martin scanned the article. She was right. The only name in the entire article belonged to the victim. None of the "five friends" were identified.

"Sure," Anna said, "newspapers sometimes conceal the name of an accident victim to protect the family and all that. But why hold back the names of the survivors? I've never seen that. Why would they do that unless the survivors' identities needed protecting?"

Martin stared at the article. He tried to remember the

photos in Damon's game room, tried to recall if Donald Jackson's smiling face was in any of those photographs. No. Only Damon, Tobias, Kwame, Solomon, and Carver were in those photos. Of that much he was sure. Martin shook his head. "No. I don't believe it. Everything you've said is circumstantial at best. This story can't have anything to do with them."

A prolonged horn blast trumpeted from the driveway, followed by Damon's bellowing voice. "Martin, let's roll! We've got a jet to catch!"

Anna said to Martin, "I hope you're right. I really do. But before you go anywhere with that man, I want you to ask him."

30

Damon Darrell stood in the center of the living room reading the printout of the news article. Martin waited for recognition or agitation or any reaction on Damon's face, but the superstar attorney remained stone-faced. Only when Damon had finished reading and began to crumble the document into a tight ball did his lips wilt into a slight frown.

Martin and Anna exchanged puzzled looks. Was that a frown of guilt or indignation or was it maybe just disappointment? "I'm sorry," Martin said. "But Anna found that and—"

Damon interrupted by raising one finger. "Gimme a sec." Then he pulled out his iPhone, thumbed a message, and stuffed the device back into his pocket. "Just letting Solomon know that we're a little delayed. It's going to take me a few minutes to explain what really happened."

Martin and Anna gaped as Damon lowered himself into one of their club chairs and crossed his legs. "So, I was right?" Anna asked. "Donald Jackson—he was part of your group?"

Damon gestured to the sofa as if he were the host and

this were his own living room. "Please, sit. This isn't easy to talk about . . ."

Martın tugged a hesitant Anna onto the sofa. Damon began by apologizing to Martin on behalf of the others and himself for not telling Martin about the incident sooner. He and Solomon and the others weren't trying to deceive Martin, Damon explained, the group just found it very difficult to discuss the way Donald died.

Anna glared at Damon. "Did all of you lie to him about how safe your trips are—the same way you lied to Martin?"

Damon shook his head. "We never lied to Donald or to your husband."

"Class III rivers only," Martin repeated coldly. "That's what you guys told me. Donald Jackson drowned in a class VI."

"Donald Jackson never saw a class VI river," Damon said. "We made all that stuff up about the raft capsizing. It never happened."

"What?" Anna said.

Martin's jaw tightened. "Damon, what the hell is going on?"

Damon sighed. "Donald had quick-fame disease. The unholy trinity—drugs, gambling, and women. But worse than all that, he couldn't write. He'd been trying to write his follow-up book for years, but nothing. The whispers of one-hit wonder and all the bills piling up finally got to him. That's why he did it."

Martin listened to Damon's words carefully. "Are you saying that he drowned himself?"

Damon shook his head. "No. I'm saying that in the middle of the night, while we were all asleep in our tents, Donald Jackson took a hike up to the top of a three-hundred-foot waterfall and threw himself off to the rocks below."

"My God!" Anna gasped. "That's horrible."

"Donald did have one hell of a dramatic streak. Guess that's what made him a good writer."

Anna turned to Martin. "I do remember reading something about the trouble he was having writing a second book. But honestly, I didn't even know he was dead until I saw that story."

"Thanks to our very considerable influence," Damon said, "the story pretty much got buried. And what did get out was just our version."

Martin shook his head, astonished. The level of string pulling and favor calling required to downplay the death of even a minor celebrity like Donald Jackson had to be an enormous undertaking. "That means you guys had to lie to the police and the press," Martin said. "Did you do it to protect his reputation?"

Damon shook his head sadly. "No, we couldn't do anything to help that kid's reputation."

"Then why?"

Damon paused a moment to stress the gravity of what he was about to reveal. "It's simple. If Donald had done something crazy like throw himself off a waterfall, that would have been suicide, and his insurance policy would have been null and void. But since he died in a tragic rafting accident, his wife and two kids collected a check for $2.5 million, tax-free, in under a week. I handled the whole thing for Mrs. Jackson, and of course it goes without saying, I did it all pro bono." Damon leaned back in his chair. "We did what we did to help a friend. I hope that you two can understand and more importantly . . . keep it in the family." Damon said these last words directing his eyes only at Martin.

"Of course." Martin nodded after only a minor hesitation. He glanced at Anna and she nodded as well. That word *family* rolled so naturally from Damon's lips that he could tell it sounded right to Anna. That's what they were becoming in a way, Martin thought. A family. And families looked out for each other.

"What you guys did for Donald," Anna said, "that's amazing."

"I'm just glad we got this cleared up," Damon replied. "Everything I told Martin about our trips is true. We're strictly safety first. Scout's honor." Damon flashed the Boy Scouts' high sign and winked at her.

Anna smiled shamefully. "I feel so damned stupid. I was just so worried about Martin and—"

"Anna, please. Stop it. It's my fault for not telling Martin sooner." Damon stood up and extended his arms. "Friends?"

Martin watched as Damon hugged his wife in the middle of their living room. Three months ago, Martin thought, when he was going briefcase to briefcase with the notorious Damon Darrell in a courtroom, he could never have imagined this scene taking place.

Damon slapped Martin on the arm. "Kiss your lady good-bye, then hurry up. Carver's gonna freak." Damon grabbed Martin's backpack and strode out the door.

"Oops," Anna said to Martin, wearing a sheepish smile.

"Somebody's getting a spanking when I get back," Martin teased.

"Keep talking like that and I won't let you leave."

Martin pulled his wife into his arms and kissed her. As he headed for the door, Anna called out, "Martin, wait."

Martin stopped and looked back.

"This doesn't mean you can forget your promise."

"Never," he said, then walked out the door.

31

A Gulfstream G200 executive jet sliced across the crisp blue heavens at 550 miles per hour and at a cruising altitude of 32,000 feet. Below, puffs of sunlit clouds stretched to the horizon like a cotton field in the sky.

Reclining in a sleek leather seat while sipping a Stoli vodka tonic, Martin gazed out the window at the awe-inspiring view. Martin had never ridden in a private jet before, so except for what he had seen in the movies, he really had nothing to compare the experience to. Of course Martin expected luxury and comfort, that was a given, and Solomon's flying wood-paneled cocktail lounge had plenty of that. What Martin didn't expect was the exhilarating sensation of velocity. The constant thrum of turbines and the steady buffeting of microturbulence made Martin feel as if he were rocketing through the upper atmosphere at light speed.

If the other men on board took even the slightest notice that they were traveling at three-quarters the speed of sound, they sure didn't show it. Damon and Tobias were on the sofa near the bar drinking beer and talking fantasy football. Solomon and Kwame were in their seats, swiveled to face each other, playing a quiet game of chess.

Carver was seated across the aisle from Martin, barking into one of the sky phones that were mounted beside each chair. It was the first time that Martin had seen any of them in casual attire. Jeans and khakis, sweatshirts and sweaters, hiking boots. Without their custom-tailored suits, Martin thought that they all looked a little smaller, the same way, Martin supposed, that a knight would appear diminished without his armor.

Martin liked flying, and every time he had the opportunity he went out of his way to book his flight early so that he would be guaranteed a window seat. How often does a person get to take in the world from this perspective? Martin never understood the people who would score a window seat but keep the shade pulled down throughout the entire flight. Not even take a peek. Who were these people? Were their lives so exciting and filled with so much beauty that watching the sun play peekaboo with the clouds right outside your window paled in comparison? Martin strived for the same level of success and power that his new friends possessed. He just hoped that when he reached that lofty goal, he would still have his sense of wonder.

Just then Martin noticed something odd outside his window. It was the sun, looming slightly right of their flight path, almost directly ahead of the jet. Martin squinted out at the fiery orb, puzzled. He was no flight navigator, but by his calculation, the sun was in the wrong place.

Solomon's jet had taken off a little after ten a.m. from Teterboro Airport in New Jersey. Destination: Seattle, Washington. They were already more than an hour into what was expected to be a five-and-a-half-hour flight. Logic told him that if they were flying west, the sun should be behind them. Then how, Martin asked himself, could he be able to see the sun out the left side of the plane?

Martin pressed his forehead against the portal glass and peered downward. He tried to study the terrain, but the cloudbanks beneath the jet were thick and never allowed more than a teasing glimpse of land. Even if he could see the land, how would that solve the mystery? It's not as if the borders of each state were outlined and the names of each state, city, and town printed across the terrain the way they were in an atlas.

"What's wrong with you?" asked a voice behind him.

Martin turned and saw Carver sneering at him. He was done shouting into his phone and had swiveled his chair around to face Martin. "You see a gremlin on the wing or something?"

"No. Actually I was wondering about the sun."

"It's hotter than hell. What else you need to know?"

"It's just if we're traveling west, shouldn't the sun be behind us?"

Carver's brow furrowed. "You a pilot, Grey?"

"No."

"A navigator?"

"Nope."

"Then how the hell can you tell shit just by staring out that tiny window?"

Martin did not like Carver Lewis. He remembered feeling an instant dislike for the young tycoon the moment he met him. Three months later, Martin liked him even less. He was also certain that the feeling was mutual. Carver never passed up an opportunity to ridicule or belittle Martin in front of the other men. Initially Martin assumed that Carver's hostility stemmed from his fear that Martin somehow threatened his position in the group, but after spending a little quality time with Mr. Lewis, Martin finally saw the inconvenient truth. Carver Lewis was a genuine, Grade A, free-roaming asshole. Plain and simple. And Martin knew that when dealing with an asshole, one rule applied. If you take their shit, they'll just keep shitting on you. After all, that's what assholes do. Martin had decided that he wasn't going to take any of Carver's shit on this trip. Not even a little bit.

"I'm just saying," Martin said with a shrug, "west is west and anyone with their eyes open can see that we're not flying west." Martin leaned back to give Carter a view of his window. "Go on, take a look."

Carver's smile disappeared. He seemed uncertain as to whether or not he had just been insulted. After a moment, he cracked a smile and swiveled to face the others. "Guys, listen up. I think we got an emergency on our hands. Martin thinks that the sun is in the wrong place."

Damon, Solomon, Kwame, and Tobias laughed.

"Go on," Carver said to Martin, "tell 'em."

Martin did. "Judging from the sun, it doesn't look like we're headed west."

"Then where the hell do you think we're headed?" Carver said, more to the men than to Martin, "*The Twilight Zone*?"

The men continued laughing. Solomon rose from his chair, strolled up the aisle, and leaned over Martin to squint nose-ward out the window at the sun. He gave a surprised look. "Hm, you're right," he said to Martin. "The sun should be behind us. We'll probably make a course correction soon. The FAA approves all flight plans. Private aircraft rarely get a direct route."

Martin nodded through his doubts. "I've never flown on anything except commercial airliners," he explained.

Solomon patted Martin on the shoulder. "My pilot's one of the best in the world. There's no need to worry."

The smirk on Carver's face gnawed at Martin like a dentist's drill. "I wasn't worried," Martin assured Solomon. "Just curious."

Solomon turned to the others. "I think we should drink a toast to Martin's first flight on a private jet."

"No, that's not necessary," Martin said, but Solomon and the others insisted.

Solomon turned to Damon. "The good stuff," he said.

Damon nodded, then slipped behind the bar and removed a crystal decanter from an overhead cabinet.

The decanter was filled with a liquor as clear as water. Damon filled six shot glasses, then worked his way up the aisle handing each man a glass. Martin was surprised to see Kwame take one.

Kwame shrugged when he noticed Martin staring. "You don't get a chance to drink the most expensive tequila in the world every day."

Damon handed Martin his shot glass last. "It's called Porfidio. It's delicious, but it really packs a punch."

"Yeah, be careful," Carver said, feigning concern. "You might wanna take itty-bitty sips."

"Bullshit! One quick swallow. That's the only way," Tobias bellowed.

Solomon, still on his feet, raised his shot glass high. The other men, including Martin, stood up and joined him. "To Martin's first ride. May there be plenty more in his future." The men clinked their glasses, then tossed back the shots.

"*Whooo!*" Tobias shouted. "Now that's something!"

The other men blurted out similar exclamations as 80 proof liquor hit their systems.

Martin winced and issued a guttural sound that he had never heard himself make before as the velvety hot liquor oozed down his esophagus and branched through his chest like lava.

Damon laughed and slapped Martin's shoulder. "You did good. You okay?"

"Great," Martin replied, his voice hoarse.

"I think he could use another," Carver said.

"Absolutely," Tobias agreed. "One more."

Martin found it difficult to even utter the word *no*. He waved off the offer of another shot and flopped back into his chair.

"No more," Damon said to Carver and the others. "Looks like he's had enough."

Martin heard the men chuckle, but strangely their voices seemed far away. Martin felt his head swim and thought it was odd that one shot could have such a quick and potent effect. They did say it was strong, but . . . He glanced out the window at the sun again. The fiery eye glared back—and began to wink and throb and grow dimmer and dimmer. It was as if someone were lowering an enormous shade over that gazillion-watt lightbulb in the sky. Before Martin passed out completely, he turned in his seat and tried to speak. He tried to tell them that he was feeling sick . . . but there were too many faces staring at him. Too many eyes. Then the world went black.

32

"Martin! Martin, wake up!"

Martin peeled opened his heavy eyes and blinked at a blurred figure. His vision began to clear like a fog lifting. It was Damon hovering over him. Nudging him.

"Wake up. We're here."

"What?" Martin noticed how quiet it was. The constant vibration of speed was gone. The jet wasn't moving. Martin shot up in his seat. The seats were all empty. He and Damon were the only two people left in the cabin.

Damon grinned. "We landed ten minutes ago. You're a real lightweight when it comes to drinking, huh?"

Martin rubbed his eyes to wake himself up. He couldn't believe that one drink had put him out for—how long? Over three hours? And why did he feel so weird? His senses had returned but there was still a residual fuzziness. It reminded him of the buzz he got from all the codeine he popped when his wisdom teeth were pulled out. After three hours of sleep, could he still be high from just that one drink? "Where is everybody?" Martin asked as he turned to the window. He noticed that the shade had been pulled.

"They're outside waiting for us," Damon replied.

Martin pulled up the window shade. What Martin expected to see outside his window was a picturesque little airport with a tiny control tower. Perhaps a dozen or so small planes parked outside a single hangar. A lonesome windsock flapping in the breeze. What Martin saw instead were trees. Just trees. An endless expanse of the tallest trees that he had ever laid eyes on, held back from the edge of the runway by a chain-link fence that ran its entire length. Martin glanced across the aisle at the other windows. All he could see were more humongous trees. He turned to Damon. "This sure doesn't look like Seattle."

"We're actually about a hundred and fifty miles east of Seattle."

"What airport?"

Damon shook his head. "No airport. A private landing strip that serves just one jet—and you're on it."

"You're telling me that Solomon has his own landing strip?"

Damon smiled like a man with a secret. "Not exactly." Damon ignored the look on Martin's face. "Listen, we got a long drive ahead. Last chance to use the john. We're ready to go."

33

The private landing strip was a six-thousand-foot stretch of blacktop surrounded by three hundred square miles of dense forest. Like a scar on the face of the earth. Landing lights flanked the length of the otherwise unmarked runway, and halogen lights were mounted atop the encompassing fence. Two steel-paneled structures were situated at one end of the landing strip. One was a garage big enough to shelter two safari-beige Land Rover Defenders and the other was a small guard shack. One hundred yards away from the two buildings stood an aboveground nine-thousand-gallon jet-fuel storage tank.

As Martin stood at the bottom of the Gulfstream's stairway taking in the scenery, he couldn't help but be impressed with how organized everything appeared. How much, he wondered, did it cost to construct a landing strip out here in the middle of a forest? How much to keep it operational and employ two guards around the clock? And where did these guards come from? Martin couldn't be certain, but the greenery in every direction seemed a good indication that the guards probably did not commute.

The two landing-strip guards, both black men, young,

and built like running backs, stood beside the nose of the jet talking to Solomon. Both guards wore khakis, green wilderness jackets, and what looked like good hiking boots. And despite the holstered sidearms that hung from their hips, Martin thought that they both looked pretty friendly. But why the firepower? What were the two NFL rejects guarding against? Bears? As far as Martin knew, jet fuel tasted nothing like honey. Trespassers maybe? Martin knew drug runners would kill for an isolated drop point like this.

"There he is," Tobias called to Martin. "You coming or not?" They were near the tail of the jet waiting beside one of the Land Rovers. The other truck remained parked in the garage. The rugged 4x4 vehicles were equipped with lifted suspensions, huge forty-four-inch off-road tires, and a raised air intake system for fording streams and shallow sections of rivers without stalling out.

The rear of the Land Rover was open, and as Martin walked over to join the others, he spotted his knapsack in the back of the truck with the other bags and rafting gear.

"You have a good nap?" Tobias asked.

"Nap?" Martin laughed. "I feel like I was drugged." Martin rubbed his eyes again. When he looked up, he caught the tail end of an odd look passing among the men. They appeared amused, but there was something else in their expressions that he was still too fuzzy to place.

"Listen, Grey. You're going to have to be able to hold

your liquor better than that if you're going to hang out with the big boys," Carver said.

Kwame pulled a small pouch from his jacket pocket, and from the pouch he removed a small twig. He handed the twig to Martin. "Chew on that. It'll help you feel better."

Martin stared at the twig. It was about two inches long with neatly cut edges. "What is it?"

"African chewing stick." To demonstrate, Kwame removed another stick from his pouch and stuck it between his teeth. "It's very soothing. Try it."

Martin shrugged and stuck the stick into his mouth. He gnashed on it and a light minty flavor flooded his mouth. It was soothing as Kwame had said.

"Nice, right?"

Kwame offered a chewing stick to the other men. Tobias and Damon each took one, but Carver declined, grumbling, "You know I'm not into that voodoo shit."

Martin gazed into the far distance at a jagged mountain range that rose above the treetops. The sight was breathtaking.

"Looks like someone's been trapped in the city too long," Damon said to him.

Martin nodded. "It's just so beautiful."

"My friend, you haven't seen anything yet."

"Not even close," Solomon added as he ambled up beside Martin. "Hell, son, this is just a rusty old fence and some blacktop. Wait until you see what's out there.

Which reminds me—" The old billionaire turned to the others. "Why the hell are we still standing here?"

"Move out!" Tobias bellowed like a drill sergeant. He slammed the rear hatch shut and began to maneuver his bulk into the driver's seat. Solomon and Carver climbed into the front beside Tobias. Damon, Kwame, and Martin took the three middle seats.

Martin watched the two guards jog across the runway to the fence, where they unlocked a heavy-duty padlock. Steel hinges groaned as both guards pulled open a wide double gate. Beyond the gate an overgrown dirt road receded into the dense woodland beyond. "How far to the river?" Martin asked.

"Just a few miles," Damon replied. "But we have to take it very slow. The road isn't exactly paved."

Tobias keyed the ignition and stepped on the gas. The Land Rover sped through the gate and disappeared into the thick of the forest.

34

The Land Rover trundled forward through the forest at an average speed of fifteen miles per hour. When they first left the landing strip, Martin could clearly make out the parallel ruts of dark soil on the forest floor that marked the road they traveled, but nearly an hour deep into the untamed terrain he could not spot a discernible path whatsoever. As Tobias wrestled the bouncing 4x4 around trees and outcroppings, it almost seemed as if the big man was following an invisible trail the same way a bloodhound follows a line of scent.

As Martin watched the vast emerald nowhere scroll by outside his window, the surrounding forest was so breathtaking that it hardly seemed real. The dense canopy shrouded the forest floor in an almost mystical half-light. Wisps of fine mist crept across the mossy ground, nudged by the faintest breeze. Utopian scenery like this was something you saw on the cover of a fantasy novel, or maybe in an adventure flick created by CGI artists. But for Martin to see it right before his big brown eyes, to be smothered by nature's raw beauty cranked up to full power . . . The experience was mesmerizing.

"What the hell are they doing?" Tobias exclaimed, wrenching Martin out of his reverie.

Tobias was pointing out the window at a mud-splattered forest-green 4x4 stopped about fifty yards away and directly in their path. Two uniformed forest rangers were struggling to lift what looked like a huge, sagging sack of matted brown fur into the back of their truck.

Solomon cocked his head as he squinted ahead. "Looks like they found a dead bear cub. Most likely they're taking it in to figure out what killed it."

"That's a cub?" Martin asked with some surprise. "That thing looks as big as both of them put together."

"Believe me, son," Solomon said, "if that was mama bear, even four rangers couldn't lift her."

The Land Rover drew closer and Martin could see that Solomon was correct. The huge fur ball that the rangers continued to wrestle with was the carcass of a young bear. Its flopping limbs and massive head made loading the creature's bulk onto the tailgate something of a Sisyphean task. The two rangers, both Caucasian and stout as lumberjacks, paused to wipe the sweat from their brows and wave with a smile at the approaching Land Rover.

Everyone waved back, but they did not stop. Martin expected Tobias to hit the breaks so that they could jump out and give the weary rangers a hand, but Tobias steered the vehicle around the two rangers and kept right on driving as if he had just circumvented a rotted tree stump. "Hey, maybe we should stop and give 'em a hand," Martin said.

For a moment there was an awkward silence in the truck. A few glances were exchanged. Finally Solomon spoke up. "Nah. Those boys are fine. It's their job. Besides, it's getting late. We need to keep moving if we're going to reach the river before the sun goes down."

Martin tried to accept that. But still, how long could it really take to help the rangers if they all pitched in? Two minutes? Hell, Tobias could probably lift the cub all by himself. Martin glanced back at the rangers until finally he lost sight of them, then found Carver staring at him with that crooked smile of his.

"Let me ask you something, Grey. If you and I were out there busting our humps and a truckload of good ol' boys drove by on their way to go murder animals, you really think they would stop to help us?"

Martin shrugged. "Maybe. Depends on who they are."

"Damn right," Carver said. "They could also stop and shoot our black asses."

Everyone laughed, including Martin. Carver did have a point. The image of a black man alone in the woods with a bunch of armed white men had a scary connotation that could not be denied. And that got Martin wondering. Were any of his fellow travelers armed? Considering their status and how much they had to protect, it seemed only natural that some of them would bring along a little protection. Still, when Martin asked, at first he got no response, just the jostle and rattle of the advancing truck.

By now it was clear to Martin that Damon and the others were keeping him in the dark about some aspect of the trip. But there was no point digging. He was already in with both feet and knew that sooner or later they'd let him in on the gag.

When Solomon finally turned in his seat and answered Martin's gun question, it was an answer that only gave rise to more questions. "Where we're going," Solomon said, "we don't need guns."

*

The Land Rover finally ground to a stop at the top of a steep decline that descended to the banks of a rushing river. At this juncture, the roaring waterway was about forty yards across and three feet deep with only a few jutting rocks to impede its calm current. So crisp and clear was the water that Martin was able to catch wavering glimpses of its mossy and cobbled riverbed. The crowding trees and ramble of the forest slackened significantly along the riverbank, and Martin assumed that, with such a spectacular view, this would make a perfect campsite. So why, he wondered, wasn't anyone reaching for the doors?

"We have a regular spot on the other side," Damon said. "This is where we drive across."

"Drive across?" Martin thought that the engine snorkel was just a piece of *just in case* gear, like the winch mounted on the front bumper or the spare tire bolted to the hood. It never occurred to him that to reach their destination they would actually have to drive across a charging river.

"Relax," Damon said. "This truck is built for it."

"Yeah. We cross here all the time," Kwame added. "Actually, it's kind of fun."

"I don't know," Carver said as he peered nervously out at the river. "The water looks a little angrier than normal. There's a good chance we could flip." Then he turned to face Martin. "You can swim, can't you, Grey?"

"Like a fish," Martin answered. "Let's do this."

Damon winked. "That's the spirit!"

"You heard the man, Tobias," Solomon said. "Let's do this."

Tobias shifted the Land Rover into gear. "Hold on."

Martin clenched the center column handle as the front end dropped sharply. The Land Rover ground down the steep embankment and plowed forward into the rushing river. Martin felt the vehicle sway sideways as the current grabbed the undercarriage. For a moment, it seemed as if they would be swept downriver, but then the whirling tires got a firm grip of the riverbed and the truck labored forward. The Land Rover bounced and rocked and slewed violently as it advanced deeper and deeper into the river. The water and the moist chill that filled the truck's interior reminded Martin of the atmosphere at an indoor aquarium, that tangible sponginess of the air that came with being surrounded by an enormous volume of water. At the river's midpoint, the deepest section, the groan of the engine dropped several octaves as it strained to pull the three-ton truck forward. The water had risen halfway up the side windows, providing the occupants with sloshing glimpses beneath the waterline. Martin could see large fish wriggling away from the churning metallic invader, and the sight brought a smile to his face. Kwame was right. It was kind of fun.

A moment later, the dripping truck was kicking up rooster tails of mud as it clawed its way up the steep bank of the opposite shore. "Everybody in one piece?" Tobias asked, to a round of exhilarated smiles. It was the first time since the trip had begun that Martin really felt like a member of the group.

Tobias continued driving, guiding the Defender deeper and deeper into the wilderness toward what Martin presumed would be a campsite. Martin felt himself relax a little. He reclined more in his seat, and somehow the forest seemed just a little more welcoming. *This camping stuff isn't so bad*, he thought. *They like me and everything is going to be okay. Screw that, everything is going to be great.*

35

Anna sat on the edge of her bed, staring at the cell phone clenched in her hand. *Should I call Martin and tell him or not?* That was the question that kept looping through her mind. When she first found out, the moment that she was absolutely sure, she wanted to call Martin with every fiber of her being. In fact she was already punching his number into her cell when a little voice inside her head interrupted. *You can't tell Martin over the phone*, the voice said. *You have to tell him in person.* Anna knew that the little voice was right: the little voice was annoying that way. The proper thing to do was just wait the four days and tell Martin when he got back. But four days could seem like a lifetime when you wanted to share the most important news of your entire life. And that was the other problem. Until Anna told Martin, she couldn't tell anyone else. Martin had to be told first. Anna didn't think that Martin would get mad if he wasn't the first to know, especially since he was off on that stupid trip, but to tell anyone else first just wouldn't feel right. She definitely had to wait until he got back. But four days? Four days was so damn long. Anna groaned and squeezed her cell phone tighter. Who was she kidding? There was no way that she could wait that long. She had to tell someone or she was going to burst. But who? Who could she trust? Her sister, Lorraine? Anna shook her head. No, Lorraine couldn't keep a secret to save her life. The whole family would know in under an hour. Then the answer came to Anna. Mom. Of course. She'd make her mother swear on a stack of Bibles not to tell a soul. Well, not a stack really; one copy of the good book would do just fine.

Anna began to dial the phone, but before she reached the last digit, that pesky little voice in her head spoke up again. *Lying to Martin is not right*, the voice said, *especially about something as important as this*. She turned and stared down at a small powder-blue plastic stick that rested on the bed beside her. It was four inches in length and flat, and if you just glanced at it, you might mistake it for a toothbrush. But it wasn't a toothbrush. Instead of bristles at one end there was just a tiny window, about the size of a Chiclet, right in the middle of the stick. The amazing thing about that little powder-blue stick was that it had the uncanny ability to change people's lives. This stick could predict the future.

Anna picked up the stick and teared up at what she saw in that little window. Every time she looked at it, more tears would come. She couldn't help it. The window's prediction was faint, barely visible in fact, but this was Anna's third test and all three of the little windows were in perfect agreement. They each showed a plus sign. Anna and Martin were going to have a baby. Finally.

Anna wiped away her tears and frowned at her cell phone. She shook her head and sighed. "Four whole days."

36

"Where the hell are we?" Martin asked.

"This is our campsite," Damon replied with a grin.

"Bullshit," Martin said as he stared out the window of the idling Land Rover in disbelief. Wherever the hell they were, Martin knew one thing for certain: this was no damn campsite. Martin saw the grins on the guys' faces as they watched him gaping. This had to be their big joke, Martin thought. This had to be what they were waiting for, to see the new guy freak out when they finally arrived here. But where was *here*? What was this place doing way out in the middle of nowhere?

Martin saw Solomon give Damon a nod that seemed to say, *Okay, let the kid off the hook*. Damon laid a calming hand on Martin's shoulder. "You're right. We did mislead you a little. This isn't really our campsite."

"No shit," Martin said, and the men cracked up.

The Land Rover had come to a stop at a gate set inside a massive, fifteen-foot-high stone wall. Completely covered with ivy and other vines, the wall appeared to have sprouted naturally from the forest floor. It stretched away from the gate as far as the eye could see in both directions and disappeared into the encroaching forest. From their position it was impossible to discern the wall's length, but Martin had a sense that the enormous barrier went on for miles. The two huge doors that appeared to be the main gate were constructed of solid wood with a thick steel frame, similar to an entrance you'd see on an old frontier fort. In fact, Martin could have mistaken this mysterious edifice for some old, abandoned stronghold if not for some troubling features. Oscillating surveillance cameras were mounted every twenty feet along the wall. At the very top of the wall angry curls of stainless-steel razor wire glistened in the fading sunlight. And there was something else—a sight that really caused Martin's flight instinct to twitch. Armed guards. Martin could see two men garbed in jungle camouflage patrolling the top of the wall. Both were armed with huge scoped rifles. What the hell were they guarding? Martin wondered. What the hell was behind that big fucking wall?

"Remember that night we mentioned Dr. Kasim?" Damon asked.

"Who?"

"At my wife's party. We talked briefly about some of Dr. Kasim's teachings. Do you remember?"

"Yes, I do remember. The underground philosopher. I think that was how you described him."

Damon smiled. "That's right." He nodded toward the gate. "This is his place."

"His place? What do you mean, his place?"

"His home."

"What?" Martin gazed out at the expansive wall with new eyes. Never mind the desolate location and the armed guards, just its staggering size made it seem incredible that someone's place of residence could be hidden behind that wall. Martin turned back and could see the others watching him with amused smiles. Relishing his reaction. "Your underground philosopher lives in an armed fortress?"

"He does indeed," Damon said. "It's kind of like a private retreat."

"A private retreat for who?" Martin asked. "Ex-cons?"

The men cracked up again. Before Martin could ask any of the million questions that cried out in his head, the huge wooden double gate began to open. Martin tried to glimpse what lay beyond the slowly parting doors, but all he could see were tall hedges and a lone black man standing in the gateway. The man was garbed in all black, from his combat boots to his hunter's cap, and had a scoped rifle of his own slung over his shoulder. Martin watched as the man strode toward them, moving with a military precision, apparently in perfect physical condition. He reminded Martin of the two guards at the landing strip, but those men were younger. Martin guessed that the guard approaching them now had to be at least in his midforties.

Tobias powered down his window to shake the man's hand. "Hey, Frank. How are you?"

Frank barely cracked a smile, enduring Tobias's enthusiastic handshake almost as if the gesture were somehow inappropriate. "I'm fine, sir. Welcome back, gentlemen." Then, standing so rigidly that he almost appeared to be at attention, Frank made it a point to nod a greeting to each man in the vehicle. "Mr. Aarons, Mr. Lewis, Mr. Jones, Mr. Darrell." Frank turned last to Martin without missing a beat. "And a pleasure to meet you, Mr. Grey."

Martin nodded back, a bit surprised that the guard already knew his name. No, it was more than that. What gave Martin pause was that he was expected. On the guest list, as it were. They were smack-dab in the middle of God knows where and some goon with a big gun was greeting him by name as if the man were the doorman at the Ritz-Carlton. *What world have I stepped into?* Martin wondered. *No, I didn't step into anything. They brought me here. They lied to me and brought me here.*

Martin was torn. He burned with curiosity to see what lay beyond that wall, to know why his companions had gone to such extreme lengths to conceal their true destination. But there was also a fluttering in his gut that didn't want to know. A part of him that just wanted to be back home with Anna, snuggled on the sofa.

The guard pivoted back to Tobias. "Mr. Lennox has been made aware of your arrival and will greet you at the main house. Enjoy your stay, gentlemen."

"Thanks, Frank," Tobias said, shifting into gear and speeding toward the waiting gate.

Martin glanced at Damon and saw a smile on his face. Solomon, Kwame, even Carver, all of them were smiling.

Faces full of anticipation, like kids on their way to an ice cream shop. Martin whispered, "Where the hell did you bring me?"

"Just sit back and enjoy the ride," Damon said. "You can thank me later."

The Land Rover cruised through the gate, and the two huge doors swung shut behind them.

37

Tara. That's what the huge house that stood in the distance before them reminded Martin of, that white-columned plantation house in *Gone With the Wind*.

After passing a small gatehouse that contained two more guards, the Land Rover started down a wide gravel road that was lined on both sides with the biggest oak trees that Martin had ever seen. The verdant canopy that hung above the road was so dense that the Land Rover appeared to be traveling down a vast shadow-filled alley. At the far end of this living corridor, a four-story mansion basked in the golden light of dusk. The huge whitewashed house with its massive Grecian columns was fronted by a vibrant flower garden and a fountain that sent a gentle spray of water high into the air. Like a light at the end of a dark tunnel, the distant mansion almost seemed to glow. The sight was so breathtaking that if someone had told Martin that he was on the road leading to heaven, he just might have believed them.

"My God," Martin heard himself whisper.

Solomon turned in his seat and looked at Martin with proud eyes. His voice seemed to swell with ceremony as he said, "Welcome, Martin. Welcome to Forty Acres."

"Forty Acres?" Beyond the colonnade of trees, Martin had a better view of the property's picturesque features. A vast, sparkling lake to the left. To the right, what looked like an apple orchard in full bloom. In every direction the lush yet perfectly manicured landscape seemed to go on forever with no sign of the enclosing wall. "This place has got to be bigger than forty acres."

The men laughed. "You're right," Damon said, "it's much bigger. Naming this place Forty Acres is just Dr. Kasim's idea of a little joke."

Martin joined in the laughter. He understood Dr. Kasim's "little joke." As almost every schoolchild could tell you, near the end of the Civil War, after Lincoln signed the Thirteenth Amendment, the United States government promised that all former slaves would receive forty acres and a mule so that they could start a farm and become self-sufficient. What was less commonly taught in schools was that this new law did not sit well with white landowners. Less than a year later, before Lincoln's corpse was cold, the succeeding president, Andrew Johnson, revoked Special Field Order No. 15 and took back the four hundred thousand acres of land that had already been deeded to the former slaves, leaving them with nothing but the rags on their backs. Now, as Martin gazed out at the palatial grounds surrounding him, every tree, every stone, every blade of grass owned by a black man, the irony of the property's evocative name was so perfect that it tickled his soul.

Martin made a show of glancing out the window. "So where's the mule?" he said, and after an exchange of glances, the men burst into howls of laughter. Martin was glad at the reaction, but he also found it a little overblown. As if they were laughing at a far better joke. A joke that Martin was not in on.

As they cruised down the final stretch of road, Martin could make out a few other smaller houses dotting the property. A boathouse nestled on the lake. A tack house adjoining a riding stable. Martin thought that if Forty Acres was located anywhere else, this place would make one hell of a resort. "So come on, what's the deal?" Martin asked. "Do you guys ever go rafting on these 'rafting' trips or do you just stay here?"

"We go rafting sometimes," Tobias replied. "But the truth is, we usually don't bother because there's so much to do here."

Solomon added, "Dr. Kasim created Forty Acres to be the perfect haven of relaxation, recreation, and reflection for the black man."

"And what about your wives?" Martin asked. "Do they know about this place?"

The inside of the truck went silent. It was Kwame who finally turned to Martin. "It's like this, brother. Dr. Kasim teaches us that far too often black men use their women as a crutch. This place is about building us up. It's about getting the black man to stand a little straighter. No wives or girlfriends allowed."

"In fact," Damon added, "I wouldn't bring up the subject at all around the doctor. For Forty Acres to have its full effect, he prefers that his guests spend as little time as possible thinking about their day-to-day lives in the outside world. And that includes wives. This is your time; he doesn't want you spending it thinking about Anna. Trust me."

Martin fought the urge to laugh as he searched their faces. "Is that a joke?"

Solomon glanced back at Martin. "Dr. Kasim might be the funniest man that I have ever met, but when it comes to his views on certain things, he's also the most serious. You'll see."

The circular driveway that encompassed the sprawling front garden and fountain was so big that it felt to Martin almost as if they were taking a slow lap around a NASCAR track. Martin spotted several gardeners kneeling in the dark soil, tending to the endless beds of colorful blooms. A rifle-toting guard strolled the garden's gravel walkway. He was dressed in the same black khaki uniform as the guards at the wall. "Some serious security here," Martin observed.

The men looked at one another as if to see whose turn it was to answer. This time it was Carver. "Think about it, Grey. A wealthy brother living like this in the middle of nowhere. America's changed a lot, but not that much."

Martin understood Carver's point. When you looked at it that way, Dr. Kasim's private little army actually made a whole lot of sense.

As they continued around the huge driveway, Martin noticed another worker, a young woman, using a leaf skimmer to clean the fountain's basin. The woman was blond, and despite her baggy coveralls and bored expression, she was unusually pretty. Martin couldn't help wondering why an attractive woman would want to work way out in the middle of nowhere. *Maybe she really loves the outdoors*, he thought. As if she could hear Martin's thoughts, the woman glanced up at the passing vehicle and their eyes met. Martin smiled and waved. Startled by the gesture, the woman dropped her gaze and returned to her chore. He thought he caught a flicker of nervousness on the woman's face. Perhaps Dr. Kasim had a rule against his staff interacting with guests.

Finally the Land Rover rolled up to the front of the mansion. Three uniformed valets in snappy vest coats, two about college age and one a few years older, were lined up at the bottom of the steps, standing at attention. Martin noticed that all three were Caucasian. Whatever Dr. Kasim's views were on race, Martin thought, he appeared to be an equal opportunity employer.

On the porch behind the valets stood a tall black man garbed in a crisp white linen suit. His clean-shaven head, chiseled features, and perfect athletic physique gave him an imposing presence.

Martin turned to Damon. "I thought Dr. Kasim would be much older."

"That's not Dr. Kasim," Damon said. "That's Oscar."

"Who's Oscar?"

Before Damon could reply, Oscar clapped his hands twice and the three valets pounced on the Land Rover. While the senior valet opened the rear lift gate and began to unload luggage, he ordered the other two to open the side doors. As each passenger climbed out, he was greeted with a very cheerful, "Good evening, sir."

When Martin thanked him, the skinny, freckle-faced kid who had greeted him registered a look of surprise before hurrying to the rear of the truck to help with the unloading.

"Welcome back, gentlemen," Oscar said as he descended the stairs. "It's been a while."

"You're right," Solomon said. The two men embraced. "Too damn long."

Martin watched as the others each took turns greeting Oscar with a hug as well. What struck him was how stoic Oscar appeared. Even while he was engaged in a brotherly embrace, the man's expression remained unchanged. An unreadable cool.

"And you, of course, are Mr. Martin Grey," Oscar said as he turned his piercing gaze on Martin. His voice was deep and his diction precise. "I'm Oscar Lennox, but you may call me Oscar. On behalf of Dr. Kasim, I welcome you to Forty Acres."

"Thank you. It's nice to meet you," Martin said, extending his hand.

Oscar ignored the gesture. "That European custom

has no meaning here. In our world we greet each other as brothers." With that, Oscar pulled Martin into a firm hug. As Martin returned it, he was surprised to feel the rock-solid lump of a shoulder holster beneath Oscar's fitted jacket. So Oscar too was carrying a gun—but why? Martin could understand the armed guards, but Oscar, in his perfect white suit, clearly wasn't a guard. But what was he then? When they parted, Martin rejoined the men.

"You guys could have told me about the no-handshaking rule," Martin said.

"That's true. We *could* have," Tobias said with a smirk.

"The doctor has heard a lot about you," Oscar said to Martin. "He's very anxious to meet you at dinner tonight."

"I've heard a lot about him too," Martin answered, "but I don't think anyone mentioned you. Are you the manager here or like a concierge?"

That's when Oscar smiled. It was only a slight smile and it didn't last very long, but still—it showed the man was human after all. "Let's just say that I oversee Forty Acres for Dr. Kasim. It's my job to make sure that every-thing runs as smoothly as—" Oscar was interrupted by a sudden bang. The skinny valet had dropped a suitcase and some of its contents were now strewn about the driveway.

"Hey, you idiot! Careful with my shit!" Carver shouted.

Martin saw Oscar shoot the guilty worker a look. The

glance was subtle but at the same time heart-stopping. Oscar's emotionless demeanor had the effect of amplifying even his slightest expression.

"Well, pick it up," the older valet barked at the younger man.

"Sorry, sir. So sorry," the skinny valet apologized to Carver, practically groveling as he dropped to his knees and frantically repacked the suitcase.

The senior valet turned to Oscar wearing a tragic frown. "Sorry, sir. Won't happen again, sir."

Oscar said nothing. He just returned his attention to his guests. "Dinner is in one hour. I'm sure that you gentlemen would like to get settled in before then. Your usual rooms are ready." As Damon, Solomon, Kwame, Carver, and Tobias started up the stairs, trailed by luggage-laden valets, Oscar turned to Martin. "I'll have someone show you to your room." He stopped the last valet. It was the same kid who had dropped Carver's bag.

As Martin watched the wiry valet strain under the weight of several bags and cases, he thought that the kid looked kind of young to be working out here.

"Show Mr. Grey to his room," Oscar instructed.

The valet nodded. "Yes, sir." Then he flashed Martin a forced smile. "This way, sir. Please." Martin could see that the kid's load was getting heavier and he was anxious to get moving.

"Let me help you with those," Martin said as he reached for one of the bags.

"No, sir," the kid exclaimed, backing up so fast that the weight of his load almost tipped him over. "I have it, sir. No worries."

"No, really. It's okay," Martin said as he reached again.

"No—" Oscar said, catching Martin's wrist. Oscar's grip was firm but gentle, like a padded vise. "Let the boy do his job. That's what he's here for. To serve you, and to learn valuable skills. You don't do him any favors by diminishing his responsibilities." Oscar released Martin's arm. "Now, please, enjoy your stay." He flashed that wisp of a smile again. The smile that wasn't really a smile.

"Thanks," Martin said. "I'm sure I will."

38

Martin was led into the cavernous foyer where a spectacular crystal chandelier sparkled overhead and a grand curving staircase ascended gracefully to the upper levels. Huge vases of fresh flowers welcomed all who entered with their delightful scent.

"This way, sir," the valet said as he shifted the load of luggage in his hands to prepare for the ascent. "Your room is on the second floor."

Martin followed the valet up the long stairway. Being empty-handed while watching the valet struggle made Martin feel awkward. He was tempted to offer some assistance again, but Martin resisted the urge. The scrawny kid did look wobbly, but what he lacked in brawn he made up for with sheer determination. Soon Martin was trailing the winded valet down a wide, carpeted hall lined with bedrooms. The valet paused twice to knock and drop off bags with Solomon and Kwame before finally reaching a closed door at the very end of the hall. "Here you are, sir," the valet said, pushing open the heavy, wood-paneled door. Martin walked into a surprisingly spacious bedroom. The room was furnished in colonial and early nineteenth-century American antiques, which matched the old plantation style of the house perfectly. The forty-two-inch plasma television that hung opposite the king-sized bed was the only thing that defied the illusion of having stepped back in time. Two large windows overlooking the front garden let in the warm light of sunset, giving the cozy room the look of a sepia-toned photograph. Martin was reminded of an old bed-and-breakfast in Atlanta where he and Anna had once stayed.

The valet pointed to a wooden door on the far side of the room. "That's the bathroom over there." He pointed to another door adjacent to the bed. "And that there's just a closet." He deposited Martin's overstuffed backpack onto the bed and headed for the door.

"Hang on," Martin said, and reached into his pocket. He thought that the kid deserved a little something for busting his tail. Martin peeled free a five-dollar bill. "This is for you."

"No, no, no, sir," the valet said, shaking his head as he backed toward the door. "That's not allowed."

Martin pushed the money into the valet's hand anyway. "It's okay. It'll just be between us."

"No, sir," the valet said. And for a moment, Martin noticed the valet's nervous eyes scanning the room. "I'm sorry, sir, but I can't. I'm sorry." The valet dropped the money and hurried out the door.

Martin stared at the rejected five-dollar bill lying on the carpet. Was it his imagination, or did the young valet actually appear frightened? Times were tough. Work was hard to come by. Maybe the kid was afraid of losing his job. But Martin sensed that something deeper stoked the young man's fear. No doubt Oscar was tough on the staff. A shouter perhaps, or, even worse, an asshole. The type of boss who gets his jollies by making his employees miserable. On the surface, Oscar appeared to be nothing but professional, but Martin knew that anyone that rigid had to have a few cracks. And what about Dr. Kasim?

Martin picked up his five-dollar bill, then began to unpack. After he had transferred the contents of his backpack into the drawers of an antique armoire, Martin sat down on the bed and pulled out his cell phone. Dinner was still the better part of an hour away, so he figured he'd use the time to call Anna and let her know that he had arrived safely. He'd decided not to tell her about Forty Acres though, at least not yet. Although the guys had neglected to swear him to secrecy, Martin couldn't help feeling that blabbing to his wife the first chance he got would constitute an act of high gender treason. Besides, Anna was already worried enough about the trip. Why give her something else to lose sleep over? Maybe he'd tell Anna after he got back. Maybe he wouldn't.

Martin turned on his phone and frowned at the two words that flashed on the small screen: *no signal*. He wasn't really surprised. Why would a telephone company erect a cell tower way out here? Bears didn't carry cell phones, or pay inflated and overtaxed phones bills for that matter. But Martin noticed that there wasn't a telephone in the room either. The two nightstands that flanked the bed held matching table lamps and crystal ashtrays. Nothing else.

Martin exited his room and started down the hall toward the great stairway. He spotted a maid exiting a room with an armful of towels and intercepted her. "Excuse me."

When the maid turned to face him, Martin was arrested by the woman's simple beauty. She was in her early twenties with fair skin, strawberry-blond hair, big green eyes, and a curvy little figure despite the frumpy maid's smock that she wore. Martin found himself wondering the same thing about this girl that he had about the girl cleaning the fountain. Why would such a pretty young woman want to work here, in such a remote and isolated setting?

The pretty maid flashed Martin a smile. "Hello, sir. Is there something I can help you with?"

Martin waved his cell phone. "My phone's not working. Is there a phone in the house that I could use?"

The maid frowned. "No, sir. I'm sorry but there are no telephones in the house."

"Outside the house?"

"No, sir. None at all."

"Really? How about a computer so that I can send an email?"

The maid shook her head. "No, sir. Telephones and computers are not allowed here."

Martin couldn't believe what he was hearing. No phones in the house was one thing, but to have no means of outside communication seemed, at the very least, reckless. "There has to be a way to reach the outside world. How do you call home?"

The young maid just blinked, caught off guard by the question. When she finally spoke there was a crack in her voice. "We don't, sir."

"What do you mean?" Martin was no linguistics expert, but the maid's clipped New England accent was easy to recognize. "You're from the Boston area, am I right? How do you stay in touch with your family? Your friends?"

The maid seemed anxious. "I'm sorry, sir, but . . . I should get back to work. Excuse me, please."

She made to leave, but Martin stepped in front of her. "Hold it. Wait a second. I'm not trying to get you in trouble or anything. I just really need a phone."

"But I told you, sir, there is no phone."

"But why? How can there possibly not be a single telephone here?"

Her mouth moved, but she gave no answer. Then her face changed. It happened so fast that it startled Martin. It was as if a dam had given way, flooding her eyes with a deep sadness.

"Forty Acres has no telephones," came a voice behind them, "because having one is against Dr. Kasim's rules."

Martin turned and saw Damon striding down the hall.

The maid took advantage of the interruption to make her escape. "Pardon me, sir."

Martin stared as the young maid hurried away down the hall.

"You have good taste," Damon said with a mischievous smile.

"What?"

"The maid. Pretty little thing, right?"

"Yeah. I guess so."

"Her name's Alice. Hottest girl on the staff. It's like having Scarlett Johansson as a maid. And man . . . would I love to have me some Scarlett Johansson. You know what I mean?"

Damon's comments were just his typical guy talk, but at that moment they rubbed Martin the wrong way. It was because of Alice's eyes. Martin was still haunted by those troubled green eyes. "So tell me," Martin began, "what does Dr. Kasim have against telephones and email?"

"He says they're a distraction," Damon said, "and he's right of course. We come here to isolate ourselves from the everyday static."

"So telephones and email are distractions but a television is not?"

"Exactly," Damon said. "Dr. Kasim calls television his magic window onto the white world."

"There has to be some way to communicate with the outside world. What if someone gets sick? How do you call for help?"

Damon shrugged. "There's a shortwave radio set up somewhere, or something like that. I don't know. I don't think we've ever used it."

"You mean except for the time Donald Jackson committed suicide, right?"

Damon smiled and nodded. "That is correct, counselor."

Martin frowned. "I really wish you had told me about the phone situation."

"Sorry," Damon said. "I guess I just assumed that you knew there would be no cell service in the woods."

"You saw how nervous Anna was about the trip. She's going to freak out when she doesn't hear from me."

"And then what, counselor?" Damon's tone was that of an instructor challenging a student to "think it through." "After your wife 'freaks out,' what will she do next?"

Martin considered. "I guess the first thing she'll do is call your wife. See if there's a way to reach you."

Damon smiled. "Exactly. Then Juanita will tell Anna that it's impossible to reach us by phone. End of crisis."

Martin didn't like the idea of worrying Anna, even if it was for a short while, but he couldn't refute Damon's logic either. "I guess you're right," he said.

"Of course I am," Damon answered. He glanced at his Rolex. "Hey, we still have time before dinner. Come on, let me show you the rest of the house."

39

When Damon said "the rest of the house," what he really meant was the impressive recreation compound located behind the house. The sprawling area was divided into five distinct activity zones, all beautifully landscaped and connected by lighted stone pathways.

Eager stars already pierced the darkening sky as Damon led Martin out a rear door and down the path toward an elongated tinted-glass enclosure that housed the indoor swimming pool. Even before Damon pulled open the door, the familiar sharp aroma of chlorine greeted Martin's nostrils. The pool was Olympic-size, maybe even bigger for all Martin knew about pools, with an ornate, mosaic-tiled bottom beneath the placid, crystal-clear water. Adjacent to the pool there was a sunken hot tub that looked big enough to accommodate a small crowd. There was also an elegant bar and lounge area worthy of a five-star resort hotel. The pool house was deserted now, but it wasn't hard for Martin to imagine the fantastic parties that could be thrown there. But then again, how many guests would come to a party way out here?

"Michael Phelps would love it here," Martin said.

Damon responded with an outbreak of laughter that

seemed a bit much for such a minor quip. "Just wait until you get a chance to take a dip," Damon said. "The water is always kept at a perfect eighty-one degrees."

Martin nodded. In truth, he had no idea why eighty-one degrees was perfect, but he took Damon's word for it.

"Did you gentlemen want to go for a quick swim?"

Damon and Martin turned to see one of the guards standing in the doorway. The guard was tall, with a head full of neat dreadlocks. Instead of a rifle like the others carried, a sidearm hung from his hip. "If you like, Mr. Darrell, I can go grab a couple of houseboys to bring some towels and open up the bar so that you and Mr. Grey can go for a swim."

"No thanks," Damon said with a smile. "Just giving the new guy the nickel tour."

The guard nodded. "All right. Have fun." He made to leave, then suddenly poked his head back in. "Oh, Mr. Darrell. You'll probably see a work crew doing some repairs on the golf course, but don't panic."

"What do you mean? What happened to the course?"

"Big storm hit two nights ago. Caused some damage. But Mr. Lennox is working them through the night to get the course in perfect shape by morning. Knowing how much you love golf, sir, I just thought I should give you the heads-up."

Damon smiled in appreciation. "Thank you," he said, and as the guard made his exit, Damon led Martin around the length of the pool toward the door on the opposite side.

"I have two questions," Martin said. "One: when the hell do you have time to play golf?"

"When I come here, of course," Damon replied. "It's just a six-hole course, but wait until you see it. It's beautiful. Tell you what, I'll give you a few lessons. You'll love it, become completely addicted, then your wife will hate me for it."

Martin laughed.

"What's your second question?" Damon asked.

Martin glanced back at the door where the guard had made his unexpected appearance. "Maybe I was hearing things, but did that guy actually use the term *houseboys*?"

Damon laughed. "You know what, I think he actually did."

*

After exiting the pool house, Damon led Martin down another path that took them past a tennis court and a basketball court. Both courts were regulation-size and equipped with lights to allow for use after sundown. The lights were off now, but even in the evening's gloom Martin could see that both courts were in pristine condition. Damon asked Martin if he played either sport, and Martin had to admit that he did not. "Actually," Martin said to Damon as they moved away from the darkened courts, "I'm really more of a Monopoly and Scrabble man."

Damon and Martin approached what, on the outside, appeared to be a cozy little guesthouse, but the instant Martin stepped inside, he saw that the building was actually a fully equipped gym.

"It's all here," Damon said, guiding Martin through the maze of steel and chrome. "Universal machines, treadmills, ellipticals—"

Damon's tour was interrupted by a loud grunt. On the other side of the room, a mirror-lined area was set aside for the use of free weights, and a fit young black man was busy doing power squats with a fully loaded barbell perched on his broad shoulders. Martin couldn't tell how many pounds the man was lifting, but the bulge of his muscular legs and those painful grunts said plenty. If the young man knew that he was being observed, he didn't show it.

Martin turned to Damon. "Who is that?"

"I don't recognize him. Must be a new guard. They're allowed to use the gym when they're off duty."

Martin's brow furrowed with confusion. "You know, I've noticed something a little odd about all these security guards."

"Really? And what would that be?" Damon said with an expectant smile.

"Any decent security guards should be in good shape, of course, but the guards here are in exceptional physical condition. At least the ones that I've seen so far."

Damon appeared amused. "That's it? That's what you find so odd?"

"Yeah. Look at that guy." Martin nodded toward the guard, who was still squeezing out power squats. "He looks more like a Navy SEAL than a security guard. They all do."

Damon nodded. "You're right. Dr. Kasim demands that every member of the security force at Forty Acres be in perfect physical condition."

"That's one hell of a job requirement. The pay must be great."

"As far as money goes, I have no idea what the guards are paid. But the knowledge that Dr. Kasim has to offer to those young men is priceless."

Martin shook his head and laughed. He didn't mean to laugh.

It was more from awkwardness than anything else. The praise Damon and the other men were heaping onto Dr. Kasim was beginning to sound a little strange.

Damon's face clouded over. "I say something funny?"

"You guys talk about this Dr. Kasim like he's a god or something. Aren't you even a little worried that you're setting me up for disappointment?"

"Once you meet the doctor, you'll understand our enthusiasm," Damon said. "I can promise you that."

"See, there you go again. And you *did* say that Dr. Kasim was the funniest man you knew."

"True, true," Damon said, "but also the most serious.

Come on." He took Martin by the arm. "Time to show you my favorite spot."

*

Damon and Martin stood beneath a dome of stars at the very edge of the six-hole golf course. Nightfall had fully descended, bathing the perfectly landscaped rolling greens with pale moonlight. The omnipresent *click* of cicadas somehow added to the course's haunting serenity. Martin knew nothing about golf, much less what a great golf course should look like, but as he gazed at the luminous field spread out before him, he couldn't imagine one ever looking more beautiful.

"It's incredible," Martin said.

Damon nodded. "I told you."

"It all is. But it seems like a lot for just one person and some occasional guests."

"We're not Dr. Kasim's only visitors. There are other groups like ours all over the country who come to visit. And once every two years or so, all the groups come together. We call it the convocation. It's an amazing experience. You'll have to come with us next time."

A little more than a hundred yards away, the work crew that the guard had warned them about could be seen toiling away. Six male workers, their shirts off, were raking and shoveling and mowing beneath the harsh glare of portable work lights. Two guards, both cradling scoped rifles, were leaning on a golf cart watching their progress. In an odd way the entire scene reminded Martin of a prison work crew that you'd see in an old movie. The only things missing were the prison stripes and ball-and-chain leg shackles.

"What exactly are they doing out there?" Martin asked Damon.

"Patching up the green. Removing debris. Cleaning mud from the holes. That sort of thing."

"And why are the guards babysitting them?"

"Why do you think? To make sure their lazy asses don't run away." Damon burst into laughter. Martin tried to join him, but all he could offer was a polite chuckle, and even that he felt slightly wrong about.

They were standing on a slight rise, which afforded them an unobstructed view of the golf course's natural boundaries. At the opposite end, a wide brook separated the tamed lawns from the wilderness beyond. A gravel road wound its way across the width of the golf course to a simple wooden footbridge that spanned the brook. On the other side, the road disappeared into the dark woods. Through the tree line that ran parallel to the brook, Martin could just make out the shapes of several squat structures grouped unusually close together. He pointed them out. "Are those houses over there?"

"No. More like barracks," Damon said. "That's where the staff lives."

"Must cost a fortune to maintain all of this," Martin

said as he glanced back toward the main house. "The staff here has got to be huge."

Damon snorted. "*Huge* is an understatement. Guards, groundskeepers, servants—it takes a small army to run this place. Not to mention the gold mine."

"Gold mine?" Martin looked at Damon skeptically. "You're kidding."

Damon smiled. "There's an old working gold mine on the property. It's about a half mile away." Damon pointed beyond the bridge. "Once you cross the bridge, the road leads right to it."

Martin knew that gold mining had once been a major economic driver in the United States but thought that the resource had been tapped out well over a hundred years ago. When Martin thought of gold mining today, he pictured shirtless, sweaty African men slaving in some insanely cramped cave in South Africa, an image retained from some Discovery Channel documentary. He never imagined that there could still be a working gold mine in the American backwoods. "Is that how Dr. Kasim makes his money?" Martin asked. "From gold mining?"

"Actually," Damon said, "it's not quite that simple." Changing the subject, he glanced at his watch. "Almost dinnertime. We better get back. I'll take you out to the mine tomorrow."

As they turned to leave, Martin glanced again at the work crew laboring to repair the golf course. An intriguing realization froze him in his tracks. The sight of the men toiling, their lean, bare torsos glistening with perspiration, continued to remind him of the African workers in the documentary that he saw, except for one striking difference. In the documentary all the laborers were black Africans, black men who were being supervised by white men. But out there on the golf course it was the opposite. The guards supervising the task were black, and all the workers were white.

Noticing that Martin wasn't following him, Damon glanced back and saw Martin staring out at the workers. "Martin, what are you doing? Let's go."

Martin ignored him. He was too busy recalling faces. The faces of the laborers he saw toiling in the garden when he first arrived, the face of the woman cleaning the fountain, the faces of all the valets lined up outside the house. The face of Alice, the timid housekeeper.

Damon grabbed Martin's arm. "Martin, what's wrong?"

Martin turned to Damon, gaping in realization, his voice low with astonishment. "I can't believe I didn't see it sooner."

"See what?"

"They're all white. Aren't they?"

Damon answered Martin's question with an amused smile. "Congratulations, counselor. I was wondering how long it would take you to notice."

"Solomon wasn't kidding about Dr. Kasim's sense of humor. An entire white staff for a black country club? That's one hell of a joke."

"Oh, it's much deeper than just a joke," Damon said. "Dr. Kasim sees the arrangement at Forty Acres as therapeutic."

"Therapeutic? How?"

Damon glanced at his watch again. "Tell you what. Why don't you ask Dr. Kasim when you meet him?"

As the two men retraced their steps and headed back to the main house, Martin took in the sprawling, luxurious property with new eyes. "Your Dr. Kasim has truly created himself a perfect fantasy world, hasn't he?" he said.

"Fantasy?" Damon repeated. "Look around you, Martin. This is no fantasy. It's all absolutely real."

40

Martin heard Dr. Kasim coming before he ever laid eyes on the man. He assumed that the slow and deliberate *thump-ka-thump* of approaching footsteps belonged to his host because on hearing that awkward cadence, everyone in the dining room rose to their feet. Damon signaled Martin to follow suit, but the prompt was unnecessary. Martin, who had been given the seat of honor at one end of the splendidly laid-out dining table, was already rising from his chair. As the *thump-ka-thump* drew closer and closer, Martin saw the five servers who were lined up against the wall stand taller and straighten their uniforms. Two of the servers were men, the other three women. They were all Caucasian. Two of the servers Martin recognized from earlier encounters, even though they now wore different uniforms. One was the redheaded kid who had showed Martin up to his room and the other was Alice, the pretty maid who he had asked about a telephone. Oscar, in a smart black suit, stood steadfast at the head of the table beside the empty high-backed chair that awaited their host. Even he briefly broke form to double-check his appearance.

The *thump-ka-thump* was just outside the dining room

door now. Martin glanced around the table at Damon, Solomon, Carver, Tobias, and Kwame. They were all staring at Martin in anticipation. Smiling at him in their fancy dinner jackets and neckties. Martin was dressed sharply as well. The fine tailored jacket he wore along with his shirt, tie, and slacks were a surprise gift from Damon, who, knowing that Martin would only have jeans and sweaters in his backpack, had smuggled them along just for this occasion. It had all been just for this occasion, hadn't it? Martin pondered. Damon's making such an effort to befriend him, the probing questions from the men at their poker games, the rafting trip invitation—all just stepping-stones leading Martin deeper into their exclusive world. And this dinner tonight—this was the final step. Meeting their—their what exactly? Their mentor, their adviser, their spiritual leader? Who was this recluse who orchestrated such eccentric, elaborate jokes yet wielded untold influence over powerful men? The only thing Martin knew for certain was that Damon, Solomon, Tobias, Kwame, and Carver deeply respected this mysterious doctor. For Martin to become a true member of their inner circle, he would have to win Dr. Kasim's blessing.

Dr. Kasim stepped into the dining room with the aid of an African walking stick. Just like Martin imagined, the man was old, early nineties was Martin's guess, but with a firm grip on his intricately carved staff, the doctor walked tall and sure, his head held at a regal height. His receding hair and wiry beard were astonishingly white, and even more so against his dark mahogany skin. Dr. Kasim's face showed few wrinkles, but his eyes betrayed his true age. Behind delicate wire-frame spectacles, heavy-lidded and ghost gray, they smoldered with a lifetime of wisdom. Unlike his guests, the doctor was dressed quite casually for dinner. He wore forest-green silk pajamas beneath a long black silk robe, and a pair of quilted leather slippers. Martin couldn't help thinking of another elderly titan with his very own walled-in kingdom who greeted his wealthy guests in elegant sleepwear. But as much as Hugh Hefner was a world-renowned celebrity, the old man who had just strode into the dining room like an African king was an absolute mystery.

The men greeted their host with respectful nods but did not utter a word. Dr. Kasim returned the gesture, but with the slightest effort imaginable. When Martin mimicked the others and also offered a welcoming nod, Dr. Kasim did not return the greeting. Instead the old man just studied him. He took a step closer. Dr. Kasim very slowly looked Martin up and down, from head to foot, the way a drill sergeant scrutinizes one of his soldiers. Martin wasn't sure why, but he just stood there. Quiet. Nervous. Paralyzed by the strange old man's probing gaze. The doctor's eyes narrowed as he focused on Martin's face. He peered deep into Martin's eyes. The awkward staring contest seemed to go on forever. Martin was desperate to look away but something stopped him.

Martin sensed that if he dropped his eyes now, he would drop everything. And he was grateful when Dr. Kasim finally cracked a smile. "Welcome, brother Zantu," he said in a low, soothing voice.

Martin appeared puzzled. "Sorry, but I'm Martin. Martin Grey."

Dr. Kasim shook his head. "No. You just think you are because you are asleep."

Martin glanced over at Damon for help. *What is this old man saying to me?*

Dr. Kasim laughed. A deep, hearty laugh that he somehow managed without ever opening his mouth. It was as if whatever tickled him was just too delicious to let out. The doctor laid a firm hand on Martin's shoulder. "Don't worry, brother. Tonight you wake up. But right now I'm starving." As Dr. Kasim approached the head of the table, Oscar pulled out his chair. Only after he was comfortably settled into his seat did the others sit down as well.

While they dined on shrimp bisque, an elegant rack of lamb, and wild mushroom risotto, Dr. Kasim never uttered another word to Martin. Instead he caught up with the lives of the other men. He seemed genuinely interested in their latest business ventures, and even more so in how much money and resources they were each funneling back into the black community. Martin had to make an effort to conceal how astonished he was by the numbers being discussed. Kwame gave away millions to several black colleges. Carver spent $2 million to build a recreation center in the Bronx neighborhood where he grew up. Solomon gave away nearly $5 million worth of laptop computers to black schoolchildren. Tobias and a group of contributors were funding the construction of a media arts school in Harlem budgeted at $30 million. And as Martin listened to these reports, a frightening thought struck him. What would he say if Dr. Kasim turned to him and asked about *his* charitable donations? There would be nothing he could say. Martin hadn't donated a dime to charity, black or white, in his entire life. Not that he didn't want to give; it was just that he was never in a position to give. Martin knew that this was a lousy excuse, though. People gave what they could afford. Even one hundred dollars to the United Negro College Fund counted for something. Martin decided then and there that in the future he would try to give back a little as well. Not the millions that Damon and the others were ticking off, at least not yet, but something affordable just to get him and Anna up on the scoreboard.

Thankfully, Dr. Kasim never did steer the charity question Martin's way, and Martin relaxed when the conversation moved on to more mundane topics like family. Dr. Kasim grilled each man about his kids. Martin noticed that his interest in their offspring did not seem all that casual. He wanted very specific updates on their behavior, education, and most importantly, their career choices. And when Dr. Kasim heard something that troubled him, he would make a firm suggestion to correct the issue. For instance, when Damon mentioned that his young son, Kevin, was considering forgoing law school after college to join the air force, Dr. Kasim shook his head and said, "No black man belongs in the military, you know that. Change his mind." Damon nodded quietly as if accepting an order, and the conversation moved on. Martin also noticed that Dr. Kasim never asked any of the men about their wives, and the men never mentioned them . . . except once. When Tobias, very relaxed after several glasses of wine, mentioned his wife's opinion about their son's college choice, Dr. Kasim interrupted by clearing his throat. The sound was loud and pointed. Tobias realized his mistake and promptly apologized.

By the time dessert was served—the best apple pie that Martin had ever tasted—Dr. Kasim still had not directed so much as a glance in Martin's direction. Oddly, Martin didn't mind being ignored by the host, and, also oddly, Dr. Kasim's behavior did not come across as rude. The dynamic at the table felt like club protocol. The members had the usual clubhouse business to attend to, and since Martin was still an outsider, he could take no part in that. He just had to sit quietly and wait to be recognized. After cleaning his plate, Martin asked Alice for a second helping of that delicious pie. Alice flashed a pretty smile at him and hurried into the kitchen to do his bidding. He noticed that the two other female servers, both blond, were very pretty as well. Whoever was in charge of the hiring had an obvious appetite for shapely young blondes. Martin assumed that hiring and firing was probably Oscar's responsibility, but as he observed Dr. Kasim's lieutenant barking orders to the staff, Martin never noticed Oscar's eyes lingering on any of the girls. Oscar was just as brusque with the women as he was with the men. If hiring so many pretty young blondes was truly Oscar's doing, then it was either an innocent coincidence, or Oscar's stone-faced facade was even more impenetrable than Martin first thought.

Alice reappeared with the apple pie, but just steps before reaching Martin she stumbled and dropped the plate. The plate hit with a crash and all the servers froze. Alice flew into an instant panic. She apologized profusely, not just to Martin, but more so to Oscar, whose unreadable eyes were fixed on the frantic girl. Tears in her eyes, Alice apologized once more to Martin, then dropped to her knees and began to scoop up the pie and plate fragments.

"It's okay," Martin assured her. "Don't cry. It's just pie." Then he knelt down beside her and began to help clean up the mess.

Dr. Kasim raised his staff high, then slammed the tip down hard upon the floor. Everyone froze at the sound, including the trembling serving girl. Startled, Martin looked up and saw Dr. Kasim staring at him. "Why are you on the floor?"

The answer to that question seemed obvious, but Dr. Kasim asked it with such sincerity that for a moment

Martin froze in confusion. Finally he found his voice. "I'm just trying to help her."

Dr. Kasim's brow furrowed. He appeared baffled by Martin's answer. "You're my guest. Why would you feel an urge to help . . . the help?"

"She was upset. I thought I could make the situation better."

Dr. Kasim shook his head and frowned in a disappointed manner. "You don't know the true reason behind why you're down on the floor, do you?"

Once again Martin found himself caught in the doctor's tangle of words. "I don't know what you mean."

"That's exactly what I just said." Dr. Kasim smiled. "Return to your seat, brother. Please."

Oscar signaled, and one of the male servers dropped down to help the shaken girl. Martin brushed off his slacks and retook his seat. The men all frowned in bewilderment at Martin, as if dropping down to help the server girl was the act of a madman.

"Bring him another slice of pie," Dr. Kasim said to Alice as she finished picking up the mess. "And bring me one too." As the girl hurried off, Dr. Kasim returned his full attention to Martin. "You must really love pie," Dr. Kasim said to him with mock awe. "I mean, to be willing to eat it right off the floor."

Martin forced a laugh along with the other men. "It is unusually good pie," Martin said, still on his guard.

"It's the apples that make the pie. That's the secret."

"The apples?"

Dr. Kasim nodded. "Zantu apples. Very rare. There's only one place on earth where they grow. A tiny, secluded region in west central Africa. The same region where a small tribe called the Zantu once flourished." Dr. Kasim searched Martin's face for signs of recognition. "Have you ever heard of the Zantu tribe?"

"I think you said that word when you first walked in, but no, I haven't."

"There's a tragic reason you haven't. On October 3, 1756, a large band of slave traders attacked the Zantu village, kidnapped the youngest and strongest, and killed everyone else. Except for the ninety-four men and women who were shipped to the United States in chains and sold into slavery, the entire Zantu bloodline was wiped from the face of the earth."

"That's horrible," was all that Martin could think to say.

Dr. Kasim's grim history lesson had the instantaneous effect of darkening the mood in the dining room. Martin wondered why Dr. Kasim would steer the conversation in such a direction. There was also the all-white staff to consider. How awkward must it be for them to just stand there, listening to a story of how their ancestors committed genocide against people who looked a lot like their current employers.

A tense quiet lingered in the room until finally Alice returned with the two slices of pie. She set one plate in front of Dr. Kasim and the other in front of Martin, then stepped back to her place against the wall. Dr. Kasim lifted his fork but paused, waiting for his guest to start. Martin, fork in hand, just stared at the crumbling, oozing slice of apple pie.

"Go on, kid. Eat up," Tobias said. "I'd have another piece myself but I'm stuffed." He patted his midsection as if his bulbous gut were a beloved pet.

"Maybe he'd rather eat it off the floor," Carver said with his usual smirk.

Martin looked at Dr. Kasim. "After the story you told, I feel a little uncomfortable eating this."

"Ridiculous," Dr. Kasim said. "Nobody on this planet is entitled to enjoy the Zantu native fruit more than you and I."

Martin had come to realize that Dr. Kasim had a peculiar knack for ambiguity. His roundabout manner forced everyone to think twice about every single word he said. But the doctor's last statement was particularly puzzling.

As if he could read Martin's thoughts, Dr. Kasim answered the unspoken question. "You and I are part of a very small group of people who still carry Zantu blood." Dr. Kasim smiled, taking a bite of his pie before continuing. "Like me, you carry a DNA marker that identifies you as a descendant of the Zantu tribe. There are very few of us left. Fewer than fifty by my estimate."

Dr. Kasim said this with such sheer confidence that Martin had little doubt that it was true—but that wasn't what bothered Martin. He set his fork down sharply. "And how would you know something like that about me?"

"Look where you are," Dr. Kasim said. "Look at the individuals around you. Are you really so surprised?"

Martin glanced around the table at Damon, Solomon, Tobias, Kwame, and Carver. Some of the most influential men in the world. Watching him. Measuring him. Dr. Kasim was right. A seat at this reserved table did not come without some sort of vetting. Martin nodded to the doctor. "I see your point."

"Excellent," Dr. Kasim said. "I have never met another man who shared my Zantu blood. It's good to see that he is a rational thinker—even in his sleep."

Intrigued, Martin replied, "You said that earlier. That I was asleep. What does that mean?"

Dr. Kasim smiled. "Eat your pie. We have a lot to discuss, my Zantu brother."

41

"You might think that you dropped to the floor to help that girl because you were trying to be nice," Dr. Kasim was saying, "but that's just a rationalization. The truth is, my brother, you suffer from a mental condition that you've had your entire life and don't even know it."

After dinner, Dr. Kasim had moved the gathering into the library. The spacious room contained not only books but also an impressive collection of African art. The doctor was seated in a high-backed leather chair with his back to a crackling fireplace smoking a pipe. His tall walking stick leaned against the side of the chair, its fierce tribal carvings eerily animated by flickering firelight. Damon, Solomon, Tobias, Kwame, and Carver were seated around the doctor puffing cigars and imbibing their favorite liqueurs. Martin, to avoid Damon's usual prodding in front of their host, had finally agreed to try a cigar. To his surprise, he found it soothing. After the drinks had been served and the cigars lit, Oscar had ordered all the servers out of the library and shut the door behind them. He did not join the group around the fireplace. Instead, he took a seat beside the door and remained quiet. It wasn't clear to Martin if Oscar's intention was to bar the servants from entering the library or to bar anyone from exiting, but the action did make Martin a little anxious. After what had been said in the dining room in front of the servants, Martin couldn't imagine what could be said now that would offend them. Martin did not have to wait long to find out. With the servants gone, Dr. Kasim was shifting the conversation back to the pie incident in the dining room. Peering at Martin through curls of pipe smoke, Dr. Kasim, in no uncertain terms, had just accused Martin of suffering from a mental illness of sorts. Martin didn't take the accusation as an insult because it wasn't presented as such. Dr. Kasim's tone was cool, as if he were simply stating a fact, the same as if he were telling Martin that his eyes were brown. When Dr. Kasim made the charge, Damon and the other men all nodded in agreement. Their faces were filled with grave concern and sympathy, as if Martin had just been diagnosed with something fatal and they were there to show support. Martin did not know how to react. What kind of doctor was this Dr. Kasim anyway? Martin had never asked, and nobody had ever told him.

Martin was seated at the end of a sofa, within arm's reach of Dr. Kasim. Seeing the puzzlement on Martin's face, the doctor reached out and squeezed Martin's hand. For an elderly man, his grip was surprisingly firm. "No need to worry, brother," Dr. Kasim said. "I'm going to help you. We all are." Damon and the others nodded again.

"Help me with what?" Martin said. "It's not like I kicked the poor girl. I just helped her pick up some pie."

"Kicking her wouldn't have been as bad," Carver said.

Martin gave Carver a surprised look but noticed that none of the other men, including Dr. Kasim, showed any reaction to the comment.

"Ever heard the term *slave mentality*?" Dr. Kasim asked.

"Of course."

"Do you know what it means?"

Martin frowned. "If you're trying to tell me that I have a slave mentality—"

Dr. Kasim shook his head slowly. "I'm not. I'm telling you that you have something far worse. The slave mentality is just one of its many tragic symptoms. And the worst part is that you are not alone. Every black man in the world suffers from the same mental aberration you do. From the day he's born until the day he dies."

Martin glanced around at the men. Stern, solemn faces. Whatever Dr. Kasim was about to reveal was very important to them. A revered secret. This was the final door opening. Martin turned back to Dr. Kasim. To those ancient ghostly eyes measuring him. He was almost afraid to ask the question. "What are you talking about?"

Dr. Kasim touched his temple with the tip of his pipe. "There's a kind of interference that clouds the black man's mind. This interference keeps black children from focusing on their studies. This interference turns black teens into drug addicts and killers. This interference keeps black men from being good fathers and providers. This interference keeps a black man behaving like a slave even when he's the master. It is this interference that keeps the black man from walking the earth with pride. There's no scientific name for it, and you won't find it in any medical books, but it's as real as depression or bipolar disease or any other psychological disorder. I call it simply *black noise.*"

"And you're saying that I have this disease? This black noise?"

Dr. Kasim nodded. "But not just you. As I said, all black men suffer from it. And that is exactly why I built Forty Acres. To help strong black men free their minds of the interference. To teach them how to quiet the noise. And once my students accomplish that, they become unstoppable. Just look at the results." Dr. Kasim waved his hands with a flourish before the other men in the room, like a stage magician at the conclusion of his grandest illusion.

The men were all smiling at Martin now, their faces lit up with some secret joy. Could what Dr. Kasim was telling him be true? That these great men owed their phenomenal success to some kind of mysterious therapy?

"Martin, listen to him," Damon said. "The doctor will change your life forever."

"Brother, once that noise goes away," Solomon said, "the whole world will look different."

"This is a new beginning for you, brother," Kwame said. "A beautiful new beginning."

Tobias patted Martin on the shoulder. "I wish I were you, learning this for the first time."

Even Carver was smiling at him. "You're lucky to be here, Grey. Quieting the noise will change your whole way of thinking."

Dr. Kasim blew a long stream of smoke as he looked at Martin. Studied him. "I can heal you of the sickness. I can quiet the black noise in your head. But you have to open your mind for the cure to work. Can you open your mind, brother?"

It was Carver's last comment that really struck Martin. That gave Martin a strange feeling that he was the guest of honor at some surreal intervention. And the more Martin thought about it, the clearer it became. That's exactly what this was. In their minds he was like an addict. But not hooked on drugs; he was an addict hooked on this so-called condition that they believed was responsible for holding the black man down. They had brought Martin out to Forty Acres to confront him with their truth and, as Carver so bluntly put it, change his whole way of thinking. Their goal was to persuade him to accept their unusual view of the world—an extreme afrocentric worldview that, no doubt, empowered them. Made them feel more confident and walk a little taller. And what was wrong with that? How was Forty Acres any different from dozens of private country clubs around the country?

Clubs where black servants catered to an all-Caucasian membership. Forty Acres was just the reverse, with a touch of dark humor. If subscribing to Dr. Kasim's "black noise" philosophy was the final step to joining their inner circle, so be it. Martin didn't know if Damon and the others really benefited from Dr. Kasim's teachings, but what he had heard so far was intriguing. "Yes, I can open my mind," Martin replied finally. "Tell me. How do I quiet this black noise?"

Dr. Kasim frowned. "Before I provide that answer, you require another answer."

"What do you mean? What answer?"

"The answer to the question that you haven't asked me yet."

Martin was quiet, trying to understand.

Dr. Kasim continued, "If you said to me that you hear a strange noise, what would you expect my immediate response to be?"

"'What noise?'"

Dr. Kasim nodded. "Why haven't you asked me that?"

Martin thought about it. "I guess I assumed it was more of a metaphor."

"Perhaps. But a metaphor for what? You didn't ask because you don't believe any of this. Am I right?"

After a beat, Martin frowned. "Sorry. It's not that I don't believe it. It's just hard to get my head around."

Dr. Kasim smiled. "Don't be sorry for being honest. Honesty is the first sign that your mind is willing to open." Then Dr. Kasim leaned closer. "Only a damn fool believes anything he's told without questioning it. Are you a damn fool, brother?"

Martin shook his head. "No, I'm not."

"Prove it. Prove to me your mind is truly open."

At first Martin didn't know how to respond. His thoughts were frozen by those piercing, ghostly eyes. Then the answer came to him. It was so obvious that he couldn't see it. The answer was the question. "The black noise. What is it?"

Dr. Kasim leaned back in his chair wearing a pleased smile. "Now we are getting somewhere."

42

Oscar carefully removed an old framed photograph from the mantel and handed it to Dr. Kasim. In the faded black-and-white photo, a young black man, his bare torso rippling with muscles, stood beside a wooden plow hitched to a stout horse. In the background a small weather-beaten house and newly built barn sat at the edge of a freshly plowed field. The young man in the photograph looked tired and dirty but there was still determination and pride in his gray eyes.

"That's me, when I was still Thaddeus Walker, on my farm back in 1937." Dr. Kasim spoke with a spark of admiration that left no doubt that he was truly the man in the photo. "My father used to be a sharecropper, but when the landowner died, he willed my father a tiny patch of land. A little more than a year later, my father dropped dead on his land and I inherited it. It was just one acre but I worked that acre hard. My father had sowed that land with his sweat and blood and I was determined to make it pay. One day I raised my eyes from the soil and discovered that my tiny patch had expanded a little. Through the years I had purchased more and more of the land around my property, and before long I was the owner of a fifteen-acre farm. That might not sound like much today, but back then in Macon the only thing that most black folks owned was the clothes on their back. A black man with a fifteen-acre spread was something exceptional. I married the prettiest black girl in town; people looked up to me. I had big plans to expand my property even further and have lots of children to help me work it. As far as I was concerned, my whole life was set. But I was a fool. I was doing better than many of the white people in town, but I didn't see the envy and bitterness in my white neighbors' eyes until it was too late."

Dr. Kasim passed the framed photograph back to Oscar, who carefully returned it to its spot on the mantel. Martin noticed a hint of sadness in the doctor's eyes as the photograph left his hand, as if he hated to part with the idealistic young man in the picture. Martin and the other men waited patiently as the doctor took a moment to relight his pipe. Although Martin was sure that the others had heard Dr. Kasim's story before, they all appeared just as riveted as he was. Dr. Kasim puffed his pipe back to life, dropped the smoldering match into a nearby ashtray, then continued his tale, eyes edged with bitterness.

"Richard Brown Jr. was the only son of the landowner who left my father that first tiny patch. Father and son were similar only in name. Even from the start Junior resented his father's generous gift to my father. And after

I had worked that land into an enterprise that was beginning to rival his own, he went insane with hatred. He offered several times to buy my farm and I always flatly refused. Not because his price wasn't fair but because I believed that that land was who I was. My identity. And without it, I would be nothing.

"But Junior saw only a stubborn Negro who was making him, a white man, look like a fool. So Junior gave up trying to buy my land and found another way to get it. He whispered in the ears of some of his friends, people who had influence in the courts and the clerk's office. White people who sympathized with his Negro problem. Suddenly the county judge revoked Junior's father's will. The deed to that tiny patch of land that my father left me was taken from me and given to Junior. Even worse, because my success with the surrounding acres was a direct offshoot of working the original land, I was forced to sell it all to Junior for less than a tenth of what it was worth. And when I refused to take Junior's money, the sheriff and all his deputies came out and kicked me and my wife off the land."

"But they couldn't have done that," Martin said, regretting the impulse even as the words left his mouth. Dr. Kasim's story took place in a time when the color of your skin was directly related to how much justice you received.

"Oh, but they did do it," Dr. Kasim said. "They did it as easily as the government takes fifty percent of every dollar you earn. They robbed me of my land right out in plain sight. In the name of the law . . ."

"The white law," Tobias sneered.

Martin found Dr. Kasim's story moving, and he could understand how anyone who had suffered such an injustice might harbor a grudge against the offenders, but what did any of this have to do with this so-called black noise that afflicted all black men? Martin was pondering a way to phrase the question without appearing impatient when Dr. Kasim smiled and said, "Patience, brother. I'm getting to it. Question is, are you ready?"

Martin didn't give an answer, and Dr. Kasim didn't wait for one. Instead the old man just blew a stream of smoke and went on.

"My reaction to losing my land was surprising. I wasn't devastated or heartbroken or depressed. None of that. I was so filled up with anger that there was room for nothing else. Not even the love for my wife. I took her back to her father's house and I never laid eyes on the woman again. I lived in the woods surrounding my land and all I did was eat, shit, and watch that white man. For weeks and weeks I watched that white man and his white family and his white friends living off what was mine, and for weeks and weeks my anger grew. I began to realize that the pure and perfect anger that I felt was fueled by something more than just my personal loss. Something deeper. Like a pressure inside me suddenly let loose. It was the anger I felt for all the crimes committed against my people. For kidnapping and raping and enslaving and killing my people. It was the anger I felt because no one had been punished for these crimes. It was the anger they tell black men to keep inside. The anger he's told that he just has to let go of because all that raping and killing happened in the past. It was that anger that I felt as I watched that white man . . . and I began to feel thankful to him. Because that anger led me to a greater purpose. A purpose far more important than owning a few acres of dirt.

"I decided that I wasn't going to play by the white man's rules any longer. No, I was going to unleash my pent-up anger and dedicate my life to avenging my people."

Dr. Kasim paused, catching his breath.

"And how were you planning to do that?" Martin asked.

Dr. Kasim gave an unexpected shrug. "I didn't have a clue. But I did have an idea how I could start. I crawled out of the woods with my hat in hand and I asked Junior for a job. Most people would think twice about keeping around a man that you had just cheated out of life, but he was so eager to completely humiliate the stubborn Negro that he took me on. I worked hard and I saved every penny until, after a few years, I had enough to quit and buy my own piece of land in the next county. It was only an acre, another tiny patch like my father left me, but this time I had a new idea as to how I could make that land pay. I went back to visit Junior, but not in the light of day. I went in the dead of night. The same way his ancestors would raid African villages. The same way masters would creep into the beds of their female slaves and rape them. I kidnapped Junior from his home and kept him chained to a beam in my barn. My place was pretty isolated, so I'd work him in the fields all day and keep him locked up in chains at night. And let me tell you, I got a lot of work done that way."

Martin couldn't believe it. He couldn't. "Are you saying that you made Junior your *slave*?"

"That is exactly what I'm saying."

"But that's—"

"Go on, say it," Dr. Kasim urged. "Illegal?"

Martin had another word in mind: *wrong*. But hearing Dr. Kasim's mocking tone, Martin merely nodded.

"Running a red light is illegal. Burglarizing someone's home is illegal. But abducting a man and enslaving him like an animal for his entire life, that's far worse, wouldn't you agree?"

Martin did not speak. Dr. Kasim had just confessed to a serious crime with the ease of delivering a punch line. True, the offense had occurred decades ago, but as far as Martin knew there was no statute of limitations on kidnapping and slavery. And what troubled Martin more was that Damon, Solomon, Tobias, Kwame, and Carver all appeared to be comfortable with Dr. Kasim's confession.

"You look shocked," Dr. Kasim said to Martin.

"Shouldn't I be? If that story's true—"

Dr. Kasim smiled. "I'm an old man. I might get some of the details mixed up but the good parts, like the first time I slapped chains on that white bastard, I never get wrong."

"That's a very serious crime. Why tell me about it?"

"Because you asked about the black noise."

"I still haven't heard anything about any black noise."

"But you have. That uneasiness and resistance that you're feeling right now, that's a normal reaction when you begin to become conscious of the noise."

"But I don't hear any damn noise," Martin snapped.

Dr. Kasim waggled his pipe at Martin. "Annoyance is also a typical reaction. Your mind wants to shut down, but you must fight that impulse. You must keep your thoughts open until I finish my story. Can you do that, brother?"

"Believe me, I'm trying. But all I've heard so far is you talking."

Dr. Kasim nodded. "Sometimes you don't notice a thing until it's gone. And that's exactly what happened to me. Back when I had my first farm, the only time I would have any contact with white men was when I'd have to go into town to buy seeds or supplies from their stores. A black man would have to be careful of what kind of mood he caught a white man in. Sometimes a white man would treat you like anybody else and charge you a fair price. Sometimes they'd treat you mean and jack up the price just because you were a Negro. And sometimes they'd just refuse to transact business with you at all. I used to dread these encounters because it made me, one of the most successful farmers in the county, feel like I was less than a man. I wouldn't even look those white men in the eye too long for fear that they'd take it the wrong way. But after Junior stole my farm and then I stole him, something about me changed. Over the years, as I forced Junior to work my land, I began to notice a profound change in my personality. Gradually, when I would go into town, I would deal with those white men with more and more confidence. My manner became firm and more direct. I would hold my head up high and look those white men straight in the eye. And the odd thing was, no matter what mood those men were in, they never took offense. All of a sudden they were treating me with respect. It was as if something inside their subconscious was responding to whatever had changed in me. But what was it? What about me had changed? Looking back now, the answer seems perfectly obvious, but back then I had to think on the problem for a long time before I solved the mystery." Dr. Kasim tapped his temple. "That constant black noise in my head that had drowned out my pride and humanity—it was suddenly gone. That's what had changed in me."

"That still doesn't explain what black noise is," Martin said.

Dr. Kasim fixed Martin with an intense stare, a lifetime

of wisdom pouring out of his ancient eyes. "Black noise is screams," the doctor said, his voice grim. "The screams of our kidnapped, enslaved, tortured, raped, and murdered ancestors crying out for vengeance."

Dr. Kasim's sudden intensity caused Martin to draw back, like he was avoiding a blast of heat from a roaring fire. He saw the other men nod in agreement.

"The screams of our ancestors haunt every black man's soul," Dr. Kasim said, with sorrow in his voice, "a constant reminder that the white man not only conquered our forefathers but robbed them of their humanity. And because of this burden of shame and humiliation, deep down every man of African descent, no matter how rich or powerful, harbors a poisonous seed of doubt that he is truly equal to the white man. Even worse, a fear of the white man."

Martin was quiet a moment. "I don't feel that way," he said at last, with deep thought. "I do not feel inferior to white people."

Dr. Kasim gave a dismissive grunt. "Of course you'd deny it. What kind of man would admit that he's inferior to another man? But if your mind was truly open, you'd see that what I'm telling you is true. The black noise is very real. Working in the background, holding you and every other black man back like an invisible leash. Only once you recognize it, only then can you learn how to quiet it."

Martin pondered this a moment. "And how do you do that?" he asked.

"That is what I had stumbled upon when I made Junior my slave," Dr. Kasim said. "My tiny act of revenge had appeased the black noise. Now whenever I faced a white man, I could look him dead in the eye, because I'd taken an action to avenge my race. I wasn't a victim any longer, groveling at the feet of my conqueror. Suddenly, I could stand toe-to-toe with the white man on the same playing field because now I was his equal. Those screams of my ancestors were replaced by the pleas of that white man chained up in my barn." Dr. Kasim leaned closer and laid a fatherly hand on Martin's shoulder. "Brother, until you quiet the noise in your head, you will never be able to look a white man in the eye with genuine pride. And because of that, you will never achieve your full potential."

Damon, Solomon, Tobias, Kwame, and Carver all blew smoke and threw back drinks. "Amen to that," Tobias said.

Martin turned his gaze back to the doctor. It still didn't make sense. "You're saying that in order for a black man to reach his true potential, he has to keep a white man prisoner in his basement?"

Dr. Kasim made a face. "Come now. Think about it, brother. Could men such as these, men under constant scrutiny, get away with something like that?"

"No," Martin replied, detecting a disingenuous tone in the doctor's voice. "That would be crazy."

"Indeed it would," Dr. Kasim whispered.

"But according to your theory, it takes an act of

vengeance to get rid of the black noise. An act of vengeance against a white man."

"Oh, it's not a theory, brother." Dr. Kasim gestured to the surrounding books in his library. "I could show you countless published studies on the ill effects of abject injustice on the human psyche. Depression, diminished self-worth, lower IQs, suicide, even erectile dysfunction. I could show you a dozen more papers by esteemed psychologists on how revenge is an essential human trait. A primal instinct as innate and necessary as reproduction. It's even in the Bible. An eye for an eye and a tooth for a tooth." Dr. Kasim shook his head. "No, Martin. What I teach is not a theory. It's a fact."

Martin glanced around at the other men. They were all staring at him expectantly. Martin wasn't sure why, but he suddenly felt afraid to ask his next question.

"So if you guys are not keeping slaves in your basements or attics, how did you do it? How did you get rid of the black noise?"

In perfect unison Damon, Solomon, Tobias, Kwame, and Carver all turned to Dr. Kasim, as if they would not dare answer without his permission. To see such powerful men behave so obsequiously toward the enigmatic old man filled Martin with dread. Dr. Kasim simply nodded to Damon, then Damon turned to Martin and smiled. It was a smile full of anticipation. And that smile scared Martin to the core. It scared him because even before Damon uttered a word, Martin knew without a shred of doubt that there was something really wrong at Forty Acres. Something so wrong that they had to hide it way out in the middle of nowhere and protect it with a private army. Suddenly Martin did not want to know the answer to his question. But it was too late.

43

"We get rid of the black noise by coming here," Damon said, spreading his hands in a welcoming manner. "By spending time here, at Forty Acres."

The meaning of Damon's words took a moment to crystalize. Martin knew that there was something off about Forty Acres and he had braced himself for a shock, but nothing could have prepared him for the terrible truth that finally crashed down on him. He gasped. He was so stunned that he felt dizzy. He set his drink down and buried his face in his hands.

"You okay, son?" Solomon asked.

Martin ignored Solomon. Instead, he lifted his head and turned to face Dr. Kasim. Stared at the old man with a tempest of disbelief in his eyes. Martin tried to ask the question that had to be asked next, but the words just wouldn't come. Perhaps it was because he already knew the answer.

Dr. Kasim raised a hand, gently silencing Martin, then in a proud voice said, "Yes, brother. Here at Forty Acres black men are the masters . . . and the whites are our slaves."

Martin did something that surprised even himself. He laughed. He laughed at the insanity and impossibility of that moment. He laughed because it was too absurd to be true. Martin glanced at the other men, hoping that they'd start laughing too. Waiting for Damon to slap him on the back and tell him that this madness was just another one of Dr. Kasim's dark jokes.

"We know how you feel right now," Dr. Kasim said. "Your first reaction will be horror. Outrage. Maybe even hatred. But you now have to think past all that. You have to see the bigger picture. What we do is not personal or about individuals. It's about making the white race pay for its unpunished crimes against the black race. For too long the modern black man has let his ancestors down. We live in comfort upon the graves of our forefathers who suffered unspeakably and were never avenged. What we do here at Forty Acres isn't for selfish reasons. It is a duty that we are privileged to bear. A duty to free our minds of that noise by any means necessary, and to use that freedom to become strong black men. Men who can lead our people out of the trash heap of human history that we have been tossed in. And maybe one day all black men will be able to quiet that terrible noise in their minds and hold their heads up with true pride. Don't just react, my brother. Remember, you've been programmed by the white man to ignore the black noise. But I'm telling you to listen now. Really listen to them!" Dr. Kasim leaned forward and gripped Martin's shoulder. His voice was soothing. "Are you going to ignore the screams of millions of your ancestors, or will you join us?"

Martin did not respond. The shock and confusion he felt had the effect of short-circuiting his mind. Everything Dr. Kasim said made sense in a strange way. And even though Martin felt that what they were doing was wrong, he had to ask himself, *Do I feel it's wrong because, like Dr. Kasim said, I've been programmed? By not seeking vengeance, am I really betraying my ancestors?* Damon, Solomon, Tobias, Carver, and Kwame were all smart men and they followed Dr. Kasim's philosophy. They had to be seeing something that Martin couldn't see. Was it really programming that caused him to hesitate, or was it just common sense?

Damon and the other men began to lay comforting hands on Martin's shoulders. "This is the toughest part," Damon said. "The doubt that you are feeling now is almost impossible to deny. The brainwashing is so deep that you can't see past it."

Then Solomon spoke. "That's why you have to trust us. You will never stop thinking it's wrong until you accept it. Once you accept it and the noise is gone from your head, then you will see the good of it."

Each encouraging squeeze of the shoulder, each lulling word, tugged at Martin's will, coaxing Martin deeper and deeper into their arcane brotherhood. And it would be so easy to go along, so easy to allow himself to be drawn into the fold. He'd be a member of a wealthy and powerful fraternity bound by a secret so great that the loyalty they shared would be limitless. The life-changing benefits of such a relationship were incalculable. Not just for him but for Anna and their future children as well. And the price of membership was equally seductive. All he had to do was embrace Dr. Kasim's ideology. It shouldn't be difficult, since Martin believed there was some truth to the old doctor's "black noise" idea. Did Martin's self-esteem whither every time he was around white folks? Absolutely not. But sometimes, when in the presence of Caucasian men, he did feel something. A hint of self-consciousness similar to the way one feels when standing before a person you highly respect. A fleeting, unwarranted desire for approval. Martin had no idea if other black men shared this experience, but for him it was real. Indeed, the more Martin pondered it, the more certain he became that Dr. Kasim might be onto something important—a poltergeist in the African American psyche that should be discussed and studied. But the old doctor, infected with hatred, wasn't interested in research, only revenge in the name of overdue justice. And that's where Martin drew the line. Kidnapping and enslaving innocent people because of ills committed by their forefathers seemed a greater crime than the original offense. Martin was proud to be a member of the black race, but first and foremost he was a member of the human race. What was true hundreds of years ago was still true today and will forever be true.

Enslaving another human being was an unredeemable act of evil.

It couldn't be justified by wrapping it up in some easily swallowed philosophical claptrap. Dr. Kasim and his followers had become the very thing they professed to hate.

And with that conclusion came a rise of anger inside Martin. Anger because men he held in such high esteem had revealed themselves to be criminals. And criminals of the lowest sort. Criminals of hate. Anger because they offered to make him a coconspirator in a crime against humanity as if they were doing him some great favor. But most of all, he felt anger because Damon and his fucked-up friends believed that he was like them.

Martin glared at Damon. A glare that screamed, *Where the hell have you brought me?*

Damon's response was a patient smile. "It's all right, Martin. You'll see."

It's all right? Martin had an urge to leap up and strangle him, but Dr. Kasim reached out and squeezed Martin's hand. "Brother, please do not allow this decision to cause you any undo stress. Whatever you decide will be perfectly fine."

The other men nodded.

Martin clenched his jaw and looked the old doctor square in the eye. Martin was about to reject their insane offer flat out when he was startled by a voice behind him.

"Of course, Mr. Grey, if you choose not to accept, we assume that you can be trusted to protect our secret."

Martin turned and saw Oscar looming behind him. With all the strange turns the evening had taken, Martin had forgotten that Dr. Kasim's right-hand man was even in the room. But now Oscar's frigid gaze struck Martin like a bucket of ice water, effectively dousing Martin's anger. In that eye-opening instant another emotion began to take hold. Fear. *Is this what happened to Donald Jackson? Did Jackson reject Dr. Kasim's mad philosophy? And in order to keep Jackson quiet did they—?*

With shock, Martin realized that his life was in grave danger. There was no way that they would let him return home with this secret. Not these men. He realized that no matter what he thought about Forty Acres, there was only one answer that would get him back home to Anna alive.

Oscar's impassive eyes remained fixed on Martin's face. Reading him. Looking for any cracks. "We *can* count on your discretion, yes, Mr. Grey?"

"Of course," Martin said, trying to keep his voice from cracking. To keep down the panic that he felt rising inside him.

"Of course he will," Dr. Kasim said to Oscar in a dismissive tone. "I never doubted that for a second." Dr. Kasim then turned back to Martin. His smile was so relaxed and inviting that it was almost hypnotic. "So tell me, brother, will you join my little country club or not?"

Martin knew that his answer had to be completely convincing. If they even suspected a little that he was faking it—

"You belong here, brother," Kwame said. "Join us."

"Kwame's right," Tobias said. "You must be a part of this."

Damon looked sympathetic. "I know all this is freaking you out, Martin, but like Solomon said, you just have to trust us."

Could it really be that simple? Martin wondered. If he told them that he wanted in, would they simply believe him and issue him a membership card? It couldn't be that easy.

Carver was out of patience. "Quit being so dramatic, Grey. You know you want in. Just spit it out already."

While the others glared at Carver, Dr. Kasim maintained his grandfatherly guise. "Don't let Carver influence you," he said to Martin. "Whatever you decide will be fine. Just tell me your answer."

Martin glanced at Carver, who was wearing his usual callous smirk. He nodded at Martin, urging him to answer. In fact, Carver almost appeared too eager. This told Martin everything he needed to know.

Martin stood up and turned to Dr. Kasim. "My answer is no! *Hell no!* This whole place is insane and all of you are out of your fucking minds!"

44

When Martin saw Dr. Kasim and the other men react with smiles and laughter to his rejection, he knew that he had chosen the correct response. Any rational man who would so readily agree to enlist himself in such a drastic and illegal conspiracy had to be lying or a fool. Martin had to let the script of their seduction run its course. Allow them to believe that they had drawn him into their cabal with persuasion; then they would be convinced. Just as Martin had expected, Dr. Kasim and the other men assured him that his reaction was perfectly normal. Martin put up a small show of resistance, but finally he allowed himself to be cajoled into retaking his seat.

"You must understand that the conflict you feel is just a result of the programming," Dr. Kasim said. "It's the fear the white man put into your mind of your own blackness."

Martin shook his head wearily. "I don't know. I don't know what to think."

"The question is how does it make you *feel*. The story I told you about the Zantu, about how you are a direct descendant of an extinct tribe. How did that make you feel?"

"Terrible, of course. And yet special too."

"What about angry? Did it make you feel angry?"

"Yes, a little."

"A little? Do you think that's a normal reaction to finding out that your family has been slaughtered? A little anger?"

"But that was so long ago."

"When Jews talk about their people being murdered in Nazi ovens, do they sound just a little angry?"

"No," Martin replied.

"You're right about that." Solomon jumped in. "The Jews are so furious that they're still hunting down Nazis to this very day. And I don't blame them."

"Only the black man is brainwashed to bury his anger," Dr. Kasim said to Martin. "That's why you resist what we offer you, because you're brainwashed by the white man not to hate him. To let bygones be bygones while they and their children benefit from the exploitation of our ancestors. They smile at us and do business with us but behind our backs they're laughing at us."

"No. I don't believe that, and even if I did, we can't just do what we want. Inflict our own punishment."

"Why the hell not?" Tobias asked. "Everything you are has been stomped on and thrown away by white people, yet you're content to live by their rules? Where were their rules when they were raping our mothers and whipping our fathers?"

Dr. Kasim nodded at Oscar, who withdrew a leather-bound photo album from a nearby shelf and handed it to Martin. Inlaid gold lettering on the cover read Family Photos.

Martin wrinkled his brow at the doctor.

"Open it," Dr. Kasim said.

Martin turned the cover over and shuddered at what he saw. An old black-and-white photograph from the 1920s of a gruesome lynching. Four brutally beaten black men hanging dead from a tree. The surrounding well-armed white mob cheering as one man used a large bowie knife to make a trophy of one of the victims' genitals. Martin had seen old photos of lynchings before, but nothing like this.

"And where were their rules when they did that?" Tobias said.

Martin shook his head in disgust and shut the photo album.

"Don't stop there," Dr. Kasim said. "There's much more. Burnings, mutilations, disembowelment, it's all in there. Everything evil that can be done to the human body they did to our people. I want you to witness it, brother. Keep turning the pages."

"No," Martin said with genuine revulsion. He thrust the album onto the coffee table as if it were suddenly too hot to hold. "I know the history. I don't need to see it."

Dr. Kasim wagged a finger at him. "But do you see what you just did?" he said. "Instead of facing the anger and pain that those images inspire inside you, instead of facing the terrible truth, you'd rather just close the book on the past. Exactly what every black man has been conditioned to do since the so-called emancipation. That's the noise working on you. Making you doubt your self-worth, doubt your humanity, doubt your right to justice. Infecting your soul with fear."

Martin could feel their stares. The room suddenly felt smaller, as if the men around him were converging. He could sense that they were waiting for something. Looking for a sign that they were reaching him. But what sign?

"It's time for you to stop fearing the white man," Damon said. "It's time to stop thinking he's better than you."

"But I don't feel that way," Martin insisted. "I don't."

"You do fear the white man," Dr. Kasim said. "You know you do." He leaned forward and laid his hand atop Martin's. After a fatherly squeeze he said, "You must trust me. I'm here to help you, brother. We all are."

The other men nodded.

"First admit your fear," Dr. Kasim pressed, "then I will show you what real freedom feels like."

Martin glimpsed Solomon reaching into his jacket for a handkerchief. That was it. They were expecting some kind of emotional breakdown. But could he do it? Martin buried his face into his hands. Shook his head. "I don't know," he groaned. "I just don't know . . ."

They all laid their hands on him. "Your brothers are here to support you, Martin," Dr. Kasim said. "To rescue you. It's time to listen to the screams of your ancestors that fear has caused you to ignore for so long. It's time for you to hear their screams and get angry. Do you hear it? Do you hear the noise?"

Martin filled his mind with the thought of never returning home. Of never seeing Anna again. He pictured the pain that Anna would feel when she found out he was dead. Then his eyes began to sting. Emotion racked Martin's body and he could feel pinpricks of tears at the corners of his eyes. "Yes, I hear it," he said as he bowed his head and let the tears flow down his cheeks. "I hear it. I hear it. Oh God, I hear it!"

Dr. Kasim pulled Martin into his arms and embraced him. "It's okay, brother. It's all going to be okay."

After Martin wiped his eyes, the men each took turns embracing him and welcoming him into their family. Damon was the last to embrace Martin, and his was the biggest hug of all. Martin thought he could see a hint of genuine relief and pride in Damon's joyful eyes. He felt strangely touched, realizing in that moment how much their new friendship had come to mean to them.

"Tonight has been a turning point for you, Martin. But tomorrow night you'll have your initiation," Dr. Kasim said. "Then your healing can truly begin."

"What is my initiation?" Martin asked, raising his eyes and feeling a quick stab of anxiety.

"You'll find out tomorrow. But I have every confidence you will do just fine, brother." His cryptic answer was followed by a sudden loud *pop!* They turned and saw Oscar holding a foaming bottle of champagne. He filled seven crystal flutes and passed them out. When Oscar handed Martin his glass, in a formal tone he said, "Welcome, brother." Dr. Kasim held his glass high and smiled at Martin. "To my Zantu brother. Welcome home." Wearing big smiles, they clinked their glasses and drank . . . all except one.

When Martin looked up, he noticed that there was one person in the room who was not drinking or smiling. Carver just stood there watching Martin, his glass of champagne untouched.

45

Where would be the best place to hide a surveillance camera? Martin wondered as he sat up in bed, his back against the headboard, pretending to watch television. Martin didn't recognize the sitcom that was playing, but the scene of a family squabbling at the dinner table made him long to be back home in the normal world, not trapped in some depraved alternate reality constructed and ruled over by a wealthy madman.

Affluent black men keeping white slaves to avenge their forefathers. How could this be going on now? And not in some backward third-world country, but here, in the United States? At least he assumed they were still in the United States. In truth he really had no idea where they had taken him. He'd slept through most of the flight—how naive he'd been to believe that the tequila had rendered him unconscious. He'd been drugged, of course. The entire situation seemed too insane to be true. Martin felt as if he were trapped in an episode of one of his favorite shows, *The Twilight Zone.* But Forty Acres wasn't fantasy, it was very real, and Martin was now determined to put a stop to it.

Martin knew what he had to do. He'd play along.

He'd use the opportunity to gather as much information as possible about Forty Acres, then get back to civilization and blow the whistle to whatever government agency handled this sort of madness. But playing along would not be easy. Martin was now certain that, from the moment he entered Forty Acres, every little thing he did was being scrutinized.

When Martin had finally gotten back to his room, finally gotten away from all those scrutinizing eyes, it took everything he had to conceal the fear and horror he felt. But he had to hold his feelings inside. Even inside his room, alone, Martin could not let the hot bile of anxiety that churned in his gut rise up because he remembered that skinny valet's face. He remembered trying to tip the valet for carrying his bags and how the kid's nervous eyes scanned the room. Now Martin understood why. The valet knew that there were cameras in the room and that he was probably being watched.

But where were these cameras?

Martin looked up occasionally from the television to steal a glance around the room, but so far he had failed to spot anything that suggested a hiding place for a camera. This did not ease Martin's suspicions, though. From what he knew about spy cameras, the very best ones were so tiny that they could be concealed almost anywhere, even inside everyday household items such as wall clocks, radios, lamps, even smoke alarms. The problem was that there was no way for Martin to closely examine the room's furnishings without giving away the fact that he was searching for a camera. If his search was noticed, they'd realize he was just pretending to be a true believer, and then he'd be a problem that had to be dealt with. Most likely, just like Donald Jackson, he'd have a fatal accident. Or perhaps, to avoid using the same cover story, they'd tell the police that Martin wandered off and disappeared in the woods. Maybe they'd be more creative and claim a grizzly bear mauled Martin to death and dragged him off in the middle of the night. Whatever lie they concocted, Martin was certain of one thing: if Dr. Kasim and the other men suspected even for a second that Martin planned to betray them, they would murder him and use all their wealth and influence to conceal their crime and protect their secret.

After a few more furtive glances around the room, Martin decided that the safer strategy would be to assume that the cameras were there and adjust his behavior accordingly.

He would not search for anything here, not yet.

*

Martin stood beneath the showerhead and let the gentle spray pelt his weary face. The warm water soothed him as it rolled and trickled over his body, making everything seem a little easier. *Just keep up the act*, Martin kept telling himself. *All you have to do is keep up the act.* Just get through the initiation tomorrow night, whatever that was, then keep up the performance for just another two days. How hard could that be?

Of course, that was the question that haunted him. Could he really fool them for three more days? And, even more troubling—could he fool Carver? Martin could still see him staring at him after the toast. Studying him with those cagey eyes. If Carver really suspected something, why didn't he just come out and say it? Maybe Carver was secretly meeting with the others at that very moment. Convincing them that Martin could not be trusted and had to be eliminated. Maybe they were already plotting his murder.

Martin shook his head under the water, as if he could rinse away the toxic thoughts that were filling his skull. He could not let fear cripple him. To survive he needed to remain clearheaded and alert. Maybe fatigue was causing him to miss some solution. Sleep, that's what he needed. Just sleep.

Martin reached for the knob to shut off the water. But suddenly he froze. Beneath the quiet roar of the shower he could just make out a disturbing sound. The sound of someone entering his room.

46

Dripping wet and wrapped in a towel, Martin exited the bathroom and found Carver smiling in the open door. "Now I see why you didn't hear my knock."

Carver's intrusion and the annoying smirk on his face made Martin, for a moment, forget his bigger worries. "So you just decided to let yourself in?"

"Sorry, Grey. The door wasn't locked. Besides, I had a good reason."

"Yeah? What's that?"

"I brought you a gift." Still smiling, Carver stepped away from the open door, allowing a beautiful young woman to enter the room.

"Good evening, Mr. Grey."

For an instant Martin did not recognize the girl. Instead of the maid's uniform that Martin had last seen her in, she now wore a simple, pretty blue dress. Her strawberry-blond hair, no longer tied back, flowed in waves over her shoulders. It was Alice, the frightened server who had dropped his pie. Martin found it hard to believe that this was the same girl. Alice's beauty was obvious before, but now she appeared almost angelic. "Hello," Martin finally managed to get out.

"From the fuss you made over her at dinner, it's obvious you like her," Carver said. "Well, here she is. All yours."

Martin was unable to stifle his surprise. "Mine?"

Carver laughed, apparently tickled by the new guy's naïveté. "One of my favorite perks of Forty Acres—beautiful women."

Martin met Alice's gaze. She put on a pleasant smile, but the sadness in her eyes was unmistakable. Martin felt an urge to punch Carver. But he couldn't. Not yet. In some ways, he was as much a captive to this scene as Alice.

"What's wrong? You do like women, don't you, Grey?"

"Yes. Of course. It's just—" Martin pulled Carver aside and whispered. "Look, I love my wife, okay?"

Carver laughed. "So do I. Hell, we all do. What's that got to do with anything? Relax. What happens behind these walls, stays behind these walls." Carver's features darkened. "You don't really have a problem with this, do you?"

Martin remembered the role that he was playing. He was now the willing participant in an inhumane crime; for him to pause at the mere act of infidelity would seem inconsistent and raise suspicion. For all Martin knew, Alice's being delivered to his bed was part of their initiation. A test of his resolve. To show any hesitancy or weakness now could cause Dr. Kasim and the others to question his commitment.

"If this bothers you, just say so," Carver said, a suspicious glint in his eyes. "It's no big deal, really."

Martin did his best to appear lustful as he turned and looked Alice up and down. He undressed her with his eyes. "No, I'm fine," he said to Carver. "She truly is quite beautiful."

But Carver wasn't sold so easily. "You sure, Grey? I mean, if this isn't your thing, I can just take her back to my room. I got a girl waiting already, but there's always room for one more."

Martin returned Carver's gaze. "Here's a better idea. Why don't you get the hell out of here so I can unwrap my gift?"

Carver grinned. "All right, Grey. Calm down. I'm going. And listen. No need to worry about STDs or birth control or any of that. All the pretty ones are tested regularly and fixed. As Dr. Kasim likes to say, no mutts allowed." He cocked his head to Alice. "Ain't that right, sweetheart?"

Alice stared at the floor, nodding. "Yes, master."

Martin found Carver's callousness disgusting. He tried to keep any hint of emotion from his voice. "That's good to know. I guess the doctor has thought of everything."

"You know it," Carver said. He stole a final admiring glance at Alice. "She's amazing, trust me." Carver winked at Martin as he strolled out.

Martin locked the door and fastened the chain. By the time he turned back around, Alice had moved. She now stood beside the bed, facing him. She managed to brighten her smile a bit, but that core of sadness was still indelible. "Do you like my dress? I picked it just for you, master."

That word struck Martin like a slap. He could hardly look at her. He couldn't bear the thought that he was partly to blame for the sad smile she wore. That she saw him like she saw the other men, a depraved captor who could do whatever he pleased with her body. Martin wanted desperately to explain to Alice that he wasn't like them. He wanted to give her hope, a promise to bring help. Instead, all he could do was put on a show for the cameras. "I like the dress very much," he said. "I'd like it even better if you'd take it off."

"Yes, master."

With her beautiful eyes fixed on him, Alice reached up and unclasped the dress. The garment billowed to her ankles and Alice stood naked before him. Her pert teacup breasts were well proportioned to her small, curvy figure.

Martin drew a sharp breath at the sight of her perfect body, a genuine reaction that caught him off guard. It astonished Martin that the vileness of the situation failed to diminish the sudden lust he felt or the stirring beneath his towel, but Alice was so amazingly beautiful.

Martin watched as Alice pulled back the top bedcover and slipped gracefully beneath crisp white sheets. Then she lay there, with her head propped up, smiling at him. Beneath the sheets, with her nipples pouting against the fabric, the hills and valleys of her luscious form were somehow even more alluring. "Are you coming to bed now, master?"

After a moment, Martin pulled off his towel and slid into the bed.

47

"Can you brighten it a bit? The picture looks like crap," Carver said.

Carver and Oscar were standing inside a cramped and dimly lit video surveillance room, peering over the shoulder of a security guard who sat before a bank of three LCD monitors. Each monitor displayed a different angle of the same darkened bedroom. The first monitor showed an overhead view, the second an eye-level view, and the third a fish-eyed low angle. Barely visible on each screen was the dark and grainy image of a couple beneath the bed sheets engaged in intercourse. The guard, a bespectacled young black man, fiddled with the various switches and knobs on a control panel to no avail. The images on the three monitors were still irritatingly dark. Carver groaned. "Do you even know what you're doing?"

"Sorry. Give me just one more second." The guard tweaked a few more knobs and finally the video on all three screens became a fraction brighter. Martin's and Alice's tensed faces were now faintly distinguishable, their two thrusting bodies a scant bit more defined. The guard looked back at Carver and frowned. "Unfortunately, sir, with the lights out in the room, this is the best that I can do."

Carver waved him off. "Yeah, yeah. Spare me."

"I really am sorry, sir, but the only way we could get a better picture is with night-vision cameras."

"Then why the hell don't you have night-vision cameras?"

Before the frazzled man could respond, Oscar intervened, laying a firm hand on the guard's shoulder. "It's all right, Sam. We can see more than enough. How long have you been monitoring Mr. Grey?"

"Ever since he returned to his room, sir. Just like you wanted."

"Have you noticed any unusual behavior?"

Sam shook his head. "No, sir. He watched some television for a little while, then jumped in the shower. That's it. If you ask me, I think Mr. Grey is adjusting just fine."

Carver snorted dismissively, then noticed that Oscar was staring hard at him. The man appeared to be pissed about something, but Carver had no idea why. Carver liked Oscar for the most part. He appreciated Oscar's no-nonsense attitude, and he respected the fact that Oscar could keep a place like Forty Acres running like clockwork. What he didn't like about Oscar were those cold, titanium eyes. Especially when Oscar had them trained on him. "Something wrong?" Carver asked.

"We're done here, Mr. Lewis." Oscar moved to the door and pushed it open. "Let's let Sam get back to work."

"Go ahead if you have to. I want to stick around and watch Grey a little while longer."

"Not possible. The doctor would be displeased to know that I allowed you in here at all. Now please, after you." Oscar gestured to the open doorway.

Judging by the stone carving that Oscar called a face, Carver knew there was no point arguing. The two men exited the surveillance room and Carver paused just outside the door. They were standing inside a storage room in the cellar of the house. Neat racks of food and other supplies lined the stone walls. The unmarked door to the surveillance room was tucked inconspicuously between two shelving units. "I just hope that kid knows what he's doing," Carver said to Oscar. "Grey needs to be watched very closely."

"And he will be, Mr. Lewis. But quite honestly, from what we've just observed, I believe your suspicions are . . . unwarranted."

"It's not a damn suspicion. It's more than that."

"Really? Please explain."

Carver frowned. He prided himself on his uncanny ability to read a man's character cold. All his life he had possessed a keen intuition that he had come to trust completely. It was that intuition—a sort of nervous tingling in his gut—that helped him to steer clear of dishonest brokers and bad deals and ultimately to accumulate his large fortune in the real estate game. Very recently Carver had felt the stirrings of his internal alarm once again. It was the day that he first met Martin Grey. He had read about Grey in the newspaper. The black civil rights attorney with his white partner. The article said they were not only partners but good friends. Jesus. That fact alone made Carver's gut tight. He tried to tell Solomon and the others that there was something off about Martin Grey, but they paid little attention. Damon vouched for Martin completely, and the others took an instant liking to the young lawyer. Of course, Carver could understand why. Martin was smart, strong-willed, and, with his activist background, appeared to be a perfect candidate for their private club. And that's exactly why Carver did not protest Martin's candidacy too strenuously—because on the surface, despite his white shadow, Martin *did* appear to be a good fit. Carver's intuition was strong, but it wasn't infallible. He supposed that maybe he was wrong this time. Maybe Grey was truly as perfect as he appeared, and in the future they'd grow to be tighter than brothers.

Maybe. But then there was that moment in the library that changed everything. The moment when Grey finally broke down before Dr. Kasim's truth. On the surface Martin's tearful submission appeared believable, but it was at that instant that Carver's belly spoke up once again—only this time it was far more insistent. What Carver felt wasn't the usual fleeting tingling sensation. It was as if an abyss had opened up inside him. What was making him react so strongly? Was Martin's breakdown just an act? Was Martin just playing a role until he could get back to the world and expose their secret? Carver couldn't be certain, at least not yet, but he did know one thing for damn sure. Martin Grey could not be trusted. He could feel it in his gut, literally. Of course, this gut feeling wouldn't be enough to convince Dr. Kasim and the others that Grey was a threat that needed to be eliminated. Carver needed real proof.

"It's hard to explain," Carver said. "I just know that something's not right about that guy. You know what's at stake here. We can't risk even the smallest doubt."

"I agree completely. That is why Dr. Kasim always insists on an initiation. I think you will agree that if Mr. Grey completes tomorrow night's ceremony, his loyalty will be unquestionable."

A smile creased Carver's face. Oscar was right. The ceremony was an extreme test, to say the least. Carver couldn't imagine how anyone, including Grey, could get through it unless he was truly committed to Dr. Kasim's philosophy. But still, Carver had an idea. A way that he could up the ante on Grey's big night and leave zero room for doubt. As Carver unconsciously ran a hand over his fit midsection, he thought, *Maybe then my gut will leave me alone.*

48

After Master Grey finally rolled off her, Alice watched him lying there with his eyes closed, panting. His sweat-soaked body glistened in the pale moonlight filtering into the room through sheer white curtains. Alice wasn't sure how she should feel. Frightened? Confused? Grateful? She wasn't even certain of what had just happened. Did she do something wrong? Would Master Grey tell her other masters about it? Would she be punished for not satisfying Master Grey—even though it wasn't her fault?

Alice played back what had happened in her mind. She did exactly what she was taught to do when masters took her to their beds. Smile. Always smile. Make them believe that there was no place else you'd rather be than in their bed. When Alice removed her dress and climbed into the bed, she could tell by the way Master Grey stared that he was sexually attracted to her. Then, when he threw off his towel, there was no doubt. He was erect and his eyes were devouring her. And as Master Grey climbed into bed with her, she remembered thinking that at least he wasn't fat or old or mean. When she'd met Master Grey for the first time in the hallway, she got the feeling that Master

Grey wasn't like her other masters. Then, later, when Master Lewis brought her to his room, she felt it again. It wasn't just his kindness—most of her masters were usually kind to her—it was something deeper. Something about the way he looked at her. When the other masters spoke to her, their eyes were cold and indifferent, as if they were addressing a piece of furniture. But Master Grey really saw her. In the hall he had spoken to her as if she were a person who actually mattered, not just a slave there to do his bidding. Whenever Alice was forced to share a bed with one of her masters, she never knew what to expect. Some preferred to just lie there and be titillated and pampered for hours. Others enjoyed the illusion that their unwelcomed caresses brought Alice genuine moans of pleasure. And there were even a few mean ones, masters who seemed to derive pleasure only by inflicting pain. But whatever their desire, beneath the masters' sheets, one thing always remained the same. They treated her like an object. Like some life-sized sex doll that they could bend and twist and inflict any depraved act upon that they pleased without any concern for her feelings. Maybe Master Grey would be different from her other masters in bed as well, Alice hoped. And he was, but not in a way that she ever could have expected. When Master Grey first reached out and stroked her body, he seemed oddly hesitant. He caressed her curves gingerly, as if he feared that he might break her. When he lowered his mouth to her breasts, instead of sucking or licking her nipples, he seemed content to let his lips just rest there. That's when Alice realized that there was no lust behind his caresses. He was just going through the motions of sex without any real desire. But it didn't make sense to her. Alice could feel his erection pressed up against her leg. He couldn't fake that. So why was he holding back? Alice thought that maybe he was shy or nervous. But when she tried to encourage him by moaning and squirming and stroking his penis, he pushed her hand away and whispered, "No. Don't."

Confused, Alice opened her mouth to ask why, but before she could get a word out, he smothered her words with a kiss. The kiss was unpleasantly firm and just as passionless as his caresses. When they parted, he nuzzled her neck and whispered into her ear. "Don't talk. Just listen to me."

That's when Alice began to get frightened. Because instead of telling her all the nasty things that he wanted to do to her, like the other masters did, Master Grey moved his mouth even closer to her ear and whispered, "I am not going to have sex with you. I just want us to pretend. Can you pretend with me?"

Pretend to have sex? Alice wasn't sure what Master Grey meant, but she nodded anyway. He was the master and she was his slave. She couldn't tell him no even if she wanted to. Beneath the sheets she felt his hand gently tug on her thigh. She obediently parted her legs and Master Grey mounted her. Staring down at her with reassuring brown eyes, he reached beneath the sheets to guide himself into her. Alice tensed, expecting to be penetrated, but that familiar filling sensation never came. Instead, as he began to pump his hips, she felt his stiff penis gliding back and forth over her shaved pubic mound. Master Grey panted and grunted with each stroke as if he were fucking her, but he wasn't. Was this some kind of kinky game he enjoyed?

"Come on. Pretend with me," he whispered in her ear.

Alice did as she was told. She thrust her hips upward to match his rhythm and groaned and squirmed with mock pleasure. "Yes, master," she moaned, doing her best to please him. "Yes, yes!" It occurred to Alice that, with their intertwined bodies concealed beneath the sheets, anyone watching would never suspect that they were only dry humping.

Alice was reminded of all the times that she had played hooky from high school with Ryan, the only boyfriend she'd ever had, and how they would make out in his bedroom all day until his mother came home from work. Alice would never let Ryan go all the way, but she remembered how exciting it was getting so close. Now, thinking back, Alice wished that she and Ryan had spent all those stolen afternoons doing it for real instead of wasting their precious time pretending. If only she had let Ryan take her virginity instead of telling him to wait until their prom night, a night that, for Alice, would never come. Then she would know what it felt like to sleep with a man she cared about. Then at least she would have the memories of truly making love.

Alice felt Master Grey's body stiffen, then begin to shudder as he pretended to climax. The knowing look on his face urged Alice to continue playing along, so she gasped and squealed and arched her back, riding out an imaginary orgasmic rush. Then Master Grey rolled off her, and whatever they had just done was over.

As Alice continued to watch Master Grey lying there beside her, she studied his face. His eyes were closed and his breathing had slowed but he wasn't asleep. He didn't appear angry or displeased. Actually, he looked relieved. But not in the way men usually looked in that quiet moment between orgasm and drifting off to sleep. Master Grey had the look of someone who had just completed a stressful task and was happy that it was finally over. This confused Alice even more. If Master Grey didn't want to have sex with her, why pretend to? For a moment she considered that perhaps he was gay and wanted to keep his secret from the other men, but then she remembered his erection. Would a gay man react that way to the sight of a naked woman? She didn't think so. Besides, everyone knew that one of the other masters slept with men, so there would be no reason for Master Grey to hide his homosexuality. The more Alice thought about Master Grey, the more confused and worried she became. She just hoped that he was as nice as he appeared and that his strange idea of sex wouldn't lead to her being punished.

Finally Master Grey opened his eyes and looked at her. For a moment his face was unreadable. Alice smiled nervously at him. "Did I please you, master?"

He smiled and nodded. "Yes, Alice, you did very well."

Alice felt a wave of relief wash over her. She cuddled closer and laid her head on his chest.

"Where are you from?" he asked.

"From, master?"

"Before you were brought here."

Alice tilted her head and regarded him with a puzzled expression. Why was he asking her this? Was he testing her? "There is no 'before here,'" Alice said with an edge of fear in her voice. "Master Lennox doesn't allow us to talk about that. Please don't make me answer that, master. Please."

"Okay. It's all right. Forget I asked you."

"Thank you, master."

As Alice watched Master Grey return his gaze to the ceiling, she glimpsed a touch of sadness in his eyes; but just as suddenly as the emotion appeared, he pushed it back and donned a neutral expression. Alice nestled her head back onto his chest. She listened to the steady pounding of his heart. She felt his hand gently stroking her hair. She thought about that fleeting sympathetic look in his eyes. Now she was certain that there was something different about Master Grey. He was nothing like her other masters.

49

Kwame was keeping himself occupied with the pastime he loved most, reading. He was seated up in bed, huddled close to the bedside lamp, the only light in the room, reading an old book that he had found in Dr. Kasim's library. One of Kwame's favorite things about Forty Acres was that whenever he visited, he had access to Dr. Kasim's extraordinary library. Whenever he traveled, Kwame had visited many libraries with collections devoted to the literature, culture, and history of people of African descent, and although most of these libraries, either government-run or owned by major universities, possessed vastly larger collections, Kwame had yet to find one that came close to the depth and rarity of the volumes found on Dr. Kasim's shelves. Some of Dr. Kasim's books were so old and rare that Kwame could not find even a mention of them recorded anywhere else.

When Kwame was still a fine arts major at Howard University, he had gone through a phase in which all he was interested in reading were slave narratives. He became fascinated by the firsthand accounts of everyday slave life to the point of obsession. He sought out and absorbed every slave narrative that he could get his hands on, and in the process, he became something of an authority on the subject. For a time Kwame even considered writing a scholarly book on the topic himself, but the demands of nurturing a career in advertising soon overshadowed that ambition.

In all of Kwame's reading and research on the subject of slave narratives, he had never come across any mention of the book that he was now reading. The binding appeared ancient, its corners and spine threadbare, but somehow the battered tome still held together. The author was a girl named Emma who was born into slavery in the early 1800s. She was sold away from her family as a teenager and purchased by a man three times her age to work not in his cotton fields or in his kitchen but in his bedroom. The narrative describes a decade of continuous rape and beatings, recounting how her master cruelly loaned her out to other white men for their sick pleasures. Emma's story was tragic and gut-wrenching, and as Kwame read, he could feel his emotions churning.

That's what had drawn Kwame to slave narratives. Unlike the literature taught in most schools, which was concerned almost exclusively with the triumphs and tragedies of white people, slave narratives were stories about people who looked like him. These were stories with consequences that reached up through the tangle of time and history and influenced the person that he was today. When Kwame read the narratives, he felt as if he were reading about his own family members, a great-

great-grandmother or -grandfather, or maybe a distant cousin. These tragic stories stirred Kwame's emotions like nothing he had ever read or seen before, often making him laugh and cry and sink with sadness—but mostly making him angry. By the time Kwame had graduated from Howard and started taking his first steps into the world of advertising, he had grown to hate the Caucasian race with a passion.

It was this simmering hatred that ultimately led Kwame to his great success. Fresh out of college and radiating talent, he easily landed an entry position at Miller and Cline Communications, a major advertising company located in Chicago. Kwame hated it there from the first day he arrived. The company was lily-white. He, two Asian employees, and the janitorial staff were the only nonwhites in the entire building. MCC had a good reason for hiring Kwame, their first black employee in the company's fifty-three-year history. They had decided to go after the growing demographic of African American consumers and thought it would be wise to have a black face along for their presentations. Kwame remained there only three weeks. Long enough to study as well as Xerox every bit of market research MCC had done on the black consumer and fulfill his two weeks' notice. Armed with a few facts and figures and the determination not to become enslaved to the white man's paycheck, Kwame opened up his own ad agency. An agency owned and run by blacks that would focus exclusively on reaching the black consumer. Friends and family told him he was unprepared, even crazy, and they were right. He wasn't even close to being ready to run his own business and it was insane to open up an office without even enough money to pay the next month's rent. But that didn't stop him. Instead Kwame used his desperation as fuel to drive him forward. He went door-to-door to the big corporations pitching his firm's unique perspective and demanding that they give him a chance, until someone finally did. In less than one month Kwame's storefront agency had landed its first major account and it had never stopped growing since.

Kwame was riding high as the CEO of one of the most profitable ad agencies in the world when his friend and mentor Solomon Aarons first whispered Dr. Kasim's name into his ear. Kwame was intrigued by the doctor's unique perspective on race relations and became a full-fledged member of Forty Acres without a moment's hesitation. Kwame's only regret about Dr. Kasim's hidden refuge was that because it had to remain a closely guarded secret, not every black man could benefit from the uniquely freeing experience of owning white slaves. Kwame often fantasized about creating a nationwide ad campaign for Forty Acres. It wouldn't take much. A few quick reenacted scenes of enslaved Africans being hunted, chained, whipped; then cut to a graphic of a black man holding a white man in shackles with the simple slogan: "Now it's our turn." Every time Kwame entertained this fantasy, it brought a smile to his face.

There was a knock at his bedroom door. Kwame put down his book. "Come in."

A young woman entered carrying a small stack of books. She smiled and said, "Master Lennox said that these are the newest books in the library."

"Good. Leave them here on the table."

The girl approached and set the books down on the night table. Instead of walking back out, she surprised Kwame by remaining at his bedside. "Is there something else?" he asked coldly.

The girl appeared hesitant to speak. "Would you like me to keep you company tonight?"

Kwame glared at her. "Who told you to ask me that?"

The girl cowered. "Master Lennox, sir. I'm sorry. I didn't mean to upset you."

Kwame sighed. The question irritated him. Oscar and the others just refused to accept the fact that he would not sleep with a white woman. It wasn't that he didn't feel attracted to them. The girl who stood trembling before him now was blond and shapely in all the right places. And if she were any other race, he'd sleep with her in an instant. But she was Caucasian and his repulsion for that race was so perfect that the idea of touching one of its members intimately, even a beautiful one, revolted him. "Go back and tell Mr. Lennox that I'd rather sleep with a dog." Kwame saw the sting on the confused girl's face and didn't care one bit. Why should he care? She wasn't human. She was his property. "Go on. You tell him exactly what I said. Now get out!"

The girl nodded and hurried for the door. The moment she was gone, Kwame picked up his book and continued to read. He was looking forward to seeing how the slave girl Emma would ultimately escape her brutal master and win her freedom.

50

Slap! Carver backhanded the girl and she flew backward onto the bed crying. Her naked body convulsed with sobs. The sight of her lying there, helpless, her tear-streaked face buried in beautiful blond hair, made Carver's blood surge with desire. He began to snatch at his belt, eager to get his pants off.

"Please don't hurt me, master," the girl whined. "Please, please."

Her tiny pleas just served to add fuel to Carver's anger. He tore off his pants and leapt onto the girl. Clamped her throat tight. "Did I say you could talk? *Did I?*"

The girl gasped for air.

Carver smirked at her feeble struggles and squeezed tighter. "You're nothing but a little white whore. Isn't that right? *Isn't it?*"

Choking and struggling to breathe, the girl nodded desperately.

"Damn right you are." Carver released the girl's windpipe and watched with relish as she gasped to refill her lungs. God, how he wished that the girl squirming on the bed before him was that bitch Diana Miller and not just some random white whore. More than once Carver had tried to convince Dr. Kasim to have that Diana captured and dragged back to Forty Acres. Carver even did all the prep work. He tracked down Diana's current address and went so far as to figure out where and when would be the best place to grab her. But the doctor refused to listen. He just kept giving the same fucking answer. "The Miller family doesn't fit the profile. And Forty Acres is not about personal vendettas." To Carver that excuse just didn't make sense. Forty Acres was about the biggest personal vendetta ever.

Carver respected the old man more than anyone else in the world, but it drove him mad just fantasizing about how sweet it would be to see Diana Miller's face the first day she woke up in Forty Acres. Her expression would probably be a lot like the one he had worn the night Diana set him up.

The most terrifying night of Carver's life had started out innocuously enough when he met a gorgeous white girl named Diana at a party. He and his frat brothers threw the best parties on the Purdue campus, and it wasn't unusual to see a few adventurous white kids in the crowd. Diana came on to Carver relentlessly. Pretty much threw herself at him. If he'd been less drunk and a lot less horny, he might have suspected something, but as far as he was concerned he was about to score some primo white ass. Carver remembered thinking that it was odd that she wanted to go back to her place. But she swore that her parents were away and they'd have privacy to do anything they wanted. Carver didn't need any more convincing. They jumped in his car and headed across town. He was a little hesitant about going over to the white side of town, but there hadn't been any real tension in Lafayette in years, and Diana was stroking his hard-on between his legs to keep him motivated. They had turned down a dark street and were stopped at a light when he saw five or six men wearing ski masks and armed with bats rush the car. Carver tried to stomp on the gas, but they already had the driver's side door open and started dragging him out. The rest of the nightmarish memory was just a mishmash of pain, screams, and shouts of "Nigger!"

When Carver awoke from his six-day coma, his story was all over the local news. As he lay in that hospital in traction for another month, he watched all the stories about marches and speeches and rallies through a numbing malaise of disbelief. The same question repeated over and over in his head: *Why me? Why me? Why me?* The only television images that cut through the fog like a lighthouse beacon were the countless interviews of Diana Miller. Her fake sympathy and lies—she claimed not to know the attackers—were so glaring that, to Carver, her words began to sound like mocking laughter. There was no doubt in Carver's mind that the white bitch had lured him there to be assaulted and maybe even killed. For all he knew she probably took a few whacks at him herself.

"Are you okay, master?" The girl could see the tempest

of memories stirred up in Carver's harsh eyes. "Did I do something to upset you?"

Carver glared at her. "Shut up." He snatched a handful of that beautiful hair and flung her back down to the bed. Quickly he mounted her and rammed inside her. He savored her gasps and squeals and the way she squirmed feebly beneath him. Fueled by a fusion of lust and rage, Carver pumped and pumped as hard as he could drive his body. Carver's eyes rolled back into his head and he roared as he climaxed. A moment later, when Carver regained his senses, he was surprised to see the girl still curled beside him, crying. "Why are you still here? Get out! Get the fuck out of here!"

Sobbing hysterically, the girl grabbed her clothes and fled the room.

51

"Does that feel good, master?"

"Don't ask silly questions," Damon answered. "It feels fucking fantastic." He was lying facedown on the bed, nude, while a young man named Everett massaged scented oil into his back. Several candles had been placed around the dark room and the walls flickered with their warm light. Soothing music oozed from the stereo. Damon had been looking forward to this trip for a long time. The last time he stayed at Forty Acres was over six months ago and another visit was long overdue. Between Damon juggling court appearances and playing cohost to Juanita's too-frequent social distractions, his schedule lately had been nothing short of insane. Finally, he was back within the comforting isolation of Forty Acres. Back where he could forget about the day-to-day turmoil and scrutiny of his semicelebrity life and just let go.

For Damon, the seclusion that came with being a part of Forty Acres was a huge part of its draw. In a media-mad world, here, finally, was a place where Damon could have real privacy. A place where he could truly be himself, without the worry that an unflattering photograph would end up in some tabloid or on YouTube. Damon dreaded to think of the resulting fallout if his occasional gay dalliances were ever made public. He could imagine the splashy headlines. "Damon Darrell Outed. Juanita Darrell Claims She Never Knew." And the ironic part was that he wasn't really a homosexual. Sure, he craved the touch of a handsome, muscular young man every so often, but he preferred women by far. He really loved Juanita, and he and his wife enjoyed a fantastic sex life. Damon was certain that Juanita would back him up on that story 100 percent, but he also knew that it wouldn't matter. In the eyes of many people, being bisexual was equivalent to being homosexual, which was equivalent to being a freak. Unfortunately, this narrow-minded view would especially apply in the African American community, where the church brainwashed his people wholesale. Damon knew that if his secret predilection ever got out, despite all that he had done and donated, his black brothers and sisters would turn on him in an instant. Damon's five-star credibility in the African American community was a priceless commodity that he used to build his legal empire. If he lost that, he'd lose everything. That's why Dr. Kasim's walled-in oasis was the perfect escape. At Forty Acres, Damon could indulge his omnivorous sexual appetite with complete security.

But for Damon, Forty Acres wasn't merely a place to score some usually off-the-menu sex. Damon truly believed in Dr. Kasim's philosophy. Placed in the context of world history, what Dr. Kasim was doing at Forty Acres was completely justified. What really sold it for Damon was that most of the captives at Forty Acres were direct descendants of former slave owners. Damon didn't know the exact process—he didn't want to know—but the way Dr. Kasim explained it was that a lot of time and effort was put into researching and locating Caucasian individuals whose lives were enriched today because their ancestors had profited from the blood and sweat of African slaves. To Damon this methodology made total sense. Was it a fair brand of justice? Not in the least, but neither was slavery. The number one rule for survival is something Damon Darrell had learned a long time ago: life isn't fucking fair.

Damon glanced up at the statuesque young man who continued to knead and rub his back. He watched the Celtic tribal tattoos on Everett's muscular forearms undulate with every caress. Damon wondered what kind of family Everett came from. Were they compassionate people who were ashamed of their family's tarnished history? Or were they a clan of cleaned-up hicks who inherited racist views and hatred along with their ancestors' money? As fast as these thoughts invaded Damon's mind, he made an effort to shut them out. Dr. Kasim constantly warned them about the danger of thinking of the slaves as real human beings with a past. It was better to treat them the same way black slaves had always been treated, as property and nothing more. Damon's eyes sank to Everett's lean athletic form. Even Everett's loose T-shirt and jeans could not hide his perfection. *And he's my property*, Damon thought with a mental smile. *All mine.*

Everett stopped massaging Damon's back. "You can turn over now, master."

Damon rolled over onto his back, revealing a full erection.

Everett issued a delighted hum as he squirted more oil onto his hands.

"Like what you see?" Damon asked.

"I do, master."

Everett began to slowly massage Damon's upper thighs. Damon moaned with pleasure as Everett's firm hands inched closer and closer to his attentive member. "Yes. That feels good," Damon said. "That feels so fucking good."

Everett smiled, pleased with the results of his handiwork. Inching his fingers even closer to Damon's erection, he asked, "Would you like me to spend the night with you, master?"

Damon let out a gasp of pleasure before he could get the words out. "What did I tell you about asking me silly questions?"

52

Solomon watched with a great deal of surprise as Dr. Kasim's hand reached across the chessboard and moved his black bishop to threaten Solomon's white queen. "Where the hell did that come from?"

Savoring Solomon's reaction, Dr. Kasim took a casual drag of his pipe and blew a long stream of smoke. Then he pointed at the board with the tip of his pipe. "I believe it's your move."

The two men were seated at a small table on the front porch with a view of the serene, moonlit garden beneath the stars. A determined moth courted the overhead lamp, casting fluttering shadows on the hand-carved wooden chess pieces.

Solomon stared, puzzled, at the chessboard again. How had Dr. Kasim come up with that move? Unlike Solomon, who had been a passionate player since his father gave him a chess set for his eighth birthday, Dr. Kasim was just a casual player. Although the doctor never presented a serious challenge, Solomon found the doctor's game sturdy enough to make their occasional matches enjoyable, but that was it. Solomon knew Dr. Kasim's playing style inside out. When Solomon threatened Dr.

Kasim's queen, he was certain that his old friend would simply move his queen out of harm's way, but instead, Dr. Kasim had chosen an aggressive counterattack that was worthy of a far more experienced player.

Dr. Kasim glanced at his watch. "You going to move or not? I'm an old man. The sooner I beat you, the sooner I can get some sleep."

Solomon laughed. "You've been practicing, haven't you?"

Dr. Kasim frowned like the idea was alien to him. "I talk Oscar into a game occasionally. But I wouldn't call that practicing. The man's terrible."

Solomon looked skeptical. "Come on. We've been playing for over twenty years. I have never seen your game so sharp. Something has changed."

Dr. Kasim couldn't contain his smile any longer. "I may have gotten my hands on a few strategy books. Just a few."

"You're reading chess books?" Solomon's surprise grew. Dr. Kasim had never even hinted at a desire to deepen his understanding of the game. And if he did want to learn more, why didn't he just ask Solomon to give him a few pointers? "Thaddeus, what's going on? You starting to get bored out here in paradise?"

Dr. Kasim grunted a laugh. Then he picked up his empty scotch glass from the porch rail and held it out toward a lone servant who stood in the shadows. The slave quickly refilled the glass from a serving cart, then handed it back to his master. Dr. Kasim took a slow sip and paused to relish the liquor's soothing warmth. "I've lived an amazing life. I've bent reality to my will and I'm damn proud of it. But there's one accomplishment that has eluded me. One desire that keeps me awake at night. Do you know what that is?"

Solomon just stared. Dr. Thaddeus Kasim was the most amazing man he had ever known. He remembered when they first met. It was in Atlanta, just days following Dr. King's assassination. They both attended a rally calling for an end to the riots that had struck so many cities. Solomon remembered the look on Thaddeus's face as he stood in the crowd listening to the speakers. In a sea of angry black faces, Thaddeus looked calm, determined. While everyone else was directionless, Thaddeus Kasim appeared to have all the answers. They became fast friends. Solomon was entranced by Thaddeus's ideas about the psychology of black men, especially his theory about the problem of black noise. And then the day finally arrived when Thaddeus trusted Solomon enough to show him the white man he had chained up in his barn. Thaddeus's "final solution" to that black noise. It was brilliant.

Unlike Dr. King, who had attempted to persuade the white man to change his racist ways, an approach doomed to failure because of the Caucasian race's seemingly innate contempt for people of color, Thaddeus's approach, in the long run, would be far more empowering. Nurture strong black men. Reinforce their confidence and pride, then set them loose to take on the white man as true equals. From that day on, Solomon was in a perpetual state of awe for Dr. Kasim's genius and completely dedicated to helping grow his idea into what it had become today—the cradle of true black pride. The man had accomplished the nearly impossible; Solomon couldn't even imagine what goal could exceed Dr. Kasim's grasp. He threw up his hands. "You got me. What is it?"

"The one desire that has eluded me is to beat you at chess. I never have."

Solomon laughed. "I should hope not. I've been playing tournaments since I was a boy. For you, chess is just a hobby."

"Be that as it may, I'm determined. I'm going to beat you at least once before I leave this earth."

"I guess it's possible if you live another twenty or thirty years."

Dr. Kasim's expression darkened. He shook his head. "Don't have that long."

Solomon froze, only now seeing the gloom hidden behind Dr. Kasim's hard eyes. "Thaddeus, what's wrong?"

"Nothing." His face sagged. "At least nothing I can describe."

"Have you seen a doctor?"

"Yes. Me."

"I mean a real doctor. Wasn't Dr. Taylor up here with the last group?"

Dr. Kasim frowned. "I'm damn near one hundred

266

years old. People my age shouldn't be allowed to waste a doctor's time. Forget that."

Solomon frowned. He knew better than anyone that there was no point arguing with the man.

"It's still your move, youngster," Dr. Kasim said, re-lighting his pipe.

Solomon returned his attention to the chessboard. He saw an opportunity to achieve checkmate in three moves, but he decided to encourage the doctor's newfound passion by prolonging the game a little longer. Solomon moved an insignificant pawn.

Dr. Kasim glared. "What the hell do you think you're doing? You could have mate in three moves!"

"What?" Solomon glanced at the board. "Guess I'm a little distracted."

Dr. Kasim shook his head in utter disgust. "Solomon, I sure hope to God that you run this place better than you tell a lie."

Run this place? Solomon was stunned. Dr. Kasim had a knack of stating the most earth-shattering things as casually as chatting about the weather.

"Oscar's supposed to take over," Solomon said. "That's what you've been preparing him for."

Dr. Kasim shook his head. "Haven't you been paying attention? He's not ready yet."

"But my wife. My kids."

Dr. Kasim frowned. "Stop it. The black race is your family. You know that."

267

Solomon nodded. It was one of Dr. Kasim's most important lessons. The members of Forty Acres had a duty to all black people, not just the ones that lived under their roof or shared their bed.

Dr. Kasim took another sip of scotch and gazed out at the garden and forest beyond. "Life here is beautiful. Peaceful. Meaningful. Important. I'm giving you a great responsibility."

"I'm sorry, Doctor. I wasn't thinking. It would be an incredible honor to take over Forty Acres. Thank you."

"Slow down, slow down," Dr. Kasim grumbled. "I'm not going anywhere yet. I still have to beat you at chess—and *without* your help." Dr. Kasim pushed over his king. He grabbed his walking stick and rose to his feet. As the doctor hobbled toward the front door, Solomon heard him call back, "Rematch tomorrow night. After Mr. Grey's initiation."

53

Martin was roused from sleep by movement on the bed. Head still buried in the pillow, he peeled open his sleepy eyes and saw the blurred, naked figure of Alice easing herself out of the bed. Pretending to still be asleep, Martin watched as Alice slipped into her dress, picked up her shoes, then tiptoed toward the door. Carefully, she inched open the door, but before making her exit, she glanced back. Alice froze with alarm when she saw Martin watching her. Martin smiled to dispel any fear that he might be upset at her surreptitious departure. Alice nodded, then quickly slipped out of the room. Martin wondered if she would tell any of the other slaves what he had done . . . or hadn't done. He had considered whispering an instruction to Alice to keep quiet about their little pantomime but he decided that that was too risky. Better to let the girl assume that he possessed an odd sexual kink rather than give her a reason to doubt his loyalty to Dr. Kasim and the other men. If she suspected that Martin intended to expose Forty Acres the moment he returned to civilization, she might tell the others. Such a rumor would spread fast among the slaves and be nearly impossible to keep from the guards. And if that happened, Martin was certain that the next time Anna laid eyes on him, he'd be dead.

Martin glanced at the bedside clock and saw that it was only a little after three in the morning. He rolled out of bed and went to the bathroom to relieve himself. When Martin returned, he heard a strange sound, a low rumbling that seemed to be coming from just outside his window. It sounded like a vehicle of some sort, but who'd be out for a drive at this hour? Martin rounded the foot of the bed, drew back the curtain, and peeked out the window. A dark green SUV, its engine left idling and its headlights blasting a row of hedges, was parked directly in front of the house. Martin noticed that the SUV was similar to the one that he and the other men had arrived in earlier. It might have been the very same truck, but his vantage point from the second-floor window and the gloom of night made it difficult to tell for sure. Besides the fact that someone saw fit to disrupt the night with that throaty vehicle, there was something else about the SUV that struck Martin as peculiar. The driver's side door and the two rear doors were hanging wide open and the vehicle was empty. It was as if the SUV had sped to a stop and the passengers all jumped out and sprinted into the house. But who were they and what could be so critical at three o'clock in the morning? Was there some sort of emergency occurring in the house? Was someone sick? If so, where were the urgent voices and sounds of commotion? Martin turned to the door and focused his hearing.

Except for the grumbling of the SUV, the house was dead quiet. But as he stared at the bedroom door, another possibility occurred to Martin. A very troubling possibility. Maybe he was the emergency. Perhaps Damon or Oscar had questioned Alice and deduced his secret. They wouldn't need to be absolutely sure; there was too much at stake. All it would take was a seed of doubt to transform Martin from a prospective member into a threat that needed to be eliminated.

Martin's heart began to pound. Armed guards could be creeping toward his room at that very moment. Coming to take him. He glanced around the room for a possible weapon. Anything to fight with. He knew his chances were slim, but if he could somehow get past the guards and make it into the woods, he could—Martin froze when he heard the *click* of the doorknob turning. Then the bedroom door began to swing open.

"Oh, I'm sorry to disturb you, sir."

It was Alice in the doorway. She was alone and, even with the door wide open, the house was still quiet.

She touched her bare neck. "My necklace. I think it fell off. May I look for it quickly, sir?"

Martin was still dazed by residual panic.

"Please, master. My mother gave it to me. It's all I have."

Martin nodded, then watched Alice move to the bed and draw back the covers. After a moment, she held a thin silver necklace with a small crucifix up for Martin to see. "Sorry, master. It comes loose a lot." She started for the door.

"Wait."

Alice paused at the door. "Yes, master."

"That truck outside. What's going on?"

"That's Master Lennox's truck."

"Are you sure?" Even as he said it, Martin knew that he sounded too anxious.

Alice appeared baffled by the question. "Sir?"

Martin reminded himself that his every move was likely being observed, his every word monitored. With a wave of his hand, Martin told Alice, "Never mind. Forget it."

"May I go now, sir?"

Martin nodded as coldly as he could for his unseen audience.

"Good night, master." As Alice shut the door behind her, Martin heard the voices coming from outside. He turned back to the window in time to see Oscar descending the front steps of the house trailed by two young women. Like most of the women that he had encountered at Forty Acres, both were blond and very pretty. Martin only got a glimpse of their faces, but neither of the girls appeared familiar to him. Although they were both dressed casually in simple sundresses and flip-flops, Martin found something alluring about their appearance. It was their hair. Instead of wearing it tied back, like most of the girls he'd seen around the compound, both girls wore their hair down on their shoulders, as Alice had when Carver first brought her into his room. Along with Oscar, who was dressed in a suit as always, it almost looked as if the trio was headed out to a club or a bar. Oscar loaded the girls into the back and then shut the door. When Oscar climbed into the driver's seat, Martin caught a glimpse of steel beneath Oscar's jacket. It was a holstered, stainless-steel nine-millimeter handgun. An instant later, the SUV was speeding away around the front garden, then up the oak-bordered drive toward the main gate. Martin watched the receding red taillights of the SUV flit away into the darkened landscape until they disappeared.

Martin slipped back into bed. He lay there wondering where Oscar could be taking the two female slaves at such a late hour and for what purpose, until sleep overtook him once again.

54

Unlike dinner, there was no formality to breakfast. Oscar had informed Martin the night before that breakfast would be served in the dining room all morning, so Martin could sleep as long as he liked. Unfortunately, Martin was too anxious to sleep in. A little after eight, he was squinting at the sunlight streaming through his window. The sky overhead looked clear, but he could see a cloud front in the distance. Perhaps a storm was coming.

After a quick shower, Martin threw on jeans, a T-shirt, a light jacket, and hiking boots—an outfit he hoped would be suitable for Damon's promised early morning tour of the gold mine. In truth, the last thing Martin wanted to do was spend another second palling around with Damon Darrell. Not only had Martin liked Damon, he had admired and respected him. Never had Martin bonded with someone so quickly. He expected that in time their friendship would have become as close as the one he shared with Glen. But last night had changed all that. Whether Damon was truly evil or just brainwashed by Dr. Kasim's madness, it didn't matter. Martin could never look at Damon Darrell the same way again. But to survive and to shut Forty Acres down forever, Martin would pretend. He'd go on taking Damon's advice and laughing at Damon's jokes, but it would all be an act. Just a ruse to learn the place's secrets. As far as Martin was concerned, his onetime friend was now a dangerous enemy.

Martin wandered into the dining room and was greeted by Damon and Carver, who were chatting over breakfast. Damon was working on a plate heaped with scrambled eggs, bacon, and syrup-drenched pancakes, while Carver seemed satisfied with just a slice of toast and a cup of black coffee. Before Martin could take a seat, he was intercepted by a white-jacketed slave who politely asked Martin for his order. After seeing Damon's and Carver's selections, Martin decided to split the difference. He ordered scrambled eggs with two slices of toast and some coffee to start.

"Try the bacon," Damon said. "It's delicious. Trust me."

Martin gave the slave the okay to add bacon, then took a seat at the table.

Carver and Damon shared mischievous smiles. "Well?" Damon finally asked.

"Well what?"

"Carver told me that he brought you a little present last night. How was she?"

Martin leveled a stare at Carver. Carver deflected it with a grin. "What's wrong, Grey? It's a secret you like pussy?"

Damon pressed, "Come on, Martin. Tell us. What did you think of Alice?"

Clearly the men traded notes on the girls. "She was nice," Martin said, and left it at that.

Carver and Damon frowned at his chaste answer. As the slave approached with Martin's coffee, Carver said to Martin, "Would you quit the Gentleman Jim act? Was Alice the best piece of white ass you ever had or not?"

Martin glanced self-consciously at the slave, who was at that very moment setting down the cup of coffee. Then Martin turned sharply to Carver. "Let's change the subject."

Carver scoffed and pointed at the slave. "Are you worried about him?" he asked Martin. "They don't hear anything we say." Carver turned to the slave, "Do you hear anything?"

The anxious young man shook his head. "No, sir. Nothing at all." Then he hurried back to the kitchen.

"You're their master," Damon said to Martin. "They worry about your feelings, not the other way around. I know that takes a while to get used to, but never forget it. Especially around them."

Martin nodded, accepting Damon's advice like an obedient student. He realized that his newness to life at Forty Acres could be a good cover for the disgust he felt.

"So come on," Carver pushed. "How was Alice? You have to give us more than 'she was nice.'"

"Okay, okay," Martin said, summoning the best smile

that he could. "It was just like you said, Carver. Best piece of white ass ever. Damn, that girl is something special."

"Special is right," Carver said with a wry grin. "If you think she's good now, wait until she gives you a blow job."

"It's true," Damon said. "That girl will make you see stars."

Martin watched the two men laugh. Carver's big mouth had just confirmed his suspicion that his room was under video surveillance. That's the only way that Carver could have known what Alice did and did not do the night before.

Carver noticed Martin staring. "Something wrong, Grey?"

"Not at all. I was just thinking I wouldn't mind spending some time with Alice again tonight. According to you guys, she's got some other talents I should know about."

Damon shrugged. "I don't see why not."

The slave walked in with Martin's breakfast. As the food was placed on the table, Carver said, "You really like Alice, don't you, Grey?"

"What's not to like?"

"No. I mean you *really* like her. That's why you were holding out on the juicy details, wasn't it? Because that sweet little thing really got to you."

Martin felt his pulse quicken. He was pretty certain that Carver was simply fishing, but still his response had to be unflinchingly convincing. Martin set down his fork.

"You're right. You figured it out. I'm deeply in love with Alice. In fact we're running off tonight to get married. Maybe you'd like to be my best man. Whaddaya say?"

Carver just eyeballed him for a moment, keen for the slightest revealing tick on Martin's face. Then he broke the tension with a small smile. "You're a funny man, Grey. Very funny man."

Martin noticed that there was still a glimmer of suspicion in Carver's eyes.

"Carver does bring up a good point," Damon said to Martin. "Have all the fun you want with these girls, but be careful. Do not let yourself grow attached to them. Got it?"

Martin put on a casual smile. "Guys, come on. I spent one night with the girl. I'm not attached to her, I'm just real horny."

Damon laughed.

Carver did not.

55

An angry-looking storm front loomed in the distance above the treetops. Directly overhead, a few scattered clouds slid across a bright blue sky like the advance unit for Mother Nature's forces. Martin followed Damon along a dirt path that trailed away from the main house and ran parallel to the golf course. Last night's work crew was long gone, and the rolling, manicured greens looked immaculate.

"How far is the mine?" Martin asked.

"Not far. About a ten-minute walk from here."

Martin looked sideways at Damon. "And where is here, exactly? Please don't say outside Seattle."

Damon did a poor job of stifling a smile. "What do you mean? Of course we're outside Seattle. Have you been staring into the sun again?"

Martin was relieved to see that Damon took his inquiry lightly. "Damon, come on, I know that we're nowhere near—"

Damon raised a hand, cutting him off, his tone suddenly serious. "For now we're outside Seattle. When the time is right, you'll know more. Cool?"

Thinking it unwise to push, Martin nodded and let the matter drop.

Soon they reached the stream. The rushing water was as clear as glass. They walked across an old wooden footbridge and then continued along a dirt path into an untamed section of the estate. Unlike the manicured landscape surrounding the main house, on this side of the stream trees and brush were allowed to flourish unchecked. To Martin it would have seemed like they had exited Forty Acres and gone back into the deep woods, if it wasn't for the strange cabins. Set back from the trail and partially hidden by trees stood a row of four squat and elongated structures. They were all boarded up, weather-beaten, and overgrown with wildlife, like army barracks that had been long abandoned. As they strolled by, Damon pointed to them like a tour guide. "Over there is where all the slaves used to live. But about twenty years ago Dr. Kasim decided to make some changes."

"Why? What happened?"

"This was before I was a member, but Solomon once told me that it had something to do with too many planes flying over and that they were worried about the slaves being spotted. They decided to move most of them inside."

That made perfect sense, Martin thought. With scores of laborers and armed guards running around, Forty Acres must have looked like a prison camp from the sky. Factor in the steady increase in private air traffic and the growing sophistication of consumer video and photographic equipment, and the result that some aerial passerby would eventually notice something fishy about Forty Acres was inevitable. "But where did they move them to?" Martin asked.

"The house. Slaves all live in the east wing of the house, down in the cellar. The guards live on the floors above them and take up the rest of that wing."

"What about the mine workers? Where are they housed?"

"In the mine, of course."

"You mean underground?"

"Exactly. Not only does it keep them out of sight, it makes escape damn near impossible."

Off to his right, through a dense grouping of trees, Martin could barely discern a section of the huge encompassing wall. The imposing barrier looked impossible to climb, but Martin knew that desperate people sometimes found ways to achieve the impossible. "Has anyone ever escaped?" Martin asked.

Damon's response was matter-of-fact. "No. And they never will."

"How can you be so sure?"

Damon paused on the trail and turned to face Martin. "Look, when I was the new guy, I worried about the same thing. If just one slave escapes from this place, my career, my life, everything is ruined."

Martin had belabored the point to gather information, not because of any concern for future repercussions. But Damon's assumption served as the perfect cover. "It's true," Martin said. "I'd be paranoid about the FBI banging down my front door one day. How the hell do you even sleep at night?"

"Think about it like this," Damon said. "The oldest nuclear power plant in the country, built atop a geological fault no less, is located just fifty miles from eight million New Yorkers and your front door. You ever lose sleep over that?"

"Not really."

"Of course not, because you know that there's too much at stake for the operators of Indian Point to leave anything to chance."

Martin thought this over. "Sounds like you're saying that Forty Acres is too big to fail."

Damon nodded. "Now you got it. This thing we have here, and the people involved—if our secret ever got out, it would be—"

"Catastrophic."

"Exactly. So, while it's impossible to eliminate all risks, every precaution imaginable has been taken."

Damon smiled at the doubt that still remained on Martin's face. "Trust me, once you see the mine, you'll get a better understanding of how seriously security is taken around here."

Martin followed Damon deeper and deeper into the wooded section of Forty Acres. For a short stretch the only visible signs of civilization were the deep tire ruts in the dirt path; then they emerged into a small clearing.

A brick guard shack with two jeeps parked out front stood adjacent to the entrance of the gold mine. The mouth of the cave was set into the base of a small stony hill and an impenetrable-looking rusty steel door barricaded the entrance. On a fading hand-painted sign over the door were the words Our Mine. Martin's jaw tightened as he stared at the sign. The wordplay about ownership revolving around the double meaning of the word *mine* was no doubt another example of Dr. Kasim's skewed humor.

A tall guard with a clean-shaven head and a gun on his hip emerged from the guard shack to greet them. He shook hands with both of them. "Mr. Darrell. Mr. Grey. How can I help you gentlemen today?"

"I want to give Mr. Grey here a quick tour," Damon said.

"Sure thing. Just let me clear it with my boss." The guard raised a walkie-talkie to his mouth and keyed it. "Roy, you copy? I got Mr. Darrell and Mr. Grey up top. They'd like a tour."

"Sure," a deep voice squawked from the device. "Send 'em down to gate two. I'll meet them there."

"Copy that." The guard holstered his radio and returned his attention to Damon and Martin. "Hold on, let me grab you some headgear." He disappeared into the guard shack and returned with two hard hats. He tossed one to Damon and the other to Martin, then led them over to the mine entrance.

The guard pulled out an odd-looking four-sided key, inserted it into a shielded keyhole, and gave it a twist. Martin heard the loud clack of an electronic-powered latch unlocking, then watched the guard repocket the key. He found himself wondering if all the guards carried such a key. Was it some sort of master key, perhaps?

The guard gripped a thick steel handle with both hands and heaved. The heavy door groaned, slowly swinging outward. The guard looked like he was opening a bank vault. The open cave belched a gust of chilly, pungent air that caused Martin to recoil. The odor was so earthy rich that Martin could taste it. Martin pressed a hand over his nose to dampen the smell.

"Yeah, it's pretty damn funky," Damon said. "Takes a moment to get used to."

Beyond the steel doorway a narrow, low-ceilinged passage reinforced by timber columns and crossbeams descended into the earth. Shielded light fixtures mounted along the ceiling provided a dingy gloom. On the dusty cave floor, rusted mine-car rails offered a foreboding trail downward.

"Just keep straight until you reach gate two," the guard said. "It's not far and there's no other way to go, so you can't miss it. I'll keep the hatch open until you reach Roy."

"I've been down a few times before," Damon said. "We'll be fine."

The guard nodded. "See you when you get back."

Martin followed Damon across the threshold and into the mine. Their footfalls crunched hollowly as they progressed downward. Very quickly the reassuring glow of daylight from the mouth of the cave was no longer visible behind them. Directly ahead, the passage's curving descent afforded them only a view of the jagged chiseled walls.

Damon smiled at Martin. "Pretty crazy, huh?"

Martin didn't say a word. He was too busy studying an old overturned mine car that abutted the tunnel wall. What puzzled Martin was that the mine car wasn't just old, it was very old. The crumbling and corroded iron carcass, with its monstrous rivets and crudely forged parts, lay in a burnt-orange bed of its own rust. That mine car had to have been abandoned over a hundred years earlier. And then there was the tunnel's construction. The hand-carved wooden beams that held back the crushing earth were so ancient that they almost looked fossilized. Martin noticed that some of the beams had been repaired over the years with modern metal brackets. The electrical light fixtures were also a relatively recent addition. Martin could tell this by the charred scorch marks spaced along the walls, most likely the result of oil lanterns or maybe even torches.

Jesus, exactly how old is this mine? Martin wondered. A day ago when Damon mentioned that there was an old working gold mine on the property, Martin assumed that the mine would be a fairly modern operation. He pictured shaft elevators, conveyor belts, maybe even a few dump trucks. Martin never imagined that he'd be hiking down a ramshackle hole that could have come straight out of the Old West.

The passage doubled in width as Damon and Martin arrived at another guard shack standing before a formidable steel wall. The wall cut off access to the deeper sections of the mine like a big steel plug. It had no windows or view ports, just one reinforced door at its center. A white number two was painted on the door. The guard shack was twice as big as the one up top and appeared to be far more sophisticated. Martin noticed several bundles of electrical cables that ran from the shack and disappeared through the steel wall, headed toward some destination deeper in the mine. Martin came to the conclusion that the windowless structure had to be the nerve center for the entire mine. This was confirmed when the door swung open and Roy stepped out. For the brief instant that the door remained open, Martin spotted another man inside the shack seated at a bank of surveillance monitors and a tall rifle rack loaded with weapons.

Roy, with his unshaved face and a stogie clamped between his teeth, didn't look like the other guards. He didn't dress like them either. There was no firearm hanging from his hip, just a walkie-talkie, and instead of wearing all black, he sported jeans and a stained blue sweatshirt. Printed on the front of his shirt in big, bold letters was the unlikely phrase Obama Is My Homeboy.

Martin couldn't help wondering what Roy's homeboy would think of Roy's chosen occupation.

Roy plucked the cigar from his mouth and raised his walkie-talkie. "I got 'em. We're all good."

"Copy that."

Wearing a big smile, Roy held his arms out wide, and his deep voice boomed off the walls. "Welcome to hell, my brothers. My name is Satan and I'll be your tour guide today."

Damon greeted Roy with a warm hug. Roy turned and pulled Martin into a hug next. "Just so you know, I'm not really Satan. It's Roy Cooper. I'm in charge down here."

"Nice to meet you. I'm Martin Grey."

Roy snorted. "Shit, I know who you are. You're the brother who beat the unbeatable Damon Darrell at his own game." Roy goaded Damon with a mocking smile.

Damon scoffed, "As you can see, the foul air down here has affected his mind. Roy's been running this mine forever."

"Thirteen years, four months, and three days," Roy said with a swelled chest. "My little way of making a difference in this fucked-up world."

"Nice shirt," Damon said.

Roy grinned. "Yeah. I'm convinced that our work at Forty Acres is a major reason why brother Obama slam-dunked it. Good shit ripples out, you know?" He glanced at his watch. "Shit. We should get going. It's almost noon and I'm sure you guys didn't come down here to see the slaves eat lunch." Roy ushered them over to the door in the steel wall and unlocked it with another four-sided key. He pushed the door open but paused before walking through. "I forgot to ask. If either of you are armed, you have to leave your weapon here. No guns allowed beyond this point." Martin and Damon both assured Roy that they were unarmed, then followed him through the door.

The mine tunnel funneled back to its narrower proportions as the trio followed it downward into the earth. The grade began to increase sharply and Martin found himself leaning backward and reaching for the wall to maintain his balance. They encountered several more overturned mine cars, including a few that impeded the passage and had to be climbed over. Occasionally Martin spotted other relics on the cave floor. An old dented bucket, a broken pick handle, even a small pile of dust that held the distinct shape of a boot. "Exactly how old is this mine?" Martin asked.

"Old," Damon replied with a laugh. "Close to two hundred years, right, Roy?"

"Close, but no cigar." Roy frowned at the fading embers of his spent stogie, then tossed it away. "All this goes back to around 1829. There was a big gold rush back then."

"I'm no history expert," Martin broke in, "but I'm pretty sure the gold rush was in California in the 1840s."

"You're talking about the gold rush of 1849. That's

the most famous gold rush that took place in the United States. But there were others. Ever hear of Reed's gold mine in North Carolina?"

"No. Should I have?"

"Not really. Gold was struck there in 1799. That's considered the first real gold rush in the United States. The second was in 1829. That's when these tunnels were dug—and all by slaves." In reaction to Martin's quizzical look, he added, "Don't tell me you think that slaves were only used to pick cotton."

Whenever Martin thought of American slavery, the standard image of Africans stooped over in cotton fields always came to mind. Of course it made perfect sense that slaves would have been used for even more arduous tasks, he just never gave the subject much thought. "Of course not," he said. "I just didn't know that slave labor was also used for mining in the South."

"Oh shit yeah," Roy said. "Slaves were used for every fucked-up job imaginable. And believe me, there were a lot of fucked-up jobs back then. Mostly they were forced to work the coal pits, but slaves were used in all sorts of mines, including gold mines like this one."

"How did Dr. Kasim come to own it?"

"The mine was shut down right after the Civil War. It was just abandoned for over a hundred years. Then Dr. Kasim came along."

"I've heard Dr. Kasim say that the reason he built Forty Acres here is because of the mine," Damon added.

"But if the mine was abandoned," Martin said, "doesn't that mean that the gold had run out?"

"Damn right," Roy said with a laugh. "I doubt they'd leave money just sitting in the ground."

Martin's brow furrowed. Either Roy wasn't making sense or Martin had missed something. "But if there's no more gold to be mined," Martin asked, "what are the slaves digging for?" He saw Roy and Damon exchange an amused glance, but neither man volunteered an answer.

"Just wait until we get to the dig," Roy said. "It's easier to explain if you see it for yourself."

They continued their trek farther and farther down the tunnel. The dank air grew colder and somehow the tunnel seemed quieter. Martin felt a chill. He wasn't sure if it was the dropping temperature or his rising fear. The idea that he could be walking willingly to his grave entered his mind, but Martin held back paranoia with reason. If they were onto him and planning to kill him, why bother with the history lesson?

The grade became even steeper and Martin wondered how deep into the earth they were. Oddly, the light in the tunnel seemed to grow dimmer the deeper they went, but the frequency and size of the lamps remained constant. Martin could not remember passing even a single blown-out bulb. He decided that there was nothing wrong with the light. Nerves were just playing tricks on him.

Martin noticed that, strung up in one corner of the cave's roof, the neat bundle of cables that originated from the upper guard shack still ran along the length of the passage. Then in the opposite corner of the roof he noticed something odd. There was another cable trailing away into the depths. But unlike the bundled cables, which were mostly black and white, this orphaned cable was bright red. Otherwise it looked exactly like the others. So why go through the trouble of stringing this cable up separately? And why so far apart from the other cables? Before Martin could raise the question, they reached a fork in the tunnel. The left branch continued downward while the right branch appeared to level off. Roy explained that he'd quickly show them the slave quarters, which were just a few yards away down the right tunnel, before taking them farther down to the actual dig. He led them through another thick, steel-plated door into a low-ceilinged chamber.

The approximately nine-hundred-square-foot space was not a natural cavity; instead it had been dug out of the earth and shored up with wooden planks that were now sagging and cracked. In spots the wounds in the wall bled loose soil. The dirt floor was crowded with what looked like human nests. Dozens of filthy bedrolls and blankets, each with its own pile of meager relics from the slaves' former lives—wallet photos of children, broken watches and jewelry, even a pocket Bible. Shielded video cameras were mounted in each corner so that even while they slept, the slaves were kept under constant surveillance. And then there was the stench. Martin struggled hard to conceal the horror he felt over the meager living conditions, but he could not disguise his revulsion at the foul odor that infected the room—a dense, living human funk that stung his eyes like ammonia. Martin and Damon both raised the collars of their shirts to cover their nostrils but Roy showed no reaction as he moved farther into the room and began to speak. "When the slaves are not digging in the mine, they're kept here. Everything they need is in this room." He pointed to a screened-off section of the room. "Back there, there's toilets and even a place for them to wash their clothes. All their meals are taken in the mine, so there's no need for cooking or storage. Every day after they do their fourteen hours in the mine, they get two hours of free time, then it's lights-out and a good night's sleep, and then it starts all over again. Sundays are half days and they get Christmas, Dr. Kasim's birthday, and Martin Luther King's birthday completely off."

As Martin listened, the words that Roy uttered when he first emerged from the guard shack echoed in his head: *Welcome to hell.*

"Do they ever get any sunlight?" Martin asked. He regretted the question as soon as he saw the stare it drew from Roy. Damon also appeared flummoxed.

"Sunlight?" Roy said with a snort. "Hell no! They lucky they got lightbulbs in this goddamned pigsty." Roy glanced at his watch again. "Come on, let's get down to the dig."

As they were exiting the room, Martin spotted something that made him pause. That strange red cable again. It was strung up flush in the corner between the walls and the ceiling and ran around the entire room. He tried to spot a termination point but there was none. The cable entered the room through a hole over the doorway, circled the room, then disappeared back out the same hole. *What the hell?*

Roy led Martin and Damon back to the fork, and then they all started down the left tunnel. Martin had begun to track the mysterious red cable after exiting the slave quarters, and now he was continuing to track it as they descended toward the dig. The isolated red cable was strung up along the roof of the cave everywhere he looked. Martin had failed to notice the strange cable in the first tunnel before they reached gate two, but he had a feeling that it was there. Something told him that that oddball red cable, whatever its purpose, ran throughout the entire mine. Martin was hesitant to ask about it for fear of raising suspicion, especially after his sunlight question, but his curiosity still gnawed its way to the surface. He directed the question to Roy. "I see this place is wired up with cameras and electric gates, but tell me something: what's that red cable for?"

Roy stopped in his tracks and turned to face Martin. "Why would you ask that?"

Martin shrugged. "I don't know. It looks different from the other cables. It's isolated, and it seems to be everywhere."

Damon stared up and down the tunnel at the red cable, his eyes puzzled. "Son of a bitch. I never noticed that before. What is that?"

Roy teased Martin and Damon with a mysterious smile. "I don't know if I should tell you guys. Might freak you out."

"Quit screwing around," Damon said. "What's it for?"

"Mr. Lennox had it put in recently," Roy replied. "He called it an extra level of security." Then Roy lowered his voice as if he were afraid someone might overhear him. "Ever hear of Primacord?"

Damon shook his head but Martin felt a sudden chill race through him. "That's a type of explosive, isn't it?"

"That's an affirmative," Roy said in a manner that, to Martin, seemed way too casual for talking about high explosives. "The whole mine is wired with it, top to bottom. The plan being that if something goes wrong, *ka-boom!* No more evidence."

"Are you fucking serious?" Damon said, with a measure of alarm. "You mean we're walking around inside a fucking bomb?"

"No need to worry," Roy said coolly. "Primacord is very stable. It has to be detonated just so, and that can only be done from two places. The office at gate two and the main house. Trust me, it's perfectly safe."

"I sure as hell hope you're right," Damon said. Then he addressed Martin. "Like I told you, around here they take security seriously. Maybe a little too seriously."

Martin said nothing as they resumed their descent. He knew speaking then would expose his true emotions. Damon, meanwhile, was anxiously glancing at the red cable, and Martin realized that Damon's concern was not for the dozens of people who would be murdered if the mine imploded; Damon was solely concerned about himself. It troubled him that despite spending so much time with Damon during the last three months, he had never realized that Damon, like the other members of Forty Acres, was a monster.

A murky green glow bathed the tunnel directly ahead, and now Martin could hear the distant *clank* of steel pounding stone. A moment later Roy led them into a large open cavern illuminated by harsh work lights. Along the perimeter of the cavity about a dozen shackled workers pecked at the stone wall with pickaxes. Another team of workers shoveled the dirt and rocks into wheelbarrows and carted the load over to a massive rock-crushing machine, where several more workers panned the resulting coarse soil in several troughs of clear, running water. Martin estimated that there were about three dozen slaves in all. Mostly men, but a few women as well. Their emaciated bodies were draped in the soiled and ragged remains of whatever clothing they had had on when they were abducted. One slave wore a tattered *Star Wars* shirt, another a dirt-caked John Deere ball cap.

Martin wanted to learn where these slaves came from and how they were captured, but he worried that probing too deeply too soon could make him look like he was gathering evidence instead of simply asking innocent questions. Damon had already made it clear that the most sensitive details of the compound's operations would only be revealed to him "when the time is right." So Martin decided that for the time being, he'd keep his questions light. Just scratch the surface for now, then later, after the initiation, after he'd gained their trust, he'd dig deeper.

Six big guards armed only with steel spring batons patrolled freely, barking at faltering slaves to keep up the pace. A few of the slaves attempted to steal a glance at the strangers who had just entered their work area and were promptly warned, "Keep your white asses working!" Directly in the center of the space stood a steel bell-shaped structure with several gun slots. To Martin it looked like a mash-up of an igloo and an armored truck. "What is that?" he asked, pointing.

Roy smiled as if he were just asked to demonstrate his favorite toy. "We call it the death dome. There's a man inside there armed with an AA-12 assault shotgun, the most powerful handheld weapon in the world. If things ever got out of order in here, he could fix it real quick, if you know what I mean."

Martin stood studying the work flow of the mine. He watched the digging, the carting, the crushing, and finally the panning. Martin was hardly an expert on mining, but it did appear as if they were looking for gold, despite

Roy's saying the mine had been abandoned a century before. Why would anyone abandon a gold mine if it was still bearing fruit? He turned to Roy. "So if they're not digging for gold, what exactly *are* they digging for?"

Roy screwed up his face. "Well, that's kind of a tricky question." Roy led Martin over to one of the water troughs, where a balding man, about forty years old, was busy filling his pan with a fresh load of ground soil. They watched as he submerged the pan in water and began to shake and swirl it around, gradually separating the light soil from the heavier sediments. The slave was a master at this task, and soon just a teaspoon's worth of black soil remained at the bottom of the pan. The slave used his fingers to sift through the dark soil; finding nothing, he frowned, washed out the pan, and then turned to scoop up another load of dirt.

"Ned, stop work and turn around," said Roy.

"Yes, sir," Ned replied with a feeble voice. He put down his pan and turned toward them but kept his eyes trained on the ground. His face was nonexpressive except for his eyes, which were full of misery.

Roy pointed to Martin. "This is Mr. Grey, your new master."

"Hello, sir," Ned said, without looking up. It was obvious that, unlike the house slaves, the mine slaves were not allowed to look their captors in the eye.

"Find anything today?" Roy asked.

"Yes, sir. Doing pretty good so far."

"Show Mr. Grey."

Roy picked up a small white plastic jar, about the size of a cold cream jar. He twisted it open and handed it to Martin. Inside the jar there were just a few tiny flecks of gold, none larger than a grain of rice. "So then," Martin said to Roy, his voice still uncertain, "they are mining for gold."

Roy paused. He raised his hand, then turned to Ned and ordered him to get back to work. Martin handed Ned back the white jar and said, "Thanks." The kind word made Ned pause as if he were basking in a fleeting spring breeze. He picked up his pan and continued working. Roy led Martin and Damon out of earshot of the slaves before finally supplying Martin with an explanation.

"You see, the people who used to run this mine didn't shut down because the gold ran out. They shut down because they reached a point where the gold ran *low*. Once the cost of digging is greater than the value of what comes out of the ground, it's time to pack up and leave. So yes, technically the slaves are mining gold, but they only find a few ounces a year. Not even enough to keep them fed. Gold is not what's important here."

"Then what is?"

"Put it this way: we can't exactly put them to work in cotton fields, can we?"

The truth struck Martin like a thunderbolt. Suddenly he understood the twisted purpose of the old gold mine. "It's just busywork," he muttered in astonishment. "It doesn't matter what they pull out of the ground. It's just to keep them working."

"Not just working," Damon said. "Working hard. The same courtesy they showed our ancestors. Isn't Dr. Kasim brilliant?"

Martin put on a smile, but inside his stomach churned. As he watched the feeble workers pecking at the walls, the weight of what he planned really hit home. These people truly were in hell. And their rescue rested solely on his shoulders. Whatever it took, he had to tell the world what was going on here.

A guard's angry shout rose above the din. *"I said keep working!"* He hit a slave across the back with his baton. The slave let out a cry and crumbled to his knees. He was older than the others and he appeared to be ill, but that did not stay the guard's hand. *"Get up! Get up!"* the guard shouted as he struck the cowering slave again and again.

"Stop it! Goddamnit! Stop!"

The guard froze. The work stopped. The entire dig fell silent except for the beaten man's whimpering. Damon, Roy, all the guards stared. Even a few slaves risked a glance at Martin. He hadn't been able to hold his emotions back any longer. His outburst was as unstoppable as a volcanic eruption.

Martin saw the puzzled eyes measuring him, perhaps the seeds of doubt taking root. Now they knew, Martin thought. Now they all knew how he truly felt . . . and he was as doomed as the men chained to the wall.

But the accusations never came. Just a wry snicker from Roy before he whispered to Martin, "Jesus, you really are new." Then Roy shouted for everyone to get back to work. The battered slave, too injured to do so, was dragged away, and the slaves returned to swinging their pickaxes. Just like that, the incident was over.

Damon gave Martin's shoulder a supportive squeeze, then turned to Roy. "I believe that Mr. Grey has seen enough."

56

A short while later Damon and Martin were trudging back through the woods toward the main house. The sky was now overcast and a light drizzle had begun to fall.

Martin thought it odd that neither Damon nor Roy had made any mention of Martin's outburst as they hiked their way back up to the surface. After they emerged from the mine, Damon's griping about not being able to get in a few rounds of golf had been the sole topic of conversation. Martin couldn't tell whether the two men were intentionally avoiding a troubling subject that would be dealt with later, or if his revealing misstep was really not that big a deal. Either way, Martin felt a pressing urge to say something. To try to slap a patch on his character before it completely deflated. But he decided to remain quiet. Why make an issue out of something that may not be an issue at all? For all he knew, Damon had already forgotten about the incident.

Martin was wrong.

They were just a few yards from reaching the main house when Damon surprised Martin by grabbing his arm.

"Hold it a minute," Damon said. The casualness Damon displayed during their stroll back had vanished.

His demeanor was stern. "What happened in the mine. That can't happen again. Never defend a slave over a master. Never."

Martin did his best to nod.

"I'm sure you can understand why," Damon said.

"Of course," Martin said. "Sorry about that. I guess I'm still just getting used to all this."

Damon shook his head. "You never really get used to it. And in some ways, your reaction was perfectly natural. If you saw a dog receiving a beating, you'd probably react the exact same way. But here's the thing: you have to keep reminding yourself what 'all this' is really about. What they did to our people. What we're doing here is a duty. It serves a higher purpose. Okay?"

After a moment, Martin nodded. "I understand."

"I hope so. If not, you'll never get through your initiation tonight."

Martin looked at him. "Is there any way I can get you to tell me what this initiation is?"

Damon's easy smile returned. "Brother, what you've seen so far is nothing. Just a small taste of what we've created. The knowledge and experiences that await you will forever change you. But before we can take you deeper, you must prove your loyalty."

"How?"

Damon frowned. "I've already said too much. But I will say this about tonight. You better toughen up, real fast." With that, Damon continued toward the main house.

57

Alice paused outside Master Lewis's bedroom door, smoothed out her maid's uniform, and took a deep breath. She tried to make herself appear calm, but that wasn't easy with her heart pounding in her chest. She had no idea why Master Lewis would ask to see her in the middle of the afternoon. In the few years that he had been coming to Forty Acres, she had only been summoned to his room once, and that was for sex. In truth, it was more of a beating than sex. It was well known that Master Lewis injured the women who went to his room and that it would probably be much worse if Master Lennox didn't keep him in check. Alice could tell, though, that Master Lewis had not enjoyed the night he spent with her. Alice didn't know why, and she didn't really care. He sure smacked her around enough. She was just thankful that Master Lewis had never demanded her company again—until last night. When she had been summoned to Master Lewis's room, she was certain that her good fortune had run out. She expected him to slam her down on the bed and rip off her clothes like last time, but instead he wanted her to sleep with the new master, Martin Grey. Alice took no pleasure in sleeping with any of them, but if she had no choice, she'd much rather sleep with Grey than a man who confused caresses with punches.

Alice took another deep breath as she stared at the doorknob. *Calm down*, she told herself. *He probably just wants you to sleep with Mr. Grey again. Yes, that has to be it.* Alice put on a big smile and rapped lightly on the door.

Carver's firm voice beckoned her to enter. Alice pushed through the door and saw Carver seated on the edge of the bed. Her tension eased a bit when she saw that he was fully dressed and smiling. "You wanted to see me, master?"

"Yes. I'm curious about your evening with Mr. Grey."

"Curious, sir?"

"Tell me what happened."

Alice took on a puzzled expression. "We had sex, sir."

Carver frowned. "I know that. I mean what did you talk about?"

"Nothing really. We didn't do much talking."

Carver's smile thinned as his eyes drank her in. "Yeah, I imagine not. Did anything unusual happen?"

"Unusual?"

"Yes. You know, like did he ask you to do anything . . . out of the ordinary?"

Alice suddenly had a pit in her stomach. Alice had a strong feeling that if she revealed the truth, something bad would happen. Not to her but to Mr. Grey. Usually she wouldn't give a shit about what happened to these men who took away her life and kept her a prisoner. But after she'd thought more about Mr. Grey's behavior, only one thing made sense to Alice: pretending to have sex wasn't some weird kink as she had originally thought. Mr. Grey faked the sex because he didn't want to rape her. He was trying to protect her. And if he was trying to protect her, Alice thought, then she should protect him as best she could.

"Answer me," Carver demanded, growing impatient.

Alice shook her head. "No, sir. Nothing like that. We just had sex."

Carver studied her suspiciously. Alice was relieved; it meant that Mr. Carver did not know the truth. Mr. Grey had kept what happened secret as well.

"Do you think he enjoyed the sex?" Carver asked.

"Yes. He seemed to, sir."

Carver leaned forward. "Do you think Mr. Grey likes you, Alice? I mean, was he kind to you? Treated you nicely?"

Alice found the question more than a little odd. Her brow furrowed. "Mr. Grey was very nice to me, sir."

"I'm sure he was. But does he like you? You can tell if someone likes you, can't you?"

"I think so, sir."

"Well? Does he like you or not?"

Alice nodded. "Yes, I think Mr. Grey does like me."

A cold smile creased Carver's face. "Yes, that's what I thought too."

Alice didn't like the look on Carver's face. It made her nervous. It reminded her of the way he looked the night he beat her. The sooner she got out of his room the better. "Is that all, sir?"

Carver shook his head, slow and ominous. "No, it's not. Come closer."

Alice's heart began to race again. "You have more questions about Mr. Grey?"

"I said come closer."

Alice forced her body, tense with fear, to take a few steps toward him.

"Don't play games. Come here. Right here in front of me."

Alice tried to remain calm. She already knew what was going to happen next—it seemed inevitable now—but showing fear might anger him and make his hands heavier. Still smiling, Alice took a few more steps forward and stopped within arm's reach of Carver. Within striking distance. For an infinite moment he just groped her body with his stare. She could see his eyes filling up with his mean lust. Then Carver said something unexpected. "Show me your hands."

Alice was so baffled by the request that she just stood there looking at him.

"Are you deaf? Show me your hands!"

Alice raised her hands. They were trembling and there was nothing she could do to stop them. She was just too frightened. Carver grabbed her hands and stared at them.

They were small and delicate. Carver took particular interest in her fingernails. They were clipped short but still had a bit of an edge. Carver ran his fingers over the tips of her nails and smiled, apparently pleased by their appearance. Finally he released her hands and looked up at her, mysteriously amused. "You and I are going to play a game," he said. Then Carver grabbed Alice and flung her hard onto the bed.

58

Juanita Darrell, displaying her usual flair, selected Xander's, a trendy new soul food restaurant on the corner of 127th Street and St. Nicholas Avenue in Harlem, to host an impromptu "girls' night out." Xander's had a three-month waiting list, but being the wives of powerful men came with certain privileges, like getting the best table in the house on the busiest night of the week without a reservation. The restaurant's unique posh-funk décor, velvety atmosphere, and delicious authentic dishes lived up to Anna's expectations. Any other night she would have been thrilled to be there, but on this night, she had far too much on her mind.

Anna sat at the table picking at her smothered lamb chops while the other wives enjoyed a lively discussion on a mad variety of topics. Dissecting every detail of Saks's new upscale nail salon took up cocktail time (verdict: good effort, but not good enough to replace Bergdorf's). Then, as wine flowed and each course arrived at the table, the conversation hopscotched dizzyingly across subjects like Obamacare, the latest episode of *Real Housewives of Atlanta*, and real estate opportunities in the Cayman Islands, and had now landed on a critique of Michelle

Obama's wardrobe. Anna remained quiet all the while.

"Anna, we haven't heard from you yet," Juanita said. "What do you think?"

Anna looked up from her plate and saw all the women staring at her. She was only vaguely aware of the current topic of conversation. Instead of pretending to care, she just shrugged. "Sorry, I guess my mind's somewhere else."

Starsha, Carver's wife and the youngest at the table, snorted. "Yeah, no kidding. You haven't said a word all night."

"No, that's not true," Kwame's wife, Olaide, said. "I did hear the sister order those lamb chops. But that's about it."

The women laughed. Juanita, who was seated to Anna's right, reached over and squeezed her hand. "Are you feeling all right?"

"Yes. I'm fine. I guess I just miss Martin."

The women traded amused looks. Betty Aarons, Solomon's regal wife, shook her head. "Lord, girl. Your man's only been gone a single day. During the war, Solomon was away for over a year and I didn't look as down as you do now."

"I've never been completely out of touch with Martin before. That's all."

Juanita frowned at Anna. "I thought we settled all this last night when you called."

"I know. It's just it feels so weird not being able to text him or anything. I had trouble sleeping."

Starsha leaned closer to Anna and lowered her voice. "See, what you need to get you through those lonely nights is a good vibrator." She winked at Mrs. Aarons. "You tell her, Betty."

The women burst into laughter, and Anna laughed right along with them. Juanita shooed off Anna's gloom with a wave of her hand. "Don't worry. By the time they go off on their next trip, you won't even think about it."

"Yeah, especially if we take a trip of our own," Starsha added. "The only reason we didn't go anywhere this time is because Margaret is in the middle of a closing."

"Sorry, girls," Tobias's wife said with a playful pout.

"Starsha's right," Juanita said to Anna. "Anywhere we go, we go in style. You'll have so much fun that you won't have time to worry about Martin. Am I right, ladies?" Juanita raised her wineglass and the other women followed suit.

Anna watched skeptically as the five wives clinked their glasses and drank to their ability to temporarily forget their husbands. It was the oddest toast that Anna had ever seen, and she wasn't sold. "Come on, be honest," Anna said. "You guys have to be just a little worried. I mean, your husbands are out in the middle of nowhere, engaged in a very risky sport."

Juanita laughed. "Risky? I don't think so. Like I told you, they splash around in a little kiddie river. They're probably in more danger when they sit around the camp-fire getting drunk."

The women laughed until Anna stopped the conversation cold with what she said next. "I'm sure Mrs. Jackson felt the exact same way."

The mood at the table shifted instantly. The women exchanged sullen looks as if they were more annoyed by the tragic memory than saddened by it. Juanita frowned at Anna. "Let me guess. You read about it on the Internet."

Anna nodded. "And yesterday, when your husband came to pick up Martin, I asked him about it."

"Then I'm sure Damon told you that Donald Jackson's death was a suicide, not an accident like the papers say."

"He did, but after thinking about it, something occurred to me that I just can't get out of my mind." Anna scanned the women's faces, hesitant to continue. She was certain her next words would not be welcome. "I think your husbands may have lied to all of you."

For a moment no one said a word. The wives just scowled at their newest member. In an attempt to deflate the tension, Juanita began to laugh. "I'm sure Anna doesn't mean that the way it sounds. Do you, Anna?"

"Well, actually I do. Just think about it. If your husbands had returned and said that Donald Jackson died while rafting, none of you would ever let them go rafting again. Am I right? It would mean the end of their camping trips. They had a good reason to lie."

Starsha laughed derisively. "Lady, you got a lot of

nerve. You don't know us from boo and you certainly don't know our damn husbands."

"Starsha is absolutely right," Olaide said to Anna in a firm voice. "Maybe lies are acceptable in your marriage, but between Kwame and me there are no secrets."

Margaret Stewart shook her head, discounting the idea completely. "No. Uh-uh. Yes, Tobias is a little wild. Yes, he gambles and drinks too much. Yes, he sometimes chases women. But one thing he never does is lie about it. Tobias tells me everything—even though sometimes I wish he didn't."

Mrs. Aarons raised an aloof nose to Anna and remarked, "Mr. Aarons and I have been married for longer than you have been alive, young lady. That makes us more than just husband and wife. Your haphazard allegation is not just wrong, it's extremely insulting."

Juanita reached out and gave Anna a little pat on the hand. "I really need to freshen up. Why don't you come with me?"

As Anna rose and followed Juanita across the restaurant, she could almost feel the glares of the women burning into her back.

*

"I think you should go home," Juanita said as she touched up her makeup in the mirror. "You're ruining everyone's night. I'm sorry, but there's just no easy way to say it."

Anna was standing beside Juanita inside the plush ladies' restroom as Stevie Wonder wafted from concealed speakers. Anna wasn't hurt by Juanita's invitation to leave. She felt that she deserved it. In fact, the instant Anna stepped away from the table, she regretted her behavior. Even if she did find the other wives' views of their husbands to be absurdly unrealistic, that didn't give her the right to be rude and obnoxious. And then there was Martin to think about. Acceptance by their influential husbands was important to Martin, Anna knew that, yet here she was making enemies of their wives. How stupid could she be? If Martin fell out of favor with his new friends as a direct result of something she did, Martin might forgive her, but Anna would never be able to forgive herself. Anna sighed and leaned against the sink. "Juanita, I'm so sorry, I really am. I guess I'm just going a little crazy."

Juanita shrugged as she applied eye shadow. "Hey, it happens when you're pregnant."

"What?" Anna asked in utter shock. "How did you—?"

Juanita burst into laughter. "Hm, let's see . . . first I noticed that you ordered iced tea instead of wine, and I definitely remember you drinking wine at my dinner party. Then, this whole clingy business about you missing your husband desperately after just one day. You seemed more levelheaded and independent-minded the first time I met you. Those things made me suspicious, but honestly I wasn't sure until just this second." Juanita chuckled

again. "Girl, you should've seen your face. Congratulations!" Juanita pulled Anna into a hug. When they
parted, Juanita noticed Anna's anxious expression.
"What's wrong?"

"I really wanted Martin to be the first to know. You
have to promise me not to say anything to anybody until
I tell him."

Juanita's eyes lit up with understanding. "That explains
a lot. He doesn't know yet?"

Anna shook her head. "I found out the same day he
left."

"You poor thing. The biggest news of your entire life
and you can't tell a soul. No wonder you're going nuts."

Anna looked at her pleadingly. Juanita zipped up her
lips and threw away the imaginary key. "Your secret's
safe with me. Promise."

"Thank you." Anna watched as Juanita expertly put
the finishing touches on her makeup. It was at that instant
that Anna decided that she really liked Juanita. Anna
couldn't believe that this was the same glamorous woman
from the pages of all those magazines. She would have
never imagined that the bigger-than-life Juanita Darrell
could be so . . . real.

"So, do you think I should go back to the table and
apologize before I leave?" Anna asked.

Juanita shooed the idea away. "The next time we get
together, it will be forgotten. Trust me, they'd much
rather live in their perfect little fantasy worlds than hold

a grudge. Besides, everything you said was completely true."

"What?" Fear flooded Anna's eyes. "What do you mean?"

"Oh, no. Not that. I don't mean Donald Jackson. As far as I know, he really did kill himself. I mean all that crap about their husbands being Eagle Scouts."

Anna's tension eased instantly. "That did seem a little odd."

"Like I said, they live in a fantasy world. They worship their lifestyles so much that they pretend not to see what's staring them right in the face. Me, I refuse to play head games with myself. I ignore it because I choose to ignore it."

"Ignore what, exactly?" Anna asked with some hesitation.

Juanita remained silent a moment. Then she sighed and said, "When they go off on their little trips, they literally disappear off the face of the earth for days. They're completely out of contact, not just from us but from the entire world. Why?"

"What do you mean? When I called, you said it was because they're in an isolated location."

"Right. I told you that crap because that's the crap they tell us. But come on, you're a smart lady."

Anna was puzzled. "I don't know what you mean. Maybe I'm not as smart as you think."

Juanita chuckled. "Ever hear of a satellite phone? You

can make a call from anywhere on the planet with one. And I mean anywhere. I asked Damon to get one for when he goes on these trips, just for emergencies, and he completely refused. It's the twenty-first century, for God's sake. And those men have enough money to buy a whole satellite, much less a satellite phone. The only reason our husbands are out of touch is because they want to be out of touch. Plain and simple. Whatever they're doing on these so-called camping trips, they don't want us or anyone else to know about it."

"But wait. Donald Jackson was pulled out of the river. I read that. That has to mean that they really go camping. At least that part of their story is real, right?"

Juanita shrugged. "I guess. But why do they need to be unreachable if it's just a camping trip?"

Anna began to feel overwhelmed. She tried to reassure herself that Martin would never betray their marriage, but she quickly realized that, like the other wives, she was idealizing her man to soothe her own fears. Put in the wrong situation, she believed that any man could lose his footing, even Martin, as much as she hated to admit it. Anna looked at Juanita. "Okay, so what do we do?"

Juanita laughed. "We deal with it." She nodded toward the restroom door. "Those women at our table, they deal with it by pretending that their husbands are saints. Me, I deal with it by calling it what it is, the cost of living a life that most women can only dream about. Our husbands are rich and powerful men, and your husband will be one soon too. These are men who can have anything and do anything they want. Okay, every once in a while they run off to some mysterious place and do Lord knows what, but then they come back home. They come back home to us, the women they love."

"But aren't you curious? Don't you want to know what they're up to?"

Juanita shook her head. "Nah, let them have their little secret. And you and I, we'll have ours."

"What secret is that?"

Juanita smiled like the devil. "That we're onto them."

59

Martin sat alone in his bedroom, watching the clock and waiting. Trying to remain calm.

Earlier that evening, at the dinner table, only one comment was made about the upcoming ritual. When everyone first sat down, Dr. Kasim, in a formal tone, informed Martin that after dinner he was to return directly to his room, where Damon would collect him at eight p.m. to escort him to the initiation ceremony. When Martin asked where this mysterious ceremony would take place, Dr. Kasim and the others simply ignored the question.

Martin resisted asking any further questions. He didn't want to appear too worried, and he was also quite certain that none of the men would offer him any clue. For all he knew, watching the new guy squirm with worry was an appetizer for the night's upcoming festivities. That was certainly true for Carver; he was clearly enjoying Martin's anxiety. More than once Martin looked up from his plate and caught a gleam of amused anticipation in Carver's eyes. Whatever Dr. Kasim had planned for Martin, it was obvious that Carver was champing at the bit to get to it already.

Martin glanced over at the clock beside his bed: 7:55.

Just five more minutes and it would be time to get some answers. The butterflies in his stomach seemed to multiply in number. Martin took a deep breath and tried to calm himself. It was only an initiation. How bad could it be? But even as he thought these words, Martin could not ignore that tiny yet persistent warning voice in the back of his mind: *It could be bad. It could be really bad. There's a damn good chance that it could be that one awful thing that you don't even want to think about.*

Martin gave his head a little shake, as if he could fling loose the dark thought from his synapses. But it held fast, like an old song you can't get out of your skull. No matter how hard he tried to convince himself that Damon and the others would never expect him to do such a thing, the possibility was too real to deny. The initiation could be murder.

Martin had never been a member of a fraternity or a cult, but he knew that a typical initiation ceremony could range anywhere from something harmless, like swearing a solemn oath or performing a humiliating act, all the way to the unthinkable: cold-blooded murder. And usually it was the groups who were engaged in malicious activities, the secret organizations with the most to hide, that levied the initiation fee of human sacrifice. Like the street gangs that required an act of random murder before you could join their ranks, or a crime syndicate in which membership wasn't truly achieved until you'd killed for the family. The high price of entry into these groups was due to their illicit nature. They had the most to lose if details ever got out, so they made absolutely certain that anyone allowed in would put loyalty to the group above all else and take their secrets to the grave.

That's what was troubling Martin. What secret could be more vital to protect than what was going on at Forty Acres?

When you put it into perspective, the truth became obvious. The initiation into Dr. Kasim's club wasn't going to be a simple swearing-in. It couldn't be. There was too much at stake here, and these men were too smart to admit anyone so easily. Then Martin remembered Dr. Kasim's comments about his ancestry. The only way they could know that for certain was to do a DNA test. And if they knew that, what else did they know about him? His financials? His medical history? And what about Anna? Did they probe every inch of her life as well? Was she, without knowing it, in the same danger he was?

Martin glanced at the clock: 7:59. One minute.

If some sort of murder was required, what would he do? He needed a plan. An excuse to get out of harming someone.

That's when that little voice in his head changed its tune. *You have to do it.* The logic was simple, of course. If faced with sacrificing one man to save dozens, he would have to do it. The police would understand, wouldn't they? Of course there was a possibility that they wouldn't. The law had a habit of being really stubborn when it came to murder. They might not believe his story. They could say he changed his mind after fleeing, anything. The legal ramifications swirled in Martin's mind until he realized one truth: it didn't matter. It didn't matter what the police said. Right now, in this moment, Martin knew it was the right thing to do. It was the only way that he was going to rescue all those people, and the only way he was ever going to get back to Anna. It didn't matter what they asked him to do. He had to do whatever it took to get back to civilization. Even if it meant murder.

There was a soft knock at his bedroom door. Martin glanced at the clock by the bed. Eight o'clock on the dot.

Martin opened the door and Damon stood on the threshold. His usual sly smile was gone. He laid a firm grip on Martin's shoulder. "You ready?"

60

Martin asked no questions as he trailed Damon across the moonlit compound. The storm clouds that loomed earlier in the day had moved on. The twinkling sky above was now as clear as glass. Martin felt as if every star in heaven were watching him at that moment. That the universe had paused. The future of everything seemed to hinge on his ability to pass the test that he was about to face.

They walked down a stone-lined dirt path that cut through a brief stand of pines. The earthy crunch of their footsteps and the pillow talk of night creatures were the only sounds. The muted outdoor lamps that illuminated the path attracted churning swarms of gnats and a few fluttering moths.

They emerged from the narrow path into an open field, and finally Martin could see where Damon was leading him. Fifty yards ahead loomed a large horse barn. Unlike the other structures on the compound that appeared to be meticulously maintained, the barn's wood-plank facade was pitted and weather-beaten. Whether the barn's decrepit appearance was intentional to add character to the place or truly the result of neglect was impossible to tell, but to Martin one thing was certain: he did not like it. The brooding and rotted structure looked like a bad place where bad things happened. The closer they got to the old barn, the tighter the knot grew in Martin's gut.

One barn door was cracked open and a glow of warm light could be seen within. "They're not going to ask me to ride a horse, are they?" Martin asked, trying to make light. "I mean, I really suck at horses."

"No horses in there," Damon replied flatly, without looking at him. Damon just kept marching forward, quiet and distant. His cold single-mindedness ratcheted up Martin's fear another notch.

A few steps before they reached the barn, Damon paused and turned to Martin. Squeezed Martin's shoulder. "Whatever happens in there," Damon whispered, "do not show weakness. You must be strong. Got it?"

For three weeks Martin had battled the man in court, and never had he seen Damon Darrell appear more serious. Fighting an invisible battle to push back his fear, Martin met Damon's gaze and nodded. "I got it."

Damon patted Martin on the arm. "They're waiting. Let's go inside."

61

The first thing that struck Martin when he entered the horse barn was its emptiness. He expected the interior of the old building to be strewn with rusted farming equipment, the walls shrouded in monstrous cobwebs. Instead the high-ceilinged structure had been stripped to its timber columns and rafters. All that remained were ten vacant horse stalls, five on each side, that ran the length of the space. Vintage oil-lamp-style electric sconces infused the barn with a dim glow that left the empty stalls in shadow.

Dr. Kasim, Oscar, Carver, Kwame, Tobias, and Solomon were gathered near the center of the barn. With the exception of their elderly leader, they were all dressed in simple black suits, with black collared shirts and black ties. Dr. Kasim was draped in a full-length black dashiki trimmed with ornate gold embroidery. Perched upon Dr. Kasim's head was a matching kufi hat. The kufi hat's embroidered design was so elaborate and striking that the doctor appeared to be wearing a golden crown.

The men stared at Martin in silence. The warm, brotherly smiles that had lured him so far away from home were gone. In their place were expressions so stern and frosty that Martin barely recognized the men.

There were also two black-garbed security guards flanking the main door. Both men wore hard stares and had handguns ready at their hips. During his stay Martin had encountered several members of Dr. Kasim's private army, but these two he did not recognize. Martin watched as the two guards pulled the creaking barn doors shut, swung down a wooden latch, then retook their original positions.

Staring at those huge locked doors, Martin couldn't help wondering if he would ever see the outside of the barn again.

Damon gave Martin a quick, supportive pat on the back, then he crossed to join Dr. Kasim and the other men. The instant Damon fell into their ranks, his face, like those of his colleagues, turned to stone.

Dr. Kasim, leaning on his walking stick, took a few steps forward. His steady, wizened eyes scanned Martin from head to toe. This inspection was slow and careful, as if the old man's ghostly orbs could somehow scrutinize every cell in Martin's body.

The unease gnawed at Martin. But he fought the urge to speak. Finally Dr. Kasim's eyes met Martin's. More tense seconds as the doctor held him with an unblinking stare. Martin could almost feel the doctor's will. The urge to avert his gaze was overwhelming, but Martin held fast. He knew what would happen at any sign of weakness.

When the old man finally spoke, his voice wasn't much more than a whisper, but each word still seemed to boom in Martin's mind. "Brother Zantu, are you ready to restore your dignity and honor?"

Martin nodded.

"Speak up," Dr. Kasim said.

Martin's mouth was dry. He swallowed. Forced his lips apart. "Yes."

"Are you ready to avenge the torture and murder of your African ancestors?"

Martin knew it wasn't enough to just say what they wanted to hear. He had to sell it. Had to make them believe that he shared their passion. "Yes," Martin replied with more conviction, not just in his voice but also in his stance, straighter, holding his head high. "Yes, Doctor. I'm ready."

The faintest smile creased Dr. Kasim's face. "Good." The doctor turned to the right side of the barn and pointed his walking stick at the center stall. "The object of your vengeance waits for you in there."

Martin felt a rush of dread. The Dutch doors on every stall in the barn were wide open, except for the stall that Dr. Kasim pointed to. Not only was that door closed, it was locked by two rusted slide bolts. Something was imprisoned inside that stall, and Martin felt pretty certain that it wasn't a horse.

Dr. Kasim motioned the other men back, allowing Martin a clear path to the selected stall. Martin understood what he was supposed to do next, but fear froze his feet to the ground.

"What are you waiting for?" Carver said. "Open it."

Dr. Kasim motioned Carver quiet, then turned back to Martin. "Go on, brother."

The other men continued staring; he caught only the slightest nod of encouragement from Damon. The lawyer's final words of advice resounded in Martin's head: *Whatever happens . . . be strong.*

Taking the first step felt like pulling his foot out of wet concrete. But then Martin was moving. One heavy step after another. The crunch of dirt underfoot was almost as loud as his racing heart. Martin could feel the stares following him. He could hear the shuffle of their feet as the men converged behind him.

The instant Martin paused before the stall door, he heard a muffled whimper from within. The pitiful, terrified sound made Martin queasy. *Be strong*, Martin repeated in his mind. *Be strong.*

Dr. Kasim whispered behind him. "Those bolts should open right up."

Martin gripped the handle of the top bolt. The cold, corroded metal flaked in his hand. He yanked the bolt and it slid open with a dull bang. From inside the stall came a startled gasp and more whimpers. Martin did his best to ignore the sounds as he seized the lower bolt. He tried to slide it open gently, but the old bolt would not cooperate. Martin had no choice but to yank the bolt as hard as he could. It slammed open, evoking another feeble gasp from within.

"Good," Dr. Kasim said. "Very good."

A thick, frayed rope with a fat knot on one end served as a handle for the stable door. Martin reached for the rope, but Dr. Kasim stopped him short.

"Wait. Not yet, brother."

Martin yanked back his hand to conceal its trembling.

"Turn and face us."

Martin did as he was told.

The six men flanking the doctor resembled a jury of statues. Dr. Kasim signaled Oscar with a nod. Oscar stepped forward and paused directly in front of Martin. For the first time since entering the barn, Martin noticed that Oscar gripped a small, black leather case. Oscar flipped open the two silver latches but he did not open the case. Instead, he carefully laid the case across his open palms and held it out to Martin. The meaning of this gesture was unmistakable: *You open it.*

Oscar's presentation of the case was executed with a solemn deliberateness that felt almost like a sacred offering.

Dr. Kasim nodded at Martin. "Open it, brother."

Martin reached out and swung the lid up. The scent of old leather and saddle soap filled his nostrils. The case's red silk lining made the black whip resting inside look like a coiled snake lying in a pool of blood. The whip's entire tapering length was constructed of thick, tightly braided rawhide. And at the whip's very tip, a mean frill of knotted leather strips.

"Do you know what kind of whip that is?" Dr. Kasim asked.

It took Martin a great deal of effort to conceal the queer sense of relief that he suddenly felt. Finally, he knew what the initiation would be, and in a twisted way, it made perfect sense. They wanted him to whip one of the slaves. The thought of brutalizing another human being terrified and sickened Martin, but whipping wasn't murder. At least, not usually.

Martin stared at the whip. "It's old," he said. "I'm guessing it was once used on slaves."

Dr. Kasim nodded grimly. "Overseers used to call that type of whip a cowskin. When it came to torturing our ancestors, the cowskin was the white man's favorite tool. Nothing like the bullwhips you see in so-called slavery movies. A cowskin is shorter and meatier. And no fancy wrist snap needed, so there was no chance of missing or striking lightly. Every swing found its mark and left its mark. Not just on the black man's flesh but on the black man's spirit. And those scars have been passed down from generation to generation."

Martin saw the other men nod and hum in agreement, like a congregation affirming the words of their pastor. Even the two guards by the door nodded their heads.

Dr. Kasim pointed a crooked finger at the whip. "But this particular cowskin is quite special. Used to belong to the great-great-grandson of a Mississippi plantation owner. He had it on display in his home. Nicely framed and everything, like some goddamned family heirloom."

The anger in Dr. Kasim's voice was palpable.

"So, twelve years ago," Dr. Kasim continued, "when we abducted the great-great-grandson, we took the cowskin too. And now it's our heirloom. The white man used it to beat down our spirit. Now we use it to take that spirit back."

Behind Dr. Kasim, heads bobbed up and down, the twist of his story music to the men's ears.

Dr. Kasim reached out and squeezed Martin's arm. "Tonight, my Zantu brother, you have the honor of being the redeemer for our suffering ancestors. Pick up the cowskin."

Martin grabbed the old whip by its rigid handle and lifted it out of the case. A few tan scuff marks were the only clues that the well-cared-for whip was an antique. The leather was as supple and flexible as if it were purchased new that very day. But what surprised Martin more was how heavy the weapon was. There was more leather packed into its construction than the tight braiding revealed. Martin let the leather cord uncoil and dangle to the dirt floor. He noticed how balanced the whip felt. Its length was just right—long enough to magnify the full swing of an outstretched arm but short enough to avoid being clumsy. The cowskin seemed perfectly designed to deliver as much punishment as possible.

"Twenty-five lashes, hard and true," Dr. Kasim said.

"Back then that was the typical Negro punishment. That's what you will give back today. No more, no less." Dr. Kasim tilted his head and peered deep into Martin's eyes, as if trying to get a glimpse of the younger man's soul. "Can you do this, brother?"

There it is, Martin thought. *Twenty-five lashes with the cowskin. No one will have to be murdered.* With this certainty, Martin calmed a bit. All he had to do was find the strength to get through the next ten minutes, then the rest should be easy. In two days he'd be back home with Anna and this nightmare would be over. Not just for him but for the dozens of people suffering in Dr. Kasim's slave pit. Martin just hoped that the poor soul locked inside the stall, the person whom he would have to whip, had the strength to survive the next ten minutes as well.

Martin nodded to Dr. Kasim. "Yes. Yes, I'm ready."

Dr. Kasim smiled. "Good. Open it."

Cowskin gripped in his right hand, Martin turned his back to Dr. Kasim and the men and stood facing the stall door. He paused to take a calming breath, then grabbed the knotted rope handle and pulled. The top and lower halves of the Dutch door began to swing open as one. Old hinges groaned as ambient light penetrated deep into the pitch-dark stall to reveal what hung limply on the rear wall.

Martin's stomach flipped; bile rushed into his throat. It took everything he had to hold down his dinner and at the same time conceal his horror from the eyes behind him.

The woman was stark naked, gagged, and strung up by her shackled wrists to a rusted hook. Her skin was so ashen and slick with sweat that she almost seemed to give off her own dim light. Although the woman hung facing the wall, Martin instantly recognized her strawberry-blond hair and her small, curvy figure.

It was Alice.

62

The shackles on Alice's wrist were old and crudely wrought, like the pair on display in Damon's game room. Martin could see rings of blood where iron cut into the girl's flesh. Alice moaned in pain as she twisted her body to peer back over her shoulder at Martin. The sight of those terrified emerald eyes made Martin numb.

Why her? Martin thought. *Out of all the slaves held captive at Forty Acres, why did it have to be Alice?* Martin had mentally prepared himself to do what had to be done, but he wasn't prepared for this. He knew that it shouldn't matter which one of the slaves he had to whip, but the awful truth was it did matter. Inflicting punishment on a complete stranger would be far easier than harming this sweet young girl whom he felt he had come to know intimately. Then it struck Martin, a question that filled him with instant panic. Did they know? Did Dr. Kasim, Oscar, and the others know that he and Alice had faked intercourse? Did they know that he was just playing along with their insanity and that he planned to expose them?

Martin whirled back around to face the men. He expected to confront a wall of hate-filled stares. He expected accusations of race traitor as the guards rushed over to seize him. But none of that happened. From Dr. Kasim and the others, Martin received only stares. Not even a hint of malice.

The exception was Carver. Carver's mocking smirk hit Martin like a knife in the back. Martin realized instantly that Alice's presence had nothing to do with the group's suspicions about his loyalty. It was Carver's doing. For the sole purpose of making Martin's initiation as difficult as possible, Carver had, somehow, convinced the other men to select Alice for the brutal ceremony. Because Carver stood at the rear of the group, the other men could not see the relish on Carver's face as Martin locked stares with him. Martin was onto him but this fact only broadened Carver's smile.

"Something wrong, brother?" Carver asked.

Martin's jaw tightened. He shook his head. "Nothing's wrong. I'm fine."

"You sure? I mean, you're looking a little pale there, my brother."

"I told you, I'm fine," Martin repeated.

"Oh, so you're just stalling, then?"

Martin could not respond. He knew that if he did, the wrong thing might come out, so he was thankful when Dr. Kasim turned and leveled Carver with a silencing stare. The doctor then turned back to Martin, exuding a fatherly calm. "The fear you feel is natural," he said. "We're not evil like the white man. Violence does not come naturally to us. But we are forced to do violence to set things right. Do you understand?"

Martin nodded. It was to Martin's advantage to play along with the assumption that he was nervous before the task at hand. The less he had to hide his true emotions, the easier his role at Forty Acres would be to play.

"What you do here tonight," Dr. Kasim continued, "is not simply a test of dedication; it is a reclaiming of power. A power that you must learn to wear as comfortably as you would a fine business suit." He gestured toward the stall. "Now, please. You must continue."

Martin began to turn but stopped short. He had know. He had to ask the question, but to avoid suspicion he had to ask it just right. He jerked his head indifferently toward Alice. "Why this one?"

There was an awkward pause, then an exchange of glances among the men. Martin's pulse raced. Had he gone too far? The thin smile on Carver's lips seemed to answer yes. It was Dr. Kasim who spoke. "Why does that matter to you, brother?"

Martin shook his head. "It doesn't. Not really. It's just . . . I had a good time with her last night. I was looking forward to a repeat performance."

There was another strained pause, but the tension was broken when Damon snickered. Tobias and Kwame cracked small smiles. But this departure from ceremonial composure was fleeting; in the blink of an eye the men's faces had returned to stone.

Dr. Kasim shook his head at Martin. "It's unwise to become attached to the property. Very unwise."

Martin nodded. "I understand."

Dr. Kasim peered past him, deep into the dark stall. He exhibited no sympathy for the whimpering woman inside. "This one has broken our rules and must be severely punished. That's all you need to know. Now, we've wasted enough time. Please begin."

Martin turned back around to face the stall. He passed through the open doorway.

Approximately twelve feet of open space separated him from the rear wall and Alice. The cowskin whip that hung heavy in Martin's grip was about half that length. He had to move closer.

Hearing his approaching footsteps, Alice glanced back over her shoulder like a frightened animal. She spotted the whip in Martin's hand and became frantic. She squirmed and shook her head and screamed "No!" through the rags jammed in her mouth. The shackles rattled and thudded against the wooden wall.

With each closing step Martin tried to hold Alice's gaze with his, but she was too terrified. Her darting eyes were too flooded with tears.

Martin paused at the halfway point. The darkness of the stall and the distance between him and his watchful audience gave Martin the confidence to whisper, "Alice."

Alice found Martin's gaze. The moment lasted no

longer than a single breath, but that was long enough for Martin's eyes to say, *I'm sorry*.

Martin lashed out with the cowskin. A fast, overhand swing. There was no crack of air, just the sharp slap of leather striking skin and Alice's muffled scream. Her body jerked; there was a bloody gash down her back.

The sight of Alice's torn flesh roiled Martin's stomach again. He had to swallow to keep from vomiting.

"One," came a shout from behind him. It was Oscar's voice. "Harder."

Martin whipped the cowskin across Alice's back again. Alice cried out as a gash appeared on her shoulder blade.

"Two," Oscar called out. "Still harder."

Martin knew they'd notice if he tried to pull his swing too much, but he thought that he might get away easing up a little. Now he saw it was no good. The mechanics of swinging a whip made it impossible to fake. He had no choice but to use all the power he could muster.

Martin swung for a third time. The force of the whip's contact nearly snatched the handle from his grip. Alice's head snapped back. She wailed mournfully.

"Three. That's good, brother. Keep going."

Martin swung the cowskin again, and again, and again. Each stinging strike was answered by a convulsive jerk and grunts of pain from Alice. By the time Martin reached ten lashes, Alice hung limp in her chains. Blood seeping from deep slashes in her back trailed over her buttocks and down the back of her pale thighs. But far worse was Alice's crying. Her entire body trembled with feeble, whimpering sobs. The urge to drop the whip, free Alice from her chains, and pull her into his arms tugged hard at Martin's soul. His eyes burned, verging on tears, but he squeezed back his grief and kept swinging.

"Fifteen."

His brain and body ached with the effort to remain focused, but with each swing of the whip, with each muffled shriek from Alice, he could feel the facade slipping away. Martin did not know how much longer he could last.

"Twenty."

Martin couldn't bear to see the whip claw into Alice's back again, so he delivered the last five lashes with his eyes closed. He didn't care if he missed. He didn't care if they saw him miss. He just wanted it to end. Martin lashed out at the dark, over and over until finally he heard Oscar shout—

"Twenty-five. You're done."

Martin's hands dropped to his sides. Hesitantly, he peeled opened his eyes.

Alice, her butchered back drenched in blood, dangled before him. Motionless.

63

The fear that Alice might be dead smothered Martin. His lungs ached for air, but he couldn't take a breath. He couldn't shut his eyes from the horror before him. He couldn't move a muscle. The only sound was the thump of his hammering heart.

Then Alice's foot twitched.

She moaned and stirred weakly. She was barely conscious, but she was alive.

Martin breathed again. He took a moment to slip back on his mask of indifference, then turned and rejoined the men outside the stall.

Instead of stony stares Martin was greeted with welcoming smiles. After the brutality that the men had just witnessed, brutality executed by his hand, the sight of their happy faces struck Martin as particularly monstrous. The simple act of curling his mouth into a smile took every ounce of willpower he had left.

Even Dr. Kasim was smiling proudly. "You have done your ancestors proud," he said to Martin. "Now, brother, you are truly one of us." The old man spread his arms wide. The staff in his hand and the grand spread of his dashiki gave Dr. Kasim the air of an African king. With a small motion of his hands, he beckoned Martin to approach.

The other men watched as Martin stepped forward and shared an embrace with their leader.

The hug was firm and gentle at the same time. The doctor's hair had a sweet, musky aroma. Oddly, Martin was reminded of being wrapped in his mother's arms, rather than his father's.

The moment the two men parted, Oscar laid a firm hand on Martin's shoulder. Dr. Kasim's second in command didn't utter a single word. He simply nodded with approval, then sealed the moment with a brief hug.

Damon Darrell threw an arm around Martin like a proud older brother. "I told you guys he had the right stuff." He yanked Martin toward him. "You made it, Grey. You're truly one of us now."

Tobias pulled Martin into a smothering bear hug. "I knew you could do it, brother."

Both Kwame and Solomon also congratulated Martin with hugs.

Carver approached him last. The young entrepreneur surprised Martin with a big crooked smile that actually appeared genuine. "You're tougher than you look, Grey. I'll give you that. Congratulations, brother."

Was it possible that after doing his damnedest to undermine Martin at every turn, Carver had finally come around? Scratching Carver's enmity from his list of worries would have been a great relief. Unfortunately, this small hope disintegrated in Martin's mind the instant Carver wrapped his arms around him. The hugs from the other men were truly heartfelt and accepting. Even Oscar's stiff embrace still managed to radiate a sense of camaraderie. But the hug from Carver was mechanical and cold, more like a wrestling hold than a display of brotherhood. In those empty seconds, as they stood heart to heart, Martin realized that despite everything that he had just gone through, Carver's attitude toward him remained unchanged. Even more troubling, as the two men parted, Carver whispered, "Now we're really gonna have some fun."

The ominous twinkle in Carver's eyes made the man's meaning clear. *There was something far worse to come.* But what? The initiation was over. Glancing back into the stall, seeing poor Alice's torn body hanging there, Martin found the idea of something worse very hard to imagine.

Then Martin realized that he still held the cowskin. He wrapped it into a coil and tried to hand it back to Oscar. "Here you go."

But Oscar did not take it.

Confusion and dread hit Martin like a slap when, instead of accepting the whip, Oscar just shook his head and said, "We're not done here yet."

64

Foolish girl," Dr. Kasim said. He frowned at the bloodied form that hung limply in the dark stall. "She has committed a crime that demands a punishment far more severe than twenty-five lashes."

"What exactly did she do?" Martin asked.

The doctor offered no reply. Instead he turned and signaled Carver with the slightest nod.

Martin felt a jolt of anger as he stood with the other men in the middle of the barn watching Carver Lewis gingerly unbutton his shirt. Carver winced as he reached for each button. Martin couldn't tell if Carver was acting or if the bastard was truly in pain, but of one thing Martin was absolutely certain: whatever Carver was about to reveal under that shirt was a lie. Martin knew that Carver had somehow persuaded the other men to choose Alice for the initiation. Now Martin was going to see how. But what gnawed at Martin's insides more was that he could do absolutely nothing about it. He was helpless to save her. "Never take the side of a slave against a master." That was the takeaway from the morning tour of the mine. A stern lesson that Martin assured Damon he understood.

Carver unfastened the final button, then flung his shirt

to Tobias. Carver's torso was lean and muscular, with taut six-pack abs. Even dressed, Carver appeared to be in exceptional shape, but Martin never expected the real estate huckster to possess the physique of a world-class athlete.

Dr. Kasim said to Carver, "Now turn. Show Martin what the girl did to you."

The other men already seemed to know the details of Alice's offense. Martin was the only one still left unaware.

Carver pivoted to present his back to the group.

The angry red scratches that raked across Carver's shoulder blades resembled claw marks from some savage beast.

"See what that bitch did to me?" Carver said as he glared into the stall at the target of his accusations. "She attacked me for no reason. She's crazy."

Alice moaned "No" through her gag and shook her head so weakly that her chains barely rattled. The sight stung Martin and at the same time confirmed Carver's cruelty. If the other men noticed Alice's delirious denial, they gave no indication.

Then Carver turned back to face Martin. "So, what do you think, Grey?" he asked. "How many more lashes should that whore get for what she did to me?"

Martin's knees began to feel weak again, and his right hand, the hand clutching the cowskin, began to tremble. He couldn't believe that this was happening. He couldn't believe that they actually wanted him to hurt Alice again.

"Come on, Grey." Carver's lips were taut with the effort to hold back a smirk. "How many more? Ten? Twenty? Thirty? Give me a number."

Martin wanted to shout out at the top of his lungs, *None! She's had enough!* Even better, he wanted to strangle Carver with the whip. But all he could do was shake his head and feign confusion. "I don't know. How do you decide these things?"

"We don't," Oscar said, frowning wearily at Carver. "The doctor decides all punishments. And as Mr. Lewis is well aware, it has already been decided." Oscar turned to the group's leader. "Your instructions were fifty lashes in total, correct?"

Dr. Kasim nodded. "Yes. So the girl is to receive twenty-five more."

Martin's heart stopped. Twenty-five more lashes? The idea was unthinkable. He glanced at Damon and at the other men, hoping to see any sign of sympathy for the girl. Hoping to spot someone who might side with him if he dared speak up. But all Martin found were cold stares, the faces of men whose humanity had been eroded away by hatred. They were indifferent to Alice's suffering through the first beating, and just as indifferent to the fact that twenty-five more lashes would almost certainly kill her.

"Let's get on with it," Dr. Kasim grumbled. "Then we can get back and have a little celebration in Martin's honor."

While the other men murmured their agreement,

Martin felt something give way inside him. It was as if the mental dam that he had formed to hold back his emotions had suddenly cracked a leak. He couldn't do it. He just couldn't hurt Alice again. And no amount of logic or rationalization regarding the greater good could change that physical reality. At that instant Martin just knew that he no longer had it in him.

But he had to do something. He couldn't just refuse. That was too risky. For all he knew, doubling the slave's punishment was a test. A regular part of the initiation designed to catch the initiate with his guard down.

The solution came easily to Martin, because there was no solution. His only choice was to tell the truth. He'd just tell Dr. Kasim that he couldn't bring himself to hurt Alice again. What Dr. Kasim's and the other men's reactions would be, he wasn't sure. More than likely they'd see his perceived weakness as a threat, but there was another possibility. Maybe, just maybe, they'd lay the blame on his fledgling status at Forty Acres. Like when he lost his cool in the mine: Damon did chastise him, but he let it slide as a rookie move. Maybe it would be the same now in the barn. Maybe there was an unspoken grace period that could save his life. Maybe. But deep down, Martin knew this was bullshit. Deep down, he could still hear Damon's last piece of advice, echoing. Advice that now sounded more like a warning. *Be strong. Be strong.*

The truth was, after whipping a helpless girl to within an inch of her life, Martin Grey was all out of strong.

345

Martin took a nervous breath, then turned to face Dr. Kasim. He opened his mouth to speak, but before he could get a word out, the cowskin was snatched from his hand.

Martin turned and saw something that froze him— Carver, still bare-chested, cowskin in hand, taking practice swings at the thin air. The loud *whoosh, whoosh, whoosh* of the whip reverberated through the rafters. Carver took a final swing, then gave the cowskin handle an upward jerk, causing the frilled tip to flip backward. Carver caught the tip with expert ease, then turned and winked at Martin. "My turn."

Realization screamed in Martin's head. He'd had it all wrong. His initiation truly was over. They didn't want *him* to give Alice twenty-five more lashes. That job went to Carver. Carver was the one offended, supposedly, so Carver got to mete out the punishment. It all made terrifying sense. And it chilled Martin to the core.

Martin could only stand there watching as Carver crossed the threshold into the stall.

When Alice glanced back and saw Carver looming with the cowskin, she found new energy. She writhed and struggled desperately, screaming into her gag.

Carver seemed fueled by the sight. He swished the whip in the dirt between him and Alice, teasing out the moment before the first strike.

As much as Martin did not want to swing the whip himself, he also didn't want to watch Carver whip Alice to death. But he couldn't look away because he himself was being watched. From the moment Carver stepped into the stall with Alice, Martin noticed that he was receiving glances from several of the men, including Dr. Kasim and Oscar. *Was* this part of the initiation then? Were they expecting him to crack?

Martin felt a hand on his arm. It was Damon. "You okay?"

Martin nodded stiffly. "Fine. I'm fine."

Damon leaned closer and whispered, "Then wipe that look off your face."

So, that was it. Martin wasn't aware of any "look," but the deluge of emotions that he was experiencing at that moment, everything from horror to sorrow, was nearly impossible to stem. Martin redoubled his focus. He slowed his breathing, clamped down on his jaw, and turned his face to stone.

The muscles in Carver's back and arm bulged as he unleashed the first strike. The crack of leather cutting flesh filled the barn, muffling Alice's scream.

Martin flinched.

Oscar shouted, "One!"

65

Martin couldn't watch and he couldn't shut his eyes, so he focused on a dark knot in one of the wood planks that made up the stall's rear wall. To anyone watching he would appear to be riveted to the brutality before him, but only the blur of the whip invaded his peripheral vision. The sharp report of the striking weapon was impossible to ignore. Martin flinched at each crack and could only hope that no one noticed. After the first few lashes from Carver, he heard not a scream or a whimper from Alice, and this terrified him.

"Twenty-five," Oscar called out. "That's it."

Carver coiled the cowskin whip into a loose loop, then swiped the back of his hand across his moist brow. His chest heaved as his exerted breathing settled back to normal. The deed was done. Carver gave his handiwork a final, satisfied glance, then emerged from the stall.

The instant Carver cleared the doorway, Oscar entered and inspected the limp, blood-soaked body. Careful to avoid staining his suit, Oscar pressed two fingers to Alice's carotid artery. After a brief pause, he repositioned his fingers. Another pause, then he moved his fingers again.

Martin observed these post-whipping activities through a dazed fog. He felt numb, shell-shocked. And at that instant, as he watched Oscar search Alice's neck for a pulse, his breathing ceased. The other men around him, even the barn, seemed to fade from perception. Every atom of Martin's being was focused on Oscar's face, desperate to see a sign, any sign. *Please let her be alive*, Martin begged the universe. *Please!*

Forsaking Alice's carotid, Oscar lifted his two fingers to Alice's right temple and pressed firmly. There was a pause that seemed to go on for an eternity. Finally, Oscar's detached features revealed a brief, indecipherable frown. Martin had to wait for Oscar to reemerge from the stall and move to Dr. Kasim's side before learning Alice's fate.

"She's alive," Oscar said to the doctor with the bend of surprise in his voice. "Barely, but definitely alive."

Martin's lungs released and he had to clench his diaphragm to avoid sighing aloud. Alice's raw open wounds were critical, he knew that, but she was alive. If she could hang on just two more days, long enough for Martin to get home and contact the authorities, then she could, she might— These desperate hopes were shattered prematurely by what Dr. Kasim said next.

"Leave the girl where she is." The doctor appeared neither pleased nor displeased with the report of Alice's survival. "If she's still breathing in the morning, have her wounds dressed and transfer her to the mine."

Martin felt a sustained plummeting sensation, as if a

trapdoor had been sprung open beneath his soul. His eyes fell to the bottom of the stall. To the droplets of blood that trickled steadily from Alice's toes into the stained soil beneath her. A red, muddy stain that grew larger by the minute. *Drip, drip, drip.* Alice's life leaking away.

It was clear to Martin that without proper care the sad, sweet girl with strawberry-blond hair would never be able to survive her injuries an entire night.

Dr. Kasim had just given Alice a death sentence.

66

"It's called sorghum beer," Dr. Kasim said. "It's an African beer. Home-brewed."

"Yeah, well, it looks like puke," Tobias said. "Kind of smells like puke too."

The men laughed, Martin along with them, but there was no levity in his heart. His thoughts were still in the barn, still with Alice. The image of her hanging by her shackled wrists, alone in the dark, dying, was as vivid as the cackling men seated beside him.

After leaving the barn and poor Alice to her fate, the men retired to Dr. Kasim's library to celebrate Martin's initiation with a drink. They were all settled in armchairs around the fireplace. Dr. Kasim, tall in his high-back leather throne that only looked like a chair, was the center of attention as usual. Martin took notice that Oscar was seated with the group as well. During the last gathering inside the library, Oscar served guard duty by the door, but this time he sat directly beside Dr. Kasim. With his legs crossed and his hands folded, Oscar, like a faithful pet, appeared quite content just to be at his master's side.

At the very center of the group, atop a low coffee table, rested an old African wooden bowl. About the size of a punch bowl, the wood was dark grained and its exterior was decorated with a simple hand-carved geometric pattern.

Inside the bowl was a surprise for the group from Dr. Kasim—a pale yellow, milky substance flecked with black and tan grain pellets. Dr. Kasim called the concoction a traditional African drink, but the scowling faces around the table seemed to side with Tobias's assessment. The stuff looked foul.

Even Martin found himself wrenched from thoughts of Alice when the African brew's sour odor reached his nostrils.

Dr. Kasim, unsurprised and undeterred by the group's initial repulsion, just smiled patiently. "I had it brewed specially, right here in my kitchen, from a very old recipe. Just for this evening." Then his smile vanished. "I'd be greatly disappointed if each of you didn't at least try it."

The men grew tense with dread. Disappointing the old man was clearly not an option.

Dr. Kasim's small smile resurfaced as he scanned reluctant faces. "So, who's first?"

Martin was surprised to see Carver's hand go up, but he wasn't surprised when, instead of volunteering, Carver straightened his arm and pointed a finger at him. "Grey should go first. I mean, it's his big night, right?"

Desperate to escape being the first guinea pig, the other men sided with Carver. Even Oscar pivoted his head to Dr. Kasim and said, "Mr. Lewis does make a good point, sir."

Dr. Kasim acknowledged the consensus with a nod, but as he turned to Martin, Martin beat him to the punch.

"It would be my pleasure," Martin said.

Everyone looked impressed, even Carver.

Martin just wanted to keep things moving. He was desperate for this nightmarish evening to end so that he could retreat to the privacy of his room. Beneath his forced smiles, Martin's emotions were in a maelstrom and he wasn't sure how much longer he could hold it together.

Dr. Kasim rewarded Martin's pluck with a pleased smile, then gestured to a gourd ladle resting beside the wooden bowl. The ladle was just as old as the bowl, but the worn native carvings on the handle were distinctly different.

"Please enjoy, brother," Dr. Kasim said.

Martin picked up the ladle and dipped it into the milky beer. The men watched with pursed faces as he lifted it to his mouth and took a sip.

The consistency was thick like mucus and gritty. The flavor was sour yet surprisingly fruity. Martin swallowed. The aftertaste was awful. A rancid paste coated the inside of his mouth and sent his salivary glands into overdrive, causing his face to screw up in utter disgust.

The men cracked up at the sight. Even Dr. Kasim couldn't resist a little laugh.

"Oh, come on, son," Solomon said between chuckles, "it can't taste all that bad."

"It's worse," Martin said, still unable to relax his clenched face. "Much worse."

The men laughed again. Dr. Kasim nodded to Martin as if to say, *Good job*, then said aloud, "Now you pick who goes next."

The laughter retreated as Martin scanned the circle of men. His weighing stares were merely a pretense. He already knew whom he was going to select. Martin extended the ladle to Carver. "Drink up," he said with a smile.

Carver seemed to feed off the new guy's push-back. He returned Martin's smile, then snatched the ladle, dipped it deep into the beer, and drank. Not just a sip, as Martin had done. Carver tossed his head back and gulped down every last drop in the ladle.

There were sounds of astonishment from the men as Carver strained to keep the toxic stuff down. His jaw tightened, his eyes squeezed, his head cocked side to side, until finally Carver relaxed and cracked his familiar crooked smile. "Not bad."

A burst of laughter and applause. Carver gloated as he watched Martin join in on the accolades.

None of the remaining men even came close to matching Carver's feat. Tobias, the biggest man in the group, sheepishly ventured only the tiniest sip. Solomon's brief taste was on par with Martin's, just enough to repulse him without making him sick. Damon, smartly, swallowed so fast that he barely had time to taste it. Kwame, accustomed to a gentle, all-natural diet, suffered the worst reaction. After only a sip the ad exec had to clamp both hands over his mouth to keep from retching the foul liquid back into the bowl.

When the gourd ladle reached Oscar, Martin and the others watched carefully. They were all eager to see the pungent ale put a dent in Dr. Kasim's lieutenant's titanium facade.

They were all disappointed.

Oscar's reaction to the drink was as calm and measured as the man himself. He simply dipped, sipped, and swallowed. No sour face, no gagging, no commentary, nothing. It was as if he had taken a cool sip of water.

Dr. Kasim received the ladle last. The men settled into silence and waited for their leader to partake.

Leaning on his staff, Dr. Kasim tilted forward in his seat and filled the ladle with the milky beer. He raised it to his mouth, but instead of drinking, he took a long sniff. "Oh, it's horrible," the doctor said, recoiling in disgust. "How could any of you drink this swill?" He flung the ladle into the bowl, splashing beer onto the table and floor.

As Dr. Kasim eased back into his seat, Martin gaped in utter confusion. What the hell was going on? Damon, Carver, Solomon, Tobias, and Kwame were also staring baffled at the doctor. Only Oscar appeared to be unrattled by the moment. He just sat there shaking his head, wearing an odd expression. He almost looked amused.

Then it struck Martin. The men had warned him about Dr. Kasim's quirky sense of humor. Was it possible? Could this all be a joke?

As if he could hear Martin's thoughts, Dr. Kasim broke out in a sudden burst of hearty laughter. He shrugged at the group and said, "You were all perfectly free to say no."

The men groaned and sighed and shook their heads in disbelief. Martin couldn't believe it either. It was just a joke. A prank.

Tobias pointed an accusing finger at Oscar. "Hey, did you know about this?"

Oscar frowned. "If I did, do you think that I would actually have drunk it?"

"What is that crap, anyway?" Kwame said, scowling at the bowl as if it were an old enemy. "Is that really a traditional African beer?"

"Of course," Dr. Kasim said, his mouth turned downward, "and I still wouldn't touch the stuff. You know, some of our African brothers eat monkey meat. Me, I prefer steak."

All the men laughed.

"Hey, Martin," Damon said, "now that you've been victimized by one of the old man's jokes, you're truly one of us."

Everyone nodded in agreement, including Dr. Kasim. "Damon's right," the doctor said to Martin. "This was an amusing way to welcome you into the fold. But there's more to it." Dr. Kasim turned to address the other men and gestured toward the bowl of African beer. "Some black folks still drink that crap, just for the sake of maintaining a pointless tradition. As black men you must never forget this. Tradition is your enemy. Tradition is for the weak and the poor to make them feel like they have something. Sure, there are a few good traditions, like a man caring for and protecting his family. Like a wife standing by her husband. But most traditions are shackles, ignorant, primitive beliefs that do nothing but hold you back. You think the white puppeteers who run this world give a damn about traditions? They *trample* on tradition. So, how do you tell the useful traditions from the non-sense? If it's hurting you and not helping you," he gestured to the beer again, "or if it's making you sick to your stomach, you should probably spit it out."

Martin watched the men acknowledge Dr. Kasim's lesson with earnest nods and murmurs. Then he remembered that he too was now one of the doctor's acolytes. Martin put on a smile and forced a nod, hoping that the gathering was finally nearing an end.

Dr. Kasim reclined in his chair and said with a smile, "Now, how would you gentlemen like some real beer?"

"Please," Tobias begged.

Dr. Kasim signaled to a uniformed male house slave who stood by the door. The slave nodded obediently, then yanked open the library door. Four more uniformed house slaves, another male and three females, entered briskly carrying two silver ice buckets jammed with frosty bottles of Guinness and trays of hors d'oeuvres.

As he watched the men grab for beer and food, Martin realized the evening wasn't winding down at all; no, the party was just getting started. By the look of things Martin would have to keep up the slavemaster act for hours before he'd be able to escape scrutiny. That meant more agonizing hours before he'd be able to shower off the dirt and blood of the crime that he'd been forced to commit. More heart-wrenching hours before he'd be able to burrow beneath the covers and acknowledge what he really felt about the girl bleeding to death in the barn.

"Would you like a beer, master?"

Martin looked up and his heart stopped. Either his eyes were playing tricks on him or the pretty girl standing over him, holding a beer and wearing a pleasant smile, was Alice.

67

Master?"

Martin just gazed at the slave girl. He couldn't help himself. Her strawberry-blond hair, her green eyes, the way her small body filled the maid's outfit, even her voice was similar. She wasn't Alice—that was clear after a few seconds—but the likeness was chilling.

"Are you okay, master?"

Lost for words, Martin nodded and took the beer. He was about to say thank you, then caught himself.

The girl flashed an awkward smile, then backed away. Martin watched as she and the other slaves began to file back out the door carrying away empty trays and the bowl of African beer. He recognized her four coworkers—he had seen them working around the house—but this girl was new.

Behind him, Martin heard Oscar say, "Her name's Felicia."

Martin turned and discovered that all the men, Dr. Kasim included, were watching him. They must have been well aware of Felicia's resemblance to Alice and been waiting to see his reaction.

"They could be sisters," Martin said aloud.

"Felicia and Alice are cousins actually," Oscar said. "They were captured together. Felicia used to work the house grounds. Now she'll replace Alice inside the house."

"Hell," Carver said with a crooked grin, "the way Grey eyeballed that, I'm guessing Felicia will take Alice's place in his bed as well."

Martin feigned amusement, but there was something that Oscar mentioned that jarred him. It was the way he said, "captured together." He sounded as if he were talking about animals and not two human beings.

There was still a great deal about the logistics of operating and concealing a place like Forty Acres that was a mystery to Martin. Those details could prove crucial for the authorities to track down all involved and bring them to justice. Up until now, to avoid suspicion, Martin had kept his probing gentle. But now he was initiated and a full-fledged member of the club. Now he should be able to ask anything.

He turned to Dr. Kasim. "How does it work exactly? How do you capture these . . . slaves?"

Dr. Kasim smiled, amused by the question. "Well, son, I don't do it personally."

"Dr. Kasim actually has a special team for that," Damon said. "Ex-military. Real badasses."

"Are they members of Forty Acres as well?"

Damon shook his head. "No. Not like us. More like the guards who work here. Exclusive confidential contractors."

"Yeah," Carver added. "Our very own in-house hit men. Only these guys are more badass. Ask Tobias. He went on a hunt once."

Tobias nodded. "Carver's right. Those dudes do not play around. They're like ghosts. They can get to anyone, anywhere, anytime. They don't just abduct people, they break their will. And if they don't break—" Tobias shook his head. "Let's just say those brothers scared the shit out of me."

The fact that Dr. Kasim controlled a private strike force that stalked the nation's cities and suburbs chilled Martin even more. "Do these 'contractors' just grab white people off the street?" he asked. "How do they choose their victims?"

"It's not their job to choose," Dr. Kasim said. "It's just their job to hunt and capture. I choose. The people brought here to serve us weren't picked at random. I have researchers as well. They trace bloodlines and family trees. Even do genetic testing. Every slave here is a direct descendant of a major plantation owner or of an individual like a ship captain or slave trader who reaped enormous profits from the bondage of the black man."

"Like the white man's Bible says," Kwame added, "the sins of the father shall be visited upon the sons."

"And the daughters," Carver joked. "Can't leave them out. The white master used our great-great-grandmothers as sex dolls. It's only fair we return the favor with their great-great-granddaughters."

361

Tobias raised his bottle. "Sounds goddamn fair to me."

Martin joined in as the men clinked bottles and sucked beer. But inside, these new facts burned in his brain. Apparently, Forty Acres was a far more complex conspiracy than he'd assumed. Slave hunters, researchers, and, according to what Damon told him earlier, about a dozen more secret members all over the country. Successful black men who crept away from society and civility for a few weekends each year to fatten their egos at Dr. Kasim's hidden retreat. Making this place go away would have a devastating ripple effect.

It struck Martin that the most important piece of information that he could provide to authorities was something he still did not know. Where exactly *was* Forty Acres? Damon had refused him this knowledge earlier for the same reason they had drugged him on Solomon's jet. Details about the location of their private slave camp were far more dangerous than accusations of its existence. Accusations could be denied, spun, and buried, especially by these powerful men. But to be able to direct authorities to the actual scene of the crime would be damn near indisputable.

Martin took a long swallow of his Guinness, then turned to Dr. Kasim. He made an effort to sound as matter-of-fact as possible. "So, Doctor, I'm curious. Where are we really?"

The men quieted. Dr. Kasim's brow furrowed. "I'm not sure I know what you mean, brother."

Martin glanced around from group member to group member. "I was drugged on the plane, I assume because you wanted to keep the real location of this place a secret. Am I right?"

Dr. Kasim looked at Martin a moment, then gave Damon a nod. Damon turned to Martin. "We all felt awful about doing that to you, but when you started questioning the flight plan, we had to do something."

Dr. Kasim offered Martin an apologetic smile. "Certainly, you understand why we must be extra-ordinarily cautious."

"Of course," Martin said. "I get it. But I'm part of this now. And it's really strange not knowing where I am."

"You're a smart young man," Solomon said. "Think about it. Where do you think you are?"

"Well," Martin considered, "when Damon took me to the mine, Roy mentioned that slaves used to work it. I assumed he meant African slaves, so I'm guessing we're not out west. We're somewhere in the South. One of the old slave states. Am I right?"

The men exchanged impressed smiles. Solomon said, "Not bad, son. Keep going."

"Roy also mentioned the first gold rush being in North Carolina," Martin said.

From the men came playful groans and headshakes. Carver made a loud "wrong answer" buzzer sound.

"Good try," Solomon said. "You were close."

"But we are in one of the Southern states," Martin said. "Which one?"

Solomon deferred the question to their leader with a glance.

Dr. Kasim measured Martin for a cautious second, as if he were putting the final stamp of trust on the newcomer before proceeding. The old doctor turned to Oscar and said, "The map, please."

With a wave of his hand, Oscar ordered the slave boy stationed by the door out of the room. Then he crossed the library to an old floor safe that dominated an entire corner. The gray steel behemoth was half the size of a refrigerator and looked old enough to be a prop in a western. Oscar dropped to one knee, worked the dial, then yanked the heavy door open. An instant later Oscar returned to the circle of men, carrying a wide and flat leather binder. To Martin it looked like an oversized photo album that was missing most of its pages. There was no lettering on the cover and, compared to the antique safe, the binder looked fairly new. Tobias and Kwame cleared the coffee table of bottles and plates, making room for Oscar to set down the binder and flip it open.

The first page was a map of West Virginia protected by a clear plastic sleeve. This wasn't a map torn from an atlas or printed from the Internet. This was a one-of-a-kind original.

The map was clearly drawn, lettered, and painted by

hand, but its clean design suggested the work of a professional cartographer. Only major cities like Charleston and Huntington were labeled, preserving the map's uncluttered design. The few colors used were applied sparingly, mostly to accent water features and forested areas.

"Welcome to West Virginia," Dr. Kasim said with a smile.

Martin's puzzled eyes dropped back to the map. "But where?" he said. "I mean, West Virginia isn't exactly uninhabited. Where do you hide a place like this?"

Dr. Kasim glanced at Oscar, who leaned forward and tapped a large patch of green at the very eastern edge of the map. The label read George Washington National Forest. "This is where we are," Oscar said. "Right here."

"That's a national forest," Martin said, perplexed.

"That is correct," Dr. Kasim said. "Largest this side of the Mississippi. Over one million acres. Can you think of a better place to preserve our privacy?"

"But you can't own private property in a national forest."

Carver made that annoying buzzing sound again. "Wrong again, Grey." Carver's voice took on a rapid clip that Martin recognized from his late-night infomercials. "Timber mills, ranches, farms, fisheries, you name it. All private companies allowed to own land smack-dab in the middle of a national forest. What most people don't know is that private individuals can too, if they have enough money and the right connections." Carver glanced around at the titans in the room, then turned back to Martin wearing a smirk. "Need I say more?"

Martin shook his head in amazement. He turned to Dr. Kasim. "All this, right under the nose of the government and the public. Another one of your little jokes?"

Dr. Kasim smiled like he had just swallowed something delicious. He tilted his head toward the open binder. "Turn the page."

Martin did so to find another custom-painted map sealed in a plastic sleeve. This one showed a closer view of Forty Acres and the surrounding wilderness. A large black rectangle encompassing several smaller multicolored rectangles represented the walled compound and the structures within. Prominent land features like hills and rock formations were also detailed. Just north of the compound, a thick, wavy blue stripe snaked across the entire map. Martin recognized it as the river that he and the men had crossed in the 4x4 to reach Forty Acres. Martin searched for the airstrip as well, but failing to spot it, he assumed that its location fell outside the map's range.

"So, how big is this place really?" Martin asked. "It's gotta be more than forty acres."

"Seventy-two acres within the wall," Oscar said. "But we own five square miles—thirty-two hundred acres in total—east of the river. This is the remotest part of the forest, and our private property signs are pretty aggressive to discourage the few campers who do get too close." Oscar swept his hand over the vast greenery that dominated the map. "As you can see, we're pretty isolated out here and we have people in the right places to keep it that way."

It was then that Martin noticed two symbols on the map that seized his attention. The first was at the very top of the sheet, the farthest object on the page from the Forty Acres compound. A spaghetti-thin gray line snaked across the wilderness, from one end of the map to the other. Was it a hiking trail or just a dirt road, or could it actually be a rural highway? The line was unlabeled, so there was no way to tell, but seeing a link to civilization so close to Forty Acres sparked something in Martin's mind. The second symbol that he noticed was even more encouraging.

Toward the center of the map, just a short distance from the river's opposite shore, Martin spotted a tiny brown-colored square. This brown square was identical to the icons used to represent the Forty Acres compound, only it was nowhere near the compound. It sat alone, isolated in the wilderness. Martin estimated the distance between Forty Acres and the river's nearest bank to be about a mile and a half, so the brown square had to be just three or four miles away. Logic told him that it was a structure, but what kind? Martin felt confident that the mysterious structure, situated on the opposite side of the river, well beyond Dr. Kasim's property line, was not a satellite of Forty Acres. Could it be possible that Dr.

Kasim had a neighbor? Could that tiny brown box be a small vacation cabin or some rich guy's hunting lodge? And if it was, were the neighbors at home? Even more crucial, did the neighbors have a phone?

Time seemed to pause as Martin's eyes ticked back and forth between the two unmarked symbols — the gray line that looked an awful lot like an active road, and that tiny brown square where there might be people and a way to contact the outside world. These slivers of hope set Martin's heart racing, because if either one was true, an entirely new possibility presented itself. Maybe, just maybe, there was still a chance for him to save Alice's life.

68

Martin waited while Tobias cracked open and passed around fresh bottles of Guinness before he asked Oscar about the two symbols. Martin's tone was curious without being eager, as if he didn't care if he received an answer or not.

Oscar, in turn, provided the answers with a similar indifference, apparently oblivious to the fact that Martin hung on his every word.

"Yes, that is a road," Oscar said, referring to the thin gray line. "An old two-lane highway that runs clear across the forest. It's a little treacherous. Undermaintained. Gets so little traffic that you could have a picnic right in the middle of it. People tend to avoid it in favor of one of the newer roads that connect directly to the interstate."

Although Martin was right about the highway, the lack of traffic made the chances of flagging down a passing truck or motor home too slim to rely on. So Martin shifted all his hope to the brown square. When he saw Oscar drop his gaze to the square and frown, Martin's heart lifted a little.

"That," Oscar said, pointing at the square with a pinch of disdain, "is where our friendly neighbors live."

"Neighbors? What do you mean?"

"You saw them," Damon said. "We drove past them in the woods on our way out here."

"Yeah," Carver said. "We practically had to hold you down to stop you from jumping out of the Jeep to help those white boys."

The forest rangers. Of course. How could he have forgotten the two rangers he'd seen working in the woods? Rangers stationed in remote areas lived for months at a time in cabins. Cabins equipped with everything that the isolated men would need to survive, including a radio. It was perfect. It seemed too good to be true.

"You're telling me that there's a ranger station three miles from here?" Martin said. "Isn't that a problem?"

"Four-point-six miles, actually," Oscar said. "Not an ideal situation but completely under control. Like I told you, this is private property. The rangers respect that. As long as we don't give them a reason to cross the river, they don't."

Dr. Kasim harrumphed. "Of course, the money we give them to mind their damn business doesn't hurt. Forest rangers love green, you know."

The men laughed and Martin laughed along with them, but inside, his mind was reeling. He glanced at the map again. Stared at that tiny brown square on the opposite side of the river. The answer to everything was so agonizingly close. He didn't have to wait another two days to reach home and the authorities. Alice didn't have to be sacrificed. Just a 4.6-mile hike through the woods and the nightmare could end that very night.

"I know exactly what you're thinking, brother."

Startled, Martin looked up and saw Dr. Kasim staring hard at him. "I wasn't thinking anything," Martin said, trying hard not to sound rattled and doing a poor job.

"Then why were you staring a hole through my map?"

"Was I?"

The other men were all watching now. Staring at Martin. Waiting for him to explain.

"I don't know," Martin continued, "I just—"

Dr. Kasim raised his hand, cutting Martin short. "You're worried about the forest rangers," he said. His tone was one of absolute certainty. "You're worried that sooner or later they're going to bust in here. Am I right?"

Grateful for the out, Martin nodded.

Dr. Kasim shook his head and sighed. "My brother, when you're behind these walls, the last thing in the world you have to worry about is a couple of white men."

The men nodded and bumped fists.

"That's for damn sure," Tobias said.

Dr. Kasim leaned closer to underscore his earnestness. "I give you my promise, our neighbors are not a problem. Can you trust me, brother?"

"Absolutely," Martin said.

"Here we are the masters, and you are one of us now. You must not ever forget that."

"I won't," Martin said. "I promise."

Dr. Kasim gave an approving smile. Then motioned to Oscar, who promptly closed the binder and carried it back across the room. When Oscar knelt down to slide the binder back into the safe, Martin spotted something that suddenly made the impossible seem very possible.

Oscar's gun.

The instant that stainless-steel weapon peeked out from beneath Oscar's jacket, a plan formed in Martin's mind. The plan was dangerous and a little crazy, but it was also very simple. Its elegance was what made Martin believe that he could pull it off. He really could save Alice and at the same time free all the slaves. And he could do it that very night.

Martin's simple plan solved every problem: getting past the guards, getting outside the wall. But there was one snag. There was still one obstacle that needed to be overcome. Martin decided that the best solution was to confront this obstacle head-on.

He took a long swig of beer, then lightly addressed the group. "So, does everyone have spy cameras in their room or is that just for the new guy?"

At first everyone just stared and exchanged awkward glances. But when Dr. Kasim began to laugh, all at once Martin's simple plan to escape Forty Acres had been set in motion.

69

Oscar pushed open the door to Martin's new accommodations and said, "Your belongings should have already been moved from your previous room."

Martin followed Oscar inside. His new room wasn't very different from his last. Queen-sized bed, flat-screen TV, small bathroom; even the garden view was the same. The only significant difference was that this room was not wired for sound and video, or at least that's what Oscar had promised.

A little more than an hour ago, when Martin complained about the hidden cameras, Dr. Kasim and the men had taken it in stride. There was an iffy moment when Oscar questioned how long Martin had known about the cameras, but Martin evaded further digging by faulting Carver. He recounted how, at breakfast, Carver had seemed to know all the details of his night with Alice. Facts that could only be explained one way: Carver was getting his jollies watching. The accusation drew a hard stare from Carver and laughter from everyone else.

It was explained to Martin that his first bedroom was the only one rigged for surveillance and that it was used exclusively for new recruits. Oscar then assured Martin that his new bedroom, like those of the other men, would be completely private.

That was a little more than an hour ago. After another cold Guinness, a couple more laughs, and few more philosophical pearls from Dr. Kasim, the group had decided to call it a night, at last. Martin was eager to retreat to his new room, eager to escape scrutiny and prepare for what promised to be the most important night of his life. Martin was caught off guard when Oscar offered to escort him to the new room personally.

Martin waited just inside the bedroom door while Oscar peeked into the closet and checked the dresser drawers. Oscar claimed that he wanted to make sure Martin's clothing had been moved like he ordered, but Martin didn't buy it. Dr. Kasim's right-hand man was too directorial to bother with unnecessary trivialities like walking Martin to his room and inspecting dresser drawers. No, there had to be another motive behind this unexpected one-on-one with Oscar, but what was it?

"Everything appears to be in order," Oscar said, squaring off with Martin. "You're all set. And no more cameras."

"Thanks. I appreciate it."

"And just so you're aware, all recordings will be destroyed as well."

"I hope so," Martin said, trying to keep things light. "I wouldn't want them to end up on YouTube."

Oscar seemed to smile more out of politeness than actual amusement. "I agree. That would be a problem."

"Well, thanks again," Martin said.

"You are welcome." Martin stepped back from the open door, inviting Oscar to exit, but the bald man did not budge. "There's one more thing, Mr. Grey."

This is it, Martin thought. Martin had no idea why Oscar would contrive to speak to him alone, and he was almost afraid to ask. "What is it?"

"What you're feeling . . . it will pass."

"What?" Martin said, caught off guard again. "What will pass?"

Oscar sighed. "Less than two hours ago you beat a beautiful woman with a whip. How does that make you feel? How does it really make you feel?"

An anxious voice in Martin's head warned him that this could just be another stage in the endless initiation.

As if he could read Martin's mind, Oscar said, "This isn't a test. I promise. Just tell me honestly. How do you feel about what you did to Alice?"

For an instant Martin considered lying, but something told him that he'd never sell it. That same intuition also told Martin that Oscar was being honest. The question wasn't meant to hurt, it was meant to help. Martin sighed. "Honestly, I don't feel great about it."

"A twinge of guilt maybe?"

Martin nodded. "Yes. Definitely."

Oscar patted Martin on the arm. "Of course you feel

that. Like Dr. Kasim says, we're not barbarians like they are. The doctor is very perceptive. He saw a little something in your eyes tonight. He asked me to send you this message. Tonight, you honored your ancestors. You did nothing wrong. What you're feeling right now, it will pass."

"Thanks," Martin said. "That makes me feel better."

Oscar's smile seemed genuine. He pulled Martin into a hug. "Good night, brother. Try to get some sleep."

"I will. Thanks."

Then Oscar was gone.

The instant Martin shut the door and locked it, he felt as if a massive boulder had slipped from his shoulders. Light-headed, he staggered across the room and fell back onto the bed. He felt the urge to scream toward heaven, but he just stared at the ceiling. When Martin shut his eyes, he saw Alice hanging by chains inside the barn. He saw Carver's muscles rippling as he whipped her mercilessly, over and over. Martin wiped away tears, but more came. He glanced at the digital clock on the bedside table: 11:14 p.m. Three long hours since he last saw Alice. And even if his plan went perfectly, it would be several hours more before she could receive any care. For all Martin knew, she was already dead. But he refused to believe that. Martin had made up his mind, and fate would just have to go along with his decision. Alice was young, Alice was healthy, and Alice would survive long enough for him to save her.

He'd wait one hour. One hour should be long enough for everyone to have gone to sleep or settled inside their rooms for the night. One more hour, then it would be time to leave.

70

Anna could not sleep. For more than an hour she had been lying awake in the moonlit gloom of her bedroom. Her anxious eyes refused to close. Instead they alternated between the shadow play of rustling leaves on the ceiling and the MacBook Pro on the nightstand.

Anna was worried sick.

She had no doubt that her pregnancy, and the fact that Martin knew nothing about it, added to her troubled state. But in truth the pregnancy was only a minor contributor to her insomnia. The real culprit was the other man that Anna could not stop thinking about.

Donald Jackson.

Three years ago Donald Jackson had gone away on a trip with the very same men that Martin was now with. And Donald Jackson had never come back. That was a fact that burned in Anna's mind. Sure, Damon Darrell had explained that Jackson's death was a suicide and not an accident, but that didn't matter. Call it intuition or a bad feeling. Somehow, tonight, Anna knew that something wasn't right.

Anna turned her head and stared at her laptop. Her urge to go online and dig up more information about

Jackson's death was strong, but Anna resisted because she knew that anything she found out would probably just increase her anxiety. No, it was better to just wait until Martin returned home and then do more research. If she uncovered something troubling, she could use it to convince Martin not to go away with them on any future trips.

The leaves and branches jittered again. The lonely quiet of the night was pierced by the distant screech of a cat.

But what if Martin was in some kind of danger, right now? Like the danger Donald Jackson found himself in? This was the relentless inner dialogue that slowly wore down Anna's resolve. It was either appease her gut feeling or, after a sleepless night, go to work at the hospital tomorrow feeling like a zombie.

Anna stared at her computer. Just five minutes. She'd go online for five minutes, just to quell the urge. Then hopefully she would be able to get some sleep.

Anna sat up, switched on the bedside lamp, propped up a pillow between her back and the headboard, and then grabbed her MacBook. At the hospital she had searched for information about white-water rafting. This time she searched "Donald Jackson death."

There were hundreds of hits. Anna found articles from every major news outlet about the promising author's tragic death. In them, as in the piece she had stumbled on days ago, the only person identified in the stories was the victim himself. Most of the articles mentioned that he had been traveling with a group of close friends, but that was it. Despite their level of notoriety, these "close friends" remained anonymous in each and every story. It was a chilling testament to the power of Martin's new associates.

If something did happen to Martin, would the press describe these men as having been Martin's close friends as well? Anna pushed the thought out of her head and glanced at the clock. She had already been online for three minutes, and so far so good. She had found no new disturbing facts about Jackson's death, nothing to add to her list of worries.

With just two minutes left, and feeling confident that there was nothing to find, Anna decided to get a bit more aggressive. In Google's search window she moved the cursor to the end of her original inquiry and added just one more word. Now her inquiry read "Donald Jackson death suspicious."

Anna moved the arrow cursor to the search button, but she hesitated. She whispered to herself, "Do you really want to do this, girl?" Anna took a deep breath, then clicked the track pad.

Anna looked at the computer screen. There was nothing scary on it. The resulting list of links appeared to be almost identical to the list from her previous search. Not one of the headlines included the word *suspicious*.

Anna sagged with relief. For a fleeting moment she considered trying other key words, like *murder* or *cover-up*, but she decided not to push it. Anna had done her due diligence and felt a lot better for it; also, glancing at the clock, she saw that her five minutes had just run out. A deal's a deal, even if it's a deal with yourself.

Anna reached to shut the laptop but paused when she spotted something unexpected on the screen. It wasn't part of the list of search results. It was at the top of the page listed below a headline that read "Image Results for Donald Jackson Death Suspicious."

It was a photograph of Damon Darrell holding the shoulders of a pretty woman, as if he were about to embrace her. The woman was not Damon's wife, Juanita. This woman was younger, and her complexion was lighter. Most intriguing of all, she was dressed for mourning, all in black.

Deal or no deal, Anna clicked on the small image. It expanded to fill the screen. Now Anna could see other mourners in the background. The photograph had been taken at a funeral. Anna moved her cursor to the bottom of the image and a brief caption materialized: "Damon Darrell comforts author Donald Jackson's widow, Christine Jackson."

Anna sat there, alone, in her dimly lit bedroom, riveted to that woman's face. The longer Anna stared, the more uneasy she began to feel. Christine Jackson's face was wrong, very wrong. While Damon offered the widow a warm and comforting smile, Christine's face replied with something completely different. There was venom in Christine Jackson's eyes. Pure, raw hatred.

Anna suspected that if the camera's shutter had snapped either an instant sooner or an instant later, Christine Jackson's expression would be exactly what one would expect from a widow. A face hung in deep sorrow. Pained eyes clenched shut. But the photographer that day, either by a fluke or the aid of a rapidly firing shutter, managed to capture the truth beneath the tears.

Why would Christine Jackson hate Damon Darrell? That was the question that resounded in Anna's mind. If Damon and the other men moved heaven and earth to cover up Donald's suicide and to ensure her and her children's financial well-being, why would Christine Jackson hate Damon Darrell? Did she feel the same way about the other men?

It didn't make sense.

At that moment Anna made two decisions. First, because she knew that it would now be impossible to sleep, she would call in sick. Second, tomorrow Anna was going to find Mrs. Jackson and get some answers.

71

Martin was seated on the edge of his bed, dressed and ready to go. He wore an outfit that Damon had helped him pick out at the camping store REI a little over a week ago. A dark blue hooded fleece jacket, hiking pants, and waterproof hiking boots. Part of what made his plan simple was that it actually didn't require any hike through the woods, but Martin still wanted to be ready for anything.

It was 12:04 a.m. He was tempted to get going that second, but he decided to stick to the plan of waiting one hour. There was no way to know if ten minutes would make any real difference—and that was the perfect reason to wait.

Martin heard a tapping sound. He glanced around the room, puzzled, before realizing that his right leg was bouncing like a jackhammer. Martin wasn't nervous. Nervous was speaking before a large audience or popping the big question. Martin was scared. Terrified. Yes, his plan was simple, and he believed that it would work, but there was always the chance that something would go wrong.

Martin heard a soft rapping sound. Unlike his tapping

foot, this new sound was not the product of his fear. Someone had knocked on his bedroom door.

Martin's eyes shot to the clock: 12:10. Who would come to his bedroom now? Whoever it was, their timing couldn't be worse. Martin considered not answering, hoping the person would think that he was already asleep, but that was too risky. It would be wiser for Martin to know exactly who was still up and around inside the main house.

The soft knocks came again.

"One second." Martin rose and crossed to the door. He reached to pull it open but paused when he remembered what he was wearing. Martin snatched off the hooded jacket and tossed it into the closet.

When Martin finally opened the door, he saw what looked like Alice's ghost standing in the doorway. It was Felicia, adorned in the same pretty blue dress that her cousin had worn the night before. Also like Alice, Felicia's strawberry-blond mane flowed gently to her shoulders, beautifully framing her sweet, sad face.

Felicia smiled. "You asked to see me, master?"

Martin was puzzled but only for a second. "Did Carver send you here?"

"No, sir," Felicia replied. "Master Lennox sent me, sir."

Martin felt a twinge of nerves. This meant that Oscar could still be roaming around the house. Not good. Not good at all.

"Would you like me to come in, sir?"

Martin shook his head. "No. No, thank you, I'm tired. But let me ask you a question. Do you know if Mr. Lennox is in his room?"

"Sir?" Felicia's eyes flooded with fear. "Did I do something wrong, sir? If I did—"

"Oh, no, no," Martin said, realizing his mistake. He had rejected the girl, and now he appeared ready to report her. "You did nothing wrong. I promise." Martin glanced up and down the hall to make sure no one was watching, then he stepped back from the door. "Come in."

Relieved and a bit puzzled, Felicia did as she was told.

Martin locked the door behind her. When he turned, she was standing beside the bed, hands folded before her, looking both innocent and vulnerable. Her smile was grateful. "Thank you for letting me stay, sir. I promise to make you happy."

"You're not staying," Martin said. "I just want you to answer my question. That's all."

Worry and confusion began to creep back onto Felicia's face. "Your question, sir?"

Martin stepped closer and gently took her hand. "You're not in trouble," he said. "I promise. Nothing's going to happen to you. Okay?"

Felicia nodded. "Alice said that you were different. You know, like nice."

Martin smiled, but hearing Felicia bring up Alice so casually meant she had to be oblivious to her cousin's situation. There was no way to be sure how Felicia would react to the news, so Martin resisted the urge to tell her. Any major disruption in the main house now would stop his plan cold. And the plan had to come first.

"Where did you last see Mr. Lennox?" Martin asked. "Was he in his room?"

Felicia shook her head. "No, in the kitchen. We were cleaning up. Master Lennox came in and said that you wanted to see me after midnight. He told me to wear something pretty."

"And how long ago was this?"

Felicia thought about it. "Half an hour ago. Maybe forty minutes."

Half an hour was good, Martin thought. Half an hour was more than enough time for Oscar to return to his bedroom and get settled in for the night. When the time came, the more settled in Oscar was, the better.

"One more question," Martin said. "On your way here, did you see any of the other masters anywhere in the house?"

Felicia shook her head. "No, sir. I believe everyone's off to bed."

"Good," Martin said. "Now you should go to bed too."

Felicia was hesitant. "Are you sure, sir? You sure that you don't want me to stay?"

Martin frowned. The girl's eagerness to sacrifice herself just to avoid disappointing him was heartbreaking. "You're Alice's cousin, right?"

Felicia nodded. "Yes, sir." She smoothed her hands over the front of her dress. "This is Alice's, actually. I don't think she'll mind that I borrowed it. I mean, well, considering . . ."

As Felicia's voice trailed off, Martin caught a flicker of sorrow in her eyes. Was he wrong? Did she know that, at that very moment, her cousin was dying?

Cautiously, Martin asked, "What do you think happened to Alice?"

Felicia shrugged feebly. "I don't know. All Master Lennox told me was that Alice was sent to work in the mine." Felicia fixed anxious eyes on Martin. "You don't know either, sir?"

It took Martin a moment to dredge up the lie. "No, I don't," he said. "But don't worry. I'm pretty sure you'll get to see your cousin tomorrow."

The girl smiled gratefully. "Yes, sir. Good night, sir."

Felicia crossed to the door, but as she reached for the knob, Martin said, "Go straight back to your room, and stay there all night."

"Sir?"

Martin made an effort to sound firm. A master giving his slave an order. "No matter what you hear in this house tonight, you stay in your room. Do you understand me?"

Felicia replied with a puzzled look, "Yes, sir. I think I do."

"Good. Now go."

A final fretful smile, then Felicia walked out and shut the door.

Martin turned to the clock: 12:15 to the minute.

Martin retrieved his jacket from the closet and zipped it on. It was time to go.

72

Martin knocked firmly, three times, on Oscar's door.

Oscar's bedroom was located at the very end of the upstairs hallway. Behind Martin, the long corridor was still and draped in deep shadow. The entire house seemed quiet. Besides his own anxious breathing, the only sounds that Martin heard were the nocturnal chatter of cicadas and crickets.

Then came the soft pad of approaching footsteps behind Oscar's bedroom door. Martin took a calming breath.

The lock clicked, and the door was yanked open just wide enough for Oscar to glare out. "What is it?" When Oscar saw it was Martin, irritation morphed into puzzlement. Oscar opened the door wider. "Mr. Grey? Is there something wrong?"

Despite his gray T-shirt and striped pajama bottoms, Oscar appeared to be wide-awake, like he'd been reading in bed until Martin's knock. There was something off-putting about seeing the always-reserved overseer now dressed so casually. Martin also took note that Oscar was now unarmed, just as expected. All Martin had to do was get inside Oscar's room.

He knew that the next words out of his mouth were crucial. He had to sound completely believable. Oscar was clearly a shrewd man; in fact, Martin's plan depended on it.

If Oscar detected one false note in Martin's actions, the night would be over before it even got started.

Martin looked Oscar square in the eye and said, "I need to speak to Dr. Kasim."

Oscar scowled, as if Martin had just spoken a foreign language. "I don't understand. What is the problem?"

Martin dropped his voice to a whisper. "I really would prefer to speak to the doctor. If you don't mind."

Oscar frowned. "Impossible. The doctor is asleep and cannot be disturbed. You'll have to wait until morning."

"I can't," Martin said, shaking his head. "It's what we talked about. The guilt. I can't stop thinking about it."

"Exactly why I sent Felicia to your room. Did she arrive?"

"Yes, but—I sent her away. I couldn't. I really just need to speak to Dr. Kasim. Any chance that you could wake him up?"

Oscar flashed a rare smile. "Absolutely not. That wouldn't be a good idea for either of us. Perhaps you could speak to one of the other men. Mr. Darrell perhaps, or even better, Mr. Aarons. He's very wise and a good listener."

"What about you?" Martin said.

Oscar's only reply was a creased brow.

Martin held his breath. Did he push too hard? Was it obvious that he had an ulterior motive?

Finally Oscar said, "You want to talk to me?"

Martin nodded. "You seemed to understand."

"I was only delivering a message."

"I know. But how many times have you delivered that message? Who knows the doctor's mind better than you?"

Oscar frowned, and it appeared that he was about to agree; but then his expression changed. He scanned Martin from head to toe, for the first time noticing Martin's outerwear. Oscar's brow wrinkled. "You going somewhere?"

Maintaining his cool, Martin reacted as if he had forgotten about his outfit. "Oh, yeah—I was going to go for a walk around the grounds."

"A walk? Now?"

"You know, to clear my head. If we could just talk for ten minutes, I would really appreciate it." Martin glanced over Oscar's shoulder. "Come on, you gotta have *something* stashed in there. Just one drink."

Oscar made a grunting sound that Martin took to be the overseer's version of a chuckle. "You drink bourbon?" Oscar said.

"Right now, I'd drink anything."

Oscar stepped back and pulled his door open. "One drink."

73

While Oscar poured two glasses of bourbon at a modestly stocked bar tray atop his dresser, Martin scanned the bedroom.

It was only slightly larger than Martin's and the layout was similar. The biggest difference was the feel of the space. Unlike the guest rooms with their neutral décor, Oscar's room, although quite neat, was filled with personal items that made it feel lived-in. There was an impressive collection of jazz and blues music, both CDs and vinyl. There was a smaller collection of hardcover books that appeared to be very old. Colorful Haitian watercolors shared the walls with framed photographs of New York City and a poster for the Pam Grier movie *Foxy Brown*.

Martin spotted the object he was searching for exactly where he expected; Oscar's leather shoulder holster hung from the bedpost of the king-sized bed that dominated the center of the room. What Martin didn't count on was that the shoulder holster would be empty.

Where was the gun?

"Here you go." Oscar handed Martin a square whiskey glass, two fingers full. Oscar then removed a bookmarked hardcover from the cushion of an old easy chair and gestured to Martin. "Sit."

Martin did so. He sat forward in the plush chair, purposely avoiding a reclined posture. At any moment he would have to move fast, and every second would count.

Oscar sat down on the edge of the bed, directly across from his guest. He nodded at Martin's untouched glass. "Try it."

The burnt oak aroma filled Martin's nostrils before the glass touched his lips. The golden liquor was smooth going down. A wave of heat radiated through Martin's torso.

Oscar hung on Martin's reaction as if he had distilled the bourbon himself. "Good?"

"Hell no," Martin said, shaking his head. "It's amazing. Better than that crap Dr. Kasim gave us."

Oscar cracked a small smile, then joined the party by taking his first sip.

In the fleeting instant between Oscar's raising his glass to his mouth and bringing it back down, Martin scanned the bedroom again. In a house full of slaves, for the overseer to hide his weapon made perfect sense, but where would he hide it? Did he tuck it into a dresser drawer every night? Did he put it on a shelf in the closet? Maybe Oscar stashed the weapon under his pillow where he could get to it fast. Martin found the answer hidden in plain sight. It was sitting right there atop the nightstand beside Oscar's bed, so innocuous that it was barely noticeable.

The small pistol safe had a dull black finish with dimensions similar to a large cigar box. The safe's surface was featureless, with one crucial exception: a single chrome keyhole.

Damn it.

"Not what you expected, huh?"

"What?" Martin turned and saw Oscar peering at him over the brim of his glass. Watching him.

Oscar took another slow sip of his bourbon, then said, "You keep looking around with an odd expression on your face. I'm guessing you were expecting something else."

"Not really," Martin said. "You just have a lot of interesting stuff. How long have you lived here?"

"Ten years, more or less." Oscar gazed at the swirling contents of his glass. His eyes were distant, as if he were staring back across the years. "I came here as a guest, same as you. Liked what I heard. Saw no reason to go back."

Martin fought the urge to glance around the room in search of Oscar's keys. Oscar had already taken notice of his snooping. If there was still any chance of pulling off his plan, Martin was going to have to be more careful. "So, you just dropped everything?" Martin asked. "Your work? Your friends? Were you married?"

Oscar withdrew from the phantoms in his glass. He frowned. "Let's not get sidetracked. We're here to talk about you, not me." Oscar left it there, his attentive stare an invitation for Martin to get to the point.

"Well," Martin said, "it's pretty much what you said. I believe in everything that Dr. Kasim is doing here, and I feel lucky to be a part of it. But when I close my eyes—"

"You see the girl," Oscar said. "You see Alice."

"Yes." Martin sighed deeply; he wasn't lying. "With your job I'm sure you've had to punish plenty of slaves. How do you, well—"

"How do I sleep at night? Is that your question?"

Martin nodded. "I guess you're used to it."

Oscar smiled at that. "No. You just put it into perspective."

"Perspective?"

Oscar leaned forward. "Every time you see Alice in your head, think about your great-great-grandfather being maimed, or boiled alive, or skinned. Think about your great-great-grandmother being raped in the same room where her family slept. Then think about how proud your ancestors would be of this place, and of you. That, my brother, is perspective."

Martin nodded and capped the moment by draining his bourbon. He frowned at the empty glass. "I know you said one drink, but—"

Oscar took Martin's glass and carried it to his dresser. As Oscar worked the minibar he said, "That photo album in Dr. Kasim's library. You wouldn't believe what's in there. Extremely rare photos of slave punishments. Very graphic stuff."

Martin was barely listening. His eyes were darting,

searching for Oscar's keys. He eyed a small table beside the bedroom door, a perfect spot to leave them, but the keys weren't there. He scanned the two nightstands that flanked Oscar's bed: nothing. He even glanced over at the long dresser where Oscar was pouring the drinks. Along with the minibar, there were a few framed photographs, and that was it. No keys.

Martin knew that his chance of finding the keys out in the open was a long shot, and he was about to give up when he spotted Oscar's suit. The white jacket and slacks were draped over the bed's footboard, most likely tossed there when Oscar undressed for the evening. Was it possible that the overseer's keys were still in the suit?

"You really should look through it at least once," Oscar said, handing Martin a fresh drink and retaking his seat on the bed. "But not tonight. If you're trying to get some sleep, it might defeat the purpose."

"If the rest is anything like that first photo, I believe you."

"Let's just say that everything in that album makes Alice's punishment tonight look merciful."

Martin considered mentioning that Alice was innocent, that Carver had only used her to get to him, but he held his tongue. Oscar might perceive the accusation as evidence that Martin's little bout with conscience was more than just a minor concern. Martin needed Oscar's guard to be as lax as possible for what he was about to try next.

"Well, thanks for your help," Martin said.

"No problem," Oscar said. He gestured to the drink in Martin's hand. "Although, I think the bourbon will help you more tonight than anything I can tell you."

Martin smiled and raised the glass to his mouth but stopped short. He rubbed his temple and said, "You know, it might be better if I just took a couple of aspirins."

Oscar lowered his glass from his lips. "Headache?"

"Yeah. I guess African beer, Guinness, and bourbon don't mix."

"Probably not."

"You got anything in the medicine cabinet? Maybe something that will help me sleep?"

Oscar looked unsure. "Maybe. Let me check." He set his glass down atop the pistol safe, then rounded the bed to the opposite side of the room and disappeared into the bathroom.

Martin catapulted from his seat and pounced on the white suit. He groped the pants pockets. Nothing. He patted the jacket pockets. Martin's hope leapt when he felt a heavy lump that jangled at his touch.

Keys.

Martin removed them, careful to avoid any jingling. There were seven keys on a simple steel ring. Two of the keys were definitely for a vehicle. Two others looked like they opened doors. The three remaining keys were smaller than the others. One of them had to be the key to the safe.

Martin could hear Oscar in the bathroom rifling the

medicine cabinet. He heard the shuffle of toiletries and the rattle of pills. There was still time.

Martin hurried to the nightstand. He moved Oscar's drink from the top of the small safe and tried the first key. It didn't fit in the lock.

Shit.

Martin tried the second key. It slid into the lock with ease, but it wouldn't turn.

Fuck.

From the bathroom came the unmistakable thunk of the medicine cabinet closing.

No.

His hand trembling, Martin took hold of the last key. The key slid snugly into the keyhole. He gave it a twist, and the cylinder turned. There was a click and the safe's lid popped free of the base, just a hair. Martin flipped open the lid. Inside the safe lay an American passport, an antique gold watch, and an old wedding photo of a younger Oscar and his bride.

There was no gun.

Oscar's voice boomed, "What the hell are you doing?"

Martin whirled.

Oscar, clutching a bottle of Tylenol PM, stood glaring in the bathroom doorway. In that naked moment, in a millisecond of eye contact between the two men, Oscar suddenly understood everything. His glare hardened into fury. "You son of a bitch."

Oscar exploded into action, but instead of rounding

the bed to reach Martin, he scrambled across the mattress. Martin realized that Oscar wasn't charging him at all; instead he was lunging toward the pillow nearest to Martin's side of the bed. Martin flung the pillow aside to reveal the stainless-steel nine-millimeter handgun. Oscar, arms outstretched, clawed for the weapon, but Martin snatched it first. In a frenzy of panicked motion Martin freed the safety, cocked the slide, and took point-blank aim at Oscar's forehead. "Don't move another inch," Martin said.

Oscar froze. Sprawled atop the bed, he glared up at Martin with dead-certain eyes. "Whatever the fuck this is, it's not going to work."

Gun steady in his grip, Martin did his best to match Oscar's confidence. "You better hope it does," he said, "because your life depends on it."

74

Moments later, both men were seated again, but with two major differences. First, to discourage any quick movements, Martin had ordered Oscar to sit as far back in the easy chair as possible with both hands in his lap, while Martin sat on the edge of Oscar's bed. Second, instead of holding a glass of bourbon, Martin held the nine-millimeter pointed at Oscar's heart.

Oscar's eyes ticked down and up between the pointed gun and Martin's face. Martin could see Oscar's mind working. Sizing up the threat.

Martin warned him, "In college Glen dragged me to the gun range a few times, so I know how to use this."

For an icy second Oscar studied him, then challenged, "Shooting paper targets is not the same as shooting a man."

"Make no mistake," Martin said. "If I can bring myself to whip that poor girl, I can definitely shoot you."

Oscar's hard, steady stare gave nothing away. But the fact that Oscar remained planted in the easy chair told Martin that his point had been made.

"What now?" Oscar growled. "What do you think you're doing?"

"It's simple," Martin replied. "You're going to get me to the ranger station."

Oscar frowned as if Martin were wasting his time. "Maybe you haven't noticed but this place is a fortress. You'll never—"

"Wait," Martin said, raising his free hand. "Before you tell me that we can't get past the guards, or we can't get through the gate, or anything else like that, let me say this. I don't care how you do it, but either you get me to the ranger station in the next hour or I'm going to kill you. It's that simple."

Oscar just stared, trying to gauge Martin's resolve. "What makes you so damn sure that I won't die to protect Forty Acres?"

"I'm not. I'm only sure of one thing. I'm willing to die to shut Forty Acres down."

Oscar's eyes narrowed. "Why are you doing this?"

"Ridiculous question," Martin said. "But if you really need an answer, here it is. Forty Acres is wrong. Plain and simple."

"Plain and simple?" Oscar shook his head in disappointment. "Clearly you haven't thought through the potential repercussions of what you plan."

"The repercussions are that Dr. Kasim and the rest of his maniac followers will end up behind bars, where you all belong."

"Keep in mind," Oscar said, "that these so-called maniac followers are influential, conscious black men.

Doctors, businessmen, politicians, even one prominent church leader. These men that you're so determined to destroy do a lot of good for our people. Ruin them, and countless innocents will suffer as well." Oscar paused to underscore his next point. "And that's just the beginning. Once you tell the world about Forty Acres, just imagine the resentment and distrust. It will be directed not only toward the men involved but toward the entire black community. You think blacks are discriminated against now? Just wait. What you do here tonight will set race relations back decades. If you truly believe that this matter is 'plain and simple,' then, Mr. Grey, you are a fool."

Martin was held by a specter of doubt. Everything Oscar said made sense. It would be naive to think that the bombshell that he was about to drop didn't have the potential to hurt innocent people. But there was one intangible saving grace that Martin hoped would help temper the inevitable shock and outrage.

"You're right," Martin said to Oscar. "Everything could happen just the way you say. But because a black man will be the one blowing the whistle, I don't think it will. I believe that the world will understand the truth—that a few twisted men, men who just happened to be black, did something really stupid."

Oscar snorted. "You're kidding yourself. This world you imagine does not exist."

"Another point on which we will always disagree," Martin said. "Now, will you get me to the ranger station, or not? And before you answer, let me offer you an incentive."

"What incentive?"

"Once we reach the station and I have contacted the authorities, I will let you go. I'll do everything in my power to help the police find you later, but tonight I will let you go."

A smile creased Oscar's face. "Now I see why you're such a good lawyer. You've thought of everything, haven't you?"

"We've wasted enough time. Just give me your answer."

Oscar sighed. "Brother, please listen to me. What's happening here is just part of what we talked about. Misplaced guilt. Why don't you let me wake up the doctor? We can deal with this."

Martin glared. "Deal with it how? The way you dealt with Donald Jackson?"

"No," Oscar said, maintaining his composure. "Jackson was different. Jackson was too far gone to help."

"So am I," Martin huffed. He extended the gun, bringing it a foot closer to his intended target. "I need an answer. Now."

Martin saw Oscar's cool, calculating eyes drop to the gun.

"Just so you know," Martin said, "if you think you're going to be saved by the guards or anyone else, you're not. Anything goes wrong, I'm aiming at one person, and that's you."

Oscar frowned. "I figured that."

It was so quiet Martin could hear the tick of the clock on the wall.

"Well?"

Oscar shut his eyes as if trying to visualize the problem. "I get you to the ranger station, you let me go. If I don't, you kill me."

"That's right."

Oscar opened his eyes and conceded with an easy nod. "Then the ranger station it is."

Martin felt as if it were suddenly easier to breathe. He had pulled it off. His simple plan had worked. The rest was up to Oscar. "Okay," Martin said. "So how do we get out of here? What's the plan?"

"Don't need a plan," Oscar replied. "Dr. Kasim owns Forty Acres and serves as its leader, but I run this place. I assume that's why you're waving that gun at me, not him. Getting past the guards will not be a problem, I promise you that."

Martin's eyes darkened with suspicion. The overseer's sudden cooperation was making him uneasy. "I'm warning you, if this is a trick—"

"You'll kill me, I know. I swear, it's not a—"

Oscar was interrupted by a knock at the bedroom door.

Startled, Martin sprang to his feet and took aim at Oscar's head. The first thought that raced through Martin's mind was that Oscar had a secret way of signaling for help. Gun trembling in his grasp, Martin whispered, "Who is that?"

Oscar shook his head and threw up his hands.

Martin made an instantaneous determination that Oscar's puzzled expression was genuine.

The knocks came again, this time followed by a voice. "Hey, Oscar, you still up? I need to talk to you. It's about Martin. He's not in his room."

Martin experienced a surge of panic. The gun suddenly felt heavier in his hand.

It was Carver.

75

Martin stood pressed against the wall beside the bedroom door, gun trained on Oscar's temple. As Oscar reached for the knob, Martin whispered, "Keep in mind, I'm very nervous."

His heart pounding in his chest, Martin watched Oscar twist open the door. From his position Martin couldn't see Carver, just the annoyed stare that Carver received from Oscar.

"It's late," Oscar grumbled. "Why are you bothering me?"

"I told you," Carver said. "Grey's not in his room."

The closeness of Carver's voice made Martin's heart hammer even faster. If Carver became even a little suspicious, things could get ugly fast.

Oscar's reaction to Carver's news was calm, bordering on bored. "And how do you know this?"

"I knocked," Carver replied. "When I got no answer, you know, I peeked in."

Martin could practically hear the stupid smirk on Carver's face.

Oscar sighed. "And this is why you woke me? There's no problem. I know exactly where Mr. Grey is."

Martin stiffened. What was Oscar doing?

"You do?" Carver said. "Where?"

The puzzlement in Carver's voice mirrored what Martin felt. His palms grew slick with sweat, causing him to adjust his grip on the gun. He didn't want to shoot Oscar, but if Oscar called his bluff—

With a casual nod of his head, Oscar said to Carver, "Mr. Grey is right here pointing a gun at me."

These words were uttered so matter-of-factly that, for a fraction of a second, Martin wasn't sure that he had heard right. This fleeting instant of hesitation was all the time Oscar needed to turn the tables.

Oscar whirled and fixed Martin with a defiant stare that dared Martin to murder him in cold blood.

Martin's trigger finger tensed, but he couldn't do it. Oscar grabbed Martin's outstretched hand. Sharp, twisting pain shot through Martin's wrist and he felt the gun snatched from his grasp. A sinking wave of emptiness spread from Martin's hand to his heart. His plan had failed. It was over.

Martin saw the steel butt of the handgun coming at him. He felt a sharp blow to his temple and a cascade of pain filled his skull. The room tilted. The hardwood floor came up and smacked the side of his face. Martin saw blurry bare feet and what looked like a pair of shoes approaching fast. He heard faraway voices. Alarmed voices. Shouting. Then blackness closed in and dragged Martin down.

76

You have arrived at your destination," the GPS announced in a friendly female voice.

"You can say that again," Anna muttered as she pulled her Prius to the curb and gazed out at the impressive house that stood directly across the street.

Wow, Anna thought. *Christine Jackson lives here?*

The house was a classic two-story redbrick colonial, nestled upon a sprawling emerald-green lawn. A curved brick path snaked past perfect hedges and a looming shade tree to reach the steps of an elegant entryway shaded by a portico. But it wasn't just the amazing house that enthralled Anna; it was the entire neighborhood. Located in affluent Westchester County, the picturesque street buzzed with the morning rituals of suburban life. Several neighboring minimansions had teams of gardeners hard at work outside, trimming and snipping the shrubbery. At one nearby home, a uniformed housekeeper chatted with the mail carrier. Down the street Anna saw two very fit young women jogging side by side. One woman pushed a racing stroller and the other led an adorable Yorkshire terrier by a brown leather leash.

Anna loved the modest house that she shared with

Martin, and was fond of their lively Queens neighborhood as well, but turning onto this street was a little like entering a dream. Whenever Anna would fantasize about her future with Martin, a street like this one, with big beautiful homes and friendly neighbors, was exactly the setting that she would imagine. Where better to raise a family and nurture a long and loving marriage? Of course, Anna was neither naive nor shallow. She knew that the neighborhood's picture-perfect facade said nothing about what truly went on behind all those high hedges and brass-knockered doors. The trappings of the American dream were a nice ideal to strive for, but ultimately they guaranteed little, happiness least of all. Donald Jackson's apparent suicide was proof of that, wasn't it?

Still behind the wheel of her idling car, Anna returned her gaze to the Jackson home as she recalled a curious fact. Tracking down Christine Jackson's address on the Internet had been a challenge because Christine and her two children had moved only a few months after her husband's death. The family's former address was a two-bedroom condo in upscale Brooklyn Heights. For a first-time author experiencing modest success, this seemed right in line with what Mr. Jackson would have been able to afford. What struck Anna as peculiar was the lifestyle that the family was able to maintain after Mr. Jackson's death. Their current Westchester address indicated a significant upgrade in the Jackson family's finances. The house alone had to be worth $3 or $4 million. Even the finest life insurance policy in the world couldn't sustain this sort of expensive lifestyle for very long.

The mystery that had inspired Anna to take the day off, get up early, and drive forty-five minutes out of the city had suddenly become more puzzling. To Anna it now seemed quite clear that Damon and his rich pals had done considerably more for the late Donald Jackson's family than merely cover up his suicide. But if loyalty and generosity were the whole story, then how to explain the vicious look that Christine Jackson had leveled at Damon Darrell in that photograph? It simply didn't make sense. No, the mysterious trips, the secret suicide, that photo, they all told Anna that something was not quite right about Martin's new friends. And judging from that unforgettable look in Christine Jackson's eyes, Anna had a strong suspicion that Mr. Jackson's widow would be able to provide some answers.

Anna killed her engine and climbed out of the Prius. Before she had a chance to cross, a yellow school bus rumbled down the block and squealed to a stop in front of the Jackson home. A single honk of the horn brought two backpack-laden kids, a boy and a girl, both about eight years old, bounding out of the house. The spritely siblings were trailed down the path by an attractive, light-skinned woman. The woman's slender figure made the burgundy silk robe that she wore look like a designer evening dress. The smoldering cigarette in the corner of her mouth completed her morning-chic look.

Anna recognized Donald Jackson's widow immediately.

Christine Jackson kissed and hugged her children good-bye and then dragged on her cigarette as they charged onto the bus.

As the yellow bus motored away, Christine noticed Anna standing across the street, watching her. If Christine Jackson found it odd to see a black woman in her neighborhood that she didn't know or recognize, she didn't show it. She simply flashed a fake smile, took another long drag of her cigarette, and started back toward her house.

"Mrs. Jackson," Anna called out as she hurried across the street. "Wait. Please."

Christine paused on her walkway and watched, perplexed, as Anna approached.

"Hi," Anna said, trying to appear as nonthreatening as possible. "You are Christine Jackson, right?"

Christine did not return the stranger's smile. "I'm sorry, but do we know each other?"

"No," Anna said, "and I apologize for ambushing you this way. I was about to knock on your door, but then the bus came, and you came out, so—"

"Yes, yes. That's fine. Now, who are you exactly?"

*

The Handyman was seated in a parked white Toyota Camry, half a block away, sipping black coffee from a

411

thermos lid while watching Mrs. Grey and Mrs. Jackson's early morning chitchat.

"Well, well," he muttered to himself. "Isn't this interesting."

The Handyman was not in the habit of taking last-minute assignments. He preferred plenty of prep time. That was the only way to ensure that everything went just so. But when the client called at 3:17 in the morning and offered to double his already substantial fee, he was tempted to make an exception. What sold him were the particulars of the gig. Essentially, the client wanted him to be on standby. He was to shadow Anna Grey for twenty-four hours and wait for an extinguish order, which might or might not come. If the order came, he'd score the double payday. If not, he'd still receive his standard rate just for babysitting. To the Handyman that sounded like a pretty sweet deal, and from the looks of things down the street, it was about to pay off big-time.

The Handyman had worked with the client for several years, on countless assignments. The fact that the client wanted Anna tracked told him that there were problems with her husband, problems that might not have a tidy solution. At such a critical time, the last thing that the client would want to see was their current dilemma grow more complicated because of a past dilemma.

The Handyman had no doubt that a meeting between Anna Grey and Christine Jackson was an unexpected development that the client would be extremely interested in.

The Handyman drained his cup and screwed it back onto a stainless-steel thermos. From the passenger seat he hoisted a Canon 5D Mark II DSLR camera outfitted with a heavy 400 mm telephoto lens. After a glance around to ensure that he wasn't being observed, he raised the camera to his eye and shot two quick photos of the women. He returned the camera to the seat and grabbed his iPhone from the dash. He opened an app called Shutter Shuttle, which was tethered wirelessly to the Bluetooth memory card in his camera, and quickly found the two photos. Both were perfect, high-resolution shots of the two women conversing on Christine Jackson's front walk. He typed out a quick email, attached one of the photos, and hit send.

The Handyman returned his iPhone to the dash, poured himself another cup of steaming coffee, and continued to watch. He couldn't hear a word they said, but it didn't matter. As the saying goes, a picture is worth a thousand words—or in this case, a big, fat double payday.

All the Handyman had to do was wait for a response.

*

Christine Jackson squinted at Anna. "And you say that your husband's name is Martin Grey? Would that be Martin Grey the attorney?"

"Actually, yes," Anna replied with surprise. She did

413

not expect Christine Jackson to know anything about her husband.

Christine saw the puzzled look on Anna's face. "I've seen him on the news," she explained. She dragged on her cigarette and sized Anna up through a tendril of smoke. "So what is this about, Mrs. Grey? I'll admit that I'm incredibly curious."

"Well, it's about our husbands really."

Christine expelled a stream of smoke. "Our husbands? I'm sorry, but there must be some mistake. My husband has been deceased for several years now."

"Yes, I know," Anna said. "And I'm very sorry."

"Thank you." The reply sounded sincere. "Now, what is this about?"

"Some old friends of your husband are now friends with my husband, Martin. And, well, I guess I'm a little worried."

Christine's brow furrowed warily. "These friends, who are they exactly?"

"Well, Damon Darrell introduced Martin to them. It's the same group of men who went on that rafting trip with your husband five years ago. Now Martin's on a rafting trip with them, and he's completely out of contact. They told me what really happened to your husband. But they lied about it at first. And—I don't know—I just get the feeling that they're lying about something more. I thought that you might be able to—"

"You thought wrong," Christine snapped. She glanced

nervously up and down the block, then fixed Anna with a stare. "Now, you listen to me. I want you to get the hell off my property and never come back. And do not try to contact me. No phone calls, no emails, nothing. Do you understand?"

Anna felt dazed, as if she had just been sucker punched. "No, I don't understand. Did I say something wrong?"

Christine Jackson took a long drag and used the pause to scan up and down the street again. Finally she frowned at Anna and said something chilling. "I have kids, okay? I have two small children. Leave us alone. Please." Mrs. Jackson's eyes welled with tears. She flicked her smoldering cigarette onto her perfect lawn, then turned and marched back toward her beautiful house.

*

The Handyman's iPhone chimed.

He set down his coffee and checked the screen. He saw what he was waiting for. Like all of the encrypted emails received from the client, the reply, regarding the photo, was brief and to the point. There were just three tiny words to decide Anna Grey's fate.

The Handyman smiled at the message, then flung his phone into the passenger seat and started up the Camry.

Time to get to work.

*

Anna's mind reeled as she headed back to her car. She actually felt a bit muddled, as if Christine Jackson's sudden shift had jarred something loose in her own head.

Anna paused at the curb to let a van zip by, then stepped into the street and began to cross. Christine Jackson was clearly afraid, but afraid of what? Did Damon and the others threaten to take away her big house and her family's comfortable lifestyle if she ever talked about what happened to her husband? Or was it more than that? It almost seemed as if the woman feared for her life. But that was crazy, wasn't it?

Anna blinked to clear her head and spotted something odd.

A gardener on the opposite sidewalk was pointing frantically up the street. The Mexican appeared to be shouting something, but the leaf blower strapped to his back was drowning out his—

A horn screamed.

Anna whirled and froze at the sight of a white car bearing down on her fast. In a panicked reflex Anna threw out her hands before her as if she could fend off the speeding car.

There was a long, smoky screech of tires before the car lurched to stop, the car's front bumper just an arm's length from crushing Anna.

A white-haired old man stuck his head out of the car and hollered, "Pay attention where you're walking, lady! Are you crazy or something?"

"Sorry," Anna said, panting. Her heart was still racing. "My fault. I'm sorry."

"Yeah, yeah." The old driver wheeled around Anna and sped away down the block.

Anna hurried to her car, unlocked the door, and jumped in. She snatched the seat belt around her as if it could retroactively protect her from what had just occurred. For a moment she just sat gripping the steering wheel, allowing the adrenaline rush to fade.

That's it. Anna was done. She was letting this whole rafting trip mystery spin out of control, to the point where she couldn't even think straight. Of course it was crazy to suspect that Christine Jackson and her children's lives were threatened. Whatever Damon Darrell and the rest of his cronies were up to, Anna was pretty sure that it was nothing worth killing over. They were millionaires after all, not murderers. Anna decided then and there that she would stop digging up fuel for her pregnancy paranoia. She'd just wait for Martin to return home, tell him their wonderful news, then never allow him to go on another trip with those men again, period. End of story.

Anna turned and gave Christine Jackson's house one final look. Then she turned the ignition and began to drive home.

*

The Handyman waited until Anna Grey's departing Prius

was a full two blocks away, then he pulled out of his parking space and began to follow.

The white Camry the Handyman was driving was the most common car on the American road. This precaution, combined with his exceptional tailing skills, made the chances of Anna's spotting her shadow practically nil. Nevertheless, there was no point in taking unnecessary chances. As long as he stayed within five hundred yards of Anna's vehicle, the GPS device planted under her bumper would transmit her exact location to the Tracker Map app on his iPhone.

Even if, by some fluke, Mrs. Grey did detect his presence, she had absolutely no chance of eluding him.

Moments earlier, when he saw that car speeding toward her, the Handyman feared that his big double payday was lost. He was greatly relieved to see the Grey woman escape death, at least for the time being. The email reply that he had received from the client was inconclusive but still very encouraging.

Stay very close.

To the Handyman, "Stay very close" meant that the job profile had shifted from a possible kill to an inevitable one. He had no idea what final moves the client needed to make before pulling the trigger, but the Handyman felt certain that Anna Grey would not escape death twice that day.

77

The stench was so thick and musky that he could taste it. Martin snorted to get the foulness out of his nose but it was useless. Every breath he took came with the nauseating odor of human funk.

Martin peeled opened his eyes to a blurry kaleidoscope of pale halftones. He blinked, and the shapes became more defined, pale circles and elongated blobs. He blinked again and saw eyes.

There were faces staring down at Martin. Dozens of dirty, ghostly faces, all watching him.

Martin groaned and sat up with a start. Bright pain lanced through his skull. He cried out and clenched his forehead with both hands. He felt a prominent knot of flesh near his temple that was tender to the slightest touch.

Martin heard voices urging him to lie back down and to keep still. He felt bony hands on his shoulders pushing him back down. Beneath him he felt a soft bundle of material that gave off a waft of stink every time he moved.

Martin blinked again, and the dirty pale faces were still there, only sharper. Men and women surrounded him on all sides. Some young, some old, some middle-aged. They were all withered shadows of formerly healthy human beings. Matted hair, rotted teeth, threadbare clothing sagging on wiry limbs. And they all reeked. Their facial expressions were eerily vacant, as if their minds had been stripped away along with their humanity.

Martin swallowed to moisten his dry throat. "Where am I?"

There was a puzzled stir. The dirty pale faces muttered and exchanged glances. Finally, an elderly man stepped closer. His bristled face was drawn, and his frame shaky, but there was a wisdom in him that the others seemed to respect. "You're in the mine," he said. "You're with us."

"What? What mine?" Still on his back, Martin glanced around. Then he remembered. He remembered the low, sagging ceiling, the nests of dirty clothes, the shielded security cameras, and that bright red cable hugging the perimeter of the ceiling. He was underground. In the slave quarters.

"They tossed you in here last night," the elderly slave said. "I let you have my spot."

Martin moaned as he sat up, wincing at another stab of pain. He rubbed the swelling on the side of his head and the memory of Oscar's gun butt came rushing back.

"You might have a concussion," the elder slave said. "Probably better if you stay down."

Martin shook his head. "No, I'm all right. I—" Martin suddenly recognized the elderly slave. It was the same old man whose merciless beating had caused Martin to cry out for the guards to stop.

"You sure you're okay?" the old man asked.

"Yeah." Martin scanned the crowd standing around him. Their number was much larger than he had first realized. Every tortured soul in the slave quarters must have been there, eyeballing one of their former black masters, yet, somehow, Martin did not feel threatened.

"Don't take this the wrong way," Martin said, to no one in particular, "but why am I still alive?"

"'Cause they ordered us not to touch you," a tall man at the back of the crowd growled. He was the biggest of the slaves, by far, with the sagging physique of a once formidable man now shriveled by years of bondage. "Otherwise," he continued, "I'd rip your black ass apart."

A majority of the other slaves instantly turned on the big man, hissing at him to shut up.

The elder slave turned to the bigger man with a chastising stare. "Vincent, you're a damn fool. He's not one of them. He risked his life to help us."

Most of the other slaves nodded in agreement.

A young man peeled from the crowd to stand over Martin. He appeared meatier than the rest and his clothing, which included a *Seinfeld* T-shirt, wasn't as worn. "Don't listen to Vincent," the young man said to Martin. "We all know what you did—or at least tried to do. I'm Louis Ward, from Southdale, Minnesota. Been here three months." Then Louis did something that caught Martin off guard. He stuck out his hand.

For an instant Martin couldn't move, the moment too

surreal to digest. When he finally reached up and grasped Louis Ward's hand, the hint of a grateful smile appeared on the slave's face.

The elderly slave offered Martin his hand as well. The frail man's hand felt like a bundle of twigs in Martin's grasp.

"I'm Otis Rolley," the old man declared, with a surprising amount of spirit. "Used to live in Fairbanks, Louisiana. Louis has the least time here and I have the most. Sixteen years."

Martin shuddered at the number. For a man to lose so much of his life to a place so horrible was unimaginable.

A middle-aged man stepped forward next. He was balding and his left eye appeared dull and lifeless. He spoke with a slight southern drawl. "I'm Robert Moore, from Sandy Spring, Georgia. I figure I've been in this hellhole for seven years and three months. Kinda hard to keep track." When Robert took Martin's hand, he didn't shake, he just gave it a firm squeeze.

Several more of the slaves felt the need to break away from the crowd and introduce themselves to Martin. Some shook his hand, some patted him on the shoulder, others just said their piece and retreated back to their spot. Martin didn't understand it exactly, until a woman wearing a tattered dress stepped forward. She appeared to be in her early thirties. Even the crust of years of hard labor couldn't hide the fact that at one time she had been very pretty.

"I'm Helen, from Far Hills, New Jersey," the woman said. She tugged forward a boy who Martin judged to be about thirteen. "And this is my son, Aaron. He was born down here." She thumbed over her shoulder. "Right in that corner over there."

Unlike the muted faces of his fellow slaves, the teenage boy wore a tight, puzzled look worthy of a caricature. "Aren't you scared?" he said. "They're going to kill you, you know. Just like they did that other man."

"Aaron!" the boy's mother snapped as she yanked him back into the crowd. An awkward silence settled over the room.

Martin understood. The slaves weren't thanking him for risking his life; they were thanking him for sacrificing his life. He was going to die. He was never going to return home from this trip, never see his wife again . . . just like Donald Jackson.

Martin turned to Otis. "Donald Jackson? Is that who he means? Did they bring him here too?"

Otis nodded. "They did. But he was in far worse shape than you. Shot. Bleeding badly and barely alive. Then they came and took him away."

Hearing the description of Donald Jackson's injuries sparked another image in Martin's memory.

Alice.

"There was a girl whipped last night," Martin said to Otis. "She was left in the barn, badly hurt. Her name is Alice. Do you know what happened to her?"

Otis frowned. "I do."

"Is she dead?"

Martin had no rational reason for caring so much about a girl whom he hardly knew when his own life was in jeopardy, but he did. It was as if his and Alice's lives were bound, somehow. He had this crazy, illogical feeling that as long as Alice lived, there was still hope.

Instead of answering Martin's question, the old man turned to Louis. "Help him up."

Louis extended his hand and tugged Martin to his feet. Martin felt a throb of pain behind his eyes that dissipated quickly.

"Come," Otis said.

The crowd parted as Martin followed Otis across the space. As Martin stepped over rows and rows of tightly spaced sleep areas, he realized something odd. The awful smell that had stung his nose only moments ago was now barely noticeable.

Otis paused over an elderly woman who was seated on the ground cradling the hand of a sleeping woman.

It was Alice. Her face was so calm and still that she almost appeared to be dead.

"They brought her down with you," Otis explained to Martin. "She has a dangerous fever. My wife cleaned her wounds but—" He frowned. "Like I told you, I've been here a long time. I've seen men die from less severe whippings."

Martin winced with guilt. He rubbed his right palm

against his pant leg to erase the sudden sensation of the cowskin handle in his grip.

"She's a strong girl," Otis's wife said.

Martin looked down and saw the old woman mopping Alice's brow with a soiled rag. Alice moaned and rocked her head before settling back into a calm sleep.

"What do you think?" Martin asked the old woman. "Is she strong enough to make it?"

"I don't know," the woman replied with a doubtful shake of the head. "That all depends."

Martin was almost afraid to ask. "Depends on what?"

"Rest." The old woman uttered the word as if it were holy. "She needs lots of rest. If they don't make her work too soon, I think she will have a very good chance. But only if."

Martin stared at Alice's unconscious form. "Well, they wouldn't try to make her work in this condition. Would they?"

The old woman's eyes fell as she went back to mopping Alice's brow.

Martin turned to old Otis and the group of slaves who had trailed them to Alice's bedside. Martin's eyes burned with the question, but the only response he received was a wall of bleak stares.

A loud metallic clacking sound drew everyone's attention to the chamber's door. The thick steel groaned open and four uniformed guards entered fast and flanked the doorway. They were trailed by their leader, Roy, the same man who'd given Martin and Damon a tour of the mine only a day earlier.

"All right, get moving," Roy barked at the slaves. "I'm not in the mood for any bullshit this morning."

The slaves filed past Martin on their way to the door. Some patted Martin on the arm or squeezed his hand or just met his eyes for a moment. Otis and his wife each left Martin with an affirming nod before they followed the others off to work. Vincent, the big man, paused before Martin and looked him straight in the eye.

"Vincent," Roy yelled, "keep your ass moving."

Vince ignored the order and extended his hand to Martin. "Vincent Clarke," he said. "Charlottesville. Three years."

Martin shook Vincent's hand.

"Vincent, I'm not going to tell you again, goddamnit!"

Vincent nodded to Martin, then trailed the others out the door.

Roy brushed past Martin as if he weren't there and glared down at Alice's sleeping form. He nudged Alice with his booted foot. "Hey."

Alice, brow beaded with sweat, moaned and stirred.

Martin's jaw clenched as he watched Roy nudge her with his boot again, harder. "You hear me?" Roy said. "Time to work."

Alice groaned and tossed fitfully. Her eyes strained to open, but she was too weak.

Roy sighed. "I can't believe this bullshit."

"Can't you see the girl's too sick to work?" Martin said.

Roy whirled and drove his fist hard into Martin's gut. Martin gasped and folded to the floor in a ball of lingering dull pain. Suddenly Martin's entire world was the spit-shined tips of Roy's combat boots.

Roy glared down at Martin's writhing form with perfect contempt. "Don't you ever say another word to me, traitor." Roy turned to the guards at the door. "Two of you escort this piece of shit to the main house. They're waiting for him."

One of the guards pointed to Alice. "What about her?"

Roy watched the girl loll and mumble incoherently. "Let her be. But if she can't work tomorrow, bury her." With that, Roy marched out.

Martin shifted on the floor to afford himself one last look at Alice. He could see that she was settling again, drifting back off to sleep.

Martin felt himself seized by both arms and hoisted off the ground. "Time to die, asshole," one of the guards snarled, then Martin was dragged across the chamber and out the door.

78

"Martin, eat something. Please," Dr. Kasim said as he gestured to the breakfast banquet laid out before them. "Surely you must be hungry after last night's adventure."

Martin and Dr. Kasim were in the dining room, seated at opposite ends of the table. Dr. Kasim was draped in a simple African print robe. His carved walking staff leaned against the end of the table. Martin still wore the hooded fleece jacket and hiking attire from the previous night.

The spread of morning favorites, everything from pancakes and waffles to poached eggs and fresh ham, was as plentiful and beautifully arranged as always. There was even a cheerful centerpiece of fresh-cut flowers.

Martin didn't touch a thing. He just sat there, empty plate in front of him, staring in shock at the other two men seated at Dr. Kasim's breakfast table.

The two white forest rangers.

Seated directly across from each other, both men were dressed in their green-and-khaki uniforms. Wide-brimmed ranger hats rested on the table beside their plates. The senior ranger was tall and barrel-chested, with more hair on his rugged face than on his head. His partner was about ten years younger, wiry thin, with a black mop of hair that seemed a bit too long for his chosen profession. Both men wolfed down eggs and pancakes and slurped coffee, apparently taking no notice of Martin.

"Is there a problem, Mr. Grey?" Dr. Kasim asked across the table. "If there's something you want that's not here, I'll have one of the girls fetch it." He waved to the two white slave girls who waited against the wall. One of the girls was Felicia.

Martin said nothing, his thoughts in a maelstrom of disbelief. The fact that the two white men seated before him were collaborators in Dr. Kasim's madness was almost too much to take. Now it was clear why Oscar had given in so easily. Martin's escape plan was doomed from the start. By inviting the two rangers to breakfast, Dr. Kasim wasn't merely rubbing Martin's nose in his failure, he was also sending Martin a clear message about the reach of his power.

"What's wrong?" the young forest ranger said, looking at Martin for the first time while reaching with his fork for more sausages. "Don't like our company?"

When Martin failed to respond, Dr. Kasim jumped in. "Nonsense, Mr. Grey loves you white folks. Even more than life itself, it would seem."

Martin's eyes flicked angrily to the old doctor.

Dr. Kasim responded with a thin smile that almost seemed pleasant.

"You should really try the blueberry pancakes," the older ranger said to Martin. "They're delicious." Then he turned and snapped his fingers at Felicia. "Get the man some pancakes."

"Yes, sir." Felicia approached the table, transferred two pancakes from the warmer to Martin's empty plate, and then returned to her spot against the wall.

Martin didn't even look at the pancakes.

"You really should try them," Dr. Kasim said. "They're actually made from your wife's recipe. Fitting, considering the significance of this meal, don't you think?"

These words made Martin wince: Dr. Kasim's way of pushing the knife even deeper.

"Try one bite. After all my trouble that's the least—"

"I don't want any damn pancakes!" Martin yelled as he stood bolt upright and swiped his place setting from the table. Plates and silverware landed with a crash. "If you think that I'm going to just sit here and chitchat with you, you're crazy!"

Both rangers shot to their feet, but before they could act, the dining room door burst open and two guards charged in, weapons drawn.

Dr. Kasim raised a staying hand. "It's okay. It's okay."

The two guards froze but remained coiled for violence. Dr. Kasim met Martin's angry stare. "Sit down, Mr. Grey. There is much to discuss and I would prefer to do that without you in shackles."

Martin sank back to his seat.

With a wave of his hand Dr. Kasim dismissed the two

guards and the shaken servant girls. Finally he smiled at the two rangers as if nothing had occurred. "Thank you for joining me for breakfast this morning. You can expect something extra this month."

The rangers nodded appreciatively.

Martin watched as the two uniformed white men picked up their hats and started for the door. Neither man even glanced in Martin's direction. It was as if, for them, he had already been erased from existence.

The instant the door clicked shut, Dr. Kasim wagged a finger at Martin. "That fire in you. That's your Zantu blood that you are so eager to deny."

"Bullshit," Martin hissed. The word tasted good in his mouth, far more satisfying than any dish on the table. His mask finally off, there was no longer a need to suffer through Dr. Kasim's tiresome musings. "That whole black noise theory of yours, total bullshit," he said. "You're no philosopher or spiritual leader or even a doctor. You're just an evil, angry old man."

For a moment, Dr. Kasim just stroked his white whiskers and held the faintest smile. "Did that feel good?" he finally said. "Must have been difficult for you to keep your true feelings hidden these last couple of days."

"You have no idea, old man."

"I'm about to prove to you that you're wrong, Martin." Dr. Kasim turned to the door. "Bring it."

One of the guards entered, dropped a manila envelope in front of Martin, then left the two men alone again.

Martin stared at the perfectly flat envelope. He couldn't imagine what was inside; all the same, it terrified him.

"Go on," Dr. Kasim said, "open it."

Martin unwound the thin red cord and peeled back the flap. Reaching into the envelope felt like sticking his hand into the mouth of a lion.

Martin withdrew a photograph printed on a standard letter-size sheet of paper. The image was taken outdoors and had the telescopic feel of a professional surveillance photo. It was a shot of Anna talking to a woman whom Martin did not recognize. But the fact that he was staring at a photograph of his wife given to him by Dr. Kasim was enough. The fear and desperation that he felt had just been ratcheted up tenfold.

"What—what is this?" Martin's voice cracked.

Dr. Kasim took his time, letting the moment stew. "That, Martin, is your wife. Causing trouble."

"I—I don't understand."

"That woman she's speaking to, her name is Christine Jackson. Donald Jackson's widow."

Martin stiffened.

"Now, why do you suppose your nosy little wife would go through the trouble of tracking down Mrs. Jackson?"

"I—I don't know," Martin said, shaking his head. "She was just worried about the trip. She's not a threat to you."

432

"Maybe, maybe not." Dr. Kasim leaned forward in his seat. "Now, if I'm an evil old man like you say, she'd already be dead, wouldn't she?"

"Please," Martin said. "Leave Anna out of this."

"Have you been paying attention? She put herself in it. And by the way, your nosy wife isn't the only family member you need to worry about."

Martin's mind reeled with confusion. "What? What are you talking about?"

Dr. Kasim's eyes dropped to the envelope. "You're not done."

Martin's trembling hand slid into the envelope once more and withdrew another photograph. It was another surveillance shot of Anna. She was alone and appeared to be exiting an office building. Baffled, Martin looked up at Dr. Kasim. "What is this supposed to mean?"

Dr. Kasim poured himself a cup of coffee. "That building she's exiting," he said, "it's a medical building."

"Medical building?"

Dr. Kasim stirred cream into his coffee. "She's leaving her obstetrician's office."

"But that doesn't make sense. Anna doesn't have an—" Martin stopped short when he saw that look in Dr. Kasim's eye, a knowing look that forced Martin to instantly see the truth. "No, that's impossible. She would have told me."

Dr. Kasim took a slow sip of coffee, then said, "Anna's two months pregnant, Martin. She just found out. I'm

433

sure she's eager for you to return home so that she can tell you the wonderful news."

Martin recoiled with emotion. Anna pregnant? It was too much to absorb, too hard to believe. "How do you know this?" Martin asked, his eyes welling with tears. "How do I know you're not lying?"

Dr. Kasim took another sip of coffee, then carefully set down his cup. "Do I really need to answer that question? Does it even matter?"

Martin knew he was right. The answer was obvious. Dr. Kasim's people, whoever they were, knew everything, and they were watching Anna. Watching her every move.

Through gritted teeth Martin said, "If you hurt my wife, I'll—"

The bored look on Dr. Kasim's face stopped Martin cold. Martin's threat was meaningless and they both knew it. "We can fix this," Martin said. "I'll never tell anyone about Forty Acres. I swear. You can watch us to make sure."

Dr. Kasim just stared. Unmovable. Waiting for Martin to accept what was inevitable.

Martin's head sagged and tears rolled from his eyes. "Please. I'll do anything you ask. Anything. Just please don't hurt her. Don't hurt . . . them. I'm begging you."

Dr. Kasim raised a hand. "No need for that. Despite what you might believe, Martin, I am not evil. I only do what needs to be done, nothing more. And certainly nothing less. This situation can all be resolved without any harm coming to your family."

Martin gazed at the photograph of Anna exiting the medical building. Her face was a bit blurry, but he could still make out the smile on her face. He could still see the joy in her eyes. The thought of that light fading from Anna's eyes once she found out the news caused Martin's soul to ache.

"Martin, are you listening to me?"

Martin nodded, too choked with emotion to speak.

Dr. Kasim leaned back in his chair, crossed his legs, and folded his hands across his lap. "Here's how it works," he said. "In a few moments, Oscar will take you into the woods to stage your tragic accidental death. You are going to cooperate fully. If everything goes without incident, your wife and child will be very comfortable for the rest of their lives. But if there's any difficulty— Well, I think you know what will happen. I do not make empty threats, Martin. The fate of your family is in your hands. Do you understand?"

Martin nodded.

"Say it," Dr. Kasim pressed. "Look at me and tell me you understand."

Martin peeled his defeated eyes from the photograph. "I understand," he said. "I will do whatever Oscar asks."

A satisfied smile creased Dr. Kasim's lips. "Good. You're doing the smart thing for your family." Dr. Kasim turned to the door and raised his voice. "He's ready."

79

Escorted by two guards, Martin stepped out of the main house onto the front porch. It was midmorning and the sky was extraordinarily clear, a perfect forever blue unbroken by even a wisp of white. The sun was golden and warm and there was a gentle breeze that carried fragrances from the nearby garden.

It was a beautiful day to die.

Solomon, Tobias, Kwame, Carver, and Damon were there on the porch, standing between Martin and the stairs. In the circular driveway, behind this farewell committee, Oscar stood waiting beside a blue Land Rover.

The five men stared at Martin contemptuously, showing no trace of sympathy or compassion. Martin felt as if he were standing before a firing squad.

"I thought you were smarter, son," Solomon grumbled while shaking his head. "I truly did."

"Can't believe you were just gonna give us up," Tobias said. "That's cold, brother."

"Brother?" Kwame practically spat the word. "You're a traitor to your people. You're nothing to us."

Surprisingly, Carver appeared the least angry. In fact, he seemed pleased by Martin's predicament. "You never had me fooled for a second," he said with a smile. "I knew you didn't have what it takes the moment I laid eyes on your sorry ass."

Martin's betrayal impacted Damon the hardest. The lawyer's face was a conflict between anger and deep sorrow. His devastated eyes brimmed with tears. "I trusted you," Damon hissed through gritted teeth. "I opened the golden fucking gates for you . . . and this is how you repay me? Why?"

Martin looked Damon square in the eye. "You know why."

He turned to the others. "You all know why. Deep down, you all know."

"Shut up!" Damon lunged and punched Martin across the jaw. Martin's head snapped to the side and he dropped to one knee.

"Damon!" Oscar yelled from the driveway. It was enough to get Damon to back off.

When Martin returned to his feet, his lower lip was trickling blood.

"You take that to your fucking grave," Damon growled.

Martin locked a stare on Damon as he wiped his lip with the back of his hand. "And you remember who sent me there."

There was a flash of uncertainty in Damon's glaring eyes.

"Bring him," Oscar called to the guards. "Let's get this done."

Damon and the other men made way, allowing the two guards to usher Martin down the steps toward the waiting vehicle. Instead of his usual white suit, the overseer was garbed in khakis and hiking boots, an outfit more suitable for an early excursion into the woods. Oscar stepped into Martin's path and looked him over from head to toe. "If we didn't have to concern ourselves with suspicious injuries, I'd do far worse than punch you. Believe it." He turned to the two massively built guards. "Jamel, Russell, ride in the back with Mr. Grey between the two of you."

As Jamel and Russell proceeded to load their prisoner into the back of the Land Rover, Oscar turned to Damon, who was still on the porch with the other men. "Mr. Darrell, you can ride up front with me."

Solomon, Tobias, Kwame, and Carver all appeared surprised by Oscar's invitation, but no one more so than Damon himself. "No. No thanks," Damon said to Oscar, shaking his head adamantly, "I'd rather just wait here with the others."

"I'm afraid I'll have to insist," Oscar said. "The doctor gave me specific instructions to bring you along to observe. Considering your connection to Mr. Grey, I'm sure the reasoning behind the doctor's request is obvious."

All eyes turned to Damon. "Are you serious? Dr. Kasim is punishing me by making me watch?"

Oscar frowned. "I think the doctor would characterize it more as a 'teachable moment.' In fact, he told me he intends to discuss it with you once we return. Now, if you don't mind, Mr. Darrell, we need to get going."

Squeezed between the two guards in the rear of the Land Rover, Martin saw Damon throw up his hands in defeat, then walk toward the vehicle. When Damon yanked open the passenger's-side door, he glared back at Martin before sliding into his seat. During that fleeting exchange, Martin thought he caught an edge of fear in Damon's eyes. It was one thing to send a man off to his death, another thing entirely to actively participate. But as Damon fidgeted nervously with his seat belt, it occurred to Martin that Damon's anxiousness was spawned by something far more basic, something instinctive to all human beings. Never move toward death, always move away, because if you get too close, death just might jump up and grab you too.

Oscar shifted the Rover into gear and they began to drive away.

Martin glanced out the rear window at the four men on the porch. They watched his departure, as still and as inhuman as garden statues. Suddenly, one of the statues moved.

It was Carver, raising his middle finger and laughing.

80

The blue Land Rover bounced and rocked as it pushed forward through the sun-dappled woods.

Except for the rumble of the engine and the creak and rattle of its frame, the Land Rover's interior was uncomfortably quiet.

Martin gazed out at the scrolling wilderness, but his thoughts were back home with Anna. He knew that Anna would take his death hard and that the pregnancy would make it even harder, but Anna was strong. She was also sensible. He was confident that, for the sake of the baby, Anna would pull herself together and go on living. Knowing that Glen and Lisa would be there to help also gave Martin a measure of comfort. And then of course, there was Dr. Kasim's promise. Martin didn't give a damn about the financial benefits of the doctor's vow—Anna earned a decent living as a registered nurse—he only cared that Anna and his child would be safe from harm.

Nearly twenty minutes into the trip, the silence was finally broken. Damon turned to Oscar and asked to know their destination.

"The river," Oscar replied, without taking his eyes off the terrain ahead. They were traveling off-road now, weaving around trees and plowing through dense stands of bushes. "I have a location picked out about a mile north of where we usually cross."

Martin had restrained himself from asking any questions, but now that the subject had been broached and his death was already a foregone conclusion, he figured he had nothing else to lose. "So that's how I die? Drowning?"

Oscar's eyes met Martin's in the rearview mirror. Martin could feel the overseer assessing his mettle, judging if the prisoner was prepared to hear his fate. When Oscar answered, he was still fixed on Martin's reflection. The moment was as intimate as if the two men were in the car alone. "It'll be a rafting accident," Oscar said, then his focus returned to the road. "Raft overturned, you got swept downriver, lost your helmet, head smashed on rocks, and then, yes, tragically, you drowned." Oscar glanced again at Martin in the rearview mirror. "Any other questions?"

"Jesus," Damon muttered, drawing a stare from Oscar.

The details of his imminent murder didn't frighten Martin so much as plant a seed of uncertainty. The scenario concocted by Oscar would probably satisfy most people, but Martin had serious doubts that Anna would buy it. Anna was a world champion worrier. Sometimes Martin found this personality quirk adorable and, other times, impossible to deal with. It was Anna's fretting that had led to her suspicions about Donald Jackson's death, and judging from Dr. Kasim's photo, she still hadn't let it go. The news of Martin's death in a similar manner would only fuel Anna's worries. Chances were good that after the initial blow, she would begin poking around and asking inconvenient questions. The more Martin thought about it, the more certain he became that, as far as Anna was concerned, the official story would not work.

But Dr. Kasim and Oscar had to know that. Why then would they proceed with such a risky plan if they knew that it would lead to more trouble from Anna? Unless—

As the Land Rover carried him closer and closer to what would be his final destination, the truth hit Martin like a fist. Dr. Kasim had lied to him. The moment Anna showed up at Donald Jackson's widow's house, she was already marked for death. The only reason they hadn't killed her yet was timing. If Martin and Anna were to perish within days of each other, in two completely unrelated incidents, the coincidence would be too big to ignore. Considering the people involved, the media attention would be off the charts. No, the smarter approach would be to kill Martin first, then a couple weeks later stage Anna's suicide. The pregnant widow, in a state of paranoia and deep depression, slits her wrists or overdoses on sleeping pills. Martin realized with rising horror that he wasn't sacrificing himself to save Anna and his child. In fact, the very opposite was true. He was about to become an unwitting collaborator in the murder of his family.

The Land Rover struck a large bump that bounced the

vehicle violently. The jarring motion seemed to shake free the sense of hopelessness that had settled over Martin. By the time the truck had resumed its firm and steady ride, a new purpose had been sparked within him.

He had to try to escape.

The vehicle was jolted by another bump in the road. Martin took the opportunity to glance at the two guards on either side of him. Their shoulder-holstered weapons were within his reach, but the tight quarters presented a problem. Even if Martin lunged for a gun, the guards would overwhelm him in an instant. He wouldn't even get a chance to fire one shot.

No, he had to think of something else.

The rising roar of water and the appearance of the river through the trees directly ahead filled Martin with a knot of dread. Time was running out.

Oscar brought the Land Rover to a stop in a small natural clearing about fifty yards from the sloping river-bank and ordered everyone to get out. The two guards stuck close to Martin as he climbed out the rear door. The sound of rushing water was louder now, and the air was thick with moisture. Martin did his best to scan the imme-diate area without appearing too interested. He considered making a run for it, but the densely wooded terrain didn't lend itself to a brisk escape. In a flat-out chase, Oscar and his two goons would have a sporting time hunting Martin down like a fleeing animal.

Martin noticed Damon watching him. He wasn't sure

if the cunning attorney could sense his scheming or if Damon was just morbidly curious to see how the condemned man would march to the gallows.

Oscar directed everyone to the back of the vehicle, where he swung up the tailgate door. There were two identical black duffel bags in the rear cargo area, and nothing else. Oscar grabbed one of the bags and tossed it to Martin's feet. "Take off everything but your shirt and underwear," he said, "and put on what's in the bag. Don't take all day." Then, to Damon, "And you, give him a hand." Finally Oscar turned to the two guards and told them that he'd be right back.

Both Martin and Damon watched, puzzled, as Oscar hiked off into the woods in the direction of the river. Martin tried to follow Oscar's path, but the foliage was too thick.

"All right, you heard him," Jamel barked at Martin. "Hurry up and get changed."

Martin zipped open the duffel bag to reveal a blue-and-gray jacket and matching pair of pants. The outfit resembled a tracksuit, but the slick waterproof material and the crisscrossed paddle logo on the jacket told him that it was rafting gear. There were paddling gloves, neoprene boots, and an orange life jacket inside the bag as well, everything Martin needed to look the part of an unlucky rafter. As he looked at the items in the bag, another thought struck Martin. He had everything he needed to make an escape by leaping into the river. From his crossing two days ago he knew that rapids were treacherous, so his chance of survival would be small, but at least he'd have a chance.

"I said hurry up, not take inventory," Jamel said to Martin.

Martin stripped down to his shirt and briefs and began to slip into the rafting gear. Damon, meanwhile, with nothing to do but observe, took a seat on the Rover's rear bumper. The tailgate door was still open. As Martin completed suiting up, he caught Damon doing something peculiar. When the guards weren't watching, Damon glanced over at the second black duffel bag that was still in the Rover's cargo area. This wasn't merely a glance of passing curiosity; this was an intense laser beam of a stare. And Martin noticed something else about Damon's gaze. His eyes held that fearful spark that Martin had seen earlier, when Damon had first climbed into the Land Rover.

When Damon turned back to face Martin, he wasn't really looking at Martin at all. He was staring uneasily at the rafting gear that Martin now wore, as if the garment possessed some sort of malevolent quality.

Suddenly, Martin understood.

Damon Darrell was worried that Martin Grey wouldn't be the only victim of an unfortunate drowning that day. Damon was worried that the second black duffel bag in the Rover was for him. He was the one who vouched for Martin and brought him to Forty Acres. Even if Damon and Martin weren't in collusion, Damon was still responsible for putting Dr. Kasim's fiefdom in jeopardy. It made perfect sense that the punishment for such a transgression would be more severe than just a ride-along in the woods.

Damon was scared.

Martin realized that Damon's drive for self-preservation could smother his anger and turn Damon into the ally he desperately needed. Working together, they'd have a far better chance of escaping. But could Martin really win Damon over to his side? If Martin played it wrong, and Damon betrayed him, any chance of escape would be blown. Still, Martin had to try. Damon was smart and had keen instincts. He had to see the writing on the wall. And there was also their friendship. Seeing tears in Damon's eyes earlier on the porch had surprised Martin. Despite everything that had happened, Martin now knew that, before Forty Acres, he and Damon had formed a genuine bond. Maybe, just maybe, that would make all the difference.

While he pretended to make final adjustments to his outfit, Martin caught Damon's eye. He held Damon with a hard, steady stare, overtly shifted his gaze to the remaining duffel bag, then returned his stare to Damon again. This was a silent statement that he hoped could only be interpreted one way: *You're next.*

Martin held his breath.

Damon displayed no reaction at first; he just stared back at Martin for a few tense seconds. Then he stood up, took a few slow steps forward, and squared off with Martin. He frowned in Martin's face and shook his head with utter contempt. "Good try, asshole," he said.

"What was that?" Oscar asked, stepping suddenly from the woods into the clearing. The sharp words had also drawn the attention of the two guards. All eyes were on Damon, waiting for an answer.

Oscar's eyes shifted between the two lawyers before settling on Damon. "Well, apparently I missed something. What was it?"

Martin tensed, expecting Damon to give him up, but Damon only shook his head. "It was nothing," he said. Then, in an effort to change the subject, Damon asked Oscar about his brief disappearance.

Oscar clearly wasn't convinced by Damon's side-stepping, but whatever had occurred between the two men didn't seem important enough to waste time on. "I just went to pick the best spot," he explained to Damon. "Better than all five of us wandering along the river."

Oscar gave Martin's attire a quick perusal. He nodded with approval. "Good job, Mr. Grey."

"Please make sure Dr. Kasim knows that," Martin replied. "He made me a promise."

Oscar did not acknowledge Martin's plea. He grabbed the second duffel bag from the back of the Rover, shut the tailgate, and said to the guards, "Bring him and follow me."

As Oscar moved to the head of the group, Martin

caught Damon staring at that duffel bag. Deciding to risk it again, Martin flashed Damon another alarmed look.

Damon rejected Martin's warning with a scowl, but as the group set off for the river, Damon hung back.

"Hey, Oscar, hold on," Damon said. "I think I'm going to stay here with the truck."

Oscar turned and leveled a disapproving stare.

"I know what the doctor wants," Damon said, "but I just don't have the stomach for this. I'll explain it to him when we get back."

Damon's excuse had zero effect on Oscar's cool stare. "Mr. Darrell," he said, "you have no idea what Dr. Kasim wants. If you refuse to follow the doctor's instructions, you will never be welcome at Forty Acres again."

"What?" Damon said. "I can't believe the doctor would say that."

"Believe what you want, Mr. Darrell. Are you coming or not?"

Damon floundered indecisively; then his eyes dropped to the duffel bag in Oscar's grip. He pointed at it. "Tell me something—what's in that bag?"

Oscar shook his head wearily. Finally he sighed and said, "I see you've made your decision. How unfortunate. Very well, wait here until we return."

There was a fleeting instant of eye contact between Martin and Damon, then one of the guards nudged Martin forward. "Let's go. Move." Flanked by the two guards, Martin began to trail after Oscar toward the river.

Damon, his face a mask of confusion, watched the departing group like a man balanced on a precipice. Should he take a chance and leap forward or make the safer choice and stay back?

"Shit!" Damon cursed at the universe, then he hurried to catch up with Oscar and the group.

81

Martin stood at the edge of a steep embankment staring thirty feet down at the rushing river below. The roar of the green water surging around jutting boulders and rock outcroppings was thunderous. The crashing rapids threw off a ceaseless spray that coated Martin's face. Although he shed no tears, the moisture on his cheeks made him feel as if he were crying.

Martin's plan would not work.

Oscar had picked the perfect spot to prevent escape. If Martin tried to leap into the river from where he stood, he'd fall to a crushing death on the rocks below.

Out of options, Martin knew he was about to die.

Oscar and Damon stood facing Martin, the duffel bag resting on the damp ground between them. The two guards, Jamel and Russell, stood directly behind him.

Oscar brushed away beads of moisture from his face and raised his voice above the roaring river. "You need to say anything?"

Martin didn't reply. He just looked for Damon's eyes. Damon dropped his gaze, whether from shame or from malice, Martin wasn't sure.

A stone slightly bigger than a softball lay in the mud

nearby. There were no similar stones in the area, so Martin guessed that Oscar, during his disappearance earlier, had placed it there in preparation for this moment.

Oscar pointed to the stone and said to Jamel, "If you don't mind."

Jamel hoisted the stone. It was heavy, but just small enough for the muscular guard to palm with one hand.

Martin tensed as Jamel raised the stone and took a step in his direction.

"No," Oscar said. "Give the stone to Mr. Darrell."

"What?" Damon stared at Oscar like he was out of his mind.

Oscar deflected Damon's outrage with an unflappable stare. "Please take the stone and use it to crush Mr. Grey's skull. Dr. Kasim wants you to prove your loyalty."

"Prove my loyalty?"

"You vouched for the traitor. Certainly, you can understand how that makes you suspect as well."

"No, I don't understand," Damon said, "and I'm not doing it. No fucking way! I'm going back to the truck."

Damon turned to walk away. Oscar shot Russell a look. The guard pulled his gun, cocked the slide, and raised the weapon to fire. The sound of the chambering weapon was enough to freeze Damon in his tracks.

As Damon pivoted back toward Oscar, he glanced at Martin; the brief eye contact seemed to finally break through Damon's wall of anger. Martin saw a glimpse of his old friend . . . and a flash of regret.

Damon fixed a knowing glare on Oscar, pointed to the black duffel bag. "That's for me, isn't it?"

Oscar sighed. He almost appeared bored by Damon's resistance. "Just do what the doctor asks, Mr. Darrell. You'll save everyone a lot of trouble, and most importantly, you'll save yourself." Oscar signaled Jamel, who stepped forward and held the murder weapon out to Damon.

Watching as Damon stared at the stone, Martin saw something that drained away his last drop of hope. He saw Damon's face hardening. He saw fear and reluctance and that flash of regret giving way to steely resolve.

"Be smart," Oscar urged Damon. "Take it."

Martin saw Damon's chest inflate with forced courage. Then Damon reached out with both hands and took hold of the stone.

Oscar nodded ever so slightly. "Good. Now, one hard strike across the skull, that's all. Then you'll be done."

Damon looked at Martin. His face was void of emotion.

Martin realized that the individual facing him was no longer the Damon Darrell he knew; he was a desperate man forced into a corner. He was a killer.

Raising the heavy stone, Damon began to step toward Martin. Martin backpedaled, his heart hammering. He froze when he felt the edge of the embankment underfoot.

Within striking distance and holding the stone high overhead, Damon said, "Turn around."

Martin, stiff with fear, shook his head. "No," he said.

His defiant eyes burned into Damon. "You do this, you do it to my face."

What happened next had the brief effect of short-circuiting Martin's mind. Damon smiled at him. His murderous stare was gone, and he was flashing that devilish smile of his. "I screwed up," he whispered, and before Martin could get a word out, he shouted, *"Run!"*

Damon whirled and slammed the stone into Russell's temple. The guard's skull bloomed blood and he went down in a heap, gun toppling from his limp hand. Damon whipped back around and charged Jamel. The rock smashed into his nose before the guard could free his weapon from its holster.

"Go, go, go!" Damon screamed at Martin as he spun in Oscar's direction.

Oscar already had his gun out. Martin watched in horror as the overseer pumped round after round into the charging Damon. But momentum still carried Damon forward far enough to send him hurtling headlong into Oscar. Both men went crashing to the ground in a tangle. The sight of Oscar shoving aside Damon's limp, bloody body while taking aim snapped Martin into action.

Gunshots rang out as Martin bolted through the woods in the direction of the Land Rover. He crashed through bushes, dodged trees, and leapt fallen logs as bullets whizzed past his head. Directly ahead he could see the vehicle peeking through the thicket. Just a few more feet and he'd be there. Another volley of concussive gunfire

453

cracked the air. Chunks of tree bark exploded around him. Martin pounded forward even faster, clawing desperately through the brush, a single terrifying question suddenly pushing aside all other fears.

Will the keys be in the truck?

Martin burst from the tree line into the small clearing. Three steps, and he was yanking open the Rover's door. He flung himself into the driver's seat and groped for the keys in the ignition. His heart thudded when his hand grabbed nothing but air.

Outside Martin saw Oscar break into the clearing, raise his gun, and fire. There was an explosion of glass as bullets obliterated the windshield. Martin ducked and spotted the keys in the center armrest tray. Keeping low, he grabbed them, cranked the Rover to life, and stomped the gas. The Rover's four-wheel drive power train found its footing instantly. The vehicle launched forward. Martin sprang up behind the steering wheel in time to see Oscar dodge clear of the barreling truck.

Martin veered hard to avoid a massive tree and suddenly he was careening forward through the dense woods. He yanked the steering wheel left and right, slaloming through nature's obstacle course. The rear window spiderwebbed and spit glass. A side window blew inward. To the vehicle's rear, Martin heard the rapid report of pursuing gunfire. In the side mirror he caught a glimpse of Oscar giving chase. The overseer was running all out and firing at the same time. Martin kept his head low and his foot firmly on the accelerator. Another glance at the side mirror revealed that Oscar had finally given up. Martin saw Oscar's diminishing figure just standing there, weapon useless at his side, watching the vehicle speed away.

Martin had escaped.

Seized by a light-headed rush of relief, Martin felt an urge to brake the vehicle and give his heart a moment to settle down, but there was no time for that. Martin also wished that he could go back and help Damon, but the famous lawyer had been shot multiple times in the midsection. Even if Damon were still alive, without immediate help, he wouldn't last very long. Damon had given his life for him.

Damon's crime was unforgivable, but if Martin made it back, he'd make sure that Damon's sacrifice was not forgotten.

Charged with determination, Martin continued to drive fast and hard over the rough terrain, pushing the Land Rover to its mechanical limits. Martin's entire focus was now on one thing and one thing only. Something even more important to him than getting back alive.

He had to get to a phone so he could save Anna's life.

82

The sky was so blue, so perfectly blue.

Damon, in all his years, had never seen a sky so perfect. It was like an ocean hovering in the air, only there were no waves, just perfect blue. He wondered if Juanita could see the same sky. He wondered if Juanita would hate him or forgive him, when she found out what he had done. He wondered why it was taking him so long to die.

Damon had never felt pain like the pain he felt at that moment. He didn't hurt in one spot; he hurt all over, as if every nerve in his body were a slowly smoldering ember. The pain was constant, but it wasn't unbearable; in fact, he could feel the pain waning with each passing second. His strength was fading as well. He felt a slow yet steady withering of consciousness, as if his soul were circling a drain.

The perfect blue was becoming darker also, heaven's light dimming faster and faster.

Damon blinked and suddenly the perfect blue sky was replaced by a face. There was a cold, unsympathetic face glaring down at him.

It was Oscar's face. Oscar was kneeling over him.

"Do you have any idea what you've done?" Oscar asked.

Damon opened his mouth to reply and he gurgled up a bitter coppery fluid. Blood. He coughed and tried to speak again. "Let him go," Damon rasped. "Let it end."

Damon saw Oscar's eyes narrow to angry slits. He saw the gun rise into view, then he felt the cold muzzle pressed against his forehead.

"Go to hell," Oscar said.

Damon saw Oscar's finger squeeze the trigger. Then the universe exploded.

*

Oscar rose from Damon's corpse, gun still smoking in his hand. He watched Jamel and Russell writhing in the dirt while clutching their wounds. "My face," Jamel moaned over and over. "My face. My face . . ."

Oscar walked over and put a bullet in Jamel's head first. When he turned to approach Russell, the terrified guard was kicking and clawing in the dirt, attempting to drag himself away. "Please," Russell pleaded. "I can make it back. I can."

Oscar stepped over Russell and took careful aim. "Sorry, but there's nothing to make it back to."

The bullet struck Russell between the eyes.

Oscar gave the three corpses a final look. Satisfied that

they were all dead, he holstered his weapon and set off into the woods.

Oscar walked briskly and with focus. He needed to get back to the compound as quickly as possible. Mr. Grey's escape meant that life for everyone associated with Forty Acres was about to undergo a tectonic shift. There were emergency protocols, evacuation plans, and cover-up procedures that needed to get under way. There were also a lot of people who needed to be silenced. Not only those at the compound but also the dozens of minor support personnel located all over the country.

Oscar picked up the pace. There was so much to do.

83

Coiled with tension, Martin wrung the steering wheel as he guided the Land Rover across the rapids. It was one thing to be a passenger during a river crossing, another to be in the driver's seat wrestling the vehicle for control. The closest that Martin had ever come to similar driving conditions was creeping through a flooded Manhattan intersection in his Volvo. That was nerve-racking enough. Grinding across an angry river in the middle of nowhere with so much at stake felt literally heart-stopping.

The Rover had reached the deepest part of the waterway. The charging water relentlessly slammed the right side of the truck, forcing Martin to make constant steering corrections while stomping rapidly back and forth on the brake and gas pedals. Martin's determination and the 4x4's stubborn torque combined to finally deliver him to the opposite shore. As Martin pushed the Land Rover forward into the wilderness before him, he glanced back at the churning water in his wake. The toughest part of the journey was over, he hoped. Now all he had to do was get to the highway.

Martin estimated that it would take Oscar about two hours to hike back to Forty Acres. That's how much time he had to reach that old forest highway indicated on Dr. Kasim's map, flag down a passing vehicle, borrow a cell phone, and call Anna to warn her to seek police protection immediately.

Martin recalled the spatial relationship on the map between the river, the ranger station, and the old highway. Starting from the river, if it took ten minutes to reach the station, it should take approximately twenty-five minutes to reach the highway. That should be plenty of time to save Anna's life. But there was still one troubling unknown.

When describing the highway, Oscar had mentioned that travelers rarely used that route anymore. He even made a joke about it. If Oscar was right, it could take five minutes for a vehicle to drive by, or it could take hours. There was just no way to be sure. Martin hated to admit it, but the success of his plan—whether Anna lived or died—would be determined by luck.

One sure way to better the odds was to have as much time to spare as possible. The faster he reached the road, the better his chances would be of encountering a passing vehicle, so Martin poured on the speed. He had never forded a river before, and he was equally inexperienced at off-roading. A rugged drive for Martin was a gravel parking lot or a speed bump, but that didn't stop him from pushing the Land Rover as hard as he could. Wrapping around a tree or snapping the axel on a boulder would be disastrous, so Martin had to try to find a balance between maximum speed and control. He whipped the Rover around obstacle after obstacle. Wildlife scrambled clear as bushes and saplings toppled beneath the bumper. Rooster tails of dirt flew up in the Rover's wake as its churning treads propelled the vehicle forward.

*

Less than twenty minutes later, Martin was standing on the faded yellow dividing line of a two-lane forest highway. As he peered up and down the tree-lined stretch of empty road, Martin was infected with a hollow feeling of hopelessness. The old highway wasn't just desolate, as Oscar had described; the weed-cracked and leaf-strewn blacktop looked like it hadn't been touched by speeding rubber in years.

Martin listened hard for any sign of an approaching vehicle. The buzz and warble of wildlife and the low rumble of the idling Land Rover, which was stopped at the side of the road, were the only sounds. Martin felt an urge to shout at the top of his lungs, to cry out to the world for help, but he knew that it would do no good. He was completely alone, and from the looks of that forgotten highway, his state of isolation wasn't about to change anytime soon.

With Anna's life hanging in the balance, he couldn't just wait there. He had to do something.

Approximately thirty minutes had passed since he'd

461

escaped. That left another ninety minutes before Oscar reached the compound. Martin could drive damn far in ninety minutes, especially on a road free of traffic. Maybe he could reach a gas station or even the main highway with still enough time to make that lifesaving phone call.

Maybe.

The interstate wasn't indicated on Dr. Kasim's map, nor were there any gas stations. Martin had no idea how long it would take to reconnect with civilization. There was also one other problem. Martin's head ticked back and forth, peering down the highway in one direction and then the other. If he did decide to take the gamble and keep driving, which direction should he choose?

As Martin weighed this decision, he spotted something on the road that seized his attention.

A wild rabbit.

The furry gray creature was sitting on the yellow line about fifteen yards from where Martin stood. Its nose twitching and its ears erect, the rabbit peered back at Martin, perhaps wondering what that strange tall creature was doing on his highway. Without any provocation, the rabbit suddenly bolted to the side of the road, scampered halfway up the embankment, and disappeared down a burrow hole.

The sight of the creature vanishing into the earth jarred something in Martin. For the last couple of hours he had been so focused on saving Anna that he had forgotten that there were other lives at stake as well. There were dozens of people imprisoned in Dr. Kasim's gold mine, and the mine was wired to explode. When Oscar finally reached the compound and reported Martin's escape, not only would Dr. Kasim carry out his threat against Anna, he would also order the execution of the slaves. Even if Martin could reach a phone in time to save his wife and alert authorities, help would never arrive in time to save those people trapped underground.

But what could Martin do to save them?

Even if he did something crazy like go back to the compound and try to rescue the slaves, he'd be doomed to failure, not to mention certain death. He was just one man, completely unarmed. Getting past the guards and freeing the slaves would be impossible.

Or would it?

They'd have to know that he was going for help. Moments after Oscar's return, Forty Acres would be in turmoil. Plus he'd have the element of surprise on his side. The last thing that they would expect was for Martin to return to the compound. In fact, they probably wouldn't expect any outsiders to show up for at least a couple of hours. Chances were pretty good that their focus would be entirely on escape rather than keeping anyone out.

Still, that didn't solve the problem of how Martin could save the slaves. Sneaking back into the compound suddenly seemed very possible, but getting down into the mine and getting the slaves out—it was just too big a mission for one man.

Martin peered up and down the desolate highway again. The frustration and helplessness that he felt at that moment returned his hopes to his original plan. If only a car would come, he thought, just one stupid car or truck or motor home. Then his problems would be solved. He'd make the phone call, Anna would be saved, and there would still be enough time for the authorities to reach the compound and stop the destruction of the mine.

It was at that instant that it came to him. The answer to how one man could save the slaves struck Martin like a thunderbolt. It was a long shot, but it could work. But what about Anna? If he turned around and raced back to rescue the slaves, he wouldn't be able to warn Anna in time to save her.

Martin had to make a decision—try to save Anna and his unborn child or try to save the slaves. Two lives versus dozens of lives.

Morally, the answer seemed obvious. But still, Martin couldn't bring himself to make a choice that might result in his wife's death. So, with time running out, he thought it best to leave the decision up to someone else, someone he trusted more than himself.

Martin Grey stood in the center of that deserted old highway in the middle of nowhere and asked himself one simple question. What would Anna want him to do?

84

Dr. Kasim sat out on his bedroom balcony enjoying an early lunch of baked catfish and steamed vegetables picked fresh from his garden. To wash the meal down, he sipped a tall glass of iced tea garnished with mint leaves and a perfect slice of lemon.

Two young uniformed slaves, one male and the other female, stood by the balcony door behind the doctor, ready to jump if needed.

A quiet solitary lunch on the balcony was a daily routine that Dr. Kasim cherished greatly. From where he sat he had a perfect view of the beautiful front garden and the broad oak-lined main driveway that led to and from the gates of his private kingdom.

To Dr. Kasim, Forty Acres was a place where all he surveyed, from the armed guards patrolling the high walls, to the slaves toiling in the dirt, was under his complete control. A place where he could liberate his followers from the psychological shackles of the white world order and instill in them the confidence and courage to be immune forever. Measured in miles, his kingdom might not have been very large, but measured by impact, Dr. Kasim believed that his work at Forty Acres was more important to the black race than anything that King, Malcolm, or Mandela had ever achieved. Sometimes it pained him to know that his name would never be listed alongside those great men, but he took solace in knowing that in the eyes of their ancestors, his deeds would certainly stand above the rest.

Dr. Kasim rattled the ice cubes in his glass, signaling for a refill. The female slave promptly approached the table, refilled the glass from a crystal pitcher, then retreated to her post by the door. As Dr. Kasim took a slow sip of tea, he noticed a lone man approaching fast up the main drive. What seemed odd was that the man wasn't dressed in all black, like a guard, and he was walking.

Dr. Kasim stuck out his hand in the general direction of the slaves and said, "Glasses."

The male slave popped forward. He removed the doctor's wire-rim glasses from his breast pocket, polished both lenses with a cloth, then laid them carefully on the doctor's palm. Dr. Kasim slipped them on and took another look over the balcony's railing. Finally he could identify the individual who had just reached the front of the main house.

It was Oscar. But why in the world would Oscar be walking?

Minutes later, his second in command barged out onto the balcony and ordered the slaves to leave immediately. The overseer's clothing was covered with fresh blood and he was in an alarmed state, which for Oscar was unprecedented. Before Oscar said even a single word, Dr. Kasim knew that something had gone terribly wrong.

Oscar opened his mouth to speak, but Dr. Kasim raised his hand. "First sit and drink some water."

"But, sir," Oscar said, "this is extremely urgent."

Unimpressed, the doctor waved to an empty chair. "All the more reason. Sit."

Knowing that it was futile to argue with the doctor, Oscar took a seat and poured himself a glass of water.

Dr. Kasim waited patiently for Oscar to drain the entire glass. "Feel better?" Oscar took a calming breath and nodded. "Now," Dr. Kasim continued, "tell me how Mr. Grey managed to escape."

Oscar looked at him, surprised at first, then withered a bit. "Doctor, it was not my fault."

Dr. Kasim cracked a small smile. "You and I have worked together for ten years. You think I don't know that?"

"It was Mr. Darrell," Oscar said. "He lost it. Rushed the guards. Grey took off before I could stop him."

"And the vehicle?"

Oscar nodded grimly. "He took it. And Grey saw the map. He knows how to reach the road. He could be talking to the FBI as we speak." Oscar looked his mentor straight in the eye. "We have to get out. It's over."

Dr. Kasim sighed. He stroked his white whiskers and gazed out over the compound.

467

Oscar asked, "Do I have your permission to shut it down?"

When Dr. Kasim turned back to Oscar, his eyes were glassy with tears. He nodded. "All the slaves into the mine. Prep the vehicles. You handle it. You know the drill."

Oscar stood up sharply. "How much time do I have? How soon do you want everyone ready to leave?"

Dr. Kasim picked up his knife and fork, cut a piece of catfish, and stabbed it with his fork. "You have until I finish my lunch," he said to Oscar as he casually ate the fish.

Oscar nodded and hurried out.

Dr. Kasim drained his iced tea, then rattled the glass for another refill. When no one jumped, he turned and saw that he was alone on the balcony.

His slaves were gone.

In a flash of rage Dr. Kasim hurled the glass to the balcony floor.

It shattered into a million pieces at his feet.

85

When the kill order came, the Handyman was seated in his parked Camry, staring across the street at the intended mark, Anna Grey.

He picked up his chiming iPhone from the dashboard and checked the screen. The client's text message was a model of economy.

Proceed, ASAP.

When the Handyman read the text, he felt a jolt of professional adrenaline. The client didn't just want the Grey woman dead; they wanted her dead fast. An ASAP order meant that the Handyman didn't have to camouflage his work to look like a freak accident or a robbery gone bad. ASAP meant that anything goes as long as it resulted in a quick corpse. Due to the sticky nature of the task, the exact timing was a bit flexible, but the understanding was that he was to exterminate the mark within one hour.

The Handyman frowned as he peered back across the street at his target. He was parked opposite Isabella's, a Mediterranean restaurant on the corner of Columbus Avenue and Seventy-Seventh Street in Manhattan. The Grey woman was having lunch with her husband's partner, Glen Grossman, and Glen's wife, Lisa. The trio was seated on the sidewalk, outside the restaurant, affording the Handyman a perfect view of the target at all times. Unfortunately, the fact that she was in plain sight also meant that, for the time being, Anna Grey could not be touched.

Despite the ASAP order, a hit on a busy Manhattan street called for an unacceptable amount of risk, so the Handyman would wait. He'd wait until the Grey woman's lunch was over. With any luck, after the meal, she'd part ways with the Grossmans and go home. Once she was isolated inside her house, the rest would be simple. Of course, there was the possibility that she had other plans. Maybe she'd go shopping or to a hair appointment, or even take a stroll through the park. Whatever she did, it didn't really matter to the Handyman. He was a professional. He'd still find a way to get to her. He took pride in not only getting the job done but getting the job done right. Anna Grey was marked for death, ASAP. Bottom line, in less than one hour, Anna Grey would therefore be dead.

*

"We really wouldn't mind having you stay with us," Lisa Grossman said to Anna. Lisa slapped the back of her husband's hand. "Glen, tell her."

Mid-sip, Glen jumped and spilled a few drops of coffee. He groaned at his wife. "Anna knows that she's welcome at our place anytime." He turned to Anna desperately.

"Would you please just stay with us before this crazy woman beats me up?"

Anna laughed. She loved Glen and Lisa. Despite being two of the smartest people she knew, they didn't take life too seriously. It was impossible to be anything but in a good mood whenever you were in their presence; that's why she'd invited them to lunch. Anna needed a distraction to get that Donald Jackson business out of her head. She had no intention of burdening the Grossmans with her worries, but by the time the waitress had taken their orders, Glen and Lisa had sensed that something was troubling her. It didn't take much to get Anna talking, but she didn't tell them everything. Anna revealed just enough so that they could understand her anxiety about Martin's trip without thinking that she was going off the deep end. And of course, Anna told the couple nothing about the pregnancy. She was determined to deliver the news to Martin first. Anna just wished that it was Monday already and that Martin was back home, safe.

"You two are very sweet," Anna said, "but I'll be fine. I'm just letting my imagination get the better of me."

Lisa looked doubtful. "Are you sure?" She waved her palms before Anna as if reading Anna's aura. "I sense something from you. It's weird."

Glen rolled his eyes. "What, are you a psychic now?"

Lisa slapped Glen's hand again. "You know that's not what I mean." She pointed a finger at Anna. "You're hiding something. What is it?"

Anna was tempted to tell Lisa about the pregnancy, but all she could do was bite her lip and shake her head. She was relieved when the waitress appeared with the check. Anna reached for it, but Glen grabbed it first. Anna opened her mouth to protest, but Glen held up a hand. "Before you say anything," Glen said, "I have two words for you. Business meeting."

Anna chuckled.

Glen pressed a finger to his lips. "Just don't tell my partner. He's really uptight about this sort of thing."

"True," Anna said, "but he's also really, really cute."

"I guess," Glen said with a shrug, "if you're into black guys."

The three of them laughed together. While Glen fished for his credit card, Lisa laid her hand atop Anna's. "Here's an idea. Since Glen's going to the office, why don't you come over and we'll watch a movie. Later, if you feel like going home, fine, and if not, the guest room is all yours."

Anna shook her head in disbelief. "You really don't give up, do you?"

"She's like a pit bull," Glen said.

Lisa shot her husband a look.

"A movie sounds great," Anna said, "but not tonight. I didn't get much sleep last night. I'm going to just go home, take a long hot bath, and then go dead to the world."

"Okay, okay," Lisa said, "but don't say it like that. I hate that expression. It's really creepy."

86

He was right. They were fleeing the compound.

Hidden behind a large tree, about fifty yards from the towering walls, Martin watched the hasty evacuation of Forty Acres. Every few minutes, another Land Rover, packed with guards still in uniform, would speed out of the main gate, roar past Martin's position, and disappear into the woods. Some of the fleeing 4x4s followed the dirt trail, while others veered off-road in several different directions.

Martin experienced a tense moment when one truck barreled straight toward the spot where he had ditched his stolen Land Rover. Fortunately, the truckload of guards failed to spot the hidden vehicle, and they continued away into the wilderness without incident.

After watching five fully loaded Land Rovers flee the compound, Martin still saw no sign of the doctor or the other men. When Martin first reached the main gate, the huge doors were still shut, so he was pretty certain that he hadn't missed their departure. That meant that Dr. Kasim, Oscar, Solomon, Tobias, Kwame, and Carver had yet to make their escape. This was good news; it confirmed, first, that the slaves were still alive, and second, that his plan to save them could really work.

Destroying the mine with the slaves still trapped inside was a housecleaning chore far too important to leave to even the most loyal subordinate. The risk was too great that a flunky might suddenly grow a conscience, or worse, become overeager and detonate the Primacord too soon. Martin figured that the last thing Dr. Kasim wanted was a massive explosion to draw authorities to the vicinity before he and the other high-profile members had ample time to escape. That meant that they would be the last ones out the door and that, before they left, they would shut off the lights. Only it wouldn't be a light switch that would be thrown, it would be a switch to trigger an underground time bomb. There was no way to know for sure how much time the slaves would have once the charge was activated, but Martin figured that a safe guess was thirty minutes. Thirty minutes was long enough for the men to distance themselves from the scene of their crimes and short enough to exterminate the witnesses before every law enforcement agency in the country descended upon the place.

Of course, this was all just a series of calculated assumptions. For all Martin knew, Dr. Kasim and the other men had used a secret exit to slip out of the compound and the slaves were already dead. But Martin didn't believe that. An explosion devastating enough to destroy an entire gold mine would be nearly impossible to miss in the serenity of the wilderness. During the breakneck drive back, he had seen no rising dust plumes and had heard nothing louder than the roar of the Land Rover's engine.

There was also another reason Martin believed that the slaves were still alive.

He had put far too much on the line for this to be a lost cause. It was true that the object he left behind on the old highway might save Anna's life, but Martin knew such an outcome was unlikely. Leaving the object was more for his sake than for Anna's; it meant that Martin did not abandon his wife completely to fate; it meant she still had a chance. Only with that knowledge could Martin make a U-turn and speed back through the woods toward the greater good.

Yes, Martin was certain that the slaves were still alive. Because if they weren't, the sacrifice of Anna's life would be for nothing.

As if the universe wanted to prove Martin right, at that instant he saw a black Land Rover cruise out of the main gate. Martin's heart began to race and he felt a heady nervousness.

It was them.

Oscar drove and Dr. Kasim, dressed in a drab white robe, rode in the passenger seat. Kwame and Solomon were in the next row of seats, and Tobias and Carver in the very rear.

Martin watched the Land Rover speed away along the wooded dirt path. He had little doubt that they were headed to the landing strip. But then where would they go? Did they truly believe that they could get away? Considering the heinousness of their crimes, despite their great wealth, Martin had serious doubts that they would get very far, unless . . . No, the thought was so awful that Martin pushed it out of his mind.

He had work to do.

Martin waited a moment longer to make certain that Dr. Kasim's Rover was truly the last one. All clear. He sprang out from behind the tree and bolted toward the left-open gate.

*

"Stop the truck," Carver yelled just moments after they had passed through the gate and left Forty Acres behind. "Quick, quick."

Oscar stomped the brakes, bringing the black Land Rover to a skidding halt.

"I don't fucking believe it," Carver said as he jumped out of the truck and stared back down the dirt path at the compound's main gate.

Everyone except Dr. Kasim climbed out and joined Carver at the rear of the vehicle, puzzled stares all around.

"Well, what is it, son?" Solomon said to Carver. "What did you see?"

Carver noticed all the confused faces. "Come on. No-body saw that?"

The group glanced back down the road. There was

nothing to see but two hundred yards of deep tire ruts leading back through the woods to the compound.

"As you know, we're a little pressed for time," Oscar said with an impatient edge in his voice. "Exactly what did you see?"

"I saw someone running into the compound."

Oscar frowned. "An animal most likely."

"No," Carver said. "It wasn't an animal." He glanced at each of them to drive home his next words. "It looked like Grey."

Tobias scowled. "You can't be serious."

Solomon shook his head in disbelief. "Son, you have any idea what's going on here? We don't have time for this nonsense."

"I'm telling you it was Grey," Carver said. "At least, it looked like Grey."

"You're wrong," Oscar said. "The last time I saw Martin Grey he was speeding west. The man was running for his life. No way he'd come back here."

"Let's just go back really quick," Carver said. "Do a quick check."

Oscar stared at Carver like he was nuts. "You know damn well we can't go back in there."

Carver glanced at his watch. "There's still time. Just a quick look."

"Impossible," Dr. Kasim barked. The men turned and saw the doctor behind them, leaning on his carved walking staff. "All of you, back in the truck. Now."

Everyone did as they were told, except Carver. He shook his head. "I know what I saw, Doctor."

Dr. Kasim laid a supportive hand on the younger man's arm. "Your feelings toward that traitor have been clear from the start. And now with all that's happened—sometimes hatred plays tricks on the mind. That's what you saw."

"But—"

"Do you trust me?"

Carver nodded. "With my life."

"Do you love me?"

Carver bowed his head before his mentor. "You know I do."

Dr. Kasim smiled. "Show me. Help an old man back to the truck."

Carver peered back down the road at the compound gate, eyes determined. Riveted.

"Did you hear me?" Dr. Kasim said. "We must go. Carver? Carver!"

87

Martin ran.

He ran as fast as he could, legs and arms pumping, a flat-out full sprint toward the main house. He felt incredibly exposed running up the wide, oak-shaded main driveway, but there was no time for stealth. No time for ducking from tree to tree or sticking to the shadows. Martin was confident about his half-hour estimate, but there was a lot to do, and there was a very real possibility that thirty minutes might not be enough.

First and foremost Martin had to find the panel or box or whatever it was that controlled the explosives. Then he had to figure out how to shut the damn thing off. He considered running directly to the mine and trying to rush the slaves out in time, but that was too risky. Just reaching the mine would eat up the clock, and if the entrance was sealed, there'd be no way that he'd be able to get past that huge steel door in time.

Martin felt sure that the most likely means to save the slaves would be found inside the main house. When he'd toured the mine with Damon, Roy mentioned that the explosives could be activated from two locations. One was the security shack on the mine's upper level, and the other location loomed directly ahead.

Reaching the circular driveway, Martin cut a direct path across the curving gravel road and trampled through the front garden, headed straight for the mansion's front door. From the moment he arrived at Forty Acres, there always seemed to be workers busy in the flower beds or performing various chores around the house's exterior. Now there were only overturned buckets, dropped tools, an abandoned pair of threadbare gloves, and a single ragged shoe. Seeing the grounds so eerily deserted and lifeless caused Martin to run even faster.

Martin charged through the unlocked front door and into the main foyer. Panting, he glanced around at the downstairs area. An overturned armchair, a broken porcelain knickknack, and a fallen painting were the only immediate signs of an evacuation. In that instant a question occurred to him. Why hadn't they burned down the house? The answer came just as quickly. It was the same reason that the mine hadn't been destroyed yet. A raging fire in the middle of the woods would draw quick attention, not an ideal scenario when you're trying to make a clean escape.

Martin had no idea where to begin his search. He didn't even know for certain what he was looking for, but he knew that there had to be some sort of security room. It just made sense that there would be a central location where every surveillance camera could be monitored. Since the Primacord was, in a sense, a security measure, such a room seemed like the perfect place to keep its triggering mechanism.

Confident that it wouldn't be difficult to locate a room full of electronic gear, even in such a large house, Martin began the search with a jolt of enthusiasm. He moved systematically from the ground floor to the second floor, then to the third. On each level he snatched open door after door, and each time he found nothing but bedrooms and closets.

After fifteen minutes of yanking doorknobs, Martin found himself in the third-floor hallway, staring up at a small hatch door that led up to the attic. Martin knew that it made no sense to put a security room in a space so difficult to reach, but he was desperate. He had already searched every inch of the house and time was running out. As unlikely as it seemed, the attic was the only place left to look.

A short knotted rope hung from the hatch door. Martin jumped and was able to catch it. As he pulled the hatch down, a cushion of musty air wafted over him. The stale odor instantly took him back to his building in Brooklyn, back to his childhood when he and his friends would play cops and robbers in the—

"Of course." Suddenly Martin knew exactly where the security room would be.

He bolted down the hall and hurtled down the stairs.

88

The Handyman crept to a stop across the street from Martin Grey's house, just in time to see Anna Grey exit her Prius and cross the lawn to the front door. He killed the engine as he watched her unlock the door and disappear inside.

The Grey woman was alone. Perfect.

The Handyman checked his watch and scanned the immediate area. There were a few neighbors about, a couple of kids walking home from school, a UPS guy making a delivery, just what you would expect to see in a middle-class Queens neighborhood at a quarter after three in the afternoon. The conditions weren't perfect, but he would make do. Ideally, he would have preferred to postpone the hit for a few hours. That way he could go home, catch a quick nap to refresh his mind and reflexes, then return after nightfall as the friendly neighborhood Cable Com guy. The Handyman had plenty of other disguises in his repertoire, but the cable guy was his favorite for one simple reason. A cable guy was one of the few strangers that people routinely allowed into their homes. Unfortunately, because the Grey woman was an ASAP job, he didn't have time for absolute stealth. To get to her quickly, he'd have to use a more brazen method.

The Handyman retrieved a small duffel bag from the backseat. From the bag he removed a pair of black Vibram toe shoes. The trendy rubber-soled shoes that resembled gloves for your feet might look odd, but they were perfect for creeping through a house without alerting the mark. He swapped the shoes on his feet for the toe shoes, then removed two more items from the bag, a .45-caliber Colt SOCOM handgun, and a four-inch-long sound suppressor. The suppressor had been machined by the Handyman himself from completely untraceable parts.

After tucking the gun and the suppressor into separate jacket pockets, the Handyman was ready. He peered back across the street at the Grey house. He saw the upstairs bedroom light switch on and caught glimpses of the Grey woman's shadow moving behind the curtained window.

The Handyman glanced at his watch. A little more than thirty minutes had elapsed since he received the kill order. He still had plenty of time to fulfill the contract as expected, so he decided to wait. People tended to move around a lot when they first arrived home. He'd wait ten more minutes to let the Grey woman get herself settled in, then it would be time to pay her a visit.

89

A dingy bare bulb flickered to life to reveal a low-beamed underground space.

Martin made his way down a creaking flight of stairs and found himself in a cellar.

Metal shelves loaded with boxed supplies lined the brick walls. There were also a few racks of wine and several pieces of stacked furniture. The stagnant air had the dank, musty odor of a basement.

It didn't take Martin long to spot the unmarked steel door tucked between two shelves. He hurried across the cellar and gripped the knob.

"Please," he whispered.

He yanked the door open and found himself staring into a room filled with glowing surveillance monitors and computer screens.

Martin flung himself into the security room. The first thing that seized his attention was an image on one of the monitors. It was a grainy black-and-white video of a large group of people. They were crowded into a large room. Some were lying on the ground, others were leaning against the walls, others were pacing, and still others were holding each other.

Martin realized that he was looking at a live video feed from the slave quarters deep inside the mine. The sight caused his chest to swell with emotion. "They're alive," he gasped. He reached out and laid his hand on the screen. He'd always believed in his heart, he truly had, but now he knew for sure.

That's when Martin noticed an odd flashing beneath his outstretched palm. Slowly, he peeled his hand away from the monitor. In the bottom right-hand corner of the screen, three green numerical digits rapidly cycled away seconds.

4:43.

4:42.

4:41.

Martin knew immediately what he was seeing—the life of every single person on that monitor, ticking away.

Martin shoved two rolling chairs out of his way and turned his attention to the control console beneath the monitors. There were countless dials, switches, and buttons blinking for attention. Fortunately, many of them were labeled. Upstairs Hall, Kitchen, Dining Room, Driveway, etc. There were also several rows of electrical breaker switches, each coded with a number. In fact, Martin quickly noticed, on the entire panel, there was only one unmarked switch. It was located near the center of the console. A simple rotary switch with two indicator lights, one red and one green. The knob was pointed toward the green light, which was illuminated. This switch had one other feature that distinguished it from all its neighbors. It was the only switch that required a key.

Please let it be here.

Martin scanned the room. A small key cabinet was mounted on the opposite wall. He pulled at the door but it was locked.

Martin grabbed a nearby fire extinguisher and hammered the cabinet's lock. Two more hard strikes and the battered cabinet door clattered to the floor.

Inside, there were two rows of silver keys. Each key had a labeled white tag. Storage, Electrical, Plumbing, Garage, and a dozen more. Only one key was different. There was no tag and the key's head was wrapped with bright red tape. The exact same color as the red Primacord cable that Martin had seen snaking through the mine.

That has to be the one.

Martin grabbed the key and slid it into the silver keyhole beside the rotary switch.

A perfect fit. He snatched back his hand, suddenly afraid to twist it. If the key didn't work, what would he do?

It has to work.

Please turn. Please.

Martin took a deep breath and reached for the key.

"Don't you move another fucking inch." The voice came from the door.

Martin froze. Slowly, he turned his head.

Carver Lewis stood in the doorway pointing a gun.

He waved the weapon at Martin. "Get away from that panel."

Martin didn't budge. He knew that if he obeyed Carver's order, he would never get within arm's reach of that key again. "Listen to me," Martin said. "It's over. All of this is over." He pointed to the monitor. "Those people don't have to die."

Carver took a menacing step forward and aimed right between Martin's eyes. "I'm not going to tell you again," he said. "Get away from that fucking panel."

The gun barrel looked huge to Martin, as if he were gazing down a black abyss. The instinct to survive was strong, but something stronger in his heart held him to that spot. Martin peered past the gun, stared straight into Carver's burning eyes, and said, "No, I can't do that." Then Martin lunged for the red key. He heard a sharp explosion followed by an impact to his shoulder that flung him backward into the wall.

Martin crumbled to the floor, blood seeping from a bullet wound in his shoulder. Drunk with pain, he watched helplessly as Carver approached the console and did the unthinkable. Carver swung the butt of his gun at the protruding key, breaking it off in the lock. The top half of the key clattered to the floor near Martin.

Vision beginning to blur, Martin lost sight of the broken red key among the drops of his blood that speckled the floor.

90

While the bathtub filled up behind her, Anna, dressed only in a terry-cloth robe, stood at the bathroom mirror pinning up her hair.

That's when she heard the strange sound.

The resonant churning of bathwater made it impossible for Anna to discern exactly what the sound was, but she definitely heard something. A knock but not a knock, sharper than that, and she was pretty sure it came from downstairs.

Unable to let it go, Anna jabbed the last pin into her hair, then opened the bathroom door and stepped out into the upstairs hallway. The instant she shut the door behind her, the watery racket from the bathtub was reduced to a low hush.

Anna listened. She heard the sound of a car passing outside, the distant roar of a jet approaching JFK, and the faintest chatter of a nearby conversation, but that was all.

It was strange, standing there in that quiet house; Anna felt an urge to call out Martin's name, as if he were just in the other room and could answer back. The feeling that she wasn't alone was so powerful that Anna was tempted to run downstairs and check to see if Martin was plopped down in front of the television snacking on potato chips and beer. Of course he wasn't, but God, how she wished he was.

Anna listened one last time for any repeat of that strange sound; hearing nothing but an empty house, she frowned and stepped back into the bathroom.

*

Once the Handyman heard the bathroom door shut upstairs, he padded softly from the Greys' kitchen into the living room.

Usually he could bump-key a door with a single strike. Perhaps because of a faulty lock, it took three strikes to open the Greys' back door. Apparently the Grey woman had exceptional hearing. If she had come downstairs to investigate, it would have made his job a bit more difficult. A mark who's alert and keyed up for trouble is unpredictable. Preferable by far is a mark who's preoccupied, a mark who never knows what's coming. One minute they're taking a relaxing bubble bath, the next they're bleeding out into the tub.

As the Handyman screwed the suppressor into the barrel of his Colt handgun he could hear the muffled roar of running bathwater coming from upstairs.

The sound was like music to his ears.

91

3:45.

3:44.

Martin, clutching his throbbing shoulder, could still see the monitor from his slumped position on the floor. With his head swimming, the flashing digits weren't much more than a green blur.

3:40.

3:39.

Carver was seated in one of the rolling chairs, his weapon trained on his prisoner. He watched Martin's suffering, wearing a tight, satisfied smile. "I told them that it was you," Carver said, "but they didn't believe me. They refused to come back. Just fucking left me. Can you believe that?"

Martin blinked and shook his head, struggling to fend off the tug of unconsciousness. "Please," Martin said, "there must be another way to shut it down. You can still stop this."

"Fuck that," Carver said. "You're gonna sit there and watch the show. Then, when it's over, I'm going to shoot your traitorous ass and take a photo to prove to them that I was right. How does that sound, brother?"

"You're crazy," Martin said.

"*I'm* crazy?" Carver leaned forward in his chair. "All white people, then and now, hate you because you're black. They might wear it on their sleeve, they might hide it deep down, but it's there. And if you don't see that one truth, then you're the one who's crazy. Even worse, you're a disgrace to your race. If I had the time, I'd peel that black off you, very slowly. Just looking at you makes me sick to my stomach."

Then Carver Lewis spat in Martin Grey's face.

Never looking away, Martin brushed away the spittle. "I take it back. You're not crazy. You're just stupid."

Carver flared with anger. He sprang out of the chair, raising the handgun to pistol-whip Martin. Martin drove his heel, as hard as he could, straight into Carver's knee. There was a sharp snap. Carver hollered in pain as he crashed to the floor. The gun flew out of Carver's hand and skittered toward Martin.

Forgetting his pain, Martin lunged for the gun. Just as his hand brushed gunmetal, a raging Carver flung himself onto Martin. Carver slammed his fist into Martin's bleeding shoulder. Martin wailed as pain lanced through his body. Carver hammered the wound again and again. Martin was jolted by rapid explosions of agony; the room began to tilt. And in that dizzy instant, he caught a glimpse of the timer.

2:13.

2:12.

"I'm gonna kill you," Carver growled. He crashed his knuckles into Martin's shoulder once more.

The pain was so intense that Martin saw a flash of white before the blackness began to draw him down. As he sank deeper and deeper, Martin could feel Carver's hand groping desperately beneath his back for the gun. Martin heard a voice, low and anguished but determined. "No," the voice said. He realized it was his own. It was his last ounce of will refusing to let those people die, refusing to let Anna's death be for nothing, refusing to let Carver get that gun. "No!" Martin yelled. In a burst of adrenalized strength, Martin kicked a stunned Carver clean off him. Martin rolled clear and suddenly it was right there, lying between them.

The handgun.

Carver's hand flew out, but Martin grabbed the weapon first. Carver scowled and screamed an obscenity and lunged at Martin, flailing.

Martin shot Carver clean through the heart, hurling his body back to the floor.

Carver lay dead.

1:43.

1:42.

Martin groaned. He grabbed hold of the console and hauled himself to his feet. He heard a faint splattering sound, looked down, and saw blood dribbling to the floor. The bullet wound in his shoulder was bleeding freely. The room wobbled. He blinked at the monitor and saw double, two black-and-white images of the roomful of doomed people, and two timers.

1:35.

1:34.

Martin dropped his failing gaze to the locked rotary switch, its green indicator light multiplying and rotating in his vision like a kaleidoscope. He grabbed the knob and strained to turn it. But of course it wouldn't budge. It was still locked.

Martin tried to focus his eyes on the lock itself. On the jagged edge of the broken key buried deep within the keyhole.

Impossible to reach, but just maybe—

Martin pressed his thumb as hard as he could against the keyhole. Applying constant pressure he tried to twist the cylinder.

His thumb slipped.

The lock did not turn.

1:21.

1:20.

Martin pushed himself away from the console. Staggering about and leaning on anything he could for support, Martin searched the security room. He dumped out the contents of several storage boxes.

1:05.

1:04.

Martin fished through the dumped supplies and found

a pair of scissors. He stumbled back to the console and tried to force the lock with one of the scissor blades.

The lock still did not turn.

:39.

:38.

:37.

Lacking the strength to hurl the useless scissors across the room, he just let them slip from his fingers. The scissors clattered to the floor directly beside Carver's gun.

Steadying himself by holding the console, Martin stooped down and picked up the weapon. When he stood back up the room spun, and spun, and spun. Flashing green numerals seemed to whirl around him.

:25.

:24.

:23.

The vertigo showed no signs of letting up, so Martin raised the gun and did his best to aim at the swaying console. Martin started squeezing the trigger, and he didn't stop squeezing until he had emptied the gun's entire clip.

The control console flashed erratically, spit sparks, and spewed white smoke . . . but the countdown on the monitor continued.

:11.

:10.

:09.

Overwhelmed by helplessness and defeat, Martin was

no longer able to resist the effects of his injury. His legs gave out and he crumbled hard to the floor. Flat on his back, beside Carver's corpse, Martin watched the last few digits tick away.

:06.

:05.

:04.

That's when every light on the console abruptly winked out. The surveillance monitor died. The lights in the security room and the lights beyond in the cellar began to flicker and strobe and then slowly dim to darkness.

Martin found himself floating in a perfect blackness. He thought that maybe he had died, but he found it strange that he could still feel the floor beneath him. He thought about Anna, about the child they might have had. For some reason he imagined a girl. He imagined himself and Anna walking along a deserted forest highway with a beautiful little girl. He could hear the little girl giggling as she ran away down the leaf-strewn road. He could hear Anna shouting the little girl's name as Anna chased after her.

"Alice, stop," Anna cried out. "Alice, please stop."

92

A twenty-two-foot 1984 Winnebago Chieftain motor home came to a screeching stop on a deserted forest highway. The sun dangled low in the sky, casting long tree shadows across the cracked blacktop.

The Winnebago's driver's-side door swung open and Freddy Tynan carefully backed out and lowered himself to the ground. There was a time when Ol' Freddy would have just leapt out, no problem, but that was back when he first bought the Winny. The year 1986 was a big one for Freddy Tynan. His wife of eight years had left him, he quit his bus-driver gig, and he decided to walk the earth. Well, drive really, and not the earth, just the continental United States.

The instant Freddy's Doc Martens boots were planted on the road, Jake, a seven-year-old cattle dog and maybe the smartest animal in the world, leapt out the door to join his master.

Ol' Freddy scratched the mess of whiskers on his chin and frowned at Jake curiously. "Who said you were invited?"

Jake sat down and barked once up at Freddy.

"Kind of late to ask now, don't you think?" Freddy said.

Jake barked again, and pawed Freddy's blue jeans.

Freddy laughed. "Okay, okay. Come on." He buried his hands in his denim jacket and walked forward to get a better look at whatever the hell it was that lay across the middle of the road. He had been warned by other RVers to avoid this old highway for just the reason that he had slammed on his brakes. They said that the route was barely maintained and that fallen trees and rockslides were common. But as Ol' Freddy and Jake stepped closer to the debris, Freddy realized that what he had seen wasn't debris at all.

Ol' Freddy scratched his beard as he beheld the unexpected sight. "I'll be damned."

Someone had used a bunch of sticks and stones to spell the word *HELP* across both lanes of the highway.

Jake barked and took off up the embankment after a scampering gray rabbit.

"Jake, don't you go too—" Freddy's words caught in his throat when he noticed a piece of paper pinned beneath one of the stones. The paper appeared to have writing on it. Ol' Freddy quickly picked it up. It wasn't a slip of paper at all. It was the torn front cover of a 2009 Land Rover LR3 owner's manual. Someone had used the blank side to scrawl a message.

When Freddy first spotted the word *HELP* spelled out with sticks and stones, he thought it was some kind of prank, but once he'd read that note, the rising hairs on the back of his neck told him it wasn't.

"Jesus Christ."

Ol' Freddy patted his pockets for his cell phone. Realizing that he'd left it on the dashboard, he jammed two fingers into his mouth and whistled. As Freddy turned and hurried back to the Winny, Jake came scrambling out of the woods and met him at the driver's door.

"Let's go, boy."

Jake leapt up into the motor home in a single bound. Then Ol' Freddy did something that he hadn't done in maybe twenty years: he grabbed the door handle and yanked himself straight up into the driver's seat. His back and shoulder would probably make him pay for that stunt in a day or two, but that didn't matter now.

Ol' Freddy grabbed his cell phone from the dash and hit the menu button. The screen came to life and Freddy's heart sank.

A red battery icon flashed zero percent.

"Goddamnit!"

Jake watched with his head cocked as his master began to dig frantically through the glove compartment.

93

The warm glow from aromatherapy candles perched along the rim of the bathtub cast wavering shadows on the bathroom walls. The soothing fragrance of lavender and vanilla, and soft music from Anna's iPod, infused the air with tranquillity.

Anna lay chin-deep in the warm soapy water, eyes shut, in a state of absolute relaxation. She almost felt weightless, formless, as if the bathwater had dissolved her body away, leaving nothing but pure thought.

Anna pondered the life growing inside her, the life that she and Martin had created, and this thought filled her with perfect joy. She thought about fun ways that she could reveal the wonderful news to her husband. Maybe she'd bake his favorite chocolate cake and inscribe it with a special message, or maybe she'd buy him one of those cheesy T-shirts that said Soon to Be the World's Best Dad. Maybe she'd do both. As Anna lay there dreaming up endless possibilities, her thoughts descended gently into sleep.

*

The Handyman, gun held ready, ascended the stairs carefully, pausing to test each step before committing his full body weight. A single creaking misstep might alert the woman to his presence; then things could get sloppy real fast. The Handyman didn't do sloppy.

Finally reaching the top of the stairs, the Handyman tiptoed down the upstairs hall. When he passed the master bedroom, just to be thorough, he peeked inside. The room was empty, as expected. He continued down the hall. As he approached the closed bathroom door, he could hear music playing inside. It was a Sigur Rós piece called "Untitled #3." It was on the playlist he listened to while jogging every morning at five a.m. The tune was very relaxing, transcendental even. Perfect music for dying.

The Handyman pressed his ear to the door and listened. There were no sounds of sloshing water or of wet feet on tiles or of magazine pages flipping, just the coaxing rhythms of "Untitled #3." The only explanation was that the Grey woman was either fast asleep or already dead. He smiled at his mental joke. Could this job get any easier?

Leading with the pointed gun, the Handyman twisted the doorknob and eased the bathroom door open. A pleasant aroma greeted him as he crept through the doorway. The sight of Anna Grey, her head tilted slightly, sound asleep in the tub, brought another small smile to his face.

Two more careful steps, and the Handyman was looming directly over Anna. Through the dissipating bubbles he could see her lovely naked body. For a second he entertained the idea of using her for sexual relief, but his professionalism would not allow him such an indulgence. Especially not on an ASAP job.

As "Untitled #3" reached his favorite part, the real quiet part at the end that sounded like the soul leaving the body, the Handyman cocked his gun and took aim at Anna Grey's temple.

The Handyman's finger was about to squeeze the trigger when he heard something, an odd musical note. He had listened to "Untitled #3" dozens of times and knew this note was wrong. Then he heard it again and realized with some alarm that the odd musical note wasn't coming from the iPod, it was coming from downstairs.

The doorbell chimed again, this time followed by loud banging and a shouting voice. "Mrs. Grey, it's the police. Open the door."

The Handyman saw Anna Grey stir drowsily. He had to act now before she woke up.

*

Another series of loud bangs and Anna lurched awake. She spun around in the tub and gasped at what she saw.

The bathroom door was wide open. She didn't remember leaving it that way, but maybe she—

Loud pounding and shouting startled Anna.

"Mrs. Grey," a muffled voice boomed from downstairs, "it's the police. Please open the door."

What the hell? Still foggy from sleep, Anna's mind whirled. "I'm coming," she shouted. She climbed out of the tub and grabbed her robe.

A moment later, barefoot and dripping all over her living room floor, Anna snatched open the front door. She stared, baffled and more than a little alarmed, at the two uniformed police officers standing on her doorstep. The older officer was white, the younger one appeared to be Hispanic. Both had their hands resting on their sidearms.

"Anna Grey?" the older officer asked.

The first thought that sprang into Anna's mind was that something awful had happened to Martin. "What's wrong?" she asked, her voice edged with fear. "What happened?"

Ignoring the question, the two officers peered over Anna's shoulder into the house. They craned their necks trying to glean as much as they could from the doorway.

"Is everything okay here, ma'am?" the older officer asked.

"Yes. Fine."

"Anyone else in the house?"

"No, nobody."

While the younger officer pivoted and glanced around the front yard, the older officer looked at her. "What about Mr. Grey? Is he home?"

"No, he's out of town." Anna's tense shoulders relaxed

as if shedding a heavy cloak. The officer's question about Martin meant that this odd visit had nothing to do with his trip. Anna brushed away dripping water from her neck. "So what is this about?"

The older officer pinned Anna with a conspiratorial stare and dropped his voice to a whisper. "If someone's hiding in the house, blink twice."

Now Anna was really getting freaked out. "Look, I was just taking a bath. I'm here alone, I swear. Would you please just tell me what's going on? You two are starting to scare me."

The two officers settled down. "Sorry, ma'am," the older officer said. "Just doing our job."

"What job? Like I told you, I'm fine. I have no idea why you're here. I didn't call the police."

"No, ma'am. Someone else did."

"And what, they told you to come to my house?"

The officer nodded. "Yes, ma'am. The DA's office received an urgent call from your attorney, a—" The officer checked his notepad. "Glen Grossman. Mr. Grossman explained that you were a witness in one of his cases and that there had been a threat against your life."

Anna stared. Nothing the officer said made any sense. "What? That's—"

The older officer raised a calming hand. "No need to get alarmed, ma'am. Usually these types of threats are baseless. But if you don't mind, I would like my partner to take a look around your house. Is that okay?"

Anna didn't know how to reply. If Glen did call the police, she didn't want to get him in trouble by exposing his lie. On the other hand, she couldn't imagine any reason why Glen would do such a thing. He wouldn't.

"I'll be real quick, ma'am," the younger officer said. "Just a walk-through for our report."

Anna shook her head. "No. Hold on. Glen Grossman isn't my attorney. He's my husband's law partner. And I'm not a witness in any case. There's been some kind of mistake."

The two officers exchanged confused looks. The older turned back to Anna. "This Grossman character is not your lawyer? You're not one of his witnesses? You're sure?"

"Of course. I told you, he's my husband's partner. This is very strange. Maybe someone's playing a prank."

"A prank? This would be a very serious prank, ma'am. Your husband's partner the kind of person who would do something like this?"

"Who, Glen? No. Never. He's—" Anna was interrupted by Glen's Grand Cherokee screeching to a stop at the curb. Glen's sudden appearance added another spin to the mystery, because it meant only one thing: Glen really did call the police. In a fog of puzzlement, Anna pointed and said, "That's Glen right there."

Anna watched Glen jump out of his car and hurry up the walk. She had never seen Martin's best friend look so anxious. Glen spotted her behind the two officers, waved, and called out, "Anna, thank God you're okay."

"Hold it right there, sir." The two officers stood shoulder to shoulder on the walk, cutting off Glen from Anna. Both had their hands on their weapons.

Glen froze. "Hey, it's cool. I'm Glen Grossman. I'm the one who called—"

"We're aware of that, sir," the older officer said. "Are you aware that making a false police report is a felony?"

Anna held her breath waiting for Glen's response.

"But it's not a false report," Glen said emphatically to the glaring officers. "I'm really glad you're here. Anna's life is truly in danger."

Anna gasped.

*

After they had moved inside, into the living room, Glen explained everything to Anna and the two police officers. How less than an hour ago he had received an odd telephone call from a man in West Virginia named Fred Tynan. This man claimed to have found a note handwritten by Martin Grey that was left under a rock in the middle of an abandoned highway. The note contained instructions for the person who found it to contact attorney Glen Grossman in New York City and warn him that Anna Grey was going to be murdered that very day.

When Glen was through with his story, the two officers did not appear very impressed, but Anna was terrified. It wasn't the threat to *her* life that frightened Anna; it was

Martin's life she was worried about. Anna had no doubt that the letter was real; it was just too crazy, just too random to be a fabrication. The fact that the letter was found in West Virginia and not Washington State also did not comfort her; in truth, she had no idea where her husband was. All at once, Anna's fears about the mysterious rafting trip, about what really happened to Donald Jackson, about the hatred and fear that she saw in Mrs. Jackson's eyes—it all came clawing back to the surface.

Verging on panic, Anna said to Glen, "Martin's in trouble."

Glen frowned. "I think you're right. But wasn't he supposed to be on the West Coast?"

Anna shook her head. "None of that matters. Glen, I know he's in trouble. I know it." Anna whirled to the two officers. "My husband's in trouble, you have to do something. Please."

The officers appeared equal parts doubtful and confused. The older one scratched the back of his neck. "Ma'am, this supposed letter, it's about you, not your husband."

"I don't care what the damn letter says," Anna snapped. She was beginning to sound frantic and she didn't care. "You have to call somebody. You have to find him. His life is in danger. I know it."

"Okay, ma'am. Just settle down. Please. I want you to explain to me very carefully how you know that."

"I can't," Anna said, tears welling in her eyes. "I just—I just know."

That's when telephones began to ring. The cell phones in the pockets of both police officers, Anna's cell phone upstairs in the bedroom, and the phone in the living room, simultaneously began to ring, chime, and buzz.

As the puzzled cops grabbed their phones, Anna crossed to the coffee table and picked up the wireless handset. She brushed tears and hit the talk button. "Hello?"

The male voice on the other end had a stiff, formal clip. "This is Agent Rivers with the Federal Bureau of Investigation. Am I speaking to Mrs. Anna Grey?"

"Yes." Anna's heart began to race. "Yes, this is she."

"Can you confirm for me that there are two NYPD police officers in your home at this time?"

"Yes, they're right here. What's going on?"

"I'll explain everything at headquarters, Mrs. Grey. Please follow the officers' instructions. Good-bye."

"No, wait."

There was a click followed by a dial tone.

When Anna turned around, she saw Glen gaping at the two officers, who were moving now with great urgency. Both men had their weapons drawn. The younger officer opened the front door and scanned the exterior of the house while the older officer approached Anna, gun lowered at his side. He addressed her with laser-like focus, as if Glen weren't in the room.

"We have an emergency, ma'am. I need you to get dressed as quickly as you can and come with us."

"Just one second," Glen said. "You can't just—"

The older officer stifled Glen with a stare. "Mr. Grossman, you're welcome to accompany her, but do not interfere." Glen deflated. The officer pivoted back to Anna. "I'm really going to have to ask you to hurry, ma'am."

"First you have to tell me," Anna said, "what's happening. What's happened to Martin?"

"Honestly, Mrs. Grey, I do not know. All I can tell you is that I just got off the phone with the director of the FBI himself. Whatever it is, it's damn important."

*

After climbing out the upstairs bedroom window and shimmying down to the Greys' backyard, the Handyman had no trouble slipping back to his parked car without being noticed.

The smart thing would have been to drive away, but the Handyman was frustrated, so instead he sat there and watched. He watched the two cops talk to Anna Grey at her front door, he watched Grossman drive up like there was some big emergency, and then he watched all of them leave in the cruiser.

It was obvious to the Handyman that someone had tipped the police off to Anna Grey's hit. But who?

Ultimately it didn't matter. The bottom line was that he had failed.

The Handyman sighed and picked up his iPhone. Now he had to endure the unpleasant task of reporting his failure to the client. Not only would he not be paid; his professional reputation would be damaged.

The Handyman dialed the number; no one answered. This had never happened before. Day or night, the client always took his call. The Handyman dialed again, and again no answer. The phone just rang and rang.

Something had changed.

As the Handyman killed the call, he felt an odd sensation, one that he didn't recognize at first. This feeling clouded his thoughts and made it difficult for him to decide his next move. Should he wait for another opportunity to kill the Grey woman; should he wait to hear back from the client; should he go off the grid? He just wasn't sure.

Then it came to him. Fear, that's what the feeling was. Something big had changed, and now the Handyman was afraid.

94

Martin Grey peeled open his eyes and squinted at the blinding white light. The light flicked back and forth from eye to eye.

"Wake up," an unfamiliar male voice called. "Time to wake up."

"Stop," Martin groaned. He turned away from that annoying light. His head felt like it weighed a ton.

The light shut off and he heard the voice again. "Good morning. Can you tell me your name?"

Martin squinted up at the man staring down at him. He was African American, about Martin's age, and he was wearing a white coat. Martin realized that the man was a doctor.

"What's your name?" the doctor repeated. "Can you tell me your name?"

Martin's lips were dry, and there was a nasty taste in his mouth. "Martin," he answered hoarsely. "Martin Grey."

The doctor smiled. "That's good. How old are you? Do you remember that?"

His vision clearing, Martin could read the name tag on the doctor's white coat. It read Dr. Gordon Hudson.

"Mr. Grey," the doctor pushed, "tell me how old you are."

"I'm thirty-three," Martin said. "Where am I?"

The doctor smiled. "You're at Emory University Hospital in Atlanta. My name is Dr. Hudson. You've been in an induced coma for four days. Welcome back."

"Four days? But—" As Martin tried to absorb this, images and memories began flying back, like pieces of a puzzle coming together. Then all at once he remembered everything. "Anna!" Martin cried as he shot up. Dr. Hudson and a nurse pounced immediately to hold him down. The nurse secured the IV tubing and monitoring cables tethered to Martin's body.

"You must calm down, Mr. Grey," Dr. Hudson said firmly.

"But Anna— They're going to—"

"Your wife is safe, Mr. Grey. She's right here."

Martin blinked at Dr. Hudson, not sure that he had heard right. "What? Where?"

Dr. Hudson didn't answer. Instead he just stepped back and allowed Anna to step forward.

Martin couldn't believe his eyes. It was really her, it was Anna, staring down at him. There were tears streaming down Anna's face but she was smiling and so, so beautiful.

Anna threw herself onto Martin and they shared a hug so long and so tight that finally the doctor had to intervene. "Easy, you two. We have to be careful of that shoulder for a while."

As they parted, Martin grabbed Anna's hand. "That place, Forty Acres. It was horrible. It's—"

"I know," Anna said. "Martin, everybody knows. I think the whole world knows what you did."

Confusion leapt onto Martin's face. "What I did?" Martin remembered the trapped slaves. He remembered time ticking away. He hesitated, afraid to ask Anna the question. "You mean . . . they're okay? The mine didn't explode?"

Anna shifted sideways to allow another person to approach the bedside. The young woman wore a pink patient's gown. Beneath the gown Martin could see that her entire torso was wrapped with bandages. Her long, strawberry-blond hair was tied back in a ponytail.

It was Alice. She was alive. Which meant that they were all alive. Martin reached out and squeezed Alice's hand, and Alice squeezed back. They shared a warm smile and Alice wiped tears from her cheeks.

"I'm so sorry," Martin said. "What I did to you—I had no choice. If I didn't—"

"If you didn't," Alice finished for him, "none of us would have gotten out of there. You saved my life, Mr. Grey. You saved all of us. That's all that matters."

"I wasn't sure what I did worked," he said. "How did everyone get out?"

Alice shook her head. "I don't know. I was out of it. They said that all the lights went out and then the doors just opened. I heard that it was Vincent who found you."

"That big guy?"

Alice nodded.

Dr. Hudson returned to the bedside. "I hate to break this up, but there are several tests that I need to run."

"We're next-door neighbors," Alice said to Martin. Then she waved good-bye and headed for the door.

As Martin watched Alice leave, he noticed something inside the room that made his eyes widen. "What the—?"

His hospital room was filled with flowers and gift baskets and balloons and what looked like thousands of get-well cards. There was barely any room for the medical equipment. Martin noticed the TV set mounted on the wall. The sound was muted, but on-screen Martin could see a reporter standing before a huge crowd outside a tall white building. The sign on the side of the building read Emory University Hospital.

Martin turned to Anna and the doctor. "That's here?"

Dr. Hudson nodded. "That's live. It's been like that ever since they brought you here."

Anna, beaming, took Martin's hands into hers. "You won't believe what's been going on. It's the biggest story ever. Martin, you're a hero."

Stunned, Martin looked back at the screen. The crowd was completely mixed—whites, blacks, Hispanics, Asians, just people. It was nothing like the helter-skelter that Oscar had predicted.

Martin turned back to Anna. "Did they catch them?" he asked. "Please tell me they caught them."

Anna shook her head. "Not yet. But it won't be very long. There was a story just this morning that they think they found a list of secret members."

"Okay, okay." Dr. Hudson laid a hand on Anna's arm. "Give me about forty-five minutes with your husband, then you can come back in. I promise."

Anna planted a kiss on Martin's cheek. "I'll be right outside."

Martin waited while Dr. Hudson turned to the nurse, who was the only other person in the room, and said, "I left my notebook in my office. Could you run and get it, please?"

The nurse appeared puzzled. "Your notebook, Doctor?"

"Yes, it's right on my desk. Thank you."

"Of course, Doctor."

The nurse exited and Dr. Hudson turned his full attention to Martin. "That's a pretty brave thing you did, Mr. Grey. I feel lucky to have you as a patient. I mean, you being a genuine hero and all."

"Thanks," Martin replied, feeling a bit awkward about his new status.

As Dr. Hudson removed a syringe from his coat pocket and uncapped the needle he said, "That business about secret members—that's pretty unbelievable, huh?"

Martin fixated on the syringe in Dr. Hudson's hand. That Forty Acres had secret followers wasn't unbelievable at all. In fact, Martin knew that it was true. Any successful black man, anywhere, could be one of Dr. Kasim's loyal followers, even a young doctor in Atlanta.

"Mr. Grey, are you okay?"

Martin pointed to the syringe. "What is that?"

"Vitamins. My own special brew. I've been giving you an injection every day." Dr. Hudson threw Martin a sideways look. "Don't tell me the hero is afraid of needles."

Martin knew that if he let the paranoia he was feeling take hold, he might not ever be able to get past it. Martin refused to live his life in fear. He shook his head and said, "No, I'm good. Go for it."

Dr. Hudson chuckled. "Well, all right, then."

While Dr. Hudson swabbed his arm with alcohol, Martin turned to the TV set across the room.

News footage from four days earlier of the slaves being rescued from Forty Acres filled the screen. Martin watched a dramatic helicopter shot of the compound grounds, speckled with dozens of tiny figures. As the angle descended, the tiny figures resolved into people—the white slaves draped in rags, waving their arms, jumping, shouting, cheering, praying, and embracing each other.

Martin had saved them.

95

Two weeks later, Martin, his arm in a sling, was slumped on the couch beside Anna, munching on potato chips while watching the evening news. It was a CNN special report about the ongoing roundup of criminals involved in what CNN had christened "The Forty Acres Conspiracy." Shots of handcuffed men escorted into police stations, courtrooms, and FBI headquarters flashed on Martin's beloved fifty-two-inch flat-screen. Martin spotted several familiar faces: Kwame, Tobias, Solomon, even the two forest rangers. What surprised both him and Anna was that the two rangers weren't the only Caucasians complicit in Dr. Kasim's madness. During the report, several other hunched-over white men were seen being led away by federal agents.

A huge portion of the news special was devoted to the two men conspicuously absent from the perp walks, Dr. Thaddeus Kasim and Oscar Lennox. There was endless speculation and theories about where the two ringleaders could be hiding, but the authorities had yet to track them down. Martin had been debriefed several times by several different agencies about the entire incident, and questions about Dr. Kasim's whereabouts were always high on the list. Unfortunately, like everyone else, Martin had no clue. He'd never tell Anna, but the fact that Dr. Kasim and Oscar were still at large made him more than a little uneasy. The sooner those two were behind bars, the sooner he'd be able to get a full night's sleep.

Martin's face appeared on the television screen. It was a clip from his very first interview, while still in his hospital bed. "Jesus, not that guy again," Martin said. "Enough already."

Anna chuckled as Martin picked up the remote and switched the channel.

Their smiles evaporated when a report about Lamont Bell filled the screen. Lamont Bell was a sixteen-year-old African American high school student who had been abducted and tortured, his dead body dumped in a park in West Chicago. Racial epithets had been scrawled all over his mutilated body, including several references to Forty Acres. The story had broken only a day ago, and already it was everywhere, a news juggernaut second only to the Forty Acres story itself. It was as if the exposure of Forty Acres were a major quake that had shaken the entire nation, and the Lamont Bell story a tsunami that followed it. And there were other Forty Acres aftershocks sprouting up around the country. In Greeleyville, South Carolina, a century-old black church had been burned down. In Athens, Georgia, a bar brawl between white and black college students erupted after a report about Forty Acres played on the bar's television. In Washington, DC, the

Martin Luther King Jr. memorial had been vandalized, Dr. King's granite visage desecrated by a splattering of bloodred paintballs. All these reports were disturbing and received plenty of attention from the media, but none had the impact of Lamont Bell's murder. The images of the teenager's brutal injuries were difficult to look at, especially for Martin. However irrational, Martin couldn't help feeling responsible.

"Martin," Anna said, squeezing his hand, "turn it off."

But Martin kept watching. He watched fidgety home video of Lamont shooting hoops with his dad. He watched Lamont's mother sob before a crush of reporters. He watched a candlelight vigil made up of hundreds of Lamont's classmates and a small mountain of flowers and cards. Martin watched because he had this crazy feeling that it was his duty to watch. He'd made a choice and now he had to live with it.

Anna reached out and pivoted Martin's head away from the television screen so that he was facing her. She answered his tortured eyes with a firm yet loving gaze. "You did the right thing," she whispered. "Now please, turn it off."

Martin nodded. He aimed the remote and pressed the off button.

The doorbell rang. Anna looked at her watch and groaned. "They're early."

Martin and Anna greeted Glen and Lisa at the front

door. There was an exchange of hugs and kisses, then Lisa sniffed the air. "Mmmm . . . Is that lamb? Smells incredible."

"God, I hope so," Anna said, biting her lower lip. "It's kinda your recipe. Actually, since you're here, you can help. Come, come." Anna grabbed Lisa's hand and dragged her into the kitchen.

Glen reached into a Toys "R" Us shopping bag and pulled out what looked like a brand-new chess set. He handed it to Martin. "Just a little gift."

Martin looked baffled at the box. It wasn't just a chess set. It was a Mephisto talking chess trainer. A shiny gold sticker on the shrink-wrap promised that the gadget was endorsed by Kasparov himself. Martin frowned blankly at Glen. "Um, thanks . . . I think."

"Not for you, Perry Mason. It's for our future partner. Why do you think my mind is so sharp? When I was a kid I played lots of chess with my dad."

"Glen, Anna's not even showing yet."

"Sure, sure, it's a little soon. But the game talks. You and Anna can play and the kid can hear every move. Kids begin learning in the womb, that's a proven fact."

Martin shook his head in disbelief. "You're crazy, you know that?"

"Says the man who single-handedly took down the biggest conspiracy in the history of ever. I *still* don't believe it." Glen gave Martin's good shoulder a friendly slap. "You okay? How you holding up, bro?"

Martin felt himself stiffen. Glen had probably called him "bro" a thousand times over the course of their friendship, but this was the first time that it had grated on his nerves. He felt a strong urge to ask Glen not to use that term again. At least not until the bullet wound in his shoulder had healed and the nightmares had stopped and the world had returned to normal. But Martin decided against it. He didn't want to put a damper on tonight's dinner, and more importantly, he didn't want to poison his relationship with his best friend. So, for the second time that evening, Martin heeded his wife's advice.

He turned it off.

"I'm getting there," Martin replied, putting on a brave smile. "I'm getting there."

Martin led Glen over to the living room wall unit and popped open a small liquor cabinet. He was about to pour Glen his usual Jack and Coke but Glen insisted that, like Martin, he'd just have a Diet Coke. "When you're off the meds," Glen said, "the first round's on me. But just the first."

Martin chuckled and reached for the Diet Coke, but the front doorbell interrupted the moment.

"Hey, who's that?" Glen said. "You never mentioned another guest."

Martin looked equally surprised. "There isn't one. At least, not that I know of."

Anna appeared in the kitchen doorway wearing oven

mitts and an accusing stare targeted at her husband. "Did you invite someone and forget to tell me?"

Martin raised his hands. "Not guilty. I swear. Hold on."

Martin crossed to the window beside the door and peeked past the curtain. "That's odd," he said, turning back to Anna. "It's the cable guy."

Anna glanced at her watch. "Now? I thought the upgrade was tomorrow."

"I did too. At least that's what they told me."

"That *is* odd," Glen said with a chuckle. "Who the hell ever heard of a cable guy coming early?"

The doorbell chimed again.

Anna sighed and said to Martin, "Well, dinner's ready. Could you ask him to come back another time?"

"I'm sure that won't be a problem."

"Then could you two come help carry in the food?"

"On our way," Glen said.

Anna thanked them with a smile then retreated into the kitchen.

Martin reached out to open the door but suddenly paused. With his hand inches from the brass doorknob Martin stood there, frozen, in a moment of deep thought.

"You okay?" Glen asked.

Martin withdrew his hand and turned to Glen. He whispered, "I have a bad feeling about this."

Glen looked confused. "What? Why?"

Martin pressed a finger to his lips, then continued in a

521

hushed voice. "Do you know how long it takes to get an appointment? If I send him away, the cable company might insist on rescheduling. But if no one's home, there's a chance they'll figure out their error and send someone tomorrow as planned."

Glen smiled and whispered, "Very smart."

Martin eased away from the front door. "Come on, let's go help with dinner."

As Martin and Glen quietly stepped toward the kitchen, the doorbell tolled for a third time, its beckoning tone lingering in the air like an unanswered question.

Acknowledgments

The journey from coming up with the idea for *Forty Acres* to having the book finally published was like a dream come true.

First and foremost, I'd like to thank Mr. Bill Teitler. Bill and I met initially to discuss one of my screenplays. Typically, during a first meeting between producer and screenwriter, the producer will ask, "so, what else are you working on?"

I told Bill about my half-finished manuscript called *Forty Acres* . . . and he loved it. For a year he poked at me to finish, but I was too busy. Finally, he convinced me to let him read what I had. Bill liked it and asked if he could show it to a literary agent he knew. Then things really took off. Without Bill Teitler's encouragement and tenacity *Forty Acres* might still be sitting in a drawer.

Also, a huge thank you to the Friedrich Agency: Lucy Carson, Nichole LeFebvre, Molly Schulman, and most of all to my agent Molly Friedrich. When I walked into their offices in New York for the first time, the enthusiasm in the room was palpable. Being new to publishing, there's a lot I don't know. Led by Molly Friedrich's wisdom, the support, guidance, and patience that these amazing women showed me has been invaluable. And even when the pressure was on, Molly's frank yet delightful wit always kept me smiling.

And thank you also to the team at Atria Books for their hard work on *Forty Acres*. Publisher Judith Curr, Daniel Loedel, Stacey Kulig, Jeanne Lee, and my editor Peter Borland. Molly said I was lucky to have Peter as an editor and from the moment I met him I knew she was right. Peter's passion and insights were truly an inspiration. Everyone at Atria did a great job. I couldn't be more proud of the final product.

I write alone, but not really. Instead of a writing partner, I use the people around me as sounding boards. I always feel self-conscious about calling up friends to test yet another idea, worried that I bug them far too much. Surprisingly, they are usually very generous with their time and show a great amount of patience as they help me find my way.

A heartfelt thanks to my friends William Massa, Gordon Chou, Suzanne Miller, Al Valentine, Robert Brody, Glen Beltran, Greg Zehentner, Michelle James, Craig Feagins, Angel Nieves, and Felicia Rivera.

One final thank you to my fiancée, Stephanie Warren, for making an exciting time in my life . . . even more exciting.

Read on for a Q&A with
Dwayne Alexander Smith

What was the first book to make an impression on you?

It's a tie. *The Lion the Witch and the Wardrobe* by C. S. Lewis and *A Wrinkle in Time* by Madeleine L'Engle. I read both in elementary school. Both filled me with wonder and caused me to fall in love with fantasy and science fiction.

What was your favourite book as a child?

Charlie and the Chocolate Factory by Roald Dahl. I can still recite most of the Oompa Loompa rhymes from memory. A book that I read over and over.

And what is your favourite book or books now?

My favorite books are *Huckleberry Finn*, *The Grapes of Wrath*, *The Three Musketeers*, and *Dune*. Pretty standard picks, I know. But I love them.

What is your favourite quotation?

"All right, then, I'll go to hell." From *Huckleberry Finn*. When Huck Finn decides to save Jim.

Who is your favourite fictional character?
I'm also a screenwriter. I love film and books equally. If I

had to pick one fiction character I'd have to say Indiana Jones or Shane from the movie of the same name.

Who is the most underrated Irish author?

I have to admit that I'm not familiar with enough Irish authors to say which is underrated. The ones I've read, like C.S Lewis, Shaw, Swift, and Stoker are pretty highly regarded. I have heard people knock Bram Stoker, and I'll admit that *Dracula* is a challenging read, but that book established one of the greatest fictional characters ever. The way Stoker expanded upon vampire mythology is pure genius.

Which do you prefer – ebooks or the traditional print version?

I like holding the book in my hands. I like the feel of turning the pages. I like feeling the weight. I like the smell of books.

What is the most beautiful book you own?

I don't really own any beautiful books. All of my books are well used. I have a coffee table book of old boom boxes from the 80s. I guess that would be closest.

Where and how do you write?

I have a home office, which I rarely use. Writing is so

lonely. I prefer a space where there's people around but no ambient music playing. Lately I've been writing at a co-working office space in Santa Monica. For a monthly fee you get to write in a pretty snazzy open office environment.

What book changed the way you think about fiction?

I'm not sure what you mean by this question. Different books expose me to different ways to tell a story, but I don't think any has changed the way I think about fiction. I have very strong opinions on how certain stories should be told to be the most effective, and I'm sticking to them.

What is the most research you have done for a book?

Forty Acres is my first book so it's the only book I've ever researched. The research was interesting because I learned a lot about American slavery that was never taught to me in school. I'm writing a crime thriller now and I'm doing tons of research on police procedure and specifically how the NYPD functions.

What book influenced you the most?

Stephen King wrote a book called *Salem's Lot*. Certain scenes scared me so much that I didn't want to sleep in the same room with it. I remember being blown away by how that book affected me psychologically. I was envious and wanted to learn to write something that would get into the reader's head as well. I wanted to make my readers' hearts pound. From the reactions I've read to certain parts of *Forty Acres*, I think I have achieved that.

Huckleberry Finn has also had a huge impact. For me, reading that book is like an emotional rollercoaster. It makes me laugh, makes me angry, makes me cry. To this day I can't read certain section without tears running down my cheeks.

What book would you give to a friend's child on their 18th birthday?

Not sure about this. All the books I'd want to give a friend's kid could be given much earlier in life.

What book do you wish you had read when you were young?

At first I had no answer to this one, but then it struck me. *Freakonomics* by Dubner and Levitt. That book has some awesome and very useful insights to everyday life.

What advice would you give to an aspiring author?

Well, I'm all about the big idea, especially when it comes to breaking in. An amazing original idea will knock down a lot of doors. If you're just pounding out another murder mystery or spy thriller, you have to ask yourself, what makes my story better than the other three hundred that are out there.

I've wanted to write a novel for a while but it wasn't until I came up with the idea for *Forty Acres*, that I felt confident enough to sit down and write one. The reactions to the idea behind *Forty Acres* were off the charts. I gambled that if I wrote it at least a few publishers would have a similar reaction.

What weight do you give reviews?

That depends. If the reviews are one-sided, then I'd suspect that they were correct, and as a author I would listen. If the reviews are mixed it's a bit trickier. I love the positive ones but I'm actually more interested in the negative ones. I'm curious to know specifically what didn't work for that reader. I also want to gauge if their gripe is legitimate or if they just didn't get it.

Where do you see the publishing industry going?

I don't know a hell of a lot about publishing, I'm far more knowledgeable about the movie industry. I have noticed that publishers have fully embraced the digital distribution of books, which is great. Bookstores are an endangered species here in the United States.

What writing trends have struck you lately?

The whole self-publishing thing is really amazing. I have a friend who has a new career as a self published author.

I also think it's cool that self publishing creates a huge marketplace for shorter fiction.

What lessons have you learned about life from reading?

I've learned that it really takes very little to ignite the imagination. Just a few carefully chosen words can evoke fantastic worlds and amazing characters. This is something the movie industry needs to understand. CGI cannot compete with the human imagination. In fact it's far less interesting. The worlds I've dreamed up in my mind with the help of great authors blows away anything Hollywood has ever done.

What has being a writer taught you?

Magic is in the details. Anyone can do the broad strokes. It's the details that will set you apart. Actually, this applies to anything in life.

Which writers, living or dead, would you invite to your dream dinner party?

Dumas, King, Herbert, Twain, Steinbeck, Dahl, Shakespeare, Dickens, Follett, Bradbury, Serling.

What is the funniest scene you've read?

Hmmm. I can't remember the specific scene but I remember laughing the hardest while reading *Huckleberry Finn*. I was laughing out loud on the subway and people were staring, and I didn't care.

What is your favourite word?

Fiasco. I love it so much I want to write a book so I can use fiasco as the title. I want to name my kid fiasco but I'm afraid it might curse him or her. The word fiasco makes me smile because for me it evokes hilarious chaos.

If you were to write a historical novel, which event or figure would be your subject?

I want to set a story against the construction of the Brooklyn Bridge. Kind of how James Cameron used the sinking of the Titanic as a backdrop. The story behind the bridge's construction is full of drama and death and it's an interesting period in New York City history. It would be an epic story.

First published as 'Brought to Book
with Martin Doyle' in the *Irish Times*